# JAY POSEY

# THREE

## LEGENDS OF THE DUSKWALKER
### BOOK 1

ANGRY
ROBOT

**ANGRY ROBOT**
A member of the Osprey Group

Lace Market House,
54-56 High Pavement,
Nottingham,
NG1 1HW, UK

www.angryrobotbooks.com
Not a sequel

An Angry Robot paperback original 2013
1

A catalogue record for this book is available
from the British Library.

ISBN: 978 0 85766 362 7
Ebook ISBN: 978 0 85766 364 1

Set in Meridien by ePub Services.

Printed and bound by CPI Group (UK) Ltd, Croydon, CR0 4YY

*For Jennifer,*
*without whom neither I nor this work*
*would be complete.*

# PROLOGUE

The blood-orange sun rode low on the horizon, a seething scar of vibrant color slashing the otherwise gray sky. A distant horn blared for the fourth time, and Jackson knew he'd pushed the limits as far as he could afford. Maybe further. Another night would soon be upon them. His eyes fluttered as he internally accessed the Almanac through his embedded connection, checking the exact time for the day's sunset. 18:32 GST. Six more minutes. He scanned the abandoned streets around him, noted the long shadows pooling in the rusted alleyways. A faint wind swept by, with a hint of the approaching winter on its breath, rattling loose bits of scrap metal some long-forgotten street merchant had once used as a sign. Jackson fiddled absent-mindedly in his jacket pocket, fingering the entirety of his find for the day: a couple of biochem batteries, both leaking something viscous, a tangled nest of magnium wire, a live 18-kilojoule shell. Not a bad haul this close to the Vault.

He inhaled deeply, taking in the crisp autumn air with its crackle of ozone. Sharp, familiar; exhilarating when paired with the knowledge that if he dawdled another five minutes, he might find himself trapped outside for the night. He wondered whether or not Gev would ever really lock him out; the gatekeeper had certainly threatened to, often enough. Still,

Jackson had never waited past three signals before. Gev might not be the only one angry back at the Vault tonight.

Jackson shut his eyes one last time, imagined himself standing alone, enshrouded by darkness; bold, defiantly alive. For a moment, it almost felt real. Then a chill overtook him, the sudden sense of someone in the alley behind, close, grasping.

He gasped and spun, slamming his back hard against the nearest corrugated steel wall, eyes sweeping the streets and alleys for any sign of movement. His heart pounded out the empty seconds, inability to move battling instinct to flee. But there was no one. Nothing to fear; no more than the day-to-day horror of living.

Unclenching his fists, Jackson felt for the first time the sting where he'd crushed the magnium wire through the top layer of his palm. Enough bravery for the day. He slid along the wall to the corner, then broke into a run. He twisted through the network of alleyways, spilled out onto a wide road beneath a sagging maglev line, and spotted the Vault just as its engines were firing up to draw the heavy steel gates down with the sun.

The Vault was aptly named: a short, squat, angular building made of concrete, wider at the base than the top. Its only entrance or exit was through the front where an eight-inch-thick steel gate controlled access. In fact, most of the Vault stretched down underground, below the city, like some kind of human hive bored out of a cement iceberg. A hundred or so tenants lived inside in an uneasy tolerance of one another, bound together by a mutual need for survival and little else.

Gev, the burly gatekeeper, leaned on a four-foot length of iron pipe, and shot Jackson a dark eye when he plunged through onto the smooth concrete of the Vault entryway. Jackson returned a nervous smile. Last one through again. Sure he was young, but he was still the bravest tenant in the Vault, at least as far as he was concerned. Gev grunted, propping his pipe against the wall, and activated the gate. Jackson turned back to savor the final glimpse of the outdoors, decaying city though it was, as it disappeared beneath the plated steel doors. It would be another eleven hours before he could go out again. With security came the familiar quiet desperation. The safety of the cage.

Then something new. A faint smell of smoke, a piercing whine of steel against steel. Jackson glanced to Gev. Gev stood silent, mouth working without sound, like some great pale fish striving for oxygen in the open air. The gates strained, shuddered, and finally heaved to a halt, angled awkwardly eight feet from the ground. The growl from the engines rose in pitch, and the odor of overheated mechanicals grew strong. Still, Gev stood, staring at the struggling gates, and the fading light beyond.

Jackson at least had sense enough to respond to the obvious signals. He rushed to the controls and shut the engines down before the damage was permanent.

Jackson roused Gev from his apparent paralysis with a slap to the shoulder. Gev swiveled to look at him, wild-eyed.

"The gates! Jammed!" he stammered.

"I see that," Jackson answered. "We should get 'em down, yeah?"

Gev grunted, and moved to the stalled structure with unusual grace for a man his size. He tugged on the gate, tentatively at first, then with growing aggression. It held fast. Jackson joined Gev at the door, lending meager strength and an unvoiced apology.

"Young fool," Gev growled between vain attempts. "Why were you gone so long?"

Gev hauled on the door with all his might, veins bulging in his neck, face purple with the strain, but the gate ignored his effort. Jackson gave up the brute force method, and instead took to examining the jury-rigged system of salvaged gears, refurbished pulleys, and mismatched cables that ran the gate. Looking at it now, Jackson was mildly surprised it had ever worked before.

A pair of men appeared from within the Vault interior, and stood silent in the entryway, staring dumbly as the last red rays of sunset deepened to purple.

"What're ye doin'?" said the first, a broad-shouldered man named Fuller.

"Ye gotter shut it," said the second, called Whit, voice cracking with the barest hint of half-crazed fear. "Ye gotter shut it!"

"It's off the track," Jackson called to Gev. "It's wedged against the rail."

"Ye gotter shut it!" shouted Whit, and in the next instant the two newcomers were upon the gates, heaving madly. Gev easily pulled Whit off by his collar, but before he could do more, Fuller kicked him in the groin. Gev inhaled sharply as he doubled over and dropped to a knee, and Whit scrambled back away from him. Fuller continued wrestling with the door, while Whit backed his way to the engine control panel.

"Stop!" Jackson yelled, moving to help Gev. "It's off the rails!"

"He's tryin' ter let 'em in!" Whit shrieked, jabbing a bony finger at Gev. "You seent it!"

Whit flipped the switch again, and the gate jerked once more, straining against itself. Jackson lunged towards Whit, but Fuller caught him around the neck and held him fast. Gev grabbed Fuller around the waist, and the three writhed together in a constantly shifting knot of human limbs. Jackson finally managed to work his way out of Fuller's grasp, and once he was free, Gev settled the matter with a heavy elbow to Fuller's jaw. Fuller dropped in a solid heap, lying motionless on the smooth concrete floor. By then the commotion had brought a cluster of other tenants to the entry. They stood and watched for a brief moment, unable to comprehend the bizarre scene before them. Smoke from the engines clung to the low ceiling, mingling with the mass of mechanical bits that strove to lower the wedged gates. Then, one spoke, voice hushed in awe, or terror.

"It's dusk."

That was all it took. Without understanding, the tenants threw themselves upon the struggling steel doors. Gev tried to push the group back, but the human tide overtook him. Jackson found himself thrown to the floor.

"It's off the rails!" Jackson cried, as he skittered out of the way of the stampede. "Stop, we've got to realign it!"

It was no use. The small crowd of tenants was rapidly growing, and each new arrival brought his or her own share of panic, until beneath the unyielding gate was a frenzy of clawing and shouting humanity, crushed together, united in purpose, devoid of cooperation. The engines whined, shuddered, and then were sickeningly silent. Still the tenants fought. Gev, big as he was, lay struggling beneath stomping feet, drowning in a churning sea of individuals-turned-mob.

"Stop! Stop!" Jackson screamed. "Just STOP!"

And suddenly, they did. For a heartbeat, Jackson thought they were listening to him.

But then he heard it, too.

Out there. A distant, ethereal shriek, electric and cold, at once human and electronic, like the squall of digital noise translated through atrophied vocal cords. Then another. Answered by yet another, not so distant.

Whit curled himself fetal in the corner of the entryway, hands covering his ears like a child in a thunderstorm.

"Late," he choked out. "Too late."

Then the chaos resumed, as the tenants of the Vault abandoned all thoughts of sealing the doors and turned instead to blind panic. The screaming throng pressed and writhed its way back, deeper into the Vault interior, forcing Jackson away from the entrance. Why they ran, he didn't know. The gates were the only real protection they had.

He tried to fight his way free of the mass, working back towards the gateway, where Gev alone had re-doubled his efforts to free the lodged door. Jackson broke from the crowd, but as the last of the fleeing tenants passed, he froze to the core. Out beyond Gev, pairs of pale blue pin-prick stars hovered in the darkness, appearing from every alley, growing. Slowly, like shadows stretching, consuming the landscape in the day's final hours, they approached. The soulless electric shrieking increased in volume and intensity, until beyond the gate all was a cacophony of sinister white noise that seemed to seize Jackson's spine and shatter all reason.

The last that Jackson remembered was Gev turning to pick up his heavy iron pipe, with a look that was resigned yet quietly determined.

"Go on, boy," Gev called, gripping the pipe with both hands like it was some great rusted warhammer. "If you've got a place to upload your soul, now's the time."

Gev strode out into the night, and the Weir were upon him.

# ONE

Golden beams of sunlight spilled through the skeletal high rises, and through the concrete and steel network of interlaced highways, bypasses, and rails that once flowed with harried humanity, now devoid of all but the meanest signs of life. Overpasses stacked ten high lay inert, arteries of a city embalmed. The wind was light but weighty with the failing autumn, like the hand of a blacksmith gently laid.

Beneath the lowest overpass, a lone figure plodded weary steps, bowed and hooded, burden dragging behind leaving long tracks in the concrete dust. He paused, raised his head, laid back his hood, and felt the cooling breeze on his sweat-beaded face. His sun-squinted eyes roved over the urban desert before him as he adjusted the straps of his makeshift harness to ease his protesting shoulders.

"I see why you left," the man muttered. He spat, wiped his nose on the sleeve of his knee-length faded olive-brown-mottled coat, and started on his way again.

The man stepped up onto the road, felt his senseThetic boots soften slightly to better absorb the hard shock of the asphalt, cringed at the hollow echo of his cargo scraping across the scarred and pockmarked ground. As he walked, he imagined the city as it might've once been. The endless dissonance of a half-million people packed into five square miles, swimming

13

in an almost tangible soup of electromagnetic traffic. He wondered what traces of personality might still be left, rippling through those invisible fields around him even now.

Progress was slow, but he was close. Another few minutes and at last the man stood before the gates of his destination: a small enclave of survivors set within the dead cityscape. From atop a twenty-foot wall of haphazardly-welded urban debris, a watchman called down.

"What's your business, stranger?"

The man jerked his thumb behind him, indicating the cargo he was dragging. The watchman grunted.

"Yeah, alright," he answered. "Reckon the agent's gonna wanna take a look before you go far."

The man waited in silence as the enormous gates ground open, just wide enough to admit him and his payload. They started to close again before he was all the way through.

"Second street on your right, agent's the first on the left. First floor."

The man nodded curt thanks, and headed to see the enclave's agent. Within the walls, the architecture was unchanged from that outside: tall gunmetal skyscrapers with windows darkened like gaping sockets of a skull, dead flat panel signs forty-feet wide that might once have hawked the day's latest technological fashion. In here, however, there were men, women, and even wide-eyed children, who stared in wonder at this new evidence of life from beyond the wall, walking amongst them. Most of the adults pretended not to notice him, though he felt their sidelong glances and heard the hushed whispers after he passed. Even in days as strange as these, it was unusual to see a man harnessed as he was, hauling such a load: scrap aluminum, worn and scratched, bent into the makeshift but unmistakable shape of a coffin.

The man reached the agent's office, and he paused, steeling himself with a final deep breath of outside air. He'd dealt with agents before, nearly thirty he could recall, and they'd all been the same. Muscle-bound gun-toters with a lot of bark, always itching for a reason to bite. Mostly ex-military or law enforcement, agents were tough guys who liked the power, and still clung to the outdated notion that order could be maintained even in a desolate society. They had their uses. But the man had little use for them.

He stepped forward, automatic doors sliding smoothly open to admit him, and dragged in from concrete to polished granite. In an earlier time, the office might've been a bank, with all its oak and stone. Or a tomb. Now, it was just a long corridor, leading to an imposing flexiglass cube. The glass was darkly smoked, but the man correctly presumed whoever was inside could see his approach. Still, he strode nearly the length of the corridor, before a sudden booming voice stopped him five paces from the cube's door.

"State your business," thundered the voice, rolling emphatically down the stone hall.

"Bounty," replied the man.

"State your name."

"Three."

There was a pause.

"You got three of 'em in there?"

"You asked my name."

The voice puzzled for a moment. Then–

"Who you got in the box?"

"One of yours."

"Open it."

"I'd rather not."

The voice resumed a more professional tone.

"All collections must be verified and processed before payment will be distributed."

"So open the cube."

A slot opened in the cube, and a sleek metal case slid out, popping open to reveal a cracking rubberized interior.

"Deposit your weapons in the provided secure receptacle."

"I'd rather not."

Another pause. Though it still boomed, the voice sounded flustered.

"You cain't come in here so armed, mister. I don't care who you are."

The man named Three let the straps of his harness slide off his shoulders. They clattered to the floor next to the coffin.

"Then you come out. I'm done dragging."

Three turned around and started back down the corridor.

"Hey!" the voice thundered, "Hey, you cain't just leave that settin' there!"

Three walked on.

"I'll have you arrested if you don't come back!"

He was almost to the exit. There was a whir and a click behind him, and a thin, crackly voice called out from the cube.

"What about your bounty? Don't you want it?"

Three stopped. But didn't turn.

"Come on get this box inside, and I'll see what we owe ya. My back cain't manage it."

Three swiveled on a heel, and returned to the cube. There, a bent old man who looked like he weighed less than his age tottered and leaned against the now-opened door. A stimstick dangled precariously from his lower lip, glowing with casual indifference. Three grabbed the straps off the floor and hauled the coffin inside the cube. The old man followed him in.

"Don't know why you folks gotta make things difficult for *us* folk. Times is rough enough without undeserved meanness."

The cube interior was a stark contrast to the cavernous entryway. Nearly every available square inch was stuffed with various devices, blinking and humming and whirring, and it was easily fifteen degrees warmer inside than out. There was a desk of sorts in the middle of the room, with a plush recliner behind it, and an overturned plasticrate that Three assumed served as a seat for rare company. From within the cube, the flexiglass was clear, and the granite corridor stretched off to the glass exit at the far end.

"So who'd you git?" the agent asked.

"Nim. Nanokid out of the Six-Thirteen."

The agent's eyes twitched back and forth as he internally accessed the appropriate file.

"Alright. Looks like fifteen-hundred."

"Four thousand."

"Nah, only fifteen for dead."

"I didn't say he was dead."

The agent looked up into Three's eyes, mouth open slightly, but he swallowed whatever question he'd been about to ask, and instead took a drag on the stimstick. He turned and rummaged through a pile of gadgets on his desk, dragging out a slender rod, pewter-colored, without any apparent seams or separate parts, which emitted a pleasant hum. This he pointed casually at the coffin, grunting after a moment with some mix of satisfaction and disdain.

"Well, that's him in there alright," he said, turning again to fish around in his desk drawer. "Pointcard's OK?"

Without waiting for an answer, the agent produced a translucent green card and swept it through a slotted device, which clicked once and beeped cheerily. He extended it to Three.

"Hard, actually," Three replied, hands in his coat pockets.

The agent's slight shoulders slumped almost into non-existence.

"I don't keep that kind of Hard just layin' around. No more than a thousand any given day."

The pointcard trembled in the agent's still-outstretched hand, in vague hope that this strange man from beyond the wall would take it and disappear. Three could tell he disturbed the agent. The wrinkled old man stared at him like he didn't belong there, like he was some alien thing wedged in the wrong reality. The agent shivered.

"I'll take the thousand now, and come back for the rest."

The agent pushed the card a little closer.

"Might be a day or two."

"I'll wait."

The agent let out a weary sigh. He rummaged in, under, and around the electric clutter of his office, until he located an ancient lockbox, secured with physical biometrics. After running his bent and knobby fingers over the touchpad, the box hissed open. The agent opened it just wide enough to slip his hand in, counted out twenty nanocarb chips, and handed them over to Three with some reluctance. Three glimpsed more Hard in the box, but made no comment, sized the agent up instead: dilated pupils, thin sheen of perspiration, colorless ring around tensed lips.

"Sorry I frighten you," Three said without apologetic tone. He leaned his head to one side and cracked his neck audibly, watching the old man carefully. The agent laughed, too suddenly, too loud.

"What? I ain't scared of ya, don't ya worry about that."

Lie, Three thought.

"I lived plenty enough years to see things a lot worse than you, friend."

That was true. Three lowered his head in the barest hint of a bow. Whatever the agent's reason for withholding a portion of his stash, Three decided, he was an honest dealer. Probably owed someone. The agent got back to business.

"Gimme your SNIP, I'll pim ya when I get the rest."

"I'll come back tomorrow."

The agent's eyes narrowed slightly.

"Be easier if you just gimme the SNIP."

"I'd rather not."

"Figgered that," the agent snorted. "Well, gimme two days, I'll have the rest for ya then. Late afternoon."

Three unfastened his coat to pocket the payment, revealing a mammoth pistol crouching in a holster on his vest, coiled like some predator hungering to pounce. The agent's eyes bulged at the hardware, but he quickly diverted his attention. He kicked at the coffin.

"'Preciate the work you done," he said half-heartedly. "Dunno why you had to do him like that, though."

Three adjusted the pistol, then refastened his coat, concealing it once more.

"You will when you open it."

Three nodded to the agent, and swiveled back down the stone corridor. As Three walked away, the agent watched him briefly, then, on a sudden whim, picked up and aimed the humming rod at his back. The agent frowned slightly, shook the rod, and pointed it again, more purposefully. His frown deepened, eyes narrowed with some undefined emotion. A thought occurred, and wide-eyed he fumbled over himself to seal the flexiglass cube, as Three stepped back out onto the street.

The honey-colored liquid swirled gently in the finger-smudged squat glass on the table in front of Three. It was his fourth of the afternoon. Still he waited for the comforting blanket of alcoholic haze to embrace him. He leaned forward, resting his face in his hands, and his elbows on the table, felt it shift slightly to the right, and wondered briefly if it were the table or himself that had wobbled. Was this the wobbly table? Or had that been yesterday? Yesterday? Yesterday. It was the second day since he'd met with the agent. Payday.

Three let out a weary sigh, ran his hands back over his shaved head, feeling the stubble of a few days' growth, then massaged his temples, probably throbbing though he couldn't be sure. It was like this when he didn't have a job; something to find, someone to bring in. The restlessness was setting in, the need to move. To hunt. It was the third day in the same town. Might as well have been a month. There were benefits to being a freelancer, but down time wasn't one of them.

From his corner booth, he had a commanding view of all the critical angles. The booth itself was U-shaped, tucked in the front corner of the bar, a natural blind spot from the entrance. Temprafoam, covered in some cheap imitation of a much sturdier textile, it was adequate comfort and gave him all the room he needed, and best of all required no reservation, deposit, or record of stay. He sat with his feet propped on the bench opposite, with his coat bundled around his hardware on the perpendicular seat that completed the U. His eyes involuntarily swept around the bar, taking stock of his surroundings, the way they had two minutes before. Habit.

But everything was the same. Same hazy atmosphere. Same chattering regulars. Same bartender. The bartender was a lean man, lean like he'd been a foot shorter and stretched to his current height, and fidgety. He was never completely still, fingers always working the air when they weren't cleaning glasses or pouring drinks. Three guessed the bartender was splitting time between customers and some fantasy app, but didn't want to guess the type.

He took another swig of his drink, then casual interest in the door. Instinct. A moment later, a woman entered pulling a small boy along behind her. She was bent at an awkward angle, clutching her long coat closed tight around her with a balled fist pressed hard to her side. Colorless, sweating, desperate. Damp shoulder-length brown hair plastered to her forehead. Wild brown eyes darting around the room. The boy was blond, vibrantly pale, with eyes deep sea-green and natural, the mesmerizing kind the Money would've paid top Hard for at the height of the market. Three guessed him perhaps five years old. The boy trembled with the frightened silence of a child who's been told everything's alright, but knows it isn't. His shocking innocence swept through the bar: fragile, beautiful, a snowflake drifting amongst ash.

Three lowered his eyes back to his glass, kept the woman and boy in his peripheral awareness. She moved from patron to patron, urgent, pleading, waved off impatiently. Three shut his eyes and drank deeply the remaining honey-liquid from his glass. He set it back on the table with a dull crack, felt the table shift again.

Good, he thought with a half-smile. Table, not me.

When he opened his eyes, she was there.

"Please ..." she began. Three's gaze flicked to the door behind her. In the next instant, it swung open, and she whipped around to face it, inhaling sharply. Whoever she was expecting wasn't there. Just a pair of teen Skinners blowing in off the street. She clenched her eyes, bent over Three's table, dropped a fist to support herself. Three watched her hazily, felt his eyes float to the boy. The boy ran his hand slowly, methodically, back and forth along the edge of Three's table, tiny fingers wrapped around some scavenged plaything: a model of an ancient shuttlecar with a few flecks of yellow paint where bare metal hadn't yet worn through. He fixed Three with a wet, penetrating stare, and never looked away.

Three reached in his vest pocket and flicked a pair of nanocarb chips onto the table, a hundred Hard. The woman opened her eyes, stared down blankly at them, then back up at him, shaking her head.

"No," she practically whispered, teeth catching her bottom lip for an instant in an almost imperceptible struggle to maintain thin composure. "We need help."

"You lose something?" Three heard himself ask heavily. The fog was settling nicely now.

"What?"

"Did you lose something?" he repeated, with overemphasized precision.

"No, I–"

"Looking for someone?"

"What? No, we're just–"

"Then I can't help you."

The woman straightened, and looked back to the door, but didn't leave. Three glanced to the boy again, found himself staring into deep green pools, fascinated. The boy seemed equally intrigued by Three. The woman made one more attempt.

"I'm not asking you to help me," she pushed the boy to the front. "Look, will you help him?"

"I'm not being rude, ma'am. Just honest."

Three tilted his glass on the table, signaled to the bartender for another. Still the woman stood, chewing her lip, pressing her fist to her abdomen, while the bartender jerked his way over and refilled Three's glass to the brim.

"Take the money," Three said, sipping from the glass, feeling the warmth roll down his throat, filling his chest with dull flame.

"Mama," a small voice peeped next to the woman. "Mama, let's just go."

The woman stared vacantly, at the door, at the table, at the Hard.

"Go on," Three said. "I've got plenty."

"Mama, please, can we go now, can we go?"

Without a word, the woman swept the two nanocarb chips up off the table and into her pocket, then whirled and tugged the boy along behind her to the bar. She spoke animatedly with the bartender, who directed her with various twitching gestures towards the back. The boy never took his eyes from Three, not until he vanished with his mother into a back room and, Three assumed, out again into the streets.

Three downed a good half of his glass, felt a faint satisfaction waft through, like the smoke-wisp of a just snuffed candle, knowing he'd helped some local skew and her runt, and hadn't even been annoyed when she hadn't thanked him. A hundred Hard was probably more than she'd make in a week of nights under sweaty Joes who couldn't afford even C-grade sims.

"Hold my table," Three called to the bartender, hauling himself out of the booth to take care of the growing pressure in his bladder that he'd just noticed.

In the stall, he watched in a sort of drunken lucidity the stream splashing onto the stainless grate, knowing somewhere below it was being absorbed, filtered, broken down into useful parts for biochem batteries, or solvent, or cooking. He chuckled aloud at the thought of his fellow patrons out there drinking his recycled urine.

But then the sudden image of the boy's sea-green eyes cut short his personal amusement, and Three couldn't shake the feeling that there was something in them he should've noted, something he missed that was important, or would've been if he'd noticed. He was still rolling it over in his thickened mind when he stepped back out to the bar and felt the twinge, the automatic heightening of senses he'd learned to trust even when he didn't know why.

He continued to his table smoothly, seemingly unconcerned, knowing any change of intent might draw unwanted attention, and slid into his booth, absorbing at a glance the altered environment. The adrenaline surge burned away all traces of the alcohol-induced mist he'd spent the afternoon cultivating. The bar was nearly the same; same hazy atmosphere, same regulars, same bartender. The regulars weren't chattering now. The Skinners had a new companion.

He was tall; taller than the bartender, broad-shouldered, with long, stringy dark hair like tendrils down his back. His face was skullish, skin stretched taut across sharp features, unnaturally smooth despite other, more subtle signs of age. Thin hands, tapering to long, dexterous fingers. The eyes were the key: a slight wrinkling at the edge, with thirty more years of life in them than the rest of the man's build suggested.

Genie, Three guessed. Dangerous.

He'd run afoul of a couple of Genies before, humans who through extensive genetic engineering, or outright tampering, had attained preternaturally advanced talents or skills. It was a mistake Three didn't plan to repeat. The trouble with Genies was you never knew what about them had been enhanced. The eggheads were never a problem. Others, though, could be lethal. Judging the tall man at the bar, Three guessed he was a strength tweaker. Could probably crush a man's skull in his massive hand.

The man spoke few words, but each brought forth a torrent of information and gestures from the Skinners, as they tripped over one another trying to convince him of their eagerness to help. They both looked terrified. Three hadn't drawn his notice, but the newcomer wasn't interested in him anyway. One of the Skinners motioned to the back of the bar, and shortly after, the tall man exited by way of the front door, without so much as a glance in Three's direction. After several tense moments, one of the regulars mumbled something that drew laughter from the others at the bar. Normalcy rebooted, a programmatic hiccup resolved.

Three reached for his glass, half-empty when he left, now half-full. The boy's eyes burned before him, innocent, unaccusing. There was no doubt the tall man was after the woman; the boy. Veins in the tall man's temples had bulged slightly as he left the bar. Anger. Three knew in his heart that the tall man meant harm to those two. He shook his head: not his problem.

A hundred Hard, Three thought. That'll go a long way, if she's smart.

He picked up his glass, swirled the slightly viscous liquid. Unappealing now. He wanted to want to drink it, but instead just watched it spin and settle. Over the rim of his glass, on the far side of the table, something caught his eye. A small model shuttlecar with chipping yellow paint.

He left the glass.

"How much do I owe you?" Three called to the bartender, standing and gathering his things.

The bartender looked his way, puzzled.

"For the drinks," Three explained.

"Your woman-friend already paid," the bartender answered. "Nice tipper, too."

Silence descended upon the bar as Three made ready, patrons goggle-eyed at this last brazen assault on their day-to-day routine. They'd all assumed Three was a drunken drifter. Now, he was checking the cylinder of his pistol and holstering it, sliding a slender-bladed short sword into its sheath at his lower back.

Three threw his coat on over his hardware, and wordlessly flowed out onto the street, in pursuit of a deadly man he didn't know for reasons he couldn't understand.

# TWO

Cass leaned hard against the wall of the narrow alley, trying to catch her breath.

"Mama?"

"I'm fine."

"I don't wanna go down there, Mama."

She glanced towards the far end, where a single steel door, painted dull, flat black yawned like the mouth of a cavern.

"It's alright, it'll be fine."

"I don't wanna go."

"We have to, baby. It won't take long."

"Mama–"

"Wren, enough!" she cut him off, irritated. His spirit crumpled, and she took a breath, softened the best she could. "You can wait here if you want. I'll just be a second."

Wren stared at his shoes: cheap pull-on low-cut boots. There was a hole where his toes would be next year. He shook his head slightly.

"OK," she said. "We'll go together. Real fast."

He didn't look up, but pushed his small hand into hers. As Cass slid along the alley, tugging him behind, Wren wiped his eyes, hoping she didn't notice. At the door, Cass straightened, ran her hands over her face, slapped her cheeks to color them. She exhaled, tried not to wince. When she pounded on the door, the dull thuds died off almost instantly inside. At first, nothing.

Then, just as she raised her fist to pound again, a heavy clank sounded from within, and the door cracked open. Cass pushed in warily, felt Wren's fingernails dig into her palm. She squeezed back.

There was a soothing hum inside, a deep vibration like machinery running up against a wall, but no electric lights; the afternoon sunlight filtered in from a high slot-window, casting the dank interior in dusty gray. The walls were bare concrete; stagnant water pooled in one corner. A single stainless steel table lay in the middle of the room, with a pair of stools nearby.

"It smells," Wren whispered.

A shuffling noise sounded from near the entry, and Cass spun around as the door clanged shut. A bent old man peered at them with pupil-less ice-blue eyes.

"Are you a doctor?" Cass asked.

"Depends on who's asking, and whatfore," the old man croaked.

"I need quint, three tabs. I've got fifty Hard."

He sucked air in through his teeth, and shook his head slowly.

"I ain't made no quint in months, darlin'. Can't get the greeds for it anymore. Duff be alright?"

Cass shook her head.

"Gotta be quint."

The doctor shrugged.

"'Fraid I can't help ya with that," he said. "Are you sick or somethin'? Hurt?"

Cass glanced down to Wren. His eyes were red, like he'd been crying. He wouldn't look at her.

"You're sure you don't have any? Not even a couple?"

"Sweetheart, if I had 'em, I'd sure sell 'em to ya," he said kindly. "Ya don't look so good. Why don't ya sit down? I'll see if I can find something else for ya."

With unfocused eyes, Cass gazed at the top of Wren's head, his hair, his perfect, fragile features; he stared off to one side at the wall, the corner, nothing. The pain in her side burned like a firebrand through her liver.

"I know you've got 'em."

She said it without looking up, felt the doctor tense, air suddenly electric.

"I'm not looking for trouble. I just need the quint. I can pay you fifty. That's a good deal for you."

She ran slender fingers through Wren's hair, then down gently over his eyes, closing them. Hot tears dripped.

"But I already told ya–" the doctor started.

He didn't finish.

Cass whipped her hand with inhuman speed, driving the edge into the right side of the doctor's neck, crippling nerves, rupturing the carotid and jugular. The old man twisted, collapsed to the floor, a bag of meat and loose bones, neck bearing a spray of deep purple beneath the unbroken skin. Silently, Cass bent down, hooked the doctor under the arms, and dragged him towards the back of the small room. His head lolled awkwardly, unnaturally.

Wren stood still as a statue, eyes closed, tears streaking his face. Cass went to him, took a knee, placed her hands on his shoulders.

"We're OK, Wren," she whispered.

"You hurt him," he answered.

Cass nodded. She squeezed his shoulders, and labored to her feet.

"I need to look for something. Want to help?"

He shook his head.

"OK, baby. OK." Cass patted him gently, then staggered to the back corner, placing her hands on the wall. Her side crackled, pain radiating, organs and nerves alive with all-consuming fire. She squeezed her eyes, tried to force the ache to wash over her and away, tried to concentrate.

Breathe, Cass, she thought. Breathe.

Focus eluded her. Without it, she would never find what she was looking for; without it, she would die. And they would take Wren.

Something brushed against her leg. Cass opened her eyes, found Wren by her side, his tiny hands outstretched, spread on the wall.

"It's OK, Mama. I'll do it."

He didn't even shut his eyes, just stared ahead, seeing not what was in front of him, but rather the information stored around him, history embedded in the invisible electromagnetic swirl. There was a faint whir, and the deep hum grew louder. Across the room, a section of concrete wall withdrew, slid open, revealing an inner chamber, stocked with gear. Cass felt tears come to her eyes.

She bent down, kissed Wren on his head, raised his face so she could look in his eyes.

"I'm sorry I had to hurt that man, baby."

Wren nodded.

"He was lying," she explained. "He wanted to keep us here. We have to hurry."

Wren nodded.

"I'm sorry I made you cry."

He wiped his eyes.

"It's not your fault, Mama," he answered, brave, bottom lip quivering. She hugged him tightly.

They separated, and Cass half-stumbled her way into the hidden room, with Wren trailing close behind. Inside, the small interior space was packed with the delicate machinery of a chemist: vials, thin flexiglass tubes, pristine stainless surfaces. An overhead panel glowed a soft blue-white, bathing the room in a surgical sterility. The hum came from a centrifuge, spinning contentedly on one of the stainless steel tables. Next to it, placed against the wall, Cass spotted a silver floor cabinet, nearly Wren's height. She moved to it, swung open the unlocked door. Tabs, vials of viscous fluids, injectors, powders. Chems. Lots and lots of chems.

She rifled through the case, searching with trembling hands for the little lavender tabs that she desperately needed. Black spots floated in her vision, a weakness seized her legs. Cass buckled to the floor, pulling shelves from the case, scattering a rainbow assortment of geometric shapes and vials across the glass-smooth floor. Wren stood in the doorway.

"Mama?" he called, hushed.

"I'm OK, baby. Just give me a minute," she soothed, hoping she sounded calmer than she was.

"No," his whisper was quieter, but more intense, urgent. "He's here."

As if on cue, thunder pounded the steel front door, three rolling booms. Cass pressed a single finger to her lips, motioned for Wren to step inside the room. He tiptoed in, careful not to step on any of the chems that covered the floor. Cass's heart raced, she bent low, searching anywhere and everywhere for the lavender tabs. Her vision swam, colors confused. Again, three shuddering blows.

She glanced up, flicked her eyes from Wren to a translucent panel on the wall by the door. He nodded, crept to it, ran a small finger across it. The false concrete wall slid back into place with a whisper, as seamless inside as it was without. A pounding heartbeat later, the blue-white light switched itself off.

Pitch-black.

Cass could hear Wren's rapid breathing. She opened her mouth to whisper to him, to calm him, when suddenly the air was rent with the shriek of steel exploding inwards.

Then, silence.

Cass strained, tried to hear anything over the rush of blood in her own ears, the hammering of her heart. Nothing, but the happy whir of the centrifuge. Even little Wren must have been holding his breath. In the darkness and honeyed-buzz, Cass lost all orientation, felt herself spinning slowly in every direction at once, slipping across the frictionless floor without moving. Her forehead thunked hard against something. A wall? No, the floor. Or was it the ceiling? It was warm. Much too warm.

A spark of light. Something moving in the darkness. Piercing cold in her hand, tiny, a splinter of icicle thrust through her palm. Wren. Lips to her ear. Calling her.

"Take it, Mama," his voice floated in nothingness. "Take it."

Quint. In complete darkness, somehow, impossibly, miraculously, he'd found what she needed. Cass moved heavy arms, threw open her coat, raised her shirt. The device implanted in the right side of her abdomen snicked open, accepted the tab, sealed itself. It would metabolize soon.

Maybe soon enough. Maybe not.

Gradually, the room slowed its spin, and Cass could tell she was lying on the floor. It was a start. She felt Wren lie down, curl up next to her. Clammy, trembling. Her mothering instinct wanted to soothe him, but a more powerful instinct refused. Survival.

Outside, in the main room, the barest suggestion of sound: a light scuffling. Someone had found the doctor, shifted his corpse. It was then that the centrifuge completed its work, with a click that sounded like the racking of a shotgun, a beep like a klaxon. Reflexively, Cass squeezed Wren to her.

Silence. Nothing. Then dread. The false wall decompressed, unsealed, slid open. The blue-white light bore down, pinning them to the floor.

In the doorway stood the tall man.

Cass felt Wren bury his face; her side, where his small body pressed against hers, grew warm, wet. The tall man glared down upon them, silent, sharp features like a bird of prey before the kill. His eyes locked with Cass's. Smoldering.

The pain was receding, but the quint hadn't taken hold yet.

"Fedor," she rasped. "You're too late. Overtapped. Me and the boy."

Fedor did not react.

"Go home. Let us die in peace."

No reply, no hint that Fedor had heard her.

"We'll die together," she bluffed. "The way it should be."

"Not yet," Fedor replied, robotically. His eyes unfocused, stared through or beyond them.

"I've got them," he said, pimming someone far removed. "Yes, and the boy."

It was a one-sided conversation, but Cass knew to whom Fedor spoke.

"*Da*, OK, OK."

His eyes refocused on Cass.

"He says I bring the boy," Fedor said, with an Eastern European accent and a smile like a corpse with its lips stretched back over its teeth. "You? You may die."

Cass tensed, willed the quint into her bloodstream, pleaded with her nerves to accept the chems. Fedor took a step into the room, and then stopped. Held, like a wolf catching an unfamiliar and unexpected scent.

"Everything alright in here?" came a voice from the main room.

Fedor turned slowly on one heel. Cass forced herself to an elbow, peered around Fedor's legs to see who had spoken. He was just sitting there, on the steel table in the middle of the main room, like he'd been there all day, hands on his knees, feet dangling.

"Reckon not," said Three, glancing to the crumpled remains of the doctor.

"Doctor's closed, friend," Fedor answered, emotionless. "Time you go somewhere else."

Three sniffed.

"I'd rather not."

Fedor advanced on him a few paces, drew up to his full height.

"Not a request, friend," said Fedor. "There is private business here."

Three shrugged.

"I've got some business with the two of 'em myself. Maybe you can wait outside."

"I don't think you understand, friend."

"I don't think you understand, *friend*."

Three leaned slightly to one side, made eye contact with Cass.

"Hey kid," he called.

Wren made no initial response, but Cass nudged, encouraging him. He peeked up, terrified. Three reached into his own left coat pocket, saw Fedor tense, pupils constricting, jaw tightening, readying himself. Three slowly withdrew his closed fist, turned it palm up, and opened it.

"You lose something?"

Wren scrunched up his face, then raised his head as recognition came. His shuttlecar, resting on Three's palm. Wren nodded slightly, frightened, timid, unsure of what to do.

"Well, come get it," Three said.

No one moved. Three looked Fedor dead in the eyes, saw them dancing frantically as Fedor internally searched for any kind of record or file on this stranger.

"You wanna let the kid by?"

Fedor hesitated, calculated. Then sidestepped slightly, and held out a hand, making space and gesturing for Wren to enter the main room. Three looked again to Cass, still outstretched on the floor, caught her eye; saw fear, desperation, but something else not there before.

Hope.

She pushed Wren up, whispered to him. Wren nodded, clambered to his feet, shuffled through the door, wary of both men and obviously ashamed of the darkened wet spot trailing down one leg of his pants.

He stopped halfway between Three and Fedor, out of reach of either. Three didn't get off the table. Just held out his left hand, where the shuttlecar waited.

"It's yours, isn't it?" he asked.

Wren shot a glance to Cass. She was sitting up now. She nodded. He looked back to Three, nodded.

"Well, come get it."

Wren started to move, but Fedor stopped him.

"No!" he barked. "That is close enough, Spinner."

Three eyed Fedor. Fedor glared back.

"Can you catch, kid?" Three asked, not taking his eyes off Fedor.

Wren didn't respond. Just stared. Three turned to look him in the eye.

"Here. Soft pitch. Ready?"

Wren nodded slightly.

Three exaggerated the motion, down, up, launching the tiny model car in a high arc towards Wren. In the same instant, his right hand flashed, snatching his pistol from its holster, bringing it to bear on Fedor. Fluid, flawless, perfect.

Yet not fast enough.

Fedor seemed to teleport across the room, hammering his forearm into Three's wrist, catapulting the weapon from Three's grasp. It clattered against the wall about the same time Fedor buried his fist in the side of Three's head, sending Three flailing backwards and sideways off the table.

Stunned, dizzy, Three managed to roll up just in time to see Fedor's heavy boot hurtling towards his throat. He twisted, felt the wind of Fedor's kick whistle by, not comprehending how a man that size had closed that distance so fast. No time to figure it out. Three rolled again, spun on his back, gained his feet just as Fedor's fingers darted towards his eyes, seeking to pry them from their sockets. With his right hand, Three slapped downwards, caught Fedor's fingers in an iron grip, sidestepped and twisted, cranking Fedor's wrist and elbow into a locked position. Driving upwards, Three whipped his blade from its sheath with his off-hand and slashed deeply into Fedor's exposed underarm, feeling the soft tissue and sinew sever and tear away in a gush.

Fedor spun from an impossible position, lifting Three off-balance, and then bashed Three with an elbow across the forehead, slamming him to the floor. Fedor's right arm hung limply, his entire side darkly saturated, as he raised his boot to stomp Three's crotch. A moment before impact, a streak shot over Three and caught Fedor in the throat, launching him backwards into the smaller interior room. He crashed heavily to the concrete floor headfirst with a wet crunch, where he lay still, rasping and struggling for breath.

Three raised his swirling head, saw Cass crouching at his feet, facing away, a single hand outstretched towards the back room. A moment later, with a barely audible whir, the door to the back room slid shut, and all was still.

Three slumped back to the floor, stared at the ceiling, wondered if it would ever stop its lazy spin. He felt robbed, having gone from sober to massive hangover without ever passing through pleasant drunkenness. Pressure from inside his head counterbalanced the throbbing from the outside in a low-intensity equilibrium of pain. His right ear rang. A tiny silhouette slid into periphery, towering above Three from his worm's-eye view.

"Is he…?" a small voice whispered, trailing off.

"Yeah, baby," Cass said, from somewhere. "I'm afraid he is–"

"I'll be fine," Three interrupted. "Eventually."

Cass appeared, sidling next to Wren, kneeling, eyes bewildered or amazed.

"We should go," she said, hushed. "Can you walk?"

"In a minute."

"They'll be here by then."

"Then go on."

The weakening sun left the room a murky brownish-gray, making features difficult to distinguish. Three thought he caught Cass biting her bottom lip again; might've imagined it. She stood, face enshrouded by shadow, took Wren's hand, and left.

Three closed his eyes. Twice now. No "thank you". At least his ear had stopped ringing.

A pitter-patter approached, and Wren called from the door.

"Thanks for my car."

Three raised a hand in silent acknowledgement, and Wren was gone.

Three didn't know who "they" were, but he'd lain on the floor five, maybe ten minutes, and no one else had shown up. After recovering his pistol, which was undamaged by the scuffle, he'd set out with the late afternoon sun towards the agent's office. Three-thousand Hard waited for him. Tonight, he was going to get very, very drunk.

When he reached the agent's office, the glass doors slid smoothly open to admit him, snicked closed behind. He ran his fingers absentmindedly over the goose-egg throbbing above his left eye, shook his head to clear it as he walked the long stone corridor. Three reached the agent's cube, waited for the greeting.

"State your business," the voice boomed.

"Bounty."

"State your name," said the voice. Almost familiar. Something different, maybe. Three was too hazy to be sure.

"We did this already. I'm just here for my money."

The same slot opened in the cube, same metal case slid out, same rubberized interior.

"Deposit your weapons in the provided secure receptacle."

"No."

A pause.

"Please approach the door."

Three stepped closer, sarcastic, nose almost touching the flexiglass door. It slid open. He looked down slightly, expecting to find the eyes of the diminutive agent. Instead, he found himself looking at a broad chest. Not the agent.

Fedor.

# THREE

A meaty hand clapped over Three's face, so huge that having its palm on his chin didn't prevent its fingernails from digging into his scalp just above his forehead. Before he even finished flinching, Three was hurtling headlong into the flexiglass room, crashing face down into a stack of aged and blinking hardware, which collapsed and buried his head and shoulders under a jagged heap. Behind him, the door slid shut, whirred, and clunked heavily, some kind of magnetic lock-and-seal dropping into place. Three lay still, mind scrambling. He'd barely survived his first encounter with Fedor, with three times the room to maneuver. Three felt Fedor prowl over him. A heavy boot stamped down on the back of his knee, grinding the kneecap into the granite floor.

"So," Fedor growled. "You are not so much."

He snorted, and spat on Three, then drew a breath to say something else.

Instead, an ear-shattering blast of white lightning erupted from the back of Three's coat, slamming through Fedor, spattering him across the inside of the cube. Then, a weighty silence descended, no doubt magnified by Three's self-inflicted deafness. He hoped it was temporary.

Three rolled slowly up on his elbow, shoved the broken hardware off himself, surveyed the scene. The wreckage that had been Fedor lay folded near the door. Three's shot had caught him right through the middle. He wouldn't be getting up again. Three checked himself, side aching from the blast he'd fired from his still-holstered pistol. His vest was scorched, and the hole through his coat smoked faintly, but he was glad to see he hadn't shot off any of his own important bits.

He sat up, inhaled deeply, jammed his fingers in his ears to work out the heavy dullness, took stock of his surroundings. The flexiglass cube was frosted opaque from the impact of the round that had torn through Fedor, but the walls were otherwise intact. In one corner lay the agent, broken by Fedor some time before.

Unnecessary, Three thought. Excessive. A waste.

He fished around in one of his coat's many pockets, and drew out his remaining stock of shells. Down to six. With practiced fluidity, he flipped open his pistol's three-chambered cylinder, and replaced the spent shell with a fresh one. He dropped the empty in another pocket, where it jangled with others he'd fired before, each eagerly awaiting a refill, though chances for that were getting increasingly slim. A sharp flick of the wrist snapped the cylinder in place, and Three slid the pistol back into its now-charred holster.

He stood, shaking his head, and set to searching for a way to get out of the cube. None of the devices that still blinked or whirred seemed to have anything to do with the door. The agent's cluttered desk was likewise no help. He flipped switches, pressed buttons, stomped, kicked. After twenty minutes of scouring to no avail, claustrophobia began to settle in. Three realized his breathing was short, his jaw clenched. He forced himself to sit. Propped up on the agent's desk, he tried to relax, told himself he'd find what he was looking for, that he wasn't going to die in a box. At least, not this one. He took a deep breath and held it.

That was when he heard the scratching.

It was quiet; rhythmical, methodical. Someone was working the other side of the door.

Three crept cat-like from the desk, half-crouched on the floor, eyes darting to reevaluate his options. For all the clutter, there was no real place to hide, no solid cover. He improvised.

As quietly as he was able, Three dragged Fedor to a corner, where he lay down and rolled the giant corpse on top of himself. He shoved his arm under Fedor, leveled his pistol at the door. Waited. The scratching continued, intermittent but determined. Minutes stretched.

Three's fingers began to tingle, nerves revolting against Fedor's dead-weight pressure crushing down into his bicep. He rested his head on the cool marble floor, chastised himself for choosing this corner of the small room, where eyes would undoubtedly fall first. The collapsed pile of hardware was the better option. The confusion of the electronic debris, coupled with Fedor's ragged form, would've bought precious seconds of advantage. Too late now. Three hoped he'd outlive this mistake.

He'd know soon enough. Finally, the door whirred, thunked. Three raised his head, just so his left eye could see over Fedor, finger tightening on the trigger. The door slid open. A tiny figure stood silhouetted at the entrance and quietly gasped. Wren. Cass appeared, saw the carnage, reflexively slipped her hand over Wren's eyes. Too late. The little boy wouldn't sleep well that night.

Three was relieved. The shock of Fedor's damage had bought him the advantage after all. Cass only just now noticed him. He pushed Fedor off and sat up, holstering his pistol and massaging his arm. Cass turned Wren around and pushed him gently outside the cube. She returned, locked eyes with Three. For a moment, neither spoke.

Then, finally.

"How long...?" Cass started. She closed her eyes, swallowed, tried again. "How long have you been here?"

"Longer than I'd prefer," Three answered. He got to his feet. "Sorry your boy had to see that."

Cass opened her eyes and nodded, though what she meant to communicate with the gesture wasn't clear. Three watched her for a moment, noted the throbbing vein in her slender neck, the fluttering eyelids in her too-often blink. Days-old weariness, offset by adrenaline. Or the quint. It was always tougher to read a Chemic. Three moved to the agent's desk with a slight shrug.

"Where's the agent?" she asked.

Three rummaged through the agent's desk, and flicked his head to the corner where the agent lay. Cass glanced over, sighed heavily, disappointed.

"You?"

Three shook his head.

"Your friend, Fedor. He was waiting when I got here."

Now Cass shook her head.

"That isn't Fedor. That's Kostya."

Three gave Kostya another look. Eyes, cheekbone, jawline… even the hair was the same.

"Clones?" asked Three.

"Worse," Cass replied. "Brothers… twins."

Three let out a deep breath, then went back to his work.

"What're you looking for?"

Three held up his reply: the agent's biometrically-sealed cashbox. Cass watched as he moved to the agent's cool form, and swiped stiffening fingers across the panel. The box hissed open, and Three let out a low whistle. It was full of Hard.

He ran a quick estimate. Twenty-five thousand, at least. Maybe thirty. Three counted out the three thousand he was due, unbuckled his vest, and secured the Hard inside. Out of the corner of his eye, he saw Cass lower her gaze to the floor.

Three placed the cashbox on the little agent's lap, and folded the old man's hands over the top. He stood, and moved to the door. Cass didn't look up.

"What about the rest?" she asked, quietly.

"This," Three said, tapping his vest where the Hard was concealed, "is mine. And I'm no thief."

After a thought, he added, "But he sure doesn't need it anymore."

Three saw her eyelids flutter, eyes darting quickly to the box and back. Yeah. She was thinking about it.

"Why'd you come here?" Three asked.

Cass looked up, bottom lip just barely catching her teeth again, almost too fast to notice.

"I didn't know where else to go."

Her eyes flicked to Kostya's torn remains, then to the agent, then back to Three. He saw the despondency closing in now, the last traces of hope slipping away, the final slender thread of courage and will strained and twisting, just before surrender. Even with Fedor and Kostya no longer hounding her she had a hunted look, and trapped. Not the smoldering ferocity of a cornered animal, but the resignation of one wounded, seeing the way out, knowing it would never reach it.

Ah. Kostya had been waiting here for her, not for him. Three felt relief, without realizing he'd been concerned about it before. Still...

Three leaned his head outside the cube, checked on Wren where he sat cross-legged, pulling at a stray thread at the bottom of his too-thin jacket. He was going to need something warmer before much longer. Probably needed it now.

"How many more of them are there?" Three asked, looking back and catching Cass's eye again. She shrugged slightly, shaking her head. Three nodded.

"OK."

He stepped out of the cube, and walked the length of the hall to the glass entryway, footsteps dull echoes in the stone corridor. Three gazed westward. The sun was disappearing out there, beyond the wall. He judged the distance.

It would be close. But it was possible.

"Get what you need," Three called back down the long hall, without turning. "Then let's go."

The trio pressed through the alleyways, Three leading the woman and child along with a barely restrained urgency, like a wolfhound straining at its leash. She'd given up asking for explanations, or plans, or even for hints of where Three was leading them. She was out of options now, and they all knew it.

Three hesitated at every corner, every intersection, every stretch of open and unprotected ground they had to cover, but never for long. Streets were emptying as residents headed indoors with the setting sun. The few that remained were quick to avert their gazes from his intensity.

Finally, they reached their destination. The wall. Specifically, the Wall, where a small side-entrance stood guarded by a squat toll-booth-sized shelter. Two night watchmen manned it, and one stepped out to halt them.

"Sorry, folks. Not enough time left for you to get out tonight," said the watchman. He was tall. Tall, but young; lanky.

"There's enough for us to get out," Three answered. "We don't need to get back in."

The tall guard looked them up and down, suspiciously.

"Naw," he replied, without warmth. "Like I said. Not enough time."

"Trust me," said Three. "There is."

"You in some kind of trouble here, miss?" asked the other guard, now emerging from the shelter. Three checked him. Older, rounder, soft, but gritty.

"No, sir," Cass answered, too quickly. "We're fine."

The older watchman's eyes roved back and forth over Cass and Wren. Three sized up both guards. Tall one was eager: he'd be the first to try something. But it was the older one he had to watch.

The older one grunted, exchanged a look with the taller. Not *a* look. *The* look.

"OK, well," said the older guard, turning back towards his shelter. "Why don't you folks just–"

Before he could finish, Three smashed his forearm across the back of the older guard's neck, slamming the watchman's face hard into the wall of the shelter. In the impact, something flew from the guard's hand: stunrod.

In the same instant, Three had his pistol jammed under the jaw of the taller guard, forcing the young watchman's head up and backwards.

"Open it, and then close it behind us," Three snarled, teeth gritting in the older guard's ear. "Or I'll do it, and leave it open. All. Night."

The older watchman remained silent through the blood pouring from his nose. Three could feel the tension in the man, like a viper coiled. Half a slip, and the tables would turn. But the taller one made whimpering, agreeable noises. When Three lowered the gun off him, he quickly bustled to the door and opened it. The door led into a darkened chamber: a small airlock within the wall. Three pushed off the old watchman, floating his weapon fluidly between the two.

"Both doors," Three growled.

The young watchman shook his head vigorously.

"It don't work like that. You gotta get in, and shut this door. Then the other one can open, from the inside."

Three started towards the guard, who stumbled backwards into the airlock, but there was no defiance there, only fear. Three knew he was telling the truth.

"Fine. Come on."

Cass and Wren pushed into the chamber, and the watchman started to sidle out. Three flashed his gun, and teeth.

"No. You stay."

The tall watchman looked to the old, color draining from his face. The older one paced closer; slow, determined, with barely restrained menace.

"Look. Whatever business you have leavin' here at this time o' day is your own," said the older guard. "You leave him out of it."

Three stared the man down, looked deep, and found steel. The old man had some bond with the taller guard. He wasn't going to budge. Three ground his teeth. They were losing time.

A tense heartbeat, then another.

Finally, Three slid his gun back into its holster, gently, and motioned the young watchman out. Young slid behind old, wounded, frightened, sheltering behind the other's strength. For a moment, Three wondered if they might be father and son.

"When this one shuts, it'll take a minute," said the old watchman, shutting the door before anyone could reply, and sealing the trio in complete darkness. Somewhere in the wall, gears ground, and a deep metallic thunk sounded; a heavy lock sliding into place.

Seconds became minutes. Still they sat. Trapped. Betrayed. Three reached for his pistol, not knowing what else to do.

Then, a hiss. A crack of ebbing light around the outer door. Three felt around, found a handle, pushed it down and outward, and the door swung open.

The dead city stretched out before them, as the last, dying rays of the sun deepened to red and purple.

"Stay with me," Three said.

And he pushed out from the safety of the Wall, into the fast-approaching night.

# FOUR

"We can't–" Cass panted. "What're you doing? We can't go out there! Not now!"

Three whipped back, stared hard into the airlock where Cass and Wren huddled together. He spoke calmly, in low tones, but an animal ferocity lurked behind the words.

"Inside those walls, there's nowhere left for you. Out here, with me, you have a chance."

He watched her shift, glance around the inside of the airlock, look to Wren. He was right, and he knew she knew it. They couldn't afford to debate.

"I'm leaving," he said. "Now."

Three turned, started on his way. "If you want to see the sunrise," he called over his shoulder, "stay with me."

He didn't bother to look back. She and the kid would catch up. Or, if not, they wouldn't be his problem anymore. He shook his head at that. They weren't even his problem now, or wouldn't be if he hadn't inserted himself into whatever trouble they were in. He'd killed two men for them already, though, and he was past trying to figure out which side of the law they were on. They were on his side now, or he was on theirs. Whatever side it was, he had to believe it was the right one.

Footsteps hurried up behind, and Three couldn't decide if he was glad to hear them. He'd have to wait and see, figure it out later, once he could tell for sure whether or not this was the thing that was going to get him killed.

The trio pressed on in silence, through the battered asphalt streets and concrete alleyways, gray labyrinthine walls pockmarked by uncounted years of neglect and decay. The day's final rays of sunlight filtered low through the crumbling architecture, highlighting the particles that swirled in the approaching evening's breeze, dust of the bygone: man's only truly lasting legacy to the world. Three moved with a steady, urgent pace, one that Cass and Wren fought to keep. As long as they kept it, though, he didn't care how much they struggled.

As the last glimpse of the sun finally dipped below the horizon, Three halted at an intersection, eyes searching north, then south, then north again. They had to be close. But close wouldn't count once the sky was dark. His mind raced, trying to remember the details, while his eyes scoured their surroundings for any sign of what he was looking for.

"What is it?" he heard Cass say, her voice floating somewhere distant, background to his thoughts. "Why are we stopping?"

Three glanced up, found the maglev line, rusted and sagging, running back towards the enclave. North, he decided. Better to pick one and hope than to stand idle, indecisive.

He moved on again, northward, as the sky deepened its blue above them, and burned fiery orange at the horizon. Fifty meters. A hundred. Two hundred. Still no sign. He'd guessed wrong. They couldn't make it now, not before...

There. Through an alley, he saw it. He checked the sky. Fifteen, twenty minutes. Maybe less.

"Come on."

Three broke into a jog, heedless of the distance he was opening between himself and the others. He found the entrance to a small concrete building; short, squat, with its heavy steel door hanging rusted on it hinges. Out of the corner of his eye, he saw Cass huffing down the alleyway to catch up,

Wren bouncing along piggyback, arms tight around her neck. Three set to work, alternately knocking rust from the hinges, and shoving inward on the door.

"What is this place?" Cass asked, lowering Wren to the ground. Her breathing surprised Three with its steadiness, its relative ease. They'd covered a lot of ground, for someone of her stature. He wondered how long she'd been carrying the boy, chastised himself for not noticing earlier. Only one set of footsteps instead of two. Should've caught that; heard it.

He didn't bother to answer her. She'd see soon enough, and every second he spent explaining was another second lost. He knocked another layer of rust off the bottommost hinge, and threw himself into the door. It shrieked in the gathering dusk, the scream of disused metal, and bent inward an inch, perhaps two. Again, Three rammed his shoulder into the rusting steel. Again, an inch, no more. He turned, put his back against it, strained, teeth-gritting, felt the frozen hinges crack, but hold. He closed his eyes, willed the door to open, to no avail.

Then, next to him, firm, strong, warm against his shoulder – Cass. Her shoulder buried into the door, feet planted. Together now. Her strength surprised him. The door shrieked again: four inches, now eight. Cool, damp air flowed out from the heavy darkness within. Three and Cass reset themselves, readied for a final shove. Wren joined in, tiny hands spread on the door, hip-level to Three. Together, they forced the door open to nearly a foot. As the screeching echoes died away, a new call answered: shrill, distant, electric.

Cass spun, faced Three. He saw fright there, complete and constricting horror. She seized his arm, nails biting into his biceps even through his coat. They were too late. The Weir were abroad. Hunting.

A second digital scream sounded, still distant, but unmistakably closer. And a third, calling in answer. Three had brought the woman and her boy out here to protect them. And that was what he meant to do. He pried Cass from him, gripped her forearms in his fists.

"Listen," he said, looking hard into her wet, vacantly staring brown eyes. There was no recognition there. "Hey! Hey!"

Cass's eyes cleared, fixed on his.

"You can still make it. You and the boy. Get in there."

He pushed her towards the opening, and then caught Wren by the shoulder, and shoved him to her.

"Go on, boy. You'll fit."

Wren stared wide-eyed at Three, at the darkness yawning from the doorway, at his shaken, trembling mother.

"Mama...?"

Another shriek, echoing down the alleyways, closer; much too close this time.

"Go, Wren, go, now baby," Cass said, pushing Wren into the gap in the door. "I'm right behind you."

Wren slipped in without effort, tiny frame instantly swallowed by the black void waiting inside. Cass followed, though not as easily, wedging herself in, struggling through. The entryway was narrow enough without the frozen gate blocking the way, and Three watched as Cass curved herself around the door with shuffling side steps. Finally, she was in. She disappeared momentarily, then peeked her head back around the door.

Three remained in place, just holding out his hand to her.

"Take this."

Cass looked down at the chemlight laid across his palm. Her eyes darted back to his, understanding. She shook her head vigorously, but he cut her off, twisting the top of the light, igniting it, thrusting it towards her.

"Take it! Follow the stairs all the way; all the way to the bottom," Three spoke rapidly now, directing, commanding. "Once you're there–"

Back down the alley, a pair of electronic shrieks called, responded. Fifty meters away, or maybe twenty. The way sound bounced through the cement corridors made it hard to know for certain. Three saw Cass start to slip again.

"Hey, are you listening?"

She refocused, nodded.

"When you're at the bottom, follow the pipes to the first alcove you find, get in it, and kill the light."

He felt her hand on his, half-closed around the chemlight.

"What about you?" she asked. He glanced back down the alleyway, back the way they had come. At the far end, a faint blue light shone, sweeping, searching. He looked back to Cass.

"If I don't get to you by sun-up, head north."

He slipped his hand out from under hers, and pushed her gently back. Then, grasping the door handle, Three pulled with adrenaline-fueled strength, and sealed Cass and Wren inside.

As the rolling echoes from the slamming door died off, Cass found herself standing in a pool of pale yellow light at the top of a cement landing, with Wren wrapped tightly around her leg. For a moment, she considered pressing an ear to the door, but the urgent directions sprang to mind, and she thought better of it. She reached down, and took Wren's hand.

"Come on, baby," she soothed, annoyed at the tremble in her own voice. "We need to head down… there."

She held the chemlight out, saw steel-grated stairs, rust-coated but sturdy, trailing off into the darkness below. The pool of light illuminated no more than the first five steps, and she wondered just how far "down there" really was.

"Can you carry me?" Wren asked. He seemed surprisingly unconcerned, and that made Cass feel stronger.

"Sure, sweetheart."

She knelt; let him scramble up on her back again. His warmth was comforting.

"Here, you hold this," Cass said, handing Wren the light. "Hold it out in front, so we can see where we're going."

"Like a maglev," he replied, almost cheerful.

"Just like."

Cass allowed herself a half smile, as she stood, hooking her arms under Wren's legs, and adjusting him on her back. She was almost jealous of his apparent fearlessness, even knowing it was born of ignorance.

"I'll be the train," she said, "and you can be the driver."

"OK…" said Wren hesitantly, swallowing hard. Cass looked back, saw him staring down into the blackness below. "But not too fast."

Maybe not as fearless as she'd thought, or perhaps hoped.

"Slow and steady, baby. We'll keep it on the rails, alright?"

He tightened around her, she felt him nodding against her back. He held the light at arm's length, showing the few steps ahead and no more. Cass took a deep breath. Slow and steady. Together, they began their descent.

The gloom was heavy, cool, damp; smelled vaguely of earth, and dust, and water. An urban cavern. But one full of energy, as if the darkness that enshrouded the pair were itself alive, eager to consume the meager light they wielded, to embrace them, and perhaps devour them as well. Each step brought a creak or groan of steel, stairs long-unused reawakening to their purpose for the first time in unmeasured years, or even decades. A narrow handrail marked the edge. Cass pressed her shoulder to the wall opposite, mistrusting the protection the rail seemed to promise, and fought the resistance she felt emanating from further below, the timeless fear of the unknown. Forward, onward, downward she drove herself, despite the growing temptation to return to the relative safety of the landing above.

Fifteen stairs down, the steps turned abruptly left, ninety degrees. After another fifteen, another ninety-degree left. This became the pattern as Cass descended, with Wren fidgeting upon her back. The air grew cooler and damper. Cass wondered how far below the streets they'd come. And she wondered where the man that brought them here was now. She hoped he was still alive. Had to believe he was, no matter what the odds against it were. She realized for the first time she didn't even know his name.

"I'm tired," Wren said, softly. "Can we stop?"

"Not yet."

"How much longer?"

"Not much."

Cass continued on, legs and knees aching, wondering for herself how much farther they had to go. Internally, she checked global-time. 19:07 GST. Outside, somewhere high above them, night had settled fully. One foot in front of the other; automatic now. They'd been descending for nearly half an hour, though at their current, cautious pace, Cass had no idea what distance they had traveled. Not nearly as far as it felt, that was certain.

She felt Wren's grip around her shoulders slacken, his head bump down on her back. His arm, stretched out in front of her, began to lower slightly, slowly.

"Wren," she said, quietly. She hated the way her voice sounded in the utter silence, as though speaking drew unwanted attention from the darkness, or whatever might be lurking hidden within it. "Wren?"

Wren's small hand continued to lower, grip relaxing on the chemlight. Cass reached up instinctively to catch it. Without her arm supporting his leg, Wren slipped sideways on her back, jolted suddenly awake. The chemlight flew from his hand, danced on Cass's fingertips.

For a breathless second–

–she almost thought she'd caught it.

Instead, it clattered to the stairs, bounced, skittered to the edge. And fell. Cass watched in horrified silence as the pale yellow light shrank into the void, and disappeared, swallowed by the blackness. She never did hear it hit the bottom.

For a time, neither of them spoke, or moved, in the utter darkness that encased them. Then, Cass felt Wren's slight shudders, knew he was sobbing, silently, mortified. She swallowed her own panic, anger, disappointment.

"It's alright, baby. It's OK."

Carefully, she knelt, feeling the wall to her side to maintain her sense of direction, and swung Wren around, embracing him. Reassuring him; feeling hopeless herself.

"It's OK, Wren. I shouldn't have made you carry it all that way. Don't cry, sweetheart, it's not your fault."

He buried his face into her shoulder, hot tears falling on her neck. She caressed his head, ran her fingers through his hair, soothed him; screamed inside. She dared not turn around, couldn't face the ascent, but her heart revolted at the idea of continuing further down without any way to see what might lie ahead. What if the stairs had given out down below? And who knew what creatures might have found their way in and made their nests in here? Cass's mind exploded with the possibilities, none of them pleasant.

In the end, she couldn't bring herself to continue on without some sense of where they were, or where they were headed. Even with the risk it posed, it seemed like the best option of very few. Cass shut her eyes, accessed distant satellites high above the earth, pinpointed herself, identified their current location. She'd already done all she could to mask her signal. Hopefully, no one would notice the query.

Within seconds of finding herself in the world, she had blueprints. They were in the storm-water system, seventy meters of one hundred below the surface. According to the schematics, the concrete floor lay thirty meters further down, a junction between miles of pipes and ducts, each carrying hundreds of thousands of gallons of water back and forth from collection points to treatment centers and on to distribution. The entire system was automated, and apparently remained functional, even now. Knowing where she was somehow soothed Cass, stole some of the menace from the darkness. She felt strengthened.

Only for a moment. Somewhere, high above, the silence was rent by the piercing shriek of steel. Cass knew in an instant. Someone, or something, had breached the door. She wanted to believe it was the man, coming to get them. The dread in her heart told her it wasn't.

"Mama?"

"Come on, baby."

Cass swung Wren up on her hip, adrenaline coursing, heart pounding. In the complete blackness, she took the steps down, two at a time. Knowing they were closer to the bottom than the top gave her some courage, but she knew how slowly she'd taken that first stretch. There was no way to tell how quickly whatever it was would descend.

Around and around they twisted, Cass plunging her feet down into darkness, hoping with every step that there would be a stair below to meet them. Then. Finally. Concrete. They hit bottom so quickly, she stumbled to a knee on her second step, expecting to find another stair instead of level ground. A pale yellow light shone weakly not far away.

The chemlight. Miraculously, it hadn't broken in the fall. Cass scrambled to it, seized it, raised it high to get her bearings. Follow the pipes, he had said. To the first alcove.

She did.

A long concrete corridor, smooth and rounded, tunneled from the base of the stairs, off into apparent oblivion. Along the wall, oxidized pipes stacked atop each other, some merely as wide as Cass's arm, others large enough for her to have crouched inside, had there been a way to enter them. They were beaded with moisture, much as Cass was, despite the coolness of the air. She pressed on in the dim light, searching for a break in the wall.

Wren's arms tightened around her neck, and he pressed his mouth to her ear, speaking in a ragged whisper.

"Mama… Mama…" the boy choked out, like a child caught between wakefulness and nightmare. "It's coming!"

Cass could hear the fear in his labored breathing, felt it herself, in her bones, like a great grasping claw just at her heels. She didn't dare look behind. She jogged on, trying to keep the balance between silence and speed.

Behind them, a strange sound. A flapping sort of echo, like bat's wings. Or bare feet upon the stair.

There. Just ahead, on the right. A break in the wall. The first alcove.

The pipes continued on, passing over top of the niche. By ducking down, Cass found she and Wren could slip in behind them, though once they did, she couldn't see the point. It was a dead end, only six feet deep; deep as a grave, and no more. But it was all they had. She took Wren to the far wall, as far back as they could go, sat him down on her lap, between herself and the wall, switched off the light.

And waited.

Cass fought to quiet her own breathing, to calm her thumping heart. The blood in her ears made it impossible to be sure whether or not those were footsteps in the corridor. In the next instant, she had her answer.

An evil croak, a mixture of loudly exhaled breath and digital static, echoed down the concrete tunnel. Instinctively, Cass cradled Wren to her, buried his face in her breasts. He clung to her with trembling hands. Silence. Then, again, the harsh electronic cry. This, now, followed by shuffling steps, growing louder, closer. Cass's mind scrambled for options, to think of anything she might have to use as a weapon. Realized she had none.

A faint ice-blue glow began to spread at the entrance of the alcove, so faint at first Cass wasn't sure she could see it. Slowly, gradually, it intensified, until there was no mistaking it. The shuffling steps continued.

The man had brought them out from the safety of the wall, sent them here, sent them here to die. And she had let him. Cass bent her head, silently pressed her lips to Wren's damp hair, kissed him goodbye. She took the slightest trace of comfort in knowing that at very least, Asher would never take Wren.

The footsteps ceased. The entryway was bathed in soft white-blue light, slowly, faintly pulsing. The inhuman cry sounded again, shocking, intense in its proximity, and Cass realized a Weir was standing at the entrance, its blue-glow eyes roving to find them, searching. Through a gap in the pipes, she caught a glimpse of the pinprick orbs, smoldering in their sockets. Her heart caught in her throat, chest constricted in terror.

And then–

Shuffling steps resumed. It moved on, further down the tunnel, croaking every so often. Light faded, and eventually sound vanished as well, leaving Cass and Wren clinging together in the uncertain safety of the alcove. Neither dared to speak. They hardly dared to breathe.

Finally, after a time, Cass allowed herself to believe they were alright. She checked the time again: 19:29 GST. Just twenty-two minutes had passed since their pitch-black flight down the stairs. It was going to be a long night. Wren leaned heavily on her, limp, breathing with the deep rhythm of exhaustion. Cass shifted her weight, brought her coat up and around them both, leaned her head back against the wall.

But sleep wouldn't come. Not for her, not here in this place. She fought the urge to turn the chemlight back on, though the promise of its meager light seemed like water to parched lips. The blackness began to work on her mind, making her see things, hear things she knew weren't there, couldn't be there. Fedor, Kostya. Asher. Asher and his hounds, hunting them, finding them, seizing Wren, and taking him back. She couldn't let that happen. She *wouldn't* let that happen.

Cass accessed the satellites again. The man had told them to head north when the sun rose. But she didn't know why, or what they should be heading *for*. She scanned, just pulses at a time, always releasing connection after a few seconds and siphoning a new one to avoid trace. North. Miles and miles of urban wasteland. Nothing surprising there. She panned the internally displayed image, eyes open, seeing the image projected onto her corneas, not the darkness beyond. Nothing stood out, no exceptional towns, no safe houses, no signs of life. Unless… She isolated; zoomed.

And froze.

A soft white-blue glow engulfed her. The Weir had doubled back.

# FIVE

Wren lay sleeping in her lap, undisturbed by the deadly creature prowling at the entrance of the alcove. Cass could see no details of the thing, save its gently radiating eyes: blue, cold, electric. These shifted; floated in a fluid, elliptical pattern, as though the Weir were peering at her through smoke, or heavy fog. Or like a cobra, before it struck. Instinctively, slowly, she squeezed Wren closer, hoping he wouldn't stir. The Weir hadn't seen them here before. Maybe it would overlook them again.

For a moment, it just stood there, silently. Cass couldn't even hear it breathing. But she could smell its scent. Antiseptic, metallic, faintly pungent, like a stainless steel scalpel, with lingering vapors of embalming fluid. Death preserved.

It glanced casually away to its right, as if disturbed by some unfelt breeze, or perhaps considering continuing on to the stairs. The creature hesitated there, just long enough for Cass to hope it would leave. Instead, it whipped its gaze back directly upon her, and she knew it was over.

The Weir crouched back, coiling to pounce, and let fly its white-noise scream. Cass crushed Wren to her, shut her eyes, turned her back to absorb the brunt of the attack.

But it didn't come.

A strange sound – the wet whip of metal through flesh and bone – silenced the Weir mid-cry. A dull bounce, followed by a heavy collapse. A sharp wave of chemical odor, sulfuric or strongly ammoniacal, crashed over them. Cass dared open her eyes to find only pitch-blackness, the Weir's blue-glow eyes doused.

Then–

–a voice, in the darkness.

"I'm here."

The man. He spoke in low tones, somewhere between whisper and growl. "You OK?"

"Where have you been?" Cass demanded, harsh, through gritted teeth, barely restraining her voice.

"Is your boy alright?" he said, more gruffly. "He's quiet."

Before Cass could respond, the man ignited his own chemlight. Meager light by most standards, but to Cass's eyes it blazed like a sun.

Three held the chemlight outstretched; scanned the couple huddled against the wall. He could barely see the kid, tucked in there between the wall and his mother, but he could see enough. Wren's eyes were open wide, staring, not even squinting against the sudden flare of Three's light. Jaw clenched, oblivious to his surroundings: catatonic. No way to tell if the kid was even still in there anymore. Three shook his head.

"I'm fine," Wren said in the barest of whispers, unblinking. "Is the other one still down here?"

Three glanced to Cass. She looked just as surprised as he felt. Three grunted, frustrated with himself. Surprised could get you killed.

"Other one?" he asked.

Cass shook her head.

"That one…" Her eyes flicked to the dark heap by Three's feet for a hint of a second, "…passed us once, but came back."

Three caught a motion out of the corner of his eye: the kid, shaking his head ever so slightly. Not openly defying his mother. Almost to himself. Like he wanted his mom to be right, but knew she wasn't. He just kept staring straight ahead.

"Wren was sleeping," she offered, gently combing his hair with her fingers. "Maybe he dreamed it."

Wren's watery gaze shifted to Three, and Three got the sense the kid knew something. He didn't push it.

"OK," he said, with a slight conspiratorial nod to Wren. "Well. Let me take care of this."

He kicked at the unmoving remains of the Weir.

"Then we'll see what we see."

Three hooked the chemlight on his coat, letting the light fall across the Weir's remains. Cass inhaled sharply, hand reflexively shooting to cover Wren's eyes. She'd never seen one up close before.

It might have been a man once, long ago. A man dead of starvation, left exposed in some frozen desert where rot had never touched the corpse. The skin was green-gray in the chemlight, stretched tight like a drum over its skeleton, with hardly enough apparent muscle to animate the bones. Its hands lay curled like dead spiders, each of its knotted fingers sharply tipped with what looked more like talons than nails. The neck ended abruptly just above the shoulders, and seeped a pungent, viscous fluid; the source of the chemical odor. Its head… well, there was no sign of that.

There came the quiet swishing sound of steel drawn across fabric, and Cass realized for the first time that Three had been wielding his short blade, and was only now sheathing it. He hooked his forearms under the Weir's armpits without any apparent revulsion, and dragged it further down the tunnel, away from the stairs. The scraping sound of the corpse across the concrete grew fainter and fainter, and at last faded to silence. Cass felt fear creeping up on her again, never having noticed its absence in the first place.

"Don't worry," she said, after a while. "He'll be back."

She told herself she was comforting Wren. The darkness stretched time, made it difficult to judge whether it'd been five minutes or twenty.

"He'll be back," she repeated.

"He's a good guy, right?" Wren whispered.

"What, sweetheart?"

"He's a good guy? He's not going to hurt us?"

Cass hesitated for a bare moment, brushed her fingers through Wren's hair, soothing.

"Don't worry, baby," she answered. "I don't think he's dangerous."

"He *is* dangerous, Mama," Wren replied, with unusual certainty. "But he's good, right?"

There was something in the tone, something deeper behind the question, but it was a something Cass couldn't puzzle out. She put her hand on his cheek. It was cool, clammy; wet with tears. He was trembling.

"What is it? Wren, what's wrong?"

He didn't answer, except with a labored sob, one he'd been trying to hold back. Panic surged up in Cass's chest: a crushing, nameless fear for her child.

"Wren, baby, what's going on? Just talk to me."

He struggled to speak, mouth working without words. Finally, he forced a whisper through his constricted throat, reluctant: part confession, part nightmare.

"I can't *feel* him, Mama."

Cass pulled out the chemlight and ignited it to get a good look at her son. Instead, she let out a yelp.

The man was there, crouched at the alcove, looking back at her.

"Sorry," he said flatly, almost at full voice, which seemed to roll like thunder down the concrete tunnel. If he'd heard what Wren had said, he didn't make any sign of it. And he didn't seem that concerned about Wren's state. Nothing unusual about a child being comforted by his mother in the dark.

"You want to move?" he asked.

It took a moment for Cass to find a reply, there was so much her brain was trying to process.

"What? Oh, uh," she stammered, and inhaled, drawing in foul fumes that stung her nostrils. "Can we?"

"Yeah," he said. "There's another alcove just a little ways down. Come on."

He reignited the chemlight hooked on his coat, and scooted back, while Wren crawled out, followed closely by Cass. A dark pool of viscous chemical fluid spread from the entry of the alcove, and trailed off in a wide swath further down the storm system.

"Don't worry," Three said, seeing Wren's wet eyes on the streak. "We'll go down the other side."

Cass held Wren's hand tightly as Three led them down the corridor at a confident pace, without any noticeable concern that more of the Weir might be around. Even walking in their little bubble of light, she felt the yawning blackness pressing down on them: weighty, draining. By the time they reached the next alcove, Cass couldn't have said whether they'd walked for twenty meters or two hundred. And she realized she was weary enough for it to have been ten times as far. Three crouched at the entryway, looking under the stacks of pipes that covered the top half of the niche, and then motioned them in.

Cass nudged Wren in ahead of her, crouched, and followed closely behind. Wren moved to the back while she settled into one corner. Once seated, she motioned to him, and he flopped into her lap, closing her arms around himself, as if wrapping himself up in a blanket. Cass hugged her son close, and extinguished her chemlight.

••••

Three watched them from the entryway, noted the almost ritualistic nature of their movements, their postures. The way Wren nestled into Cass, how she rested her cheek atop his head. Three guessed the woman and child had spent many nights just this way, sleeping in some abandoned building or alley.

"Will you sleep?" Cass asked, raising her head slightly.

Three shook his head.

"You go ahead and rest, ma'am. I'll keep an eye out."

Cass nodded slightly, and resumed her posture, closing her eyes. Three watched her for a moment. Ragged, weary, she looked suddenly vulnerable. Fragile. And the boy. Three looked to him, and glimpsed the boy's eyes shutting suddenly. The eyelids fluttered. Pretending to be asleep. Three smirked at that.

He turned his back to them, and sat cross-legged at the mouth of the alcove. He drew a deep breath, then switched off his chemlight; allowed himself to be swallowed by darkness. Silently, so as not to disturb the woman and child, he drew his pistol and laid it in his lap. Three didn't expect anyone, or anything, to find them down here, but the familiar weight of the gun was reassuring. He reached back, unsheathed his blade, rested it over the top of the pistol. His own ritual. He steeled himself, set his mind and will to staying awake in the long and silent darkness.

After a moment, a breathy whisper sounded behind him. The boy.

"What's your–?" he started, then caught himself. "My name's Wren. What's yours?"

"Three," whispered Three over his shoulder.

There was a long pause, almost long enough for Three to think Wren had gone on to sleep. He hadn't.

"Should I call you Mister Three?"

Three smiled to himself.

"Just Three," he answered. Then almost as an afterthought, added, "Should I call you Mister Wren?"

Three could hear a hint of smile in the boy's reply.

"Just Wren."

After that, it was quiet for a long time.

Cass stirred awake, felt the dull ache of a night's sleep on a marble-hard floor, let her eyes float open. Expecting the total darkness of the storm-water system, she jolted when she realized she was outside. The sun was a sliver of fiery orange on the horizon, dawn breaking under a mercury sky. She took groggy stock of her surroundings, blinking heavy eyelids. A courtyard. Brick. Squat buildings, three or five stories high, crumbled around her. Heavy mist the color of concrete swirled off the ground at knee-level. Sleep fell away, and a realization broke over her like an arctic squall.

Wren was gone.

Cass exploded to her feet, and whipped around to get her bearings, looking for any sign or trace of her boy, finding none. She stood frozen, panicked, afraid to call out. Afraid not to.

Then, a voice sounded behind her.

"It's alright," a man called. "He's with me."

Cass recognized that voice. She spun.

"Asher!"

There, leaning against a wall across the courtyard, was her nightmare incarnate. Tall, lithe, wearing his wolfish grin, Asher's stillness coiled with menace. He was shaggy-haired and sharply handsome, with young, smooth features, and a boyish charm that could put almost anyone at ease. But not Cass. She knew what he was, and what he could do. She'd seen it for herself. Her hands balled into knuckle-cracking fists.

"Where is my son?"

"Don't worry about little Spinner," Asher said. "Ran and Jez are watching him."

Rage boiled up within Cass; rage, and an ice-cold fear. She had sworn to Wren she would never let them take him back. Her heart broke at what he must be going through now, alone, without her.

Asher scanned her up and down with a brief, casual amusement, then turned his interest to picking the lint from his long black coat. She judged the distance. The courtyard was maybe twenty meters wide. Too far. She'd never cross it fast enough.

"It's not too late for you, you know," he offered, not looking up. "All could be forgiven."

His eyes flicked up to her then, over her body, predatory. Hungry.

"For the right price."

A wave of revulsion crashed through her, and Cass fought to still herself. It wasn't enough. Asher caught the flicker of disgust on her face. She might as well have said it aloud.

"Not even for a chance to be with your own kid?" said Asher, with a humorless laugh. "Same as always – too stubborn for your own good."

"I swear to you, if you so much as think about hurting Wren–"

"Spare me the cliché," he interrupted, flicking a speck of dust. "It bores me."

He straightened to his full height, brushing one sleeve lightly with the back of his hand, and then tugging its cuff down past his wrist. Cass's mind raced. She might as well try for it. Maybe she'd catch him off guard.

"Fedor said you'd be like this," Asher sighed. He fidgeted with his other sleeve, glanced off at the horizon. "I wanted to argue, but… I guess I can't *force* you to make good decisions."

Asher seemed briefly lost in thought. This was her only moment. Cass rerouted synapses, flooded herself with adrenaline, readied to pounce.

"Besides," he added with a scoff. "Someone else has been missing you far more than I have."

Cass tipped forward to launch herself at him.

Her toes never even left the ground. Steel fingers seized her shoulder from behind, paralyzing her.

The scream died in her throat.

# SIX

Cass opened blind eyes to the nothingness that surrounded her, stifled a gasp, tried to get her bearings. For a moment, her last memory of Asher lingered, sharp, as real as the flight from the city wall, the Weir, the man. But in a flash, it was fleeting, fading, replaced by the reality pressing down around her. The damp blackness, the weight and warmth of Wren sleeping in her lap, the stone floor beneath her. Still, wakefulness didn't rid her of the intense grip she felt on her shoulder. The whole train of thought took only a fraction of a second, and in the next instant she realized the man was by her side, hand on her shoulder, lips pressed to her ear, his growling whisper hot on her face.

"We're in trouble."

Her instincts snapped alive, sudden clarity and focus even in the darkness.

"Wake the boy," he said. "But keep him quiet."

Before she could ask, he evaporated into the darkness, leaving only a release of pressure on her shoulder, a trace of warmth and wetness like a passionless kiss on her ear. Cass bent gently, pressed her cheek to Wren's, nuzzled him awake. He stirred in her lap, inhaled sleepily, but didn't speak, wouldn't until she said it was alright. She had taught him that long ago. She helped him to unsteady feet, and then rolled up to her knees, tried to work the hard knots out of her back and thighs. There was a dryness in her mouth, a stretching feeling at the back of her throat almost like the need to yawn, a certain restlessness deep in her lungs. The quint was getting low. Already. That much had used to last her days. Now, her body seemed to be burning through it faster than she could find it.

The man rematerialized.

"Do you remember the way to the stairs?" he whispered.

Cass nodded, forgetting he couldn't see her.

"Good," he said, before she had a chance to speak. "We're leaving."

Cass checked her internal clock. 06:17 GST. Sun wouldn't be up for another half hour, at least.

"What's going on?" she asked.

A distant, digital croak answered for him. Cass stiffened, felt the hairs rise on her neck.

"There *was* another one," Three said. "It brought help."

Another croak echoed down the tunnel, eerie in its origin, otherworldly with its reverberation.

"Let's move," said Three. Cass actually heard him shuffle backwards this time, presumably out of the alcove. She took Wren's hand in one of her own, and used the other to feel her way out, leading him along behind. The barest movement of air, a trace of coolness, signaled when she'd reentered the cavernous tunnel. Back to her right, towards the stairs, the endless blackness continued. Off to the left, however, a faint twinkle of blue glowed at her, bobbed, a wisp in the willows. It was joined by a second. Then a third.

Cass felt Wren pull away from her, and instinctively her hand clenched tight.

"It's alright," Three whispered, barely letting the air escape through his lips. "I've got him."

Cass reluctantly let Wren go. From the rustling, she gathered that the man had slung Wren up on his back.

"Hold on, and stay close."

Cass slipped her fingers through Wren's belt, and bumped up tight against him.

"Here we go."

Like a gentle tide, Cass felt Wren receding from her, so smoothly and silently, at first she thought she was falling backwards. She caught herself, and stepped forward, feeling clumsy and jostling in her gait compared to the flowing pace of the man in front of her. After a few steps, however, she found a rhythm that, if not matched, at least complemented his, and together they slipped off in the darkness.

The trio floated down the tunnel towards the stairs, haunted by the occasional squelch of white-noise echoing from the Weir behind them. Though they weren't sounding any closer, Cass was unnerved to notice they weren't sounding any farther away either. The squawks and croaks usually came in clusters, almost as if it were a conversation composed entirely of static. And now that she was paying more attention, she could pick out peculiarities in the sounds, or voices, if she dared call them that. One was thinner, drier; somehow more brittle. The others were fuller-throated, less harsh in aural frequency, but more fierce and guttural in tone.

Cass felt lost in the swimming darkness, her only anchors to any sort of concrete reality the floor under her feet and her hand on Wren. He was being awfully brave, she thought. She wondered how far they had left to go. It certainly felt like they should've made it by now.

She pinged the nearest satellite, located their position in the schematic she'd downloaded from before, ran an internal app to measure the distance. Eighty-three meters to go.

Suddenly, an electric shriek shattered the tunnel, ricocheted like sonic shrapnel; pierced her ears. Reflexively she clapped her hands over them and glanced behind. The blue orbs were there, now closing fast.

"What'd you do?" Three barked, snatching her around to face him.

"What?" she stammered. "No, nothing. I—"

He ignited the chemlight on his vest, and the ferocity on his face frightened her. He growled a wordless curse, and slid his hand down to her wrist, gripping it. Hard.

"Come on."

He jerked her to a run. All grace and fluidity disappeared. The three of them crashed headlong into the darkness, seeing no more than five steps ahead of themselves. Wren clung desperately to Three's back. Cass struggled to keep pace while being towed along.

She chanced a glance over her shoulder, caught a fleeting glimpse. Not three orbs now. Six pinpoints. Eyes.

The Weir were gaining.

Her heart pounded in her chest, she felt like she was falling behind, could feel Three straining to hold himself back so she could keep up. Cass wasn't going to be the one to get them killed. She proc'd more of the quint, overdrove her adrenals, felt her nerves electrify with the surge. In two bounding steps, she was dead-even with Three, jerking her arm away from him with strength renewed.

He didn't seem to notice or care. They sped down the tunnel. Three pointed ahead to their left.

"There!"

She cut that way, found the base of the stairs, launched up them. But Three snatched her arm again, stopping her mid-stride, spinning her back towards him. In a fluid motion, he had Wren off his back and into her arms, so quickly she barely had time to grab her son. Three wrenched the chemlight off his vest, and shoved it between her fingers.

"Go. Climb."

He pushed her on up a stair, and from the look in his eye, she knew better than to hesitate. She took them two at a time. Two flights, three flights, she put everything she had into every step, trying to remember just how many flights she'd come down. Somewhere between the fifth and sixth flights, she heard an impact on the stairs. The Weir were climbing.

Cass pressed on, thighs burning with the effort, breath coming in great gulps. She threw a glance over the rail, saw them a few flights below, the two in front like wild dogs bounding over each other to be the first to the kill. Their blue eyes streaked in the blackness around them, dancing as they vaulted up the steps.

Wren squeezed tight on her back. She felt him bury his face to her neck, almost sensed him willing her faster, or perhaps wishing he could wake from the nightmare. His weight dragged at her. Shifting on her shoulders, it made her next step tough to judge. Her toe caught, just barely. Just enough. She went sprawling with a cry.

Cass's chin hit hard on the metal-grated stair above her, as she rolled reflexively to her left, throwing Wren towards the wall, away from the edge. Dazed, stunned for a moment, she caught a view of the Weir circling the flights behind her. Not quite three flights now, one outpacing the other by several steps. She launched herself to her feet, and yanked Wren up on to her back. As she fled higher, the image flashed again in her mind. The Weir racing up the stairs. Two of them. Only two? Or had she missed the third?

Her foot slipped again, though she caught herself this time with a hand on the rail. She'd lost count of flights by now, and her mind was set on nothing more than reaching the top. Spots floated through her vision, and she blinked them away, terrified that another misstep would be the end of them both.

There was a commotion on the stairs below: a sharp digital shriek that escalated in pitch, a solid impact that shuddered the staircase. No time to look back. Cass flew on, a hind leaping to high places. Another flight. Another. Then, out of nowhere, the door. She'd almost forgotten it was her goal.

She slung Wren to his feet on the landing, hurried him to the heavy metal door. It was cracked open, inward. Just enough.

"Go ahead, baby, go through," she panted.

Wren hesitated at the crack.

"Wren, go!" she pushed him, and he dug his heels in, resistant.

"It's dark!" he cried, the first words from his mouth since he woke. "It's still dark out!"

She ground her teeth, tried to force him through, but she couldn't get leverage between the wall and the door. In a moment, it didn't matter anyway. A Weir was there. On the landing.

Cass spun to confront it, expecting it to leap upon her full force. Instead, it halted, hunched but not crouched, scanning her. Cass reached behind her, felt for Wren, ensured he was there, shielded. At least there was no sign of the others. Cass just had to buy a little time. Just long enough for Three to catch up. She just didn't know how she was going to do it.

The Weir seemed uncertain, hesitant. It glanced quickly away down the stairs, as if noticing for the first time that it was alone. This one was different from the others: larger, more muscular. Still a corpse, but one better preserved. It looked back at Cass, opened its mouth and squawked at her. A vicious howl of circuitry and menace; an electric wolf. Cass tensed.

"Come on," she said internally, a silent plea for help. "Come on."

The Weir flexed its hands, nails green in the chemlight. Still no sound on the stair below. Cass hoped that was a good sign. But she wasn't fool enough to count on hope alone. She dosed again. She'd have to deal with the consequences later. If there was a later.

The Weir scanned her again. No, not her. *Behind* her. It was trying to get a bead on Wren. No more waiting.

Cass pounced.

••••

Three was aware. Aware that he was aware. That was a start. Not a great one, but a start nonetheless. The left side of his face felt like it was covered in dry paint, or plaster. His neck felt strange. Definitely crumpled into a corner. A corner made of something hard. His legs wouldn't move.

Bad sign. Broken neck, probably. He tried his fingers. They wiggled. Still had those, at least. He wondered how he would drag himself up all those stairs with just his fingers. After a thought, he tried his toes. Surprise. They wiggled too.

Oh. Something heavy, on his legs. Heavy, wet, and unpleasant. He finally opened his eyes, only just realizing he hadn't done that yet. In the darkness, he could make out the outlines of things. Not really details, but shapes, beginnings and endings; depth, movement. The thing on his legs definitely wasn't moving. Hazy memories started coming back now. Weir. On the steps. He'd gotten the first one no problem. The second one, that'd been a problem. The thing on his legs was the second.

The second. There had been three. Three. Another one, still alive, somewhere up above him. After the woman and the boy. The boy. Wren.

With no small amount of effort, Three rolled the Weir off him, found his blade buried through its middle. All was quiet up the stairs. Three didn't like that at all. He forced himself to his feet, hissed at a searing in his side, between his ribs. He felt around, found something hard that hadn't been there before. With gritted teeth he pulled at it, worked it free. Nail from the Weir. Punctured his vest. Must've broken off in the fall.

He left it with the Weir, and got his blade back, wiping it clean on the Weir's ragged garment. His hands were sticky.

Three forced his feet up the steps, a slow, painful plod at first. Feeling worked its way back through his legs, and not a good one. He pushed on, brought himself to a weary jog. As he climbed, he looked up, spotted the landing at the top. Three more flights. A yellow-green light glowed there.

He hurried as best he could, reached the landing, stopped to take stock of the scene. The chemlight lay in the middle of the floor, showing it all.

Too late. He was too late.

The Weir was gone. Cass lay slumped against the wall, her shirt stained crimson from neckline to navel. A limp arm dangled over Wren, who sprawled motionless in her lap. The first graying light of morning slipped through the cracked door, and fell like a ribbon of mist over Cass's pale form.

Three clenched his jaw, swallowed what felt like emotion crawling up his throat. Foolish. Too risky, bringing a woman and her child out beyond the wall at night. He should've known better, should've thought it through. Seeing those first rays of morning made him angry, reminded him of just how close they'd been to making it. He thought back over what had happened, tried to figure out where he'd made the critical mistake. He should've trusted the kid more, gone hunting for that second Weir. Or maybe they should've just stayed in the city, holed up and waited it out. Most likely, he just should never have gotten involved in the first place.

He slipped his blade back into its sheath, ran a hand over his scalp, down over his face, closed his eyes. Gathered himself. He'd have to find a place to bury them. A quiet place. Where they could rest. Three opened his eyes and forced himself to look again at the silent and grim monument to what the world had become. All widows and orphans, with no one to defend them.

A twitch. Three blinked, and refocused.

*Fool!* he cursed himself.

Not dead. Unconscious. Or asleep. He'd let himself see what he expected to find, instead of what was there. Yet another mistake that could've gotten him killed. He'd lost count of how many of those he'd made in the past two days. Too many to still be alive, that was certain.

He crept to the pair, knelt at their side, placed his hand on Wren's back. It rose and fell steadily. Three took a closer look at Cass, brushed the hair back from her face. She was drawn, pale, damp with a cool glisten of sweat. High cheeks, olive skin, full lips rimmed in white. From here he could see the split in her chin, still oozing, the source of the blood on her shirt. A welcome relief. He'd feared her throat had been cut. The knuckles and back of her left hand were spattered and crusted with a dark, drying fluid, and a quick inhale told him at least part of the story. Wherever the Weir was now, it wasn't happy.

Three placed a hand on her arm, and squeezed gently. Cass jerked awake with a sharp inhalation, pulled back, stared at him with wild eyes. Recognition finally came, and she glanced down to check on Wren. Still sleeping, undisturbed.

"Are you hurt?" Three asked. The woman's hand went gingerly to her chin, but she shook her head no.

"I'm fine," she said. She looked at him with concern. He wasn't sure why. "Are you going to be alright?"

"Yeah," he answered, with a half shrug.

Cass reached up and touched the side of his face, high on the cheekbone, near his eye socket. The light brush of her finger felt like a blowtorch across his skin. Three jerked away with a hiss. He grimaced. More damage than he'd thought.

"Oh, I'm sorry," Cass said with a pained expression. "I thought maybe the blood wasn't yours."

"Well," Three replied, testing the wound with his own fingertips. The whole left side of his face was crusted. "I guess it's not anymore, huh?"

The flesh around his cheekbone was hot and puffy. He pressed into it, ignored the sting, probed the bones beneath. His cheek was lacerated, and would bruise deeply, but otherwise the facial structure seemed to be intact.

"Where'd the Weir go?" Three asked, gritting his teeth through the ache that now radiated through his face and jaw.

"Back downstairs," Cass answered flatly.

"It ran away?"

"Not exactly."

"It fell," said a sleepy voice from Cass's lap. "Mama knocked it over the edge."

Wren sat up and rubbed his eyes with the heels of his hands. Three gave Cass another look. She certainly didn't look like one to take down a Weir. Slight of frame, maybe a hundred and fifteen pounds by Three's estimate. Sure, she was juiced, but it took a lot more than a little chemical boost to deal with something that dangerous. Under his gaze, she just shrugged.

"Can we go now?" Wren asked.

Three didn't take his eyes off Cass.

"Sure you're alright?"

"Yeah," Cass said, too quickly for Three's liking. "Just tired. That was a lot of stairs." She added a throwaway smile.

Lying. But she didn't seem to have any serious injuries. Probably exhausted; hungry, thirsty. Three chalked it up to her being brave. He stood, and held out a hand to her.

She accepted the help, got to her feet with forced ease. Wren stood as well, and Three knelt beside him.

"You want a ride, kid?"

Wren looked to his mother for a cue. She nodded. Relieved. Wren clambered up onto Three's back, and Three regained his feet, shifting Wren around to a comfortable spot.

"By the way, what's your name?"

"Three."

"Three? I'm Cass. My son is Wren."

"Mister Wren," Three said with a half-nod, "and I already met."

"Where are we going?" Cass asked, picking the chemlight up off the floor, and extinguishing it.

"Somewhere you can rest," Three said. Then caught Cass's eye. "And we can talk."

He gave the door a yank, and it swung open with a jarring screech. He didn't bother to close it as they set out in the weak light of the early dawn.

# SEVEN

Cass had made some early attempts to start idle conversation, but by mid-afternoon, the trio had fallen mostly silent, save for the sound of their footsteps on the dusty concrete. They pushed northward through the decaying sprawl, passing countless buildings; towering headstones in an unbroken urban graveyard, empty shells of life disappeared. Many shone with dull or flickering light from signs or rooms, half-lit by technology that long outlasted its creators and carried on ignorant or indifferent to their absence. Three kept a steady pace, slowing rarely, stopping less, and only when Cass or Wren absolutely required it. He himself seemed tireless.

Cass couldn't help but wonder at the intensity of Three's focus and concentration. Even after these hours, his eyes constantly roamed, scanning, searching out tracks of previous travelers, signs of passing scavengers, or worse. At first, Cass had thought it obsession on the verge of paranoia. Then Three had steered them clear of the first of the traps.

"Deadfall," he'd said, flicking his head towards what looked to her like any of the other innumerable piles of scrap metal and abandoned scaffolding they'd already passed without concern. As they worked their way around it, though, Cass looked closer, saw the thin filament running across what had been their path, saw what it would've triggered had they tripped it.

"Why would anyone do that?" she'd asked.

"People gotta eat."

"Yeah, but what could you catch out here? A Weir?"

Three shook his head grimly. It took a moment for Cass to understand. That's when she'd stopped trying to make conversation.

The journey had been a slow, long march, punctuated by Three's occasional forced breaks, when he would insist she and Wren wait together while he scouted ahead. Once in a while he would point out what had caught his attention: a steel-cable snare, or a deadly spring trap, one time even an improvised explosive. More often though he would just reappear, gather Wren upon his back, and wordlessly return them to their march, making any necessary adjustments to their path.

According to the satfeed, Cass calculated they'd covered just over twenty miles since they'd left the storm-water system. She was hesitant to check it too often though, for fear of attracting unwanted attention from those that might be skimming the stream for her. Still, she couldn't help but take occasional peeks, in hopes of finding their destination. Three would say nothing more about it other than that she'd see it when they got there. And judging from the topdowns "there" could be anywhere. Or more likely, nowhere.

"How you doing?"

Three's voice jarred her from her latest search.

"Uh, fine," she lied, flashing a thin smile. "Tired."

"Not much farther."

Though relieved to hear it, Cass was puzzled. There wasn't a town, or enclave, or even a fortified structure that she could see for miles around. But she was too weary to consider much. A weakness had come upon her before noon, one that seeped from her muscles down into the marrow of her bones, hollowed her arms and legs. Her fingers trembled and twitched. Every step took effort, and she longed for a chance to sleep. The last of the quint was burning out.

At one time, long ago, quint had been a tool, chems for synapses and reflexes that helped her do the job. These days, it was as essential to her body as water, or air. And she had none.

"Alright," Three said, kneeling and letting Wren slide from his back. "It's going to take me a minute. Wait *right* here."

Before Cass could respond, Three was off and headed towards a nearby derelict building. He stopped of his own accord, and turned back, drawing his pistol as he returned. He held it out to Cass.

"Just in case."

Cass took the weapon, felt its heft: weighty, but balanced. It felt almost alive to her, like some once-wild beast, now controllable but hardly tame.

"You know how to use it?"

She nodded, slowly. It'd been some time since she last held a gun of any kind, and never one of such magnitude.

"If you don't, say so."

"I do," Cass said, "I just don't want to have to."

"You won't," Three replied, with a bare hint of reassurance. "But, just in case."

He dropped a hand on Wren's head and ruffled the boy's hair.

"Be right back."

Cass watched Three go back to the building. He surveyed it for a moment, and then leapt suddenly up its side, finding some handhold higher up that Cass couldn't see. He scaled it expertly, precise but swift, fluid, as if climbing a ladder up to the third floor, where an empty-framed window gaped. Three disappeared inside.

For a while, Cass and Wren stood watching the window.

"Are we going to do that too?" Wren asked.

"No, sweetheart," Cass answered, sounding more certain than she was. "I don't think so."

In truth, she was waiting for Three to reappear, to lower some kind of ladder or anything that might make the climb easier. Cass scanned the building, tried to see what about it might make it any safer, or even different, from the countless ones they'd passed along the way. Nothing stood out. It was as gray, drab, and run down as any of the others.

Minutes stretched. Wren sat down on the ground and tugged his shuttlecar from a pocket. He made soft whooshing noises as he ran it in lazy circles over his legs. Cass watched him for a while, smiled to herself, almost envious of his ability to find moments of childhood in nearly any circumstance. Moments which were far too rare, she thought sadly. Wren's stomach growled loudly, and Cass's heart sank; eyes welled. They hadn't eaten in over a day. Wren hadn't once complained.

He glanced up at her, smiling slightly.

"That was a big one."

Cass laughed in spite of herself, felt a tear drop to her cheek as she bent down to kiss the top of her son's head.

"Yeah, it really was."

"You think Mister Three will be back soon?"

"Soon, I'm sure."

Wren went back to his shuttlecar, flying it, driving it, crashing it, and Cass stood over him, scanning for any signs of Three. She ran her thumb back and forth on the grip of the pistol, absentmindedly feeling the checkering, trying to ignore the unrelenting weariness that clung to her, dragged her downwards, tempted her to lie down right there and sleep for a week, or forever.

Cass shook herself, inhaled. Then caught her breath. There was a scuffling sound, like shuffling feet, coming from the building. No, not footsteps. Something like claws on metal, like a giant rat on a sewer pipe.

"Three?" she called. There came no answer.

Wren stood up, and hooked an arm around her leg.

The sound continued, grew louder. Not from the building. From *under* it. Grinding. Wren squeezed.

Cass checked the pistol, readied it, took it in both hands. There. Near the front corner of the building, by the alley. The concrete itself, or rather the ground beneath it, shifted, lurched. Something was coming.

Cass raised the weapon; aimed it. The ground lifted, raised, separated cleanly as if cut by a laser. A shape emerged from the hole: hooded, coated in gray dust, unnaturally silent, a ghost rising from its grave. Cass's finger involuntarily tightened on the trigger.

"Really?" said the shape. The figure laid back its hood. Three. Of course.

Cass lowered the pistol immediately, felt her face flush hot.

"Told you you wouldn't need it," Three said flatly, though something in the tone suggested a smile behind the words. "Sorry. Took longer than I expected."

He waved them over to the opening in the cement. Cass gathered herself and shepherded Wren over to where Three awaited them. When she reached the opening, she was surprised to find a set of steep metal steps, leading down under the street.

"Come on," he said, "you first."

Three held out a hand to her. She took it in hers, and he steadied her as she descended. Cass reached the bottom more quickly than she had expected. She found herself in a tight corridor, perhaps six feet in height and half as wide, smooth-walled and warm.

"Here," she heard Three say from above. "Elevator for you, Mister Wren."

Wren's feet appeared in the opening, dangling in mid-air and descending slowly, body stretched and arms over his head as Three held his wrists above. Three made whirring noises as he lowered Wren, and Wren floated down into his mother's arms laughing. Cass couldn't remember the last time she'd heard him do that.

"Got him?" Three called down.

"Yep."

Cass felt Wren's weight settle on her as Three released him, and in the next moment, Three dropped lightly to his feet in front of her, bypassing the stairs entirely.

"Straight ahead," he said, nodding down the narrow hall. "Make yourself comfortable."

Above them, the opening in the concrete shrank to nothingness, sealed magnetically, without sign or trace of ever having opened. The hall was faintly lit in a bluish-hued glow that nevertheless seemed somehow warm, and Cass realized the light was coming from the end of the hall, perhaps ten or fifteen meters away.

She carried Wren down the corridor to the end, where it turned sharply and opened out into a room. It was simple, Spartan in its furnishing, almost monastic. The floor was concrete, smooth and gray. A pair of small metal-framed beds with thin mattresses sat pushed to the matching gray wall on the left, separated by a thin screen. Across from the beds sat a simple table, and two mismatched and worn chairs. An alcove ran off to one side; within it sat a waste-recycler, and a jerry-rigged filtering system that Cass guessed served as a shower. There was a drain in the floor. Through a small doorframe without any door there was another, compact room, more of an oversized closet than anything. Cass set Wren down, and poked her head into the room. Metal shelving lined the walls wherever there was space, stocked with all manner of supplies. Piles of clothes, worn but in decent condition, military rations, shoes, lengths of synthrope, biochem batteries, water canisters. Wren just stood there taking it all in, mouth slightly open.

"What is this place?" she asked.

"Wayhouse," Three answered, emerging from the entryway. "Not much to look at, but should be safe enough for a day or two."

"Is it yours?"

"For now, yeah."

As usual, Three wasn't really answering her question, and it annoyed Cass. She felt light-headed, empty, the room seemed to tilt ever so slightly to the left. Three must've read her.

"You alright?"

Cass nodded, closed her eyes.

"I just need to rest."

What she needed was quint, and soon. She couldn't think about it now though, her brain was too foggy with fatigue and hunger. She'd figure it out. She always had before. Wren slipped up next to her, and took her hand. It felt small in hers.

"Before you sleep, let me show you something."

"Can't it wait?" she asked, opening her eyes.

"No."

He took her by the arm, firmly, but with care. Supporting her more than leading her. Wren trailed along beside her, eyes roving.

"Let me show the ways out. Just in case."

"In case of what?"

Three ignored the question.

"You saw the way we came in. There's a button to the right of the ladder. Just press it, and you're out."

He led them back to the storage room, and it didn't take Cass long to scan the whole thing. All available wall-space was taken up by the metal shelving, each heaped with a packrat's nest of unsorted supplies. She glanced up at the ceiling, looking for any sign of a hatch or other entry, but found none.

"Right here," Three said.

He stretched out his hand, fingers extended to form a triangle with the three longest, and pressed them against the wall, just above and beside where one of the shelves was braced. Cass saw what looked like tiny cracks in the cement wall, and realized that they were in fact markings, indicating invisible pressure plates where Three now pressed.

A whir and click sounded from below, and Three stepped back as a segment of the floor smoothly retracted, revealing another set of steep stairs, like the ones from the first entry.

"Down there, it's a short corridor, then a branch, left and right. Both ways lead out. To the left is how I got in. It'll take you up to the third floor of the building that's above us now. The right goes out through the basement of the neighboring building."

Cass nodded faintly. If she didn't rest soon, she knew her body would shut down and force the issue. She swallowed hard, feeling a bilious gurgle in the back of her throat. In front of her, the floor panel slid back into place.

"You can open it?"

Cass nodded again.

"Show me."

Her hands were trembling, impossible to hide now. Still, she ran her fingers across the plates, triggered the hatch.

"Good."

"And here's the other!" Wren called from behind.

Cass hadn't even noticed him slip off. She and Three turned to find the boy just outside, crouching near the entry of the supply room. He was beaming, like he'd just found the most well-hidden Easter egg.

"Where does this one go?"

Three stepped out, and Cass followed. A panel in the wall to the right of the supply room entrance had disappeared, leaving behind a three-foot tall corridor that trailed off into darkness. Three knelt and peered into it. He grunted.

"I have no idea," he answered, flatly.

It took a moment before Cass realized this was the first time Three had seen this route before.

"How'd you open it?"

Wren shrugged.

"It just kinda happened."

"It opened itself?"

Wren shook his head.

"So you pressed something?"

The boy shook his head again.

"Then how'd you find it?"

Wren shrugged again, looked down to the floor, shrinking into himself as if he'd done something wrong. Cass moved to him, put a hand on his shoulders.

"It's alright baby. It's fine."

"It's not fine," Three said gruffly, "if you can't tell me how to close it again."

"I'm sorry," Wren said, voice quivering. "I just… I just…"

"Just what?" Three pressed.

"That's enough," Cass snapped.

"Felt it…" Wren finished, trailing off.

"Wren, it's fine. You didn't do anything wrong, sweetheart, OK? Why don't you go sit on one of those beds and take your shoes off?"

She directed his shoulders with her hands and steered him gently towards the beds, and patted him on the bottom as he went. Then she turned back to Three, and lowered her voice.

"Listen," she said, quietly but smoldering. "In case you haven't figured it out by now, Wren's very sensitive. Especially to how people talk to him. You watch what you say."

Three just stared back at her without emotion, his dark eyes boring into hers. She saw the muscles in his jaw work, teeth clenching. But he didn't reply. Just turned to look back down the corridor.

"I'll be back in a minute," he said finally. Then disappeared down into the half-height hallway.

Cass stood there with her hand on the wall, gathering herself.

"Mama?"

"Yeah, baby?"

"I can't get my shoe off."

She sighed to herself. So weary.

"Alright."

Cass turned to face Wren, saw him with his right foot at an awkward angle, stuck in the upper part of his boot. Only a child could figure out how to get a foot stuck in shoes that were too big for him. She started to walk over to him, to help get him free.

Instead, everything went black.

Her first thought on waking was that she'd fallen onto a bed of coals. From hip to breast her right side seared with pain, though try as she might, she could not will herself away from it. Darkness coated her vision, an oily blackness filled with disease. Voices floated there, muted, distorted.

"...a blanket, water..."

The words were harsh, commanding. Cass felt the floor give way beneath her. Falling. Pain clinging like a web.

She landed in an arctic lake, subterranean, its blackness complete. Surrounded, drowning, but somehow able to breathe. Silence. Nothingness.

A roaring wind blasted her ears. Scalding. She was trapped, cocooned in agony. She fought to free herself, struggling, thrashing to no avail. Iron shackles clamped her wrists, biting her skin, crushing her bones. A weight pressed down on her, smothering. Forcing the air from her lungs. Compressing her ribcage, preventing inhalation. Though blind, she felt the blackness returning. Closing in. Stalking. Overtaking.

••••

Naked, under a night sky. Glimmers of light streaked, stars falling from heaven. Beautiful. Deadly. A storm of glassy shards plummeted, showered her, pierced her flesh like needle-point icicles. She screamed, but her voice sounded far away. She twisted to escape, but some steely trap encased her, held her tightly beneath the impaling rain. Too much to bear. Consciousness slipped out of reach, never fully grasped.

A gentle breeze soothed her skin, her forehead, her cheeks. A wetness brushed across her lips, and Cass opened her eyes. Asher loomed over her with his wolfish grin, a steel cup in his hand. Cass tried to pull away, but had no strength. He leaned down, pressed the cup to her lips. She fought, clenched her teeth, tried to shake it away. A viscous fluid flowed over her lips, down her throat, acrid, bitter. Her body tried to reject it, but the liquid seemed alive, crawled its way into her belly, nested in her gut. Asher stood, and smiled until his face ripped. Within the crimson wounds, something wet wriggled. Blackness swallowed her.

Something cold in her hand. Small, but soothing, life-giving. A beacon. Calling her. It pulsed, grew warmer, lent her strength. Blue light glowed, faintly electric, peaceful. She warmed slowly, steadily, and the light brightened. A shape appeared at the center of the light, and Cass smiled to herself. Wren. He was there with her, bringing her light in the darkness. His mouth moved in slow motion, as if saying her name, though he made no sound. She called to him, but the words felt foreign, or too big for her mouth. She heard herself moan, and in that moment, the light shattered. A thousand sparkles of blue-hued glass exploded and faded into the darkness, and once again she knew no more.

"Mama."

Something moved in the darkness.

"Mama, please."

A pressure on her forehead, a brush of flesh across her cheek. Eyelids fluttered. She saw.

Three's face filled her view, his dark eyes piercing, his breath splashing hot over her lips. At her waking, he did not smile. Instead, he retreated.

In the next instant, Wren was upon her, arms around her neck, sobbing. Cass swung a weak arm across his shoulders, let it fall heavily over him. She felt like she should say something to him, anything, but her tongue was a lump of sandy rubber in her mouth. She tried to remember when she'd last had a drink. Hours? Days?

Asher.

She remembered the bitter fluid creeping into her belly, felt a surge of panic. Scanned her surroundings. The metal bed, the gray concrete walls. Asher couldn't have gotten to her. A dream, a nightmare. Nothing more.

Three reappeared, a canister of fresh water in his hand. He knelt, gently pulled Wren off Cass and spoke something to him too softly for her to hear. Wren nodded and with a quiet but hopeful look to his mother, disappeared on the other side of the screen. Three returned to her side, slipped a hand under her head and carefully lifted her. As cool water splashed over her parched lips, Cass realized for the first time that she felt no pain. The water rushed cold through her throat straight into her veins, cathartic, washing away the fever, the chills, the black disease within. Her body demanded that she drink forever, but Three pulled the canister away, and laid her back. His fingers were strong; his hand seemed to linger on her neck after he pulled away.

"How do you feel?" he asked, in his usual direct, flat tone. He didn't sound like a man who had just coaxed life back into a dying woman.

"I should be dead," she answered.

He nodded.

"You would be, if it wasn't for your boy."

He held the water canister out to her: a simple test of her strength. Cass took it, surprised at the hollowness in her arms.

"Quint's evil stuff," he said. As she sipped, he got up from his knee and sat on the foot of the bed. "I wouldn't have pegged you as one to run something like *that*."

It was the first time she'd heard Three say anything that sounded even slightly judgmental. He raised a shoulder in a barely perceptible half-shrug.

"Good thing Wren knew."

"Where'd you find more?"

"I didn't. I made a synth."

She waited for more. It took a raising of her eyebrows to prompt him.

"It won't boost you like quint, but it should keep your cells from imploding. Probably have to drink it every few days though."

In a flash, Cass remembered choking down the acrid ooze, and realized only part of her nightmare had been imagined.

"What's in it?"

Three shook his head.

"You don't wanna know, girl."

Cass sipped more of the cool water, and already found herself feeling refreshed, more alert. On a whim, she rolled up to an elbow, started to sit up. Three shot a reflexive hand out to steady her. After a few wobbly moments, he let go, and they sat together in uncertain silence. Then he spoke, in even lower tones than normal.

"What's your burn rate?"

Cass shrugged, bought herself some time with another swig of water. She didn't want to lie, but she couldn't tell him the truth.

"Fifty a day, I guess," she slipped it out between drinks, hoping it sounded casual. "Maybe a little more."

"That's what, tab every eight days?"

"Depends on the grade, but yeah, that's about right."

In reality, Cass was burning at nearly twice that just to maintain; far more if she boosted. Three looked at her with the usual hardness, but if he suspected she was lying he didn't show it. She paused, made herself take a breath before changing the subject, not wanting to seem eager.

"I, uh…" she paused, genuinely now, uncertain. "I don't know what all you had to do to, uh…"

Cass wanted to be eloquent, felt that there should be much more to say than she could think of, but in the end, she just decided to keep it simple.

"Thank you."

"Sure," Three said, still with a hard look in his eye. "And since we're all friends and neighbors now, you wanna tell me who's after you?"

His directness surprised her, though she knew it shouldn't. So far, she hadn't seen him any other way. This just wasn't the change of subject she'd been hoping for.

"Just some people from my past. Got involved with them when I was young, and they don't want to let me get uninvolved."

"How many?"

"Can we do this later? I'm pretty tired. I think I need to lie down again."

"In a minute."

There was an edge to Three's voice now, like the soft, deep rumble of a dog that doesn't want to bare its teeth, but wants you to know it'll go there if you push it. The room seemed a lot smaller all of a sudden.

"How many?"

"Six," she answered with a weary sigh, knowing there was no use in resisting. Then corrected herself. "Well, I guess it's just five now."

"What were you workin'?"

It was becoming an interrogation. And Three's penetrating eyes made her fear how much she'd give away, no matter how little she actually said.

"What do you mean?"

"Fedor, Kostya, you, the kid." Three held up a finger for each name as he said them. "Two genies, a chemic, and your boy. I've never seen anything like him before, but he's some kind of something, for sure. That ain't people from your past, that's a crew. So what were you workin'?"

"Security," she said. Then for some reason, she continued. "At first, anyway. I was just a kid when we started, I didn't know what it was going to turn into–"

Three cut her off.

"Look, I don't care about who you are, where you're from, or whose pocket you picked in your youth. All I want to know is what I'm up against. Get me?"

Cass nodded, hoping he didn't see how much his words had stung her.

"What kind of security? Sec/Net?"

If he hadn't offered it, she would never have thought he'd buy that, but since he'd said it first, she just nodded.

"Awful lot of muscle just for tapping Sec/Net."

"You wouldn't think that if you'd met our clients."

Three grunted. Then sat in tense silence. He stared into her eyes so intensely it almost hurt, but Cass didn't dare look away. It was almost unbearable. At any second, she was certain she would tell him everything, and he would do what anyone with even a hint of brain would. Run.

Instead, he was the first to break the silence.

"You've been masking?"

She nodded.

"And you taught the boy how to?"

Cass shook her head, and for the first time saw Three surprised, almost lose control. He raised his voice in frustration.

"So what's the point of hiding you, if they can track your kid–"

She interrupted.

"*He* taught *me*."

Again, they returned to silence. Three looked away, down at the floor, processing. Cass just sat there, afraid to move for fear of attracting his attention again. Finally, he spoke, though now he didn't look at her.

"When you're ready, we'll push on north. I know a spot, pretty off-grid," he said, standing to his feet. "If we make it, we'll figure out where to go from there."

Three started to leave, but Cass reached up and touched his hand, stopping him. Still he didn't look to her.

"How long was I... have we been here?"

"Six days," he answered.

He lingered for a moment, but when she said nothing else, he walked off, around to where Wren had gone. Moments later, Wren bounded back and curled up beside her, a wolf cub nestling against his mother. Cass hugged him tightly, letting his warmth and touch soothe her. She felt tired, but healthily so, as if she'd fought a long battle, and deserved respite. She lay back, and Wren repositioned, snuggled on her shoulder, and together they slept a deep, restful, dreamless sleep.

Three sat on an overturned plasticrate in the supply room, rocked back on one edge with his feet up on a low shelf. Methodically, meticulously, he ran a gritstone along an edge of an eight-inch piece of scrap metal he'd found on some dusty shelf. Shaping it. Sharpening it. His hands moved with practiced precision.

Three small piles lay neatly arranged on the floor: supplies collected and carefully assessed for their weight, durability, and usefulness. He'd taken only what they'd need. Inwardly, he chuckled humorlessly. This wasn't his way. Hopelessly entangled with the weak and wounded. He'd already done what he could for the woman. Another day or two, and she'd be strong enough to walk. And he'd done what he'd said he'd do. He'd gotten them safely out of the enclave, away from the crew that was chasing them. For now.

He looked at the back wall, where the hidden pressure plates waited. So simple. Stand up, walk down those stairs, move on. On to the next thing. Like always. This wasn't his way.

He set the gritstone and scrap metal on the shelf behind him and stood. Silently moved to the main room, crept to the bed, stood over the woman and boy. Her color was better, her breathing steady. Both lay on their sides, the mother with a protective arm draped over the son. Peaceful.

They'd have everything they needed. He moved back to the supply room, quietly packed a harness with a few traveling essentials: water, food, an extra chemlight or two. As was the custom, honor code of travelers, he'd exchanged some of his own valuables for those he took. Not one, but two of his shells. Exorbitant for what he'd taken for himself, but he felt it only right to pay for the woman and her kid. He'd brought them in, after all. That left him three in the cylinder, one in the pocket. Three shook his head. He'd have to do something about that soon.

He leaned his head to the side, left ear almost touching his shoulder, and cracked his neck out of habit. He didn't know why he was still standing there. In his gut, he already knew he'd made his decision. With a full exhalation, he reached down and picked up the harness, slung the straps over each shoulder, adjusted the weight of the two broad pockets that rested on either hip.

Move on. To the next thing. He'd done enough.

Three strode to the shelf at the back wall, fingered the secret plates, stepped back as the floor opened up and offered his escape. The blackness beneath him seemed inviting. His chance to return to a life in the background, in the shadows, without notice. And he stared into it. What was he waiting for?

He glanced back at the door to the supply room. Listened. Heard the deep and steady breath of Cass and Wren. A woman and a boy. Just some other people trapped in the same dying world.

With a silent and half-hearted goodbye, Three slipped like a wraith into the darkness below, and disappeared.

# EIGHT

Cass stirred, shifted awake, let her eyes float open slowly, watched as they focused the haze into clarity. The first thing she noticed was Wren's absence. The blanket was still compressed and rumpled from where he'd been curled next to her, but he was nowhere to be seen. She lay still for a moment longer, listening for the usual sounds of her son. Though there was no obvious reason to think so, she knew with a cold certainty that something was very wrong.

She rolled herself up silently, slipped her feet to the floor, tested her strength. About fifty percent. Quietly she stood, and crept stiffly around the wayhouse.

When Cass found him, he was standing in the supply room towards the back, in the dark, hand nearly to his face. Fist tightly balled. Staring. She'd seen him that way before; terror seized her.

"Wren?"

Blood ran freely from his palm, down to the elbow, where it dripped in a spatter on the concrete. He didn't seem to notice her. She rushed to him, swept him into her arms, felt his hair damp with clammy sweat.

"Wren, baby, what is it? What's wrong?"

Tears welled in her eyes. Still cradling him against her, Cass seized his hand, pried its stiff fingers open to reveal a blade, gently curved, one solid piece: a length of scrap metal crafted into a deadly thing. Cass took it and placed it on the ground, then reached for a nearby garment from a shelf and tore it, fashioning a makeshift bandage. Wren just stood, injured hand limp in hers, never looking to her.

Finally, as Cass tied off the bandage, Wren rasped, barely audible.

"He's gone."

Cass stopped, tried to absorb that.

"And they're here."

Terror and despair collided, with Cass caught in between. She felt her breath escape, her heart icy cold as it leapt and pounded in her chest. She squeezed him tighter still.

Somehow, by some unholy miracle, *they* had found her. Asher, or at least some of his crew, prowled somewhere just above them, undoubtedly searching for a way in, and most certainly capable of finding it. It was just a matter of time, and not much at that.

Her mind raced, tried to find an explanation. Maybe Three had sold them out. Kept them here until Asher could reach them. It made some sense, but not much. Her nightmare flashed back. Asher, grinning over her. It clicked. In her fevered torment, her digital mask had cracked. He had found her signal.

A grinding sound pulled her out of her paralyzed thought. Down the corridor, towards the entrance from the street. They were coming.

"Come on, baby. Quiet as you can."

Cass noted the piles of supplies on the floor, hastily scraped them into a backpack. Wren remained motionless, unblinking. Staring into nothingness. Or seeing something beyond sight.

Cass slung the backpack over her shoulders, took Wren's hand, and gently pulled him towards the back corner of the supply room. She searched the wall, found the signpost cracks, felt for the pressure plates. The instant before she pressed into them, Wren's hand tightened on hers, unnaturally strong, painful. She flinched, but his eyes stopped her dead.

Terror.

"Not that way, Mama."

He was with her now. Frightened, but lucid. She nodded, understanding. They were coming from both sides. Cass bent down, nose to nose with her son. Whispering.

"The other way, the secret you found. Can you open it again?"

"I'm not sure... I... I don't think so."

"Let's just try."

Cass swung Wren up in her arms. He felt so much heavier than she remembered. Her legs trembled at the extra weight. A few steps outside the supply room, she placed him on his own feet. The grinding continued, faint but relentless.

"Go ahead, baby. Just see what you can do."

Wren nodded, uncertain, shoulders sagging with a lack of confidence. He closed his eyes, stretched out a hand, touched the wall.

The grinding continued. Cass thought she caught the trace of a deep rumbling voice floating from the supply room, muffled through the concrete.

Wren raised his head, opened his eyes. Crying.

"I'm sorry, Mama, I can't."

"Yes you can, sweetheart, you've done this same thing a hundred times. You can do it."

"No, it's different. They're always different, Mama."

"Try again, Wren. Just try."

Wren lowered his head, stared at his feet. Defeated. He shook his head. He was just a child, Cass thought. A child with a gift he didn't understand, frustrated by his own incapability to control it. What more could she ask of him?

"Just try, baby, OK? For me?"

"I can't," he murmured. "I can't feel this one, I can't."

It was the recent near-death experience, perhaps, or maybe the sheer anger at the circumstance, the futility, or the helplessness she felt; whatever the reason, Cass did something she had never done in her entire life.

She slapped her son.

Wren's little face snapped to one side, and in an instant he looked back to her, wild-eyed, shocked, bewildered, tears at the verge. His cheek flushed hot purple. Cass's heart shattered at the raw pain in her precious child's eyes. But she couldn't stop. Their lives were at stake.

"They are here, Wren. Asher is here. And he is going to take us away, and separate us. And we will never be together again, not ever. Not unless you open this door and get us out of here. So you find a way, and you make it happen. Right. Now."

She snatched his arm and whipped him to face the wall. It was a dangerous game, and for long seconds Cass thought she had played it wrong. Wren just stood there, chin trembling, hand on his cheek, not daring to look at his mother, but not daring to let her out of his peripheral vision either.

Then, the grinding sound stopped. And Wren set his jaw. He squeezed his eyes shut tightly, and slammed his palm against the wall. Brow furrowed in intense focus, lip curled in the slightest hint of a snarl. He looked very much like his mother.

Finally, his face softened, the timid boy returned, and he let his hand fall from the wall. Down the corridor, there was a hiss; the magnetic seal unlocking.

"Sorry, Mama."

Cass ran her fingers through his hair, kissed the top of his head.

"It's OK, baby."

A *thunk* from the supply room signaled the activation of the stairs. Back there, in the darkness, the floor panel was sliding open. And without any sound at all, a small hole appeared in the wall where Cass and Wren stood.

A half-moment of shock was all Cass could spare before she grabbed Wren by the arm and shoved him inside. She bent double and followed him in, shuffling sideways as quickly as she could with one eye on the opening.

"It's OK, Mama," Wren said. "I see it now."

He sounded much older. And with that, the opening disappeared, and the two of them were plunged into complete darkness.

After a neck-breaking crawl down a pitch-black tunnel, and several painful collisions with abrupt turns in the walls, Cass and Wren finally found themselves at a gentle upward slope, where the ceiling suddenly gave way in a matching curve. Cass stood at full height, and managed to scramble higher onto the smooth metal surface. The top was covered by a smooth steel mesh, more like a drain than a grate, and with one solid push outward, Cass was disheartened to discover that's exactly what it was. An exit convincingly concealed in some sort of waste recycling reservoir.

It appeared that the levels never actually rose high enough to enter the pipe, but that was small comfort. There was no obvious route from this exit to the next, except through the filth and refuse. Cass swung her backpack around to the front, and had Wren climb up on her back. Then the two set out, scrambling out of their secret tunnel and into a pool of stinking sludge, thigh-deep for Cass. She struggled her way to the nearest edge, where it was shallowest. Following the curving concrete around the outside, they eventually came to a small iron hatch: a maintenance access.

"Once we get outside," Cass whispered to Wren. "We'll have to be very, very careful."

Wren just nodded.

Cass grabbed hold of the access release, and slowly, gradually, almost imperceptibly, applied strength to it. She could feel the flexing metal, feel the parts that had been unused for untold years reawakening. Her great fear was that the hatch would spring open with some horrible shriek, instantly alerting anyone who might be outside. As she felt the hatch release and begin its automatic opening, she realized she had no idea whether it was day or night.

Her first look at the outside world in six days turned out to be dark. Wren constricted around her neck, and she heard him hiss involuntarily. But a closer look revealed that their limited view was just in heavy shadow. Cass poked her head through the hatch timidly, and saw the bright gray horizon to the east that signaled a new dawn fast approaching. For once, things were going her way. Light enough for the Weir not to be about. Dark enough to conceal their escape.

Cass swung Wren off her shoulders, and lifted him through the hatch to the ground outside. She quickly followed, and readjusted the backpack once she had joined him. As quietly as she was able, she closed the hatch. It *thunked* dully when it sealed.

"OK, baby," she said, taking Wren's hand firmly. "Stay right with me, no matter what."

Wren just nodded. He knew what they were up against.

Together, the pair slipped cautiously from the concrete recycler to a nearby building. Its bottom floor had been gutted by vandals, or fire, or both, but there was ample concealment there. Though everything in Cass's body told her to run, she forced a creeping pace, using every ounce of her will to search out danger. She was especially glad to have Wren now, knowing he would warn her before her own eyes could.

Ten minutes stretched to twenty, then thirty. Still they picked their way from building to building, alley to alley. Spending no more than a fleeting moment in the open, no less than a few minutes observing from each new position.

Finally, they reached the outer ring of a small courtyard. It was in a chaotic state of urban disrepair; once-beautiful archways collapsed to formless piles of rubble. That was where Cass saw the first of them.

She recognized her instantly. It was Jez. Mesmerizingly beautiful Jez, with her skin-tight fibrasteel suit, and white-blonde hair dangling down her back in tight braids; braids that often concealed razortips cunningly woven in. Jez moved like a heron. Graceful, fluid steps, punctuated by a piercingly sharp gaze that snapped from point to point with almost inhuman precision. Cass's breath caught in her throat. Instinctively she dropped to a low crouch and pulled Wren tight to her side.

Jez, on the other side of the courtyard, stopped. Stood stone still. Listening.

Finally, Jez moved on, out of sight. Cass felt a rush of hot breath on her neck, as Wren released the one he'd been holding.

"Back out. Slooowly," Cass whispered. "We'll find a way around."

Without taking her eyes from the corner around which Jez had disappeared, Cass took cautious steps backwards, back the way they'd entered. As she stood, she bumped into something that hadn't been there before.

And before she could even draw a breath to cry out, a hand clamped tight over her mouth, jerking her head back into a shoulder. Lips on her ear hissed a warning.

"Shhhhhhhh."

She nodded as much as she could, caught as she was. Immediately, the hand relaxed, slipped from her mouth down gently to her neck. Cass felt the tension release from her body. Three hadn't left them after all. He must've been watching for them.

His lips lingered on her earlobe, wet, slightly parted. She heard him inhale deeply, as if drawing in her scent. As if he'd missed her. Cass hazarded a sidelong glance.

Not Three.

Dagon. The Grave.

Cass spun out of his loose grasp; instinctively jerked Wren behind her, shielding him. She hunched down, readied, tried to trigger a boost before she realized she had nothing to tap. For a moment, Dagon just stood there, watching her.

Then, he spoke.

"I've been looking for you."

Low tones, conspiratorial. He glanced off to where Jez had gone, as if he hoped no one would notice him here, with Cass and her son.

"I was worried. About you," he said, "and Spinner too, of course."

Dagon leaned to one side, trying get a look at Wren.

"Heya, Spins."

Wren clung to his mother's leg, but offered a half-wave in response.

"Hi Dagon."

"I'm not coming back, Dagon," Cass said. "Neither of us are. You know that."

Dagon shifted his gaze around, met her eyes briefly, quickly looked away. He had an awkward posture, always uncomfortable, like his bones didn't quite fit together. Pale skin almost translucent at times, dark circles under dark eyes. Impossibly thin, like a knife-blade. Unequivocally deadly.

"I'd watch out for you, Haven. I always have."

"My name is Cass."

He looked at her again, fleeting. Nervous.

"Cass," his voice quavered. "Just come back with me. We can work it out. Me and Ran. We'll take care of you, I promise."

"I don't think you'll get the chance."

"Why? Asher won't do anything."

"That's not what I meant."

He looked back to her, held her gaze for once. He looked lost. For a split second, she almost felt sorry for him.

"What are you–?"

Dagon almost asked the question, but at the last possible moment, he twisted his body, bent backwards, held a gravity-defying pose as Three's blade severed the air where Dagon's neck had been a half-instant before. How Dagon had sensed Three, Cass would never know. Even watching Three's approach, she hadn't heard him. It didn't matter now anyway. She could hardly believe what was unfolding before her.

Three must've been surprised by Dagon's sudden evasion, but he almost seemed to expect it the way he redirected his blade in a fluid motion, a single strike. Dagon bent again, twisted, dropped on his shoulder and whipped his shin across Three's collarbone. Three stumbled back, rebalanced, just as Dagon whirled and regained his feet. For a heartbeat, they sized each other up.

Then collided.

Dagon was the first to impact, his knee crushing into Three's solar plexus a half-second before Three buried his elbow into Dagon's jaw. Dagon spun with the force of the attack, but carried through with a kick that knocked the sword from Three's hand. Three responded with a stinging backhand, followed it up with a flurry of strikes too fast for Cass's eyes to see. Dagon bounded backwards, but in the next instant lunged forward, catching Three with a hard palm to the face, and then darting his fingertips into a nerve cluster at Three's shoulder joint. Three fell back again, dazed, clutching his arm as it dangled uselessly. Dagon melted to the ground, rolled, somehow came up to his feet with Three's blade in hand.

Cass couldn't help it. She called out, reflexively.

"Dagon, no!"

Too late. Dagon slashed the blade across Three's throat. Three's hand jerked once, spasmodically. For a moment afterwards, no one moved. Then, Cass gasped at the thin line of crimson that welled on Three's Adam's apple.

"Please," Dagon said, glancing at Cass, almost pleading. "They'll hear us."

Dagon looked back to Three, watched him with unreserved fascination, the hint of a smile on his thin lips.

"I could've killed you, you know."

Three hesitated, nodded. He reached up, felt his throat with his fingertips. A seam of blood stretched from one side of his throat to the other, a shallow cut, almost surgical. A warning.

"I didn't do so bad myself," Three replied in dry monotone.

Dagon chuckled humorlessly, dropped his gaze to his own torso. There, for the first time, Cass saw a slender length of polished steel protruding from between Dagon's ribs.

"Missed the heart," Dagon answered.

"Not by much."

Dagon shrugged, smiled. Shot a look to Cass. Struggled, wavered. Finally.

"You know I can't just let you go."

He turned back to Three, eyed him. Cass saw something pass between them, some kind of understanding she couldn't identify or explain. Three smirked.

"But I can give you a head start."

Dagon plucked the blade from between his ribs, bowed slightly, extended Three's short sword back to him. Three took it without ceremony; slid it into its sheath.

"I'll keep this one," Dagon said, holding the simple knife. "A reminder."

Three touched his throat again.

"Guess I'll keep this one then."

"Next time," Dagon started.

Three just nodded. Cass picked Wren up and quickly joined Three. Dagon wouldn't look at her anymore.

"You should go," he said quietly. "They won't be far behind."

"Dagon…" Cass began.

"Don't."

He turned his back to them, but made no motion to leave.

"Seeya, Spins."

"Bye," Wren murmured.

Cass swung Wren to her back, and hoped in her heart she'd never see Dagon again.

Three didn't know what exactly had just transpired, who Dagon was, or why he'd let them go, but he wasn't about to wait around for someone else to find them. He grabbed Cass under the arm and led her as fast as she could go back the way he had come. They'd made it deep into a tight alley, maybe fifty meters away, before Cass ripped her arm from him and stopped running.

Three halted, whirled to face her.

"We've got to keep moving."

Cass set Wren down on his feet. And then, with everything she had, she punched Three square in the face. He took it, but reflexively grabbed her wrists.

"You left us!" she spat. "You left us to die, you son–"

Three spun her, shoved her hard against the nearest wall, crushed his body into hers, pinning her.

"You listen to me," he growled, in a cold monotone. "I promised you nothing. I owe you *nothing*. You're alive. For now. You want to stay that way, we move. Now."

Three looked down deep into Cass's dark eyes, saw the defiance there, the hard resolve, the intense fire he knew would burn him later. But also acceptance. She knew he was right. There would be time for arguments later. He hoped.

He stepped back, released her wrists.

"He said a head start. How much of one?"

Cass massaged her wrists, shook her head.

"Not enough to get away."

And as if on cue, there came a cry from the far end of the alley. In the strengthening light of the early morning, the source was unmistakable. Tall, muscular, right arm dangling, gray and useless. Fedor.

Three snatched Wren off the ground and broke into a dead run with the boy tucked awkwardly under his arm, Cass right on his heels.

Cass fought to keep up the breakneck speed that Three required of her, but without the quint, she couldn't get any more out of her body. Fedor's massive form was closing the distance with every step, and Cass knew Jez couldn't be far behind.

The trio twisted and turned, seemingly at random. Cass wanted to tell Three that they'd never lose Fedor when they were already this close, but she didn't have the breath or the words for it. Then, she started to notice their surroundings. Landmarks she hadn't even realized she'd noted the first time she'd seen them. A crumbling brick wall. Piles of rusted corrugated steel. A lewd advertisement from some former shop.

Three was leading them back the way they'd come. Something nagged at her, in the back of her mind. A warning. Too faint, too vague to heed.

"Come on, this way!" he called from ahead.

Cass couldn't figure out the point in retracing their steps. They were way too far from the Enclave to make it back. Even if they could, the guards at the gate would never let them in after the way they'd left. It all seemed pointless. Fedor had dropped out of view, but she knew he was still tracking them. And he never tired.

The trio rounded another corner.

"Keep running," Three barked. "Don't stop, don't look back!"

Cass didn't have the will to argue. Three practically tossed Wren to her as she passed him, and she slung him on her back, on top of the backpack. Three slowed. She hazarded a glance back, and saw him drop to a crouch.

She pressed on, alarms screaming in her head, danger. What was she forgetting? She ran ten more yards, nameless panic rising.

Then it dawned on her.

The traps.

She skidded to a stop, almost fell to her knees under the weight of Wren and the backpack.

A moment later, a thunderous explosion shattered the air. Behind her, plumes of concrete dust filled the sky and alleyways. Heart pounding, she sank to the ground and hugged Wren, doubting anyone would be catching up to her now.

# NINE

A minute; five, twenty. Cass couldn't be sure how long it'd been since the explosion. Not long enough to catch her breath, too long to be safe. She forced herself to her feet, calves searing, thighs hollow and trembling from the effort. A deep breath. Focus. She readjusted her backpack.

"Can we wait? Just a little longer?" Wren asked, hopeful, barely audible.

Cass just shook her head. She didn't have the courage to look behind her, so she took his hand in hers, and started off again. One step at a time. It was all she could manage. Out of the corner of her eye, Cass saw Wren glance back over his shoulder. She stole the chance to wipe the tears from her eyes.

It wasn't the loss. At least, that's what she told herself. They'd been on their own, on the run, too long for their brief time with Three to really make much difference. For the first time, though, she felt an emptiness that hadn't been there before. A quiet resignation. Her body would go through the motions for as long as she could force it to, but somewhere between the wayhouse and wherever they were now, her heart had given out. Hope can only be offered and snatched away so many times before it becomes a mockery. It didn't seem to matter now. There was nothing more this shell of a world had left to give that could make her feel safe.

"Mama?"

"Yeah, baby."

"Are we going to die now?"

The question jolted Cass from her haze. Wren had an uncanny knack for asking the very questions she was asking herself.

"Of course not."

She wanted to reassure him, but that was all she could muster.

"OK."

He took it at face value, and for that she was thankful. They walked a little ways in silence, and then Wren spoke again.

"Will you tell me when?"

"When what, sweetheart?"

"When it's time for us to die."

Cass's heart practically stopped. What mother could possibly answer such a question? And what did it say about her, that her child, so young, would even think to ask it? She couldn't stop the tears then. She sank to her knees, and drew Wren close, hugged him, drawing comfort more than offering it.

Wren squeezed back.

"I'm sorry, Mama. I didn't mean to make you cry."

Cass just squeezed harder.

"It's not you, sweetheart."

"It's me," a nearby voice said.

Cass and Wren both jerked at Three's sudden reappearance. She swiveled on a knee, instinctively grasping Wren's arm to pull him behind her. Three stood at the entrance of an alley, just a few feet from them.

"Don't flatter yourself," she replied, hastily clearing the tears. "I'm used to you disappearing."

He grunted at that, the closest thing to a chuckle she'd heard from him.

"Come on this way," he answered, motioning them over.

Cass stood and readjusted her pack, but made no movement towards him.

"We've got about nine hours of light, and ten hours of travel. Sooner is better."

Still, she held her place.

"You were right, you know," she said. "No promise. No debt."

She glanced away, back towards the Enclave. She and Wren had made it a long time without help. They could do it again. Especially now that Fedor, Kostya, and probably Jez were all gone.

"Maybe we should just say our goodbyes, while we still can."

There was a stretch of silence. Wren shifted beside her, fidgeting as children do.

"Well," Three said. "I *did* say I didn't owe you anything."

His nonchalant agreement surprised Cass. She'd expected at least some marginal protest, some semblance of noble gesture. But he had left them behind once before. It was probably a relief to do so again, this time without the guilt.

"I never said *you* didn't owe *me*."

She looked back. He was staring right at her. Grim. Determined.

"I've put too much on the line to just let you crawl off and die. So come on."

He didn't sound angry. There was no malice or menace in his voice. Just raw determination, as if by his words he'd eliminated any other choice. And to Cass, it was as if he had. Still, she hesitated, more out of pride than uncertainty.

"How do I know you're not just going to leave again?"

"Because I'm here now."

She gave a final glance in the direction of the Enclave, feigning the act of weighing her options. Finally, she nodded, and taking Wren's hand in hers, made her way over. "Fine."

"Yeah."

And without fanfare, Three led them off down his side alley, perpendicular to their previous route. Within the first few yards, he was back to his old self, hesitating every so often when some instinct kicked off a silent warning. He seemed to be straining every possible sense, listening, watching, feeling for any hint or sign of danger. After some indeterminate span of time, Cass began to feel that her own measured breathing was too loud for his liking. Even so, she had to hazard a question.

"How many of them did you get?" she whispered.

Three shot her a sidelong glance, then went back to scanning the way ahead.

"None."

He must've misunderstood. She clarified.

"I meant with the explosion."

"So did I."

Cass couldn't understand Three's matter-of-factness. All the trouble he'd gone through, the risk he'd taken, and he hadn't killed even one of their pursuers. She would've thought there'd have been some hint of embarrassment, or disappointment at least. He must've picked up on that.

"I wasn't trying to kill them."

Surely this was some sort of defensive response, a casual *I-meant-to-do-that.*

"Oh?"

"Nah, I was killing us."

She rolled it over in her mind, making some sense of it, but not a lot. The explosion, the rubble, the plumes of concrete dust. Maybe the wreckage would disrupt signal enough to buy them some time. Or maybe Asher was busy sifting through the wreckage for her body, or for some trace of residual impulse. Too many maybes, never any answers.

She opened her mouth to ask another question, but Three

pressed ungentle fingers over her lips and shook his head. Enough talk. The rough, callused skin left a trace of heat when he pulled his hand away. He set off again wordlessly, silently, a mist of a man dissipating across the jagged asphalt terrain.

For his part, Wren was holding up well, keeping pace without complaint, picking his feet up instead of scuffing them along as he was wont to do. He had declined a piggyback ride, which was practically unheard of. He seemed more relaxed than Cass could remember him being, more confident. Older somehow, though she couldn't be sure when he'd grown.

Progress was slow, but steady, and after the first two or three hours, Cass grew nearly accustomed to the broken rhythm of the journey, the patternless flow that Three kept without any apparent effort. At first it had irritated her, being unable to predict how long they might crouch in the corner of an abandoned building, or how far they'd travel across open space before they stopped. But eventually Cass discovered the benefits of it. Alertness. Focus. Rhythm bred complacency, and that was one thing none of them could afford.

"We'll rest here," Three said, almost at full voice. The sudden volume was shocking in the dull and heavy silence that pervaded the dead city around them, and Cass couldn't help but flinch.

"Are you sure it's safe?" she whispered.

"Not at all," he answered. "But you need it."

He glanced to her briefly, caught her eye, added a little nod. Cass had started to protest, but Three's tone was neither condescending nor accusatory. Not gentle, perhaps, but there was a hint of care or concern in his voice that she hadn't noticed before. And suddenly, she was glad for it. Cass only now realized how exhausted she was.

They found a niche in what had once been a large fountain, though no water ran there now; a curving serpent wrapped around a stylized mountain, which offered them cover from three sides and some slight concealment from the fourth. Cass and Wren nestled together with their backs against the concrete base. Three produced some sort of ration from his harness: a synthetic combination of carbohydrates and protein; spongy, flavorless. They ate it without conversation or enjoyment, though Cass could tell it was at least nourishing.

After they'd eaten, Wren lay down and put his head in her lap, while Cass leaned back and let her eyes drift closed.

"So what's the plan?" she asked without opening her eyes again.

"North a few more miles, then west."

"Where does that get us?"

He inhaled deeply.

"Northwestish."

Cass cracked an eye open. Three crouched by the opening, hands clasped, elbows resting on his knees; the closest thing to relaxed Cass had yet seen of him. Whether he had intended to say more or not, Cass wasn't sure, but he reacted to her when he saw her looking. A half-smile, one corner of his mouth turned down slightly. A lightness in his eyes. A joke.

"The Vault's up that way," he continued. "Heard of it?"

Cass shook her head.

"Yeah, not many have. Not the nicest place, but it should be safe for a night, maybe two. Gatekeeper's a friend of mine."

"You have friends?"

Three exhaled abruptly through his nose; apparently his version of a chuckle.

"Enough to get by," he replied. Then added with a nod, "Get some rest, girl. We'll move soon."

Cass let her eyes fall closed again, felt herself drifting off already, welcoming the deep embrace of sleep under Three's watchful eye.

••••

Three ran a thumb back and forth over the checkered grip of

his holstered pistol, mind working to calculate all the variables that would affect the rest of their travel. He'd already let the woman and kid sleep nearly half an hour. Every minute that ticked by robbed them of precious daylight, their only ally out here in the open. They'd been making better time than he'd expected. Much better. Tough as the two were, though, they'd been showing signs of exhaustion. Three didn't know how far he could push them.

Five more minutes. Then he'd wake them.

Three scanned their surroundings from his constrained viewpoint. Less visibility than he would've liked. And it was rarely a good idea to back into anything that only had one way out. But he knew Cass and Wren would feel safer here, surrounded by walls, hidden from view.

He chuckled humorlessly at that, touched the shallow, weeping cut across his throat. Seemed like he'd been making a lot of compromises lately.

He glanced over at the slumbering pair, and found Wren sitting upright, staring at him with glassy eyes, blond hair standing straight out from the side of his head where he'd been lying in his mother's lap. Three nodded. Wren wiped an eye with the back of his hand and tossed a casual wave in response. For a moment, they just sat there, looking at each other, Wren's sea-green eyes fixed unblinking on Three.

Three flashed back to when he'd first seen those eyes, back at the Enclave, back in that dive bar. Days ago? Another lifetime. Something in those eyes had captured his notice and escaped his definition then. Even now, sober and alert, Three found he couldn't quite identify what he saw there. Something hovered at the outer edge of his consciousness, just beyond his grasp, a vanishing dream he fought to recall. Something…

Cass spasmed abruptly, eyes wide, hands shooting up from her lap; the sudden movement made Wren jump.

"They know," she rasped. "They know I'm alive."

Three was already in motion.

"Tracerunnin' you?"

She shook her head.

"Can't be. But he knows."

Three's mind scrambled through the scenarios. They'd been headed in a different direction before the blast. Not directly opposite, but far enough off-track to make other routes equally plausible. They'd avoided the obvious double-back. And there was an outside chance that the Vault was off-grid enough to escape Asher's notice... No. No reason for optimism now. Three never counted on the outside chance, unless it was bad.

"If he can't track your signal, he'll have to split his crew, three, maybe four ways to cover the bases. Worst case, I figure we get to the Vault a good hour before they do, and by then, well..."

He trailed off; probably best if she didn't know just how close they were cutting it.

"We'll stay ahead of 'em," he added. "We'll be alright."

Without hesitation Three stood and stretched a hand out to Cass, helping her to her feet; action conveying his certainty better than words. He dropped low, and glided out, quickly surveying the area before committing to an exit. Cass gathered their things, prepped Wren.

And once again, they were on the move.

# TEN

Cass had traveled through more of the mummified carcass of the world than 99.9% of the remnant populace, but somehow she had never noticed before just how much everything looked the same. Gray or brown, concrete and rust, punctuated by flickering sparks of tech still happily humming with some internal purpose; gaudy, like Christmas lights on a gravestone. Maybe it was the exhaustion from the travel, blurring everything into one dreary, colorless smear, but most likely, she thought, it was some sort of newly acquired way of seeing things. Seeing them as they actually were, in the real world, rather than what they had been, before, as told by their lingering swirl of residual signal. Something learned from Three, perhaps. Or maybe just a fanciful musing from her weary mind.

She glanced at the sky above, framed from her vantage on either side by empty, towering high-rises. A vibrant orange, filtering to a muted purple, boxed in by the ever-present cold and lifeless gray. No, she was the one in the box... the sky was up there, gloriously free. She felt a twinge of envy, though she knew it was ridiculous to be jealous of the heavens. They simply were, as they had always been. Unchanged by the events that unfolded beneath. Cass shook her head with a humorless chuckle, wondering how exhausted she must be to be thinking that way.

They had held up well. By any sane person's standards, she and Wren had made a heroic effort, a feat of nearly inhuman strength and endurance, to travel so far in their condition. Even at the best of times, running at full strength in Asher's crew, she'd never traveled this far in the open in a single day. But compared to Three, she felt like they should've covered twice the distance. The man was tireless. He walked a few paces ahead of her, steps still even, strong, and sure, even though he had added her backpack on top of his own harness, and was now carrying Wren on his back as well.

Their pace had quickened significantly in the last two hours or so. Three insisted it was because he knew the area was safer than the others they'd passed through, but Cass couldn't help but feel he was risking more than he would admit. And she understood. In another thirty minutes or so, it wouldn't matter how much ground they had covered if they weren't locked safely inside somewhere.

Three disappeared around a corner into yet another narrow, rusting alley, and Cass followed with one trudging step at a time, one foot in front of the other, willing herself onward. Exiting the alleyway, Cass found herself at a wide road. An old maglev line, bowed in the middle, ran overhead. And just across the road sat a squat block of concrete, more like a bunker than a building, with a heavy steel gate implanted in its middle. The Vault.

Three hesitated at the edge of the road, glanced skyward. Cass edged to his side.

"That it?"

Three nodded with a furrowed brow. She noticed the slash across his throat was bleeding again.

"So, shouldn't we be going in?"

Three nodded again. But he didn't move. Just stood there, scanning the road, the building, something, everything; Cass wasn't sure what.

"Sooo… why aren't we?"

Three shook his head, let Wren slide down off his back.

"Feels wrong."

He unbuttoned his coat, and eased his pistol out of its holster. Flipped open its cylinder, snapped it shut again with a flick of his wrist. Without looking at her, he pushed Wren gently back against her legs, held the gun out for her to take. Cass dropped a hand on Wren's shoulder, took the heavy weapon with the other.

"Wait here."

Cass felt tears come to her eyes as she watched Three glide out across the road and make his silent way to the Vault. She let them fall without knowing or caring why they came. She was spent, depleted of all her body had to give and beyond, with a weariness she felt down through the middle of her bones, deep into her heart. If there was something wrong here, at the Vault, after all they'd done to reach it, she felt she'd just as soon sit down and let the Weir come for them rather than take another step.

"What do you think it is, Mama?"

Wren's voice sounded small.

"I don't know, sweetheart."

"Maybe he's just being extra careful."

"That's probably it."

"My feet are sad."

"Mine too, baby. Mine too."

Across the street, Three moved from place to place, sometimes within view, sometimes not. Cass wondered what he was looking for, what he was seeing. She felt like she could see it all from where she stood: a concrete bunker, impenetrable save through its one entrance, which was securely blocked by the lowered steel gate. And if he truly had friends inside, it seemed like he could just let them know they were outside. But Three was nothing if not cautious and thorough, and she had to trust there was a good reason they were still in the open with the sun slipping beneath the horizon.

After about five minutes, he motioned for them to join
him and quickly. Cass steeled herself, took Wren's hand, and
crossed.

"What now?" she asked when they reached him. She
handed him his massive handgun, glad to be rid of the thing.

"The gate."

"Yeah, why don't we just get them to open it? I thought you
said the gatekeeper's a friend of yours."

"Yeah."

Something in Three's tone concerned Cass. His demeanor
had changed; darker now. If she didn't know better, she'd
almost say he sounded worried.

"I don't understand."

Three didn't say anything. Just pointed to the bottom of the
gate, nearest to where they were standing. Meanwhile his eyes
were busy scanning around the top.

At first, she didn't see anything. Concrete. Steel. No way
in. The fatigue and frustration were getting to her. Why Three
couldn't just tell her what was wrong, she couldn't fathom.
The man's aversion to words was quickly becoming his least
attractive quality.

Cass opened her mouth to tell him to spell it out for her,
but caught herself. She saw it now. A gap, maybe three inches
wide, at the base of the gate. It wasn't sealed, looked more like
it had fallen than been lowered. She bit her lip to keep the
tears back.

Three turned, put a knee in front of Wren, rested his hand
on her son's shoulder.

"How you feelin', Mister Wren?"

"Tired," Wren shrugged.

"How's your hand? Hurting any?"

Wren held up his bandaged hand. Blood showed through
the fabric. He shook his head. Cass knew he was trying to be
tough, trying to impress Three.

"I've known grown men who would've given up a long time ago. You're a soldier. A real soldier."

Wren half-smiled at that; embarrassed. Honored. Three was building him up for something, Cass figured.

"Think you could help us out here?"

"I dunno."

Cass didn't know why Three was taking so long to get to the point. Maybe he just didn't feel comfortable asking Wren for help directly. She jumped in.

"Can you get this door opened up for us, sweetheart?" she asked.

Three looked up at her briefly, shook his head.

"That's a no go. Engines that drive the gate are older than I am. Mechanical, not electronic."

"What do you want him to do then?"

Three looked back at Wren, then pointed up above the gate, to the left side. About nine feet up, there was a small grate, maybe two feet wide and a foot and a half tall; much too small to be a point of entry for anyone. Except perhaps a child.

"Do you see that vent up there?"

Wren looked up, back at Three, nodded. Cass cut the conversation off.

"No. No way. You're not sending him through there."

Three ignored her.

"It's big enough for you to fit. Can you crawl through, and open the gate from the inside?"

"Did you hear me?" Cass said. "He's *not* going in there."

"I'm talking to your son," answered Three, forcefully. Cass was so stunned she didn't know how to respond. Three didn't take his eyes off Wren. "Can you do that?"

Wren shrugged, apparently torn between Cass's words and this man who called him a soldier.

"I think so, maybe."

"Don't tell me what you think," Three said in a firm voice. "Tell me if you can."

Wren looked up at the vent again, and then back at Three. Cass noticed her son did not look at her. He just nodded.

"I can do it."

Three stood up and took off his harness.

"Three," Cass said. "No. I'm not going to let you send him in there by himself. There's no telling what's in that thing. He could get hurt."

Three pulled a chemlight out of his vest and ignited it, attention still focused on Wren.

"If he doesn't go, he'll die."

Three had a way of making choices seem nonexistent. Cass struggled to think of a better alternative, any alternative, while Three went on prepping her son, as though she had no say in the matter. He gave Wren the chemlight, drew something from his vest which he held hidden in his hand, all the while talking Wren through the steps.

"Once you get the cover off, crawl to the nearest vent. You may have to turn left or right once or twice, but it shouldn't be too far before you can drop down. If anyone's in there, ask for Gev. Can you remember that?"

Wren nodded. Cass gave up trying to prevent it, just watched the exchange, noticed how attentive Wren was, how eager.

"And if you don't see anyone, look for two engines. Big engines. There's a lever on one side. Just pull it, and the gate should open up. Can you do that?"

"I think–," Wren stopped himself. "Yes."

"Who are you asking for?"

"Gev."

"Alright, I want you to take this."

Again Three knelt, holding out his hand. Across his palm, lay one of the knives Cass had seen twice before; once in the wayhouse where Wren had cut his hand, and again during Three's fight with Dagon.

"He certainly doesn't need that–" she protested. Wren flicked his eyes to her, but Three paid her no mind.

"This is very sharp, and very dangerous. You understand?"

Wren nodded. Three lifted Wren's unbandaged hand and pressed the handle of the knife into it.

"You'll need it to open the vents. Do a good job, it's yours."

Wren nodded solemnly while he gazed at the simple, elegant blade, as if it were an ancient sword being passed down from some great and mighty warrior-king.

"Listen," Three caught his eye again. "You'll do it. I already know. You ready?"

Wren nodded again. Confident. Cass wanted to say something, anything, to change their minds, but nothing seemed forceful enough, meaningful enough, to override whatever had just taken place between Three and her son. Something in Wren's face had changed, so subtle, so slight only a mother would notice. But there was some measure of strength there now that hadn't been there before, as if Three had given some of his own for Wren to carry with him. Wren didn't even look at her as he stepped closer to the wall.

"Hey, one last thing," said Three. "Give your mom a kiss."

Wren obeyed, shuffled over to Cass. She knelt, hugged him, received his little wet kiss on her cheek.

"Be careful, sweetheart. Don't get hurt."

It sounded wrong to her, somehow, like telling a soldier in the arctic to remember his mittens, but she couldn't stop herself from saying it. He pulled away before she was ready for him to go.

"*Always* kiss the lady goodbye," Three said, easily swinging Wren up onto his shoulders. "So she remembers you."

Wren scrabbled up to a standing position on Three's shoulders. His head just below the vent, he reached up with his knife and jammed it into the seam between metal and concrete. He pulled hard on the handle, but the vent wouldn't budge.

"It's stuck."

"Work it back and forth, little bit at a time… yeah, yeah, that's the way."

Wren worked the blade and the vent inched away from its concrete base. After a few moments, it swung suddenly free, catching him off-guard. He swayed backwards, but caught the lip of the vent, balanced himself.

"Be careful, baby."

"Mom. I am."

It was the first time Cass remembered Wren calling her anything other than Mama.

"Alright, soldier. In you go."

Three had Wren step up on to his hands, then boosted him higher. Wren stretched his hands into the opening, scooted in up to his shoulders.

There he hesitated, and for a moment Cass thought, hoped even, that he would back out, say he couldn't do it, that they'd have to find another way.

"It smells bad in here."

"You won't be in there long."

Three's eyes flicked skyward, judged the ratio of blue to purple. The first stars were just visible.

"Quick as you can."

With that, Cass watched as her baby son scuffled and shimmied his way into a dark shaft, headed into the unknown, alone, without her, and she was frightened.

Three stepped back, watched Wren's small feet kick their last way into the opening, and disappear from view. He and Cass stood in silence for a few moments. Then, wordlessly, with the slightest glance and nod, Three patted her shoulder twice, and squeezed it once.

"He'll be alright."

"If he's not, I'll kill you myself."

••••

For once, Wren was thankful for his size. The airshaft, or whatever it was he was in, was bigger than he'd first thought, big enough for him to move pretty freely in. But the darkness made it seem tighter, more confining. The yellow-green chemlight splashed out in all directions, and didn't show nearly as far ahead as Wren wished it would. There was a very slight breeze, more draft than anything, but it was hot, and the smell from inside was getting stronger. Wren couldn't place it as any one thing. It just reminded him of being sick.

It'd seemed so easy, so possible when Three had told him about it. A simple crawl, a drop, a lever to pull. Nothing he hadn't done playing in any of the places he'd been with his mother, even more so when he'd been out with Ran and Dagon. But here, now, alone in the dark, he just felt afraid. Something about the darkness just changes when grown-ups aren't in it with you.

He glanced back at the entrance, now a hole of waning light small enough to hide behind his thumb. Mister Three had said it wouldn't be far, but how far *was* it? Not far to *him* sometimes seemed like a really long way to Wren. Wren started to wonder if maybe he'd passed the way out already, if maybe he should try to turn around, or crawl backwards. But Mister Three had said to be quick, and Wren already felt like he'd taken too long.

He crawled on a little further, and suddenly felt a change in the subtle draft. A swirling, like wind colliding. He stretched the chemlight forward as far as he could. And his heart fell.

Mister Three had said there might be a left or right turn. He never said there might be both, in the same place.

Wren was at a T in the ductwork, blackness stretching off to his left and right without hint or clue as to which way he should go. A coldness crept up inside, and he looked quickly back to the entrance, hoping maybe it was closer than he remembered. It wasn't. In fact, it was harder to see it now; smaller, darker. Night was falling. A quiet sort of dread crept into his heart.

He wanted to call out, call for his mommy to tell him what he should do, but felt somehow that he shouldn't, that now that he was inside, he needed to be quiet. And pimming her was a no-no: Asher would be looking for that, and that'd be even worse than not masking, since it'd make them both easy to find. Should he crawl back? Tell them he was lost?

No, he didn't want to make Mister Three mad. There was no telling what he might do if he got mad. Or disappointed. He'd said he was a soldier. Soldiers probably didn't call for their mommies, and they probably weren't afraid of the dark. Tears came to his eyes.

Wren gripped his knife tighter, held the blade up, looked at it. He was a soldier. He was a soldier.

"I'm a soldier," he whispered, as the first hot tear streaked his face. "I'm a soldier."

For some reason, he just decided to go right. It felt better somehow. He took one last look at the entrance, and then moved on. And once the decision was made, he found it suddenly easier to move, to crawl faster. To quit crying. It'd been a fleeting glimpse of the entryway, but Wren knew now that time was short. The Weir would be out soon. And Mama was counting on him. Mister Three was counting on him. He wouldn't let them down.

He crawled on, elbow after elbow, and in another minute or so, he nearly passed over top of the very thing he'd been looking for. Another vent. A way out. Below him, and smaller than the one he'd come in through, it nevertheless looked like his best and only option.

Wren scooted back, tried to get some leverage on the fitting, but it was no good. A couple of minutes of trying to wedge the blade into the seams didn't work. In the end he took to stabbing the vent over and over, each strike echoing sharply throughout the Vault beyond, and sending a chill up his spine.

Finally, the metal bent outward, making a hole big enough for him to slip through.

For a time, he sat listening, straining for any sound of human life below. Then, he scooted forward, and peered downward into more of the same deep blackness that he'd just crawled through. He remembered back when Mister Three had hidden them before, back in that big wet place, when he'd dropped their chemlight down the stairwell. It'd been an accident then. Now, it seemed like a good idea.

Wren reached through with the chemlight, then let it fall from his hand, watched as it floated into nothingness, and then clattered suddenly, and rolled to a halt. Its meager light pooled on what looked like a smooth concrete surface. It didn't seem that far down. Too far to go head first, though. Wren dragged himself forward over the vent, then, once his feet were clear, dropped them through the hole and scooted backwards.

He had intended to lower himself slowly down until he was just hanging from the edge, and then drop. Something didn't go right. It happened too fast, about when his waist went through the hole, and all of a sudden he was slipping and falling, and something punched him in the arm and chin, and then his feet hit before he was ready, and he fell to his hands and knees on cool, hard concrete.

It took a second for Wren to figure out he'd hit the ground, and that he was where he meant to be. His arm felt funny. And his chin was burning. Really burning, like he'd put it on the stove. He tried really, really hard not to cry. But he couldn't help it.

Through the tears he picked up his chemlight, held it high, tried to figure out where he was. Then, there was a sound. A sort of scuffle. A mouse running through paper, or a raven's sudden flight. Wren froze. Strained. Gripped his knife so hard it hurt. Again, the sound. Coming from slightly behind him, over his right shoulder. Then a scraping, metal on metal.

An arctic wave of panic rushed over Wren then, as every nightmare creature he'd ever imagined exploded in his mind, there, trapped in the room with him, and he holding the only light. He wanted so desperately to scream, but his only thought, his one lone rational thought was to be still, and he clung to that thought. Be still. Be still. Be still.

Again, a rustling. No closer. And this time, followed by a voice.

"Wren?" it called. It sounded small, tinny, strange. "Wren, baby, are you in there?"

Mama.

"Mama! It's me, I'm here!"

"Where are you, sweetheart?"

"I don't know," he called. He wasn't even trying anymore. The tears fell freely. "Mama it's all dark!"

"Come to me, Wren. Just come to my voice."

He moved towards the voice he knew and loved the most, each step making it sound fuller, warmer, more and more like Mama.

"Keep coming, baby. You're real close."

Finally, in the last few steps, Wren could barely make out a stripe of pale purple light slipping in. The gap in the gate. He dropped to his knees, set the chemlight on the floor, and stuck his hand through.

"Here Mama, I'm here."

He felt her strong hands close around his, warm, certain.

"Are you alright? Are you hurt?"

"I fell."

Another voice now.

"The engines. Can you see 'em?"

Mister Three.

"No, sir. It's all dark."

"Wren, are you OK?"

He laid the knife down by his side, wiped the tears away with his free hand. He still had a job to do.

"Yes, Mama, I'm OK. I'm OK now."

"Wren, you're on the left side of the gate," Three said, louder. He must've been kneeling near the gap now. "If you follow the gate over to the other side, the engines should be right there."

"OK. I'll find them. Hang on."

Wren stood up, picked up his chemlight, followed the gate across the room, running his other, empty hand along it more for comfort than direction. Mama and Mister Three were on the other side of that gate. Eight inches away. Everything was fine.

He reached the end of the gate, where steel met concrete, and held the light above his head again. A few paces away he saw the beginnings of some kind of machinery: old, brown, massive. Had to be the engines.

"OK, Mama, I found them!" he yelled.

And in the next instant, froze again, as the echo from his voice trailed off. He felt it.

Something was there, moving in the darkness. Closing.

No faint rustle now. Just a steady, slow *pat... pat... pat*, like bare feet carefully placed. There was no hope for control now. Wren screamed.

"Mama! Mama!"

"Wren?"

Absolute terror seized him, a waking nightmare.

"Mama! Something's in here! *Mama!*"

"Wren! Wren!" she called, hysterical. "*Wren!*"

Back, back, he slid back to the wall, down to the corner, hugged his knees. The knife, *his* knife, he'd left it on the floor across the room, just now when he needed it most. And the patter never stopped, never sped up. It just came closer, closer, closer.

In his panicked fright, Wren threw the chemlight at the sound, watched it sail and clatter away, bouncing off some block of rounded, rusted metal. Clamped his hands over his ears, screaming for his mama to come get him, knowing there was no way she could.

# ELEVEN

The woman was hysterical, and Three couldn't really blame her given the situation. Wren had gone suddenly silent, and wasn't answering her calls now. But they were on a knife's edge, minutes from the waking of the Weir. Without the safety of the Vault, he was out of options. And without options, Cass wouldn't survive the night.

She was on her knees, sobbing into the gap in the gate, calling for her son. Pleading for an answer. But the intensity was waning. Three knew she would be useless in searching for another way. There was always another way. Knowing that had gotten him this far, and he hadn't come this far to stop searching now. He could feel his eyes sliding over details, instincts screaming to slow down, go back. But Cass's cries were interfering, dulling his focus.

"Cass," he called her gently. She didn't respond. "Cass, come on."

He reached down to take her arm, thinking to help her to her feet, but the instant he made contact, she sprang up, screaming again, right in his face.

"He's gone! You killed him!"

She flailed at him, weak, pathetic blows that he didn't even bother defending himself against. Behind the chaos, the storm of a woman that raged in front of him, a hint of sound caught his attention, something he felt more than heard.

"Cass," Three said, his voice calm, even.

"You sent him to die!"

"Cass," he said it again, firm, urgent; a warning, if she'd been listening.

"He's gone! My son is *gone!*"

He didn't have time for this, or to explain, so he did what came naturally. He punched her in the sternum, a sharp, shallow blow that stole the breath from her body, and crumpled her to the ground. There. Quiet. Controlled. He put a hand on her neck to keep her in place while he scanned, strained. Every sense stretched outward, seeking to disprove what he'd thought he'd heard. Knowing in his gut that he had. Yes, there again... he'd heard it. The faint, distant but unmistakable call of the Weir. The very first of them were out. More would follow.

Cass had fallen into a silent, shuddering sort of sobbing, and Three took advantage of her stillness. He took his hand from her, scanned everything he could think of: the gate, the vent, the alleyways, the maglev line... In all that surrounded them, there had to be something to use, some place to hide. But his mind kept sliding back to the Vault. It wasn't an option, but it refused to remove itself as one. He fought to forget it, to force his eyes to see everything else.

Under normal circumstances, he never would've let it happen. But the stress, the exhaustion, the pressure... whatever the reason, he let himself forget about the woman for a moment. A mistake. She hit him from the side, a blur of movement in the waning light, and drove the edge of her hand into his neck, just under the jaw. Three's vision jolted; blacked out for an instant. As he fell to a knee, he felt the pistol sliding clear of its holster. Her words flashed through his dazed mind, her promise that if anything happened to Wren, she'd kill him herself.

She got two shots off before he managed to grab her wrist, and the third round tore a chunk from the upper corner of the

Vault's reinforced exterior. As the rolling echo from the blasts rumbled into the distance, Three wrenched the gun from her, and threw her back to the ground. For a long moment, he just stood there, staring, jaw clenched tight, temples throbbing, fighting back the urge to do her some violence. She stared right back, smoldering, defiant; he had no doubts about her will or ferocity. But there was something else... a vulnerability he hadn't expected. Resignation to a familiar fear. Acceptance of what was about to come. And he knew in that instant that this woman was no stranger to abuse.

For the first time, something inside Three cracked. He felt it without understanding it. And there wasn't time to analyze it now. But he knew something had changed, and whatever it was probably wasn't good news for him. Wordlessly, he slid his pistol back into its holster, and went back to the job at hand, trying to forget for the moment that he'd just lost three of his four remaining shells in a flash of unchecked emotion. Not to mention the unwanted attention those gunshots would surely attract.

At first he'd thought she'd meant to kill him, but he saw now that wasn't the case. Near the left-hand lower corner of the gate, just where the gap was, were two new holes, no more than three inches apart, still glowing orange-red where the thirty-kilojoule rounds had bored through. If only Cass had asked, Three could've told her that wouldn't work, but he felt a twinge of relief as he realized he didn't owe his life to lousy shooting.

Another squawk sounded from somewhere in the gathering gloom. A melancholy, almost lonely cry that resonated far too well with their current circumstances. Three ran a hand over his bristly head, cracked his neck. The wind was picking up, and the autumn air had the promise of a colder-than-usual winter on its breath. He flexed his fingers, worked out a tightness he hadn't noticed until now.

"Come on, girl," he finally said quietly, turning back to her and offering his hand. "We'll figure this out."

Cass had her legs drawn up, hugging her knees. She stared off back the way they'd come, refusing to look at him. Despondent.

"We need to go."

Out this far, the Weir were scattered, harder to predict.

"Cass."

She wouldn't look at him, wouldn't acknowledge him. But in a quiet voice, more to herself than to Three, she answered.

"I'm done."

They were losing time they didn't have.

"No you're not."

It was bad enough they were talking instead of moving. Cass was making it worse with long pauses between responses, as if the effort to speak was almost more than she could manage.

"Wren was all I had. No reason to go on if he's gone."

"And if he's not?"

Still she hadn't moved. Another uncanny howl echoed down the alleys, swirled in the chilling air. Three's tone hardened.

"You're his mother. If he was dead, you would know. He's in there. And it won't do him any good, waiting here to die. So come on."

She didn't look to him. But after a too long moment, she reached up, put her hand in his, let him help her to her feet. When he let go, her hand slid away with the barest hint of reluctance. Three told himself it was from her exhaustion.

"Where?" asked Cass.

Three put on his harness and slung the backpack over a shoulder, all the while scanning their surroundings a final time, searching for that other way. It was here. That voice inside was screaming that he'd seen it already, if he could just think. It was *here*. Just put it together.

No… not here. He'd passed it somewhere. Somewhere close. But what was *it*?

Finally, there was a spark of an idea, a floating scrap of conversation he'd overheard in some nearly forgotten place, some indeterminate time ago.

"Can you climb?"

Wren sat shoved hard into the cold corner of concrete and steel, desperately trying not to breathe. The scaly hand pressed over his mouth had a sour smell that made his stomach feel upside down and the hot breath on his face reeked of strong vapors that burned his eyes. In those last few terrifying moments, the chemlight had rolled away under some piece of machinery, leaving only the faintest glow pooling on the floor. All Wren knew of his captor was that it was human. He could at least feel that much.

Whoever it was shifted, placed its mouth right into Wren's ear. Its breath tickled when it spoke.

"Quiet, little one," it hissed. "Quiet, or we die."

He wanted so badly to call out to Mama, to answer her calls, to let her know he was OK. But even if there hadn't been a hand over his mouth, the fear in his throat would've stopped any sound he'd wanted to make. The thing was human, minimally. But it felt somehow… wrong. Being this close to It flooded Wren with an indecipherable sense, like hearing an argument in another language, unable to grasp the words but unmistakably getting the tone. Whatever was wrong with It, Wren felt simultaneously afraid of and sorry for It. It seemed wild, and lost.

"We'll go to the safe place… it's too late for the others. But you can live. If you are *quiet*."

It shifted again, and Wren was glad when the hand slipped off his mouth. But in the next instant a strong grip seized him, and then he was being lifted up, awkwardly but not unkindly swung onto his captor's back, and held securely in place by Its wiry arms.

"Quiet," It reminded him.

It carried him away at the same unchanging pace as It had approached. *Pat... pat... pat...* Its bare feet following practiced steps across the concrete floor. Wren saw the yellow-green glow of the lost chemlight grow and then recede as they passed by and moved into some chamber beyond the entrance.

It stopped briefly, Its head swiveling slightly, Its rank whisper washing over him.

"I'm... we need to... I can't always remember..."

It stopped Itself, exhaled in frustration, seemed to shake Its head as if to clear it.

"Safe first, then we'll see. Then we'll see."

With that jumble of thoughts hanging in the air, It proceeded onwards. Whatever was carrying him walked differently than anyone else Wren had ever known. And he had gotten a *lot* of piggyback rides before. This one didn't bounce very much. He almost felt like they were gliding, even when they started going down the stairs. His mama's calls became muffled and duller, and drifted above him, and finally stopped altogether.

Without his mother's voice, without that connection to her, Wren felt completely lost. He started sobbing, a silent, shaking cry, frightened of making any noise, but terrified of what might happen to him, and to his mama, and to Mister Three. He jammed his fist in his mouth, tried biting his fingers. Sometimes that worked.

"Don't cry, little one," It whispered. "I have a safe place."

It was pitch-black, and the air was thick with the sickly odor that Wren had first smelled back in the vent, though it was much stronger here. Wren squeezed his eyes tightly shut. He bit his hand a little harder. Somewhere far above him, three rolling booms thundered.

"Too much noise," It murmured. "That won't do. It isn't safe."

Its arms released and Wren felt himself sliding slowly from Its back. When his feet touched the ground, he just stood there, hand in his mouth, crying and missing his mom.

"Lie down, little one, yeah? Sleep is quiet, and we stay quiet until morning. No noise and no stream, because they hear both. OK? Then we'll see. I think maybe… maybe it will be the same again… the way it used to be. Maybe, in the morning. We'll see."

Wren heard It shuffle not far away and make noises he could only guess meant It was taking Its own advice and lying down. Without knowing what else to do, Wren curled into a ball on the cold concrete floor and bit into his knuckles, fighting desperately the urge to scream.

Cass stared up at the maglev line towering over her, at the twisted scaffolding, the flexing support structure, the tangled mass of metal… and the man perched like a hawk in the midst of it all, twenty feet from the ground. Three was up there, unnaturally nimble, a four-limbed spider in his web of steel, barely visible as the final traces of the day faded into night. He swore it'd be safe but he was checking it out nonetheless, having left her alone on the ground, cloaked in the night air with nothing more for protection. She couldn't ignore the fact that he hadn't left the pistol with her this time.

Even standing, it was hard to resist sleep. Cass's body was near collapse, threatening to shut down without regard to her wishes if she didn't willingly rest soon. The ache was back. The hunger, the thirst. The dull, glowing heat in the pit of her stomach and at the back of her throat that cried out for quint. Whatever synth Three had crafted, he'd said it'd last her a few days. It'd been less than two. And it was gone, already used up by her ever-accelerating burn rate. Her arms and legs shivered, though not from cold. She just had to endure, had to let him think the worry was getting to her, which was true enough. Worry for Wren made her head swim. But it was fear that kept her from telling Three the truth, fear that knowing she'd lied about her burn rate would lead him to question how else she may have misled him. And as much as Cass hated it, she needed Three now, needed him to get them through. She knew whatever it took to keep him on their side, she'd do without question or regret.

Three had been right, of course. In her heart, Cass knew Wren was alive. Frightened, certainly. Hurt, maybe. But alive. As a mother, it just wasn't enough. She yearned for contact, for a touch, a glimpse of him, even a word. Just a word.

Cass glanced up at Three, thirty feet above her, all but invisible now. Far enough away. Even if he was monitoring her signal by proximity, he was too high to trace anything simple, and from the look of it, he was focused more on his climbing than on anything she was doing. She'd expressly forbidden Wren from pimming her, knowing that opening those channels carried too great a risk of exposing them both to Asher's ever-watchful eye. It'd seemed like a smart rule before, when they were never apart even for a moment. But now, in the cold, in the dark, cut off from one another by some unknowable distance and who knew what else, the danger didn't seem so great or so relevant. Not compared to the hope offered by the simple act of reaching out across that distanceless space where Wren was separated by no more than a thought.

In less than a breath, it was done.

"Wren."

A heartbeat. Another. And another. Long enough for her son to have responded, if he was alright. Fear grew in her with each passing moment, every second of silence conjuring new nightmares that might have befallen her child.

And then–

"Not now."

His message came through, clear, simple, like a thought of her own spoken in his voice. Reassuring and baffling at the same time. Somewhere in the distance, a crackling wail sounded.

Above her, Three hissed, calling Cass's attention. Straining her eyes she could just make him out motioning to her, an urgent, forceful wave beckoning her to climb. She drew a deep breath, tried to steady herself. Worked her hands to ease the trembling. And started to climb.

The metal of the scaffolding was warmer than she'd expected, which was a welcome surprise. But after the first step up, with her full weight off the ground, she knew it was going to be a tough climb. Forty feet, maybe. It wouldn't have been hard if she'd had her chems. Without them though, everything was hard: climbing, walking, breathing, thinking. Cass hoped sleep would fix some of her brokenness. Assuming sleep would come.

Five feet up. Thirty-five to go. She glanced up to the underside of the maglev line, but it was too dark now to locate Three. Maybe he was already on the top. She wondered what climbing would do for them out here. Maybe the Weir wouldn't think to look for them up so high, though she doubted that. To her, it seemed that the Weir were led by something other than their eyes. She thought back to the night they'd spent in the cavernous storm water system outside the Enclave. When the Weir had passed her by once. Of course, it had come back. And so had others.

Hand up. Hold. Then foot. Reach. Stretch. Ignore the burning. Fifteen feet up. Still no sign of Three. Up here, she realized some of what she'd thought were support beams were actually just thick cables. Round, they were easy to grip, but their odd angles made her footing unsure. She did her best, forced herself to take her time despite the searing in her forearms, her back, her thighs. Even so, she never really felt completely in control.

Twenty-five feet above the ground now. Just twelve or fifteen more to go. Cass thought briefly about how they'd get down, then shoved the idea out of her mind. The thought of doing this again, not to mention backwards, was too much to process. And maybe too optimistic. Coming back down assumed they'd survive the night.

Below her a sudden croak sounded, startled her, made her lose focus just as she was mid-step, floating between foothold and handhold. Her foot slipped sideways on the cable beneath her, twisting her around out of reach of the grip she'd been reaching for, and she slammed her back into the edge of something hard. Above her, a shadow within shadows swept across the cables; she sensed it more than saw it. Three. He would save her. For a moment Cass dangled out in space, one quivering hand her only connection to the physical world. Then that too was gone.

She felt his fingertips brush hers as she slipped away into the darkness below. The first impact caught her across the back, knocking the breath from her lungs and throwing her forward. Another six feet down Cass slammed into a pair of cables where they met in an X. It bent her double with a searing pain across her belly, and the speed of her fall flipped her headfirst. In a flash of instinct, she managed to hook one elbow around the cable as she spun over the top. That probably saved her life. The cable bit deeply, but she slowed herself just long enough to make a desperate grab with her other hand. With a solid grip supporting her for a moment, her feet scrabbled and found stability on the scaffolding below. She readjusted, got two good handholds, steadied herself. Still alive, somehow.

Cass's back muscles were still seized, and she fought to suck air into her lungs, if not to breathe at least to scream. She could hear above her now Three's quick movements drawing closer, descending with such swiftness she felt certain at any moment he'd plummet past her to his own death. He reached her about the time she got her first breath.

Even in crisis, Three remained stoic. He continued down past her without a word, climbed in just underneath her with his shoulder near her waist. He shifted his weight, seemed to be testing for secure footing. Then, he pressed into her, his shoulder firm and sure against her stomach, raising her up and taking her weight from her hands and feet. The pressure sent fire coursing through her middle, and she bit into her lip to stifle a cry. Surely he didn't mean to carry her.

"Arm around my neck," he whispered, barely audible. Slowly, painfully, Cass draped her arm over the back of Three's neck, along his left shoulder. He grasped her wrist, shifted her across his shoulders, distributing her weight as evenly as possible in a sort of fireman's carry.

"Now," he breathed, words hardly more than wind in the air, "be *still*."

And with that, he began to climb.

# TWELVE

The ascent was slow and painful for Cass, every upward movement sending shockwaves through her damaged body. She couldn't imagine how Three must've been feeling. He made no complaints, but there was no doubt the climb was taking its toll, even on him.

Not a machine after all, she thought.

Sweat poured, soaked through his coat where she was laid across his shoulders. Muscles strained, trembling slightly. Pauses between movements grew longer. Three seemed to be gearing himself up for each effort. Cass had no idea how far they had left to climb. It was tough to judge their height from her vantage point, where she felt lost somewhere between sideways and upside-down. She thought about giving it another try herself. Her mistake had only almost cost them one life. A mistake now would cost at least two, and probably a third, later. But she knew her body was spent. Her head was swimming, and occasional waves of nausea were washing over her with increasing frequency and strength. Three had asked her to be still, and that was something she absolutely could do.

Glancing down to judge their distance, Cass was surprised to see she could still make out details far below despite the darkness. The street underneath them was tinted in a faint blue, not unlike moonlight. It took her groggy mind a few seconds to realize what that meant, to replay her fall and what had caused it.

Weir.

Two shapes moved in the darkness, their electric starlight eyes roving. A muted burst of white noise from one. A soft answering call from the other in that otherworldly, organic static. Almost like the quiet *whuffing* of wolves in the night. Cass wondered briefly if that was how they whispered.

To her surprise, Three thrust upwards to a new position. He must have known the Weir were in the street below. Apparently far less concerned by them than she was. Cass only then realized she was holding her breath. The Weir crept along beneath them, and continued out from under the maglev line, picking their way cautiously in the direction of the Vault. Soon enough they were lost in the night.

Three jolted again, driving upwards, and something round and hard thudded off the top of Cass's head with a dull, metallic *thunk*. A broad and throbbing pain radiated through her skull, down her spine, and into her toes. She squeezed her eyes shut, saw stars, bit off the cry that tried to escape her lips.

"I am *so* sorry," Three hissed. "You OK?"

Cass realized he'd bounced her head off the underside of the maglev line. They'd reached the top.

"Fine," she whispered, still not opening her eyes. Another wave of nausea washed over her, the strongest yet. She hoped she didn't have a concussion.

"Can you pull yourself up?"

Cass shifted slowly, carefully, and saw that they were just underneath the main line, where a gap about two feet wide allowed access to the top side of the track. In answer to Three's question, she reached up and dragged herself up through the gap. Flopped on her belly. Pulled leaden legs along behind. And lay still.

Three joined her a few moments later, lying on his back, drawing deep breaths. For a while, the two of them just lay there, recovering. The wind was colder up here; more constant, more biting. Cass rolled to her back, shoulder to shoulder with Three, eyes still closed as she fought off the vertigo.

She felt him shift closer, press into her, felt his warmth against her arm.

"Hey," he said, close now. "Take a look."

Cass couldn't tell from his tone what she'd see when she opened her eyes. When she did, she gasped. Above her, the sky was afire.

Stars. More than she'd ever seen; beyond counting, beyond even imagining. Like a spray of diamonds cast across a sea of velvet. Light, wispy clouds glowed from a half-moon, blending some stars into a milky translucence and highlighting the burning intensity of those out of the clouds' reach.

Instinctively, Cass stretched out a hand as though she could feel them, or collect them. And instantly thought of Wren, longed for him, knew how awestruck he would've been to see what she now saw.

"I wish Wren…" she started, and couldn't finish. She shut her eyes again, felt tears roll, chilling her cheeks in the wind.

"He'll see 'em one day," Three whispered. "Promise."

Cass didn't respond. She thought back to Wren's two word pim, wondered what it meant. Maybe he was hiding. Or in danger. Or worried about Asher discovering their location. Why had she ever let him go?

"Come on. Let's get you out of this wind."

Three rose to his knees.

"Give me another minute."

"Feeling sick?"

Cass was too tired to lie. She nodded without thinking.

"Repeater probably. You'll get used to it after a while."

She had no idea what he meant, and it took too much effort to talk so she didn't ask. Just another minute. Her injuries and nausea and exhaustion mingled into some unholy perfection of personal pain. But she could force herself up in another minute. Maybe two.

She didn't have to. Without permission or fanfare, Three scooped her up off the ground and carried her down the line, cradling her like an overgrown child.

"I can walk," she said, fidgeting in protest.

"I don't know. Pretty sure you got heavier since we got up here."

He kept walking.

"Put me down, Three. I can manage."

"Fine."

He dropped her legs, and helped her upright. Cass made a show of adjusting herself, as if he'd somehow mishandled her and maybe owed her an apology.

"Where are we going?"

"Here."

Cass looked around and sighed. They were standing at the edge of what looked like a very short tunnel. Six concentric rings of gray steel stacked tightly together along the track, forming an enclosure around the rail about nine feet tall and twice as long. It seemed to be emitting a faint, low hum, just at the edge of hearing; one that seemed imagined if you listened for it, but obvious if ignored. Cass ran a hand along its smooth curving surface. It was cool to the touch, not the cold she expected.

"This is a repeater?"

"Yeah," Three answered. "Something about the magnets. Weir don't like 'em."

Nausea swept over Cass again, the strongest yet, and she thought for a moment she might actually faint. She leaned her head against the repeater wall until it passed.

"I don't think I like them either," she said, more to herself than Three. Cass leaned back and looked again at the repeater, the rail itself. Thought about the general state of disrepair. "I'm surprised this thing is still... doing whatever it does."

Three shrugged in the moonlight.

"Me too. Lucky."

"How'd you know it was running?"

"I didn't."

Cass thought that over briefly.

"Well, what would've happened if it'd been dead?"

"Nothing good."

His tone was his characteristic brand of flat, matter-of-fact. Somehow understated, yet completely honest. Cass reflected back to their climb and wondered if maybe she'd been wrong, if maybe he really *was* a machine after all.

"Come on," he said. "Might as well get comfortable. Not much left to do tonight except sleep."

He walked down into the middle of the repeater, where it was darkest. Cass followed along one pained step at a time, her body ceasing to give her any localized sensations and having resorted to one generalized mass of hurt. She lowered herself to the ground, sat cross-legged, leaned her back against the repeater wall, surprised by how much she could still see with the moon- and starlight filtering in from both open ends. It might've been comforting if not for the void in her lap, where Wren usually slept. She felt empty.

Three slid in next to her.

"We'll be safe here, don't worry."

He swept something heavy over her, covering from her shoulders down over her legs. It was damp, but extremely warm. His coat.

"Sleep. I'll keep an eye on you."

Deep down, Cass felt she should make some sort of protest, to remind Three that she didn't need him or anyone else watching out for her. But deeper still, she knew that was fast becoming a lie. She let her eyes fall closed, and welcomed the embrace of dreamless sleep.

Three's eyes snapped open, but careful discipline kept the rest of him as still as death. He counted to ten before shifting his gaze to check the periphery, letting his ears do the preliminary work. Nothing seemed immediately out of place. At some point, Cass had slipped sideways into him, and was now sleeping soundly with her head on his shoulder and a hand tucked just inside his elbow.

It hadn't been a sound that had awakened him, but he felt the pumping adrenaline as if someone had called his name, or smashed out a nearby window. Instinctive alarms were screaming in his head.

Intruder.

Slowly, Three shifted his head ever so slightly to the right, just enough to take in the full view of the line leading off that direction. It was clear. Now, just as slowly, just as carefully, back the other way, checking left. He stopped. Someone was standing on the track.

Three waited. Judged. Let his mind run the calculations. Not a Weir. The idea was so bizarre, so preposterous, that he wondered briefly if he were still asleep, dreaming, or maybe hallucinating. But his gut told him he was wide awake, seeing what he was seeing. The silhouette of a man standing patiently on the tracks, maybe ten meters from the repeater, as if he'd been there all night.

Somewhere in an alley far away and far below, a Weir cried out in some unknown and unknowable emotion, if Weir could in fact be said to have emotion. The silhouette turned its head slightly in the direction of the sound, revealing a brief profile. It turned back as Three's brain worked to identify the intruder from that momentary glimpse of features, and he noted from the movement that whoever it was, they were staring right at him now.

Thin, angular. Something in the posture seemed familiar. Three's hand floated almost of its own accord up to the thin slash on his throat as it clicked.

Dagon.

There was no telling how long he'd been out there. Waiting. And there was no reason for him to be there other than because he had tracked them to their hiding place. If that was the case, why hadn't he crept in and killed Three in his sleep? Taken Cass? If Dagon could evade the Weir at the height of their activity, that made him even more dangerous than Three already considered him. More dangerous than anyone Three had known before. And if Dagon had found them, what did that mean for the others? Were they waiting outside as well, ready to ambush him?

No. Something within told Three that the right thing was to go out to him. It didn't make sense, but none of it did anyway. Dagon had some strange sense of honor, or some personal code. Three didn't know much about the man, but he felt certain that whatever was about to happen, it wasn't a trap. At least, no more a trap than confronting the deadliest foe he'd ever met could be.

Three slid carefully out from under Cass, propped her gently with the backpack as a pillow, and crept up to his feet. Dagon didn't seem surprised as Three walked out to meet him. Three prepared himself, drew a deep breath, forced his body into a relaxed readiness. He cracked his neck as he walked the final steps, hands slightly stretched out to his sides, showing he was unarmed. For now.

As Three closed the distance, Dagon moved forward a few steps almost as though the two were old friends meeting again for the first time in a long while. Close enough for Three to see his half-smile. Close enough to whisper and be heard.

"Sorry if I woke you," Dagon said, still smiling. "I was trying to be quiet."

"Light sleeper."

"Me too. Guess it's not a bad thing. At least in these parts."

Three didn't respond. Just waited. Silence had a way of drawing more out of people than any question ever would.

"Is Haven in there?" asked Dagon. "Cass, I mean."

"Would you believe me if I said no?"

Dagon chuckled quietly, shook his head.

"And Spinner?"

Three didn't know why Dagon used different names, but he guessed correctly that he meant Wren.

"If I said no for that one?"

"I guess I wouldn't believe you either."

Again, Three just waited. The whole situation was surreal, like some sort of collision between alternate realities. Dagon didn't belong here. But then again, neither did Three. None of them did. And certainly this didn't seem like the time or place for small talk.

"What's your name?" asked Dagon.

"Three."

Dagon grunted. Then extended a hand.

"Three, I'm Dagon."

Three hesitated, evaluated. But everything seemed sincere, genuine. He took Dagon's hand, shook it firmly. A strange tradition that somehow managed to survive in a world where real, physical contact was practically indistinguishable from the virtual kind.

"I remember you, Dagon. We traded a couple of tokens of friendship last time we met."

Dagon smiled. There was a strange kinship between them, though Three couldn't place it. Few enough men in the world were left who could travel the way Three did, out in the open at night. Here stood another. Maybe that was all it was.

"Is she alright?"

"Hanging in there."

"You taking good care of her?"

"I doubt she'd see it that way."

Three understood now. Dagon loved her. And he guessed the feeling wasn't mutual. That explained Dagon's turmoil, his need to find her, to bring her back, and his wish to let her go, for her to be free.

"Let her go, Dagon."

He seemed surprised at Three's words, maybe slightly embarrassed, his secret revealed in the barest of exchanges. Dagon dropped his eyes, looked off over the side of the rail at the Vault below.

"Pathetic, isn't it?"

A moment of silence. Then Dagon shook his head.

"But no. I can't. Asher won't do anything else until he has her back, and that's not good for business."

"Cracking Sec/Nets for Cutters really worth her happiness to you?"

Dagon's reaction seemed even stronger: surprise, but also a hint of amusement.

"Sec/Net? Is that what she told you?"

Three didn't answer. But he felt that cold wave wash over him that told him he'd been played for a fool. Worse. He'd let himself be played as one.

"Maybe things aren't all I thought," said Dagon. "You really don't know who we are? Who Asher is?"

Three just stared him down. Dagon let out a low whistle.

"Brother, you just might want to sit down for this one then."

"I'd rather not."

"As you like... you ever heard of RushRuin?"

Before he knew why, Three felt it in the pit of his stomach. Utter dread. Some part of his brain kicked on automatic, rifled through backlogs of jobs he'd done, people he'd brought in.

There was a glimmer of vague recognition. A passing familiarity. And recognition came. Older, maybe outdated, maybe a rumor. A dangerous crew, well outside his line of business.

"Brainhacking crew?"

Dagon snorted at that.

"Professionally speaking, we offer 'thought acquisition and recovery'. But yeah, *brainhacking* gets it too."

It was coming back to him now. A job two or three years old. Some nanokid in the heart of Fourover got his hands on a piece of tech he shouldn't have. Ten grand alive, three dead. By the time Three had tracked him down, RushRuin had already gotten to him, which was saying something. Mostly just a bag of meat and bones left. They'd taken back the tech and ripped out whatever the kid had known about it, along with pretty much everything else he'd ever learned in his short life. Three had brought him in anyway, and managed to wrangle five thousand out of the agent in charge.

"Still working out of Fourover?"

"We go where we like these days."

He didn't want to admit it, but Three was rattled. Something hadn't been sitting right with him since the wayhouse when it came to Cass. He'd known she was holding something back, but he'd assumed it had more to do with her chems than anything else. But this? This was way bigger, way deeper than anything he could've predicted.

"I wish you hadn't killed Kostya. Asher might've let you off since you didn't know. But Fedor…" Dagon shook his head, sincerely sorry for Three. "Well. That was his brother, you know?"

Three fought to maintain control. Stillness.

"So now what?"

Dagon shrugged.

"I guess I go back and tell Asher where I found you. And you keep running."

"Not really my style."

"Well. You might want to make it yours. You seem like a good man."

Three thought it through. He could try again. Try to drop Dagon while he was relaxed. But the last time he'd thought he'd gotten the drop on him had almost cost Three his life. It didn't seem like Dagon had any intention of fighting him. At least not here. Not now. And Dagon likely could've killed Three while he slept. Somehow attacking him now seemed dishonorable.

"There aren't any good men left, Dagon."

Dagon just nodded. Then stepped back, turned, and began walking away. After a couple of steps, he turned back, raised his voice just enough to be heard.

"Best of luck to you, Three. I'm sure we'll see you again."

"Yeah."

And with that, Dagon walked back down the maglev line, more casual than cautious, and faded into nothingness, even to Three's eyes. To the east, the barest hint of gray was beginning to show at the horizon.

Three had never so dreaded the breaking of dawn.

# THIRTEEN

Wren lay curled in a ball, arms tucked together, legs drawn in, his hands used as a pillow. Shivering, half or less from the cold, the rest from fear. Exhausted as he was, he just couldn't sleep. Not really. He'd dozed off for stretches of a few minutes here and there for the last hour, or two, or ten. But the concrete and an erratic but persistent dripping sound always woke him. He had no idea how long they'd been in "the safe place", and he was too afraid to check GST ever since his mother's pim. Almost immediately after she'd sent it, his captor-companion had shifted and grunted in the darkness, as though the pim had woken It. And even though it may have been pure coincidence, Wren couldn't bring himself to risk streaming anything else. Not until he knew it was morning.

Wren picked up his hand, moved it slowly towards his face until his palm bumped the tip of his nose. Pitch-black. Why had he thrown his light? And his knife. The two things that Mister Three had given him, both gone. And the thing he wished most was gone was still there. He could feel it. Even in relative silence, the It had a wild edge; its soft breathing sounded more animal than man. Wren wondered when It would wake and what it would do when it did.

And Wren thought of his mama. Wondered where she was. Her pim hadn't sounded scared, or hurt. Just worried. But that wasn't unusual. Mister Three was with her, and that probably meant she was OK. Maybe he'd found a way in before it got dark. Or maybe a safe place to hide. He seemed like he knew how to stay safe even at nighttime. Mister Three seemed like he could pretty much do anything.

"Gev?"

The sudden sound of Its voice startled Wren, and he jumped badly. It wasn't whispering, and Wren realized that the It was most likely a He. Wren couldn't bring himself to answer in anything but a whisper.

"I don't think he's here."

"Oh…" He said. There was a long pause, and finally He made rustling sounds that Wren took to mean he was sitting up. "Did you sleep, little one?"

Wren didn't want to lie, but he didn't want to offend anyone either.

"A little bit."

"I'm sorry it's not more comfortable. But it's safe, yeah?"

"Is it morning?"

"Early still. I don't think the sun's up, but it should be very soon."

The He sounded nicer, or at least less scary. Less confused. They sat in silence for a few moments longer. Then the He sounded like he was getting to his feet.

"I'm sorry if I scared you. Last night, I mean. Night is a bad time for me. A bad time."

From the sound of His voice, Wren could tell the other had turned and was walking away from him. There was a click and suddenly a blue-white light flared. Dull and dim by usual standards, it momentarily dazzled Wren's eyes. He squeezed them tightly shut against the glare. And then wondered whether or not he actually wanted to open them again. In the long darkness, he'd almost forgotten that the person-thing that had carried him downstairs was more than just a voice. He knew when he opened his eyes, He would be standing there.

"You OK?" He asked.

Wren couldn't answer. He hugged his knees.

"Hey, you're OK, little one. Nothing's going to happen to you now."

Wren heard Him approach, felt Him kneel down. A hand on his shoulder, gentle, soothing. Wren risked a peek.

The first thing that struck him was how young a face it was that stared back down at him. Not a boy, certainly, but maybe not quite old enough to be a man yet. He kind of reminded Wren of Asher, at least age-wise. His face was grubby and gaunt; greasy, dark hair hung in long curls to his shoulders. He didn't seem mean, or even unkind. Mostly, he just needed a bath.

"My name was Jackson," he said, then shook his head, corrected himself, "*is* Jackson. What's yours?"

"I'm Wren."

Jackson held out his hand: fingers tipped with long, dirty nails.

"Hi there, Wren."

Wren took his hand and shook it timidly. Jackson smiled.

"Been a while since I've had company."

Wren nodded. Jackson stood, and helped him to his feet. Wren glanced around, checked out what the so-called safe place looked like. No surprise, it was concrete: concrete floor, concrete ceiling. He guessed the walls were concrete too, though they were mostly obscured by rows and rows of dark pipes, stacked atop one another. That explained the dripping sound. Water pooled in a back corner, where the elbow joint of one pipe leaked slightly. The room was smaller than he'd expected, though when he thought about it he couldn't figure out why he'd ever imagined it'd be larger. As far as he could tell, it was some kind of hub for the Vault's water system, a miniaturized version of the storm water system Mister Three had hidden them in their first night outside.

"Can I see my mama now?" Wren asked. Jackson grimaced.

"I hope so. I can't open the gate, though. Not yet. It isn't safe."

Wren felt the tears clawing their way up his throat. He was cold and tired and hungry and there was nothing he wanted more than just to sit in his mama's lap and fall asleep knowing she was safe, and he was safe, and everything was going to be OK. Jackson moved alongside him, dropped an arm over his shoulders.

"Come on, kiddo. Let's get you something to eat, and then we'll find your mom, yeah?"

Wren wiped his eye with the back of his hand, and nodded, and let Jackson lead him out into the darkness of the Vault.

Cass felt sleep slipping away from her without being able to recall ever falling asleep. As always, her first instinct was to reach out and check on Wren. It took a moment for her brain to catch up, to replay the events of the night before, to remind her of their situation now. She thought back to his pim, wondered if he was still hiding somewhere, or scared, or hurt. She resisted the urge to pim him again, to tell him she was coming to get him right now.

Her eyes floated open. She was lying on something lumpy, still covered in Three's coat. He was nowhere to be seen. Cass tried not to panic. She couldn't imagine he'd go to all the trouble to get her through the night, only to leave her in the morning. Well, she *could* imagine it, which was the problem. She forced herself not to. Judging from the graying light, dawn wasn't far off.

She sat up, tried to work the kinks out of her muscles. Twisting to one side brought a shooting pain that reminded her of her fall. She ran a hand under her shirt and gingerly checked the injury with her fingertips. Massive abrasion, deeply bruised, but as far as she could tell nothing was broken.

A slow, careful, deep inhalation. Pain, but not broken-rib pain. She'd be alright.

Cass got to her feet, stood uneasily for a moment, letting the blood circulate. Back down the rail, she saw a form laid out on the tracks. Still as death. It had to be Three.

Her heart went cold. Surely she would've woken up if there'd been any trouble? And Three didn't seem like the kind to get taken by surprise. Cass crept out of the repeater and moved down the line on legs that felt noticeably stronger than they had the night before. Sleep had done her good. She could probably push it out another day or so before she'd need another hit of the synth, assuming they didn't have another thirty miles of ground to cover.

As she drew closer, Three's silhouette shifted slightly; he glanced her way, then returned to his previous position. He was watching something down below the rail. Cass slid in next to him, lying across the track as he did. He pointed towards the Vault, near the gate. She looked that way, scanned for what he was seeing.

A Weir. A big one. Bigger than any Cass had seen before. And well-preserved too, from what she could tell. Though it was tough to see much detail in the weak light, across that distance, Cass almost could've mistaken it for a man, if not for the telltale blue-glow eyes. It just stood there, staring at the gate as if waiting for it to open. After a long moment, it turned slowly and walked a few paces away. Then, it swiveled right back around and returned to its original position, precisely the same spot, and stared at the gate again. The Weir cycled this behavior twice more before Cass spoke.

"What's it doing?" she whispered.

"Stuck in a loop, I'd guess."

"Looks like it wants to get in."

"Probably does."

"You think it knows Wren's in there?"

"I think he wants to go home."

Cass puzzled at that. She'd never thought of the Weir as having homes.

"What do you mean?"

Three didn't answer. Just sat there, watching the Weir as it shuffled away, then back again.

"Three…?"

He inhaled deeply. Held it. Released slowly. Controlled.

"That's my friend…" he finally said. "That's Gev."

As Jackson led him by the hand through the corridors and along the catwalks, Wren was in awe of the Vault. In the darkness of the previous night, he'd imagined it as a squalid urban cave. Now he was surprised to see it was not much different from most of the other places he'd been; just under the ground instead of above it. There were rows and rows of rooms, deep and wide, that the previous tenants had personalized the way one might expect a row of houses to have been.

They'd found food just a few rooms down from the safe place. And not just scraps, as Wren had expected. A huge storehouse, with rows and rows of shelves each piled with varieties of rations. After they'd eaten, Jackson took Wren through "the District", which, he explained, was the residential area comprising the three lower levels of the Vault. Now, however, they were on their way to see what Jackson called the Treasure Room.

"Here we go," Jackson said, flicking on another light and tugging on a thick steel door. It slid open with a deep rumbling groan, and Jackson let Wren go in first.

The room was the largest he'd seen yet, even larger than the food storehouse. And it was packed nearly wall-to-wall with what seemed to be long tables, deeply set. Wren approached one and laid his hand on it. He saw now it was more like a very shallow crate, maybe five inches deep, than a table. And on top of almost every table was a well-organized pile of just about anything you could hope to find in the outside world. Clothes, tools, old mattresses, scrap metal, chemlights; Wren understood why Jackson called it the Treasure Room.

"So yeah," Jackson said, still in the doorway. "This is it. Pretty much my life's work, I guess."

"Where'd you get it all?" Wren asked in a quiet voice.

"Well of course I didn't get *all* of it. But that's what we did, me and the people who used to live here. Just go out in the morning, come back with what we could find. It's getting harder these days, but there's still a lot out there to be harvested."

"What do you do with it?" Wren asked, running his hand over a dark brown coat.

Jackson chuckled.

"We use it, little one…"

He trailed off for a moment, smile fading, eyes clouded. Wren looked up from the coat, noticed Jackson.

"Are you OK?"

Jackson just stared.

"Jackson?"

His eyes cleared, and he shook his head slightly, forcing a smile again.

"Sorry. I said we, but I guess it's really just me now. Well, actually… there is 'us', at least for now."

"Where did they go?"

"Who?"

"All your other people?"

Jackson's eyes dropped to the floor, jaw clenched. He shook his head.

"I don't… little one. Away," he replied in a low voice. "Taken."

"I'm sorry."

Jackson shrugged, wiped his nose with the palm of his hand.

"Hey, you like that coat? You can have it if you want it."

Wren looked back down at the coat. It was the neatest looking coat he'd ever seen. It was brown, with a hood, and had tons of zippers and pockets on it, and even secret pockets on the inside.

"You should take it," Jackson said. "Looks like it might fit you pretty good. If not this year, maybe in a couple anyway."

"That's OK," Wren said, hand sliding back to his side. "I don't want to take your things."

Jackson laughed good-naturedly.

"That's what it's here for. No way I'm gonna be wearing it anyway. Go on, take it. It's in a lot better shape than yours is."

"Well..." Wren paused, thought through it. It really was a great coat. "If it's OK with you, then, thank you very much."

"You're very welcome. Come on," Jackson said, turning and kneeling at the door. "Hop on. Let's go see about your mom."

Wren rolled the coat up as best he could under his arm in a hurry and jumped on Jackson's back, piggyback style. Jackson stood and set off down a corridor to a staircase. Now, riding on his back, in such close proximity to Jackson, Wren felt a wave of anxiety wash over him. He couldn't explain it, or find the right word for it; just images of wildness, and jostling crowds, and frustration, and fear. His skin crawled, and at last he couldn't bear it.

"Can you put me down now?" he said quickly. "Please?"

"We've still got a few more flights to go–"

"Put me down! Put me down please!"

Jackson dropped quickly and let Wren slide off his back, then turned to face him. Wren dropped back two steps, and pressed his back against the wall.

"What is it, kid? What's wrong?"

Wren felt the tears welling up, and he swallowed hard, trying to hold it together.

"What's going on?"

"Are you sick?"

The question took Jackson back. He shook his head slowly.

"Not that I know of... why?"

"There's something..." Wren took another step back down, afraid to say the words. "Something's wrong. With you."

Jackson gave a curious look at Wren. Studied him. Then, he sat down on the stairs and crossed his arms, resting them on his knees.

"Yeah," he said slowly. "Yeah, I know."

"What is it?"

He didn't answer for a while. Just dropped his gaze to his feet. Eventually he rubbed his face with both hands, ran them back through his greasy hair.

"The night they came..." he started. "I just needed a few minutes. You know?"

Wren waited, not sure where Jackson was going.

"I thought I was going to die. I *knew* I was going to die. So I shipped. I just needed a few minutes to do it. I hid in the safe place."

Wren didn't understand. People often shipped in the final moments of their lives, sending their consciousness off to a digital warehouse for preservation, effectively ending their own life.

"But... if you shipped, how can you be here now?"

"They didn't find me. So I came back."

He paused, sucked his teeth.

"But... I don't think I came back alone."

Jackson dropped his head into his hands, clenched his eyes tight. Pulled his hair back, tight.

"Night is a bad time for me."

The two stayed silent for a time, Wren not sure how to respond, and Jackson seemingly lost in his own thoughts. Finally, Jackson was the first to speak. He stood.

"It's alright, I'm not going to hurt you. Sometimes I just have trouble remembering which one is me. But I'm OK. Right now, I'm OK."

Jackson stretched out his hand.

"Come on, little one. Let's go get your mama."

Three crouched at the entrance of the Vault, running his fingers along the edge of the gate where it separated from the wall. Eyes closed. Hunting for a mechanism or release that might activate the door. For now, he focused on solving the problem at hand, on reuniting Cass with her son. Once that was taken care of, then and only then would he let his mind consider the gathering storm that RushRuin surely presented for them.

His fingers brushed across a small, angular piece of metal just inside the gate. As he probed it with his fingers, he snuck a glance at Cass, standing nearby, wearing his coat. Chilled, pale; fragile. And somehow in her raw humanity, utterly captivating. Her eyes flicked to his, as if she felt his gaze. He didn't look away.

"Any luck?" she asked.

Three shook his head, opened his mouth to explain he was unlikely to find any sort of way to open the gate from the outside. Instead, the sudden sound of straining steel. The gate shifted, rose in jerking steps. And suddenly, a gasp from inside, and a cry from without. A blur of motion. Cass on her knees, Wren in her arms, both sobbing. Inside the Vault, Three saw a gaunt young man operating a jury-rigged crank. The two nodded to each other. But for a time, it just didn't seem right to speak. Even in this collapsed and decaying world, the reunion of mother and child demanded some semblance of reverence.

Three looked at the two of them, the delicate pair that he had brought out into the open. Without question, he was responsible for them now. And in a sudden flash he felt, without question, they were the mistake that would cost him his life.

And he wasn't sure it was a mistake at all.

# FOURTEEN

Three sat cross-legged on the floor, staring down the empty corridor, letting the hollowness fill him until he could taste it. He wanted to feel rage, wrath, a burning righteous fury to unleash upon the Weir when next they met. But here, now, in this heavy, silent hallway where the air barely dared to stir, he felt nothing. The emotions he had expected to surge and seethe were as dead as the shell of this underground city.

Loss was nothing new. He'd lost more than a few acquaintances out in the open, and even a couple he'd have dared to call friends. But Gev? If there was anything like family left in the world for Three, Gev had been it. And he'd never seen the Weir hit anything on this scale before. Gev, the Weir... Dagon. Too much to process.

And Cass. She'd played him, and he'd let her. He'd killed for her, nearly died for her, even left and come back for her. Even now he didn't know why. Or wouldn't admit that he did. He'd seen women and children plenty of times before, in the shelters, in the gutters, never thought of them as anything more than human debris. But these two... he felt something for them, but couldn't, or wouldn't, identify it. Pity? Compassion? Was it the boy? Or his mother? He found her intensely frustrating. And even more fascinating. Such a small thing to be so fierce. He cursed himself for getting involved, for taking responsibility for someone else's mistake. And all the while he felt that he'd never had a choice.

Cass and Wren were somewhere upstairs, in the top third of the Vault, high above him. At Three's direction, Jackson had taken them to the Vault's medical apartment, where they could get cleaned up and reconnected. He knew they needed that time together, to be close again, to know the other was alive, and safe, and real.

And he knew every minute he sat in the disquieting silence of these vacant catacombs was another minute lost. Standard procedure dictated that any action was better than none. But Three couldn't shake the feeling that in this case the wrong action would be impossible to correct. It was chess, and he was running out of room to maneuver. His mind churned, rushing from one thought to the next, trying to sort through the collision of events. Searching for the solution. For an escape.

If Dagon had reported their location, it was possible that RushRuin was already on the way. But Dagon had crossed through the open by night, during the Weir's peak hunting hour, without any apparent concern of being tracked. That gave Three a critical piece of information: Dagon must be disco'd. Which meant he had to do all his communicating the old fashioned way, face-to-face rather than via pim. That was some comfort, as Dagon couldn't just tail them and constantly update the rest of the crew as to their location. It was equally troubling, though, to know that Dagon had tracked them precisely to their hiding point by purely physical means. Up to that point, Three had known they were being followed, but had assumed that it was the woman or the boy whose residual signal was giving them away. But now he couldn't be sure. If Dagon was off-grid and a hound, he was a master tracker that even Three might not be able to shake. How exactly he had done it was a mystery. Three hated mysteries.

There was some calculated risk in lingering at the vault. By his way of thinking, with the time it took for Dagon to return and report their location, RushRuin would assume Three and his companions were on the move again. And even if they did send someone to the Vault to check, chances were Three had a better shot at picking them off or slipping them entirely here than in the open.

His thoughts flashed back to the early morning hours, outside the gate. Gev, his friend. Or rather, the husk of him, inhabited now by something completely other. Three wondered how many of the Vault's old inhabitants were dead, and how many had instead been cored. And he wondered if there was any real difference between the two.

Jackson he'd known tangentially, remembered him as the kid who liked to wander. Gev had spoken of him often, usually complaining about his recklessness but always with a hint of fondness, like the proud uncle of a mischievous nephew. He seemed decent enough. A bit scattered, but clever enough to survive on his own for however many days or weeks it'd been since They had come.

And Three wondered for the first time if he'd have to add Jackson to the list of dependents. It seemed likely. Surely the kid wouldn't want to remain behind, no matter where Three decided to lead them. As if there were anywhere left this side of the Strand that RushRuin wouldn't follow.

He shook his head, trying to clear the scattered thoughts. Took a final deep inhalation, resigned himself to the fact that he'd have to rejoin the others sooner or later. The fatigue was getting to him. Tonight they would remain at the Vault. At first light, they would set out again, somewhere, and he knew that for every step by dangerous step of the journey they'd undertaken, what they had accomplished was nothing compared to what lay ahead.

••••

Cass wondered what Three was up to. He'd disappeared a couple of hours before, saying he needed to scout out the rest of the Vault, leaving Jackson to look after her and her son. While he was away, Cass had bathed in crystal clear water that ran hot, hotter than she could stand. It'd been so long she'd almost forgotten it was possible to feel clean. Jackson had provided her and Wren both with clothes, worn but comfortable. And after she'd bathed Wren, Jackson had led them to the Commons, a section separating the entrance and work areas above from the living quarters below, and given them hearty rations in generous portions. Now, meal completed, feeling contented in nearly every way possible, Cass sat back in her chair with Wren on her lap, and for the first time really took notice of her surroundings.

The room was large enough for a hundred or so people to find places to sit, with tables of various sizes and shapes and salvaged chairs gathered into small knots and clusters. If not for the obvious scavenger atmosphere, the room wouldn't have been out of place in any number of the outpost towns that Cass had been through before she'd left RushRuin, or after. But it had a cavernous feel now, with places for so many occupied by so few. And clean. Almost sterile. For all the trauma the Vault must've endured, it was strangely tidy. Jackson had kept busy.

Wren drove his shuttlecar back and forth along the oval flexiglass table making soft, rumbling engine noises. Jackson watched from across the table, fixated on the toy but eyes unfocused, distant. He'd certainly proved to be an almost overwhelmingly generous host, but there was an edge about him that Cass couldn't place. Something wild lurked behind his youthfulness. The fitful attempts at small talk always trickled to nothing; Jackson seemingly content to sit in silence, and Cass unsure of what questions were safe to ask.

The bath and food had done her well, but the gnawing hunger of her nerves was growing steadily, and she could feel her eyes dancing in their imperceptible rhythms. At least she hoped they were imperceptible. Three's synth had been surprisingly effective at preventing her cells from imploding, but it was becoming painfully apparent that the dose had been a substitute and not the real thing. Her limbs burned with pinprick fire, angry, like long-compressed nerves reawakening. Occasional flashes of pain shot through her tongue without warning, stainless-steel pangs without apparent cause or reason. She figured another two days. Maybe less.

"How long have you known Three?" she asked, rousing Jackson from his daze.

"Couple years, I guess. Maybe longer. Hard to say. He was always just sort of there, then not, if you know what I mean."

"I do."

"Strange one, that. Gev always had good things to say about him, but he always made me nervous. Not in a bad way, like he was going to hurt anyone or anything. Just kind of. I don't know. Doesn't feel right, yeah?"

"He isn't real," Wren said, still pushing his shuttlecar back and forth along the table.

He said it so matter-of-factly, but the comment hit Cass like a concrete wave. Wren had only ever described one other person that way before.

"What do you mean, sweetheart?"

"He's just pretend. You know, like Dagon... sorta. Except not so weird."

Jackson looked at Cass with questioning eyes, looking for any clue as to what her son meant.

"Who's Dagon?"

Cass shook her head, processing. "Just someone we used to know."

"Just someone who's still lookin' for you."

His voice came from some corner, unexpected, startling. Jackson flinched visibly at Three's sudden words. How long he'd been standing there, none of them knew.

"Guess I should knock."

"Doubt it'd help," Cass answered. "You sneak too much."

Three half-shrugged a shoulder and approached, grabbing a chair and sliding it to the head of the table. He sat heavily, nodded to Jackson, rested his eyes on her. Studying. Cass tried to hold his gaze, but felt herself wilting. Every time she looked into those dark eyes she felt she was telling him everything she'd ever done.

"Jackson gave us a tour," she offered. "You wouldn't believe the Treasure Room–"

"We need to talk," Three interrupted, more forcefully than she'd expected, almost impatient.

"OK."

Three didn't take his eyes off hers, just watched and waited. Like he had a lot to say, and didn't know where to start. Or like he knew a secret.

"You guys want to work this out alone?" Jackson said. "I can take Wren–"

"Might be a good idea," Three replied.

"No," Cass answered. "You can go if you want Jackson, but Wren stays."

Three and Cass stared at each other. Wren had stopped playing. Jackson just sat with both palms on the table, unsure whether to stay or leave. Three let a tense breath go by, then another. She wasn't going to back down. The last time he'd separated them had nearly been catastrophic.

"Fine," he said at last.

Three paused, gathered himself. She'd never seen him like this before.

"We're in real trouble," he said. No one seemed surprised. But no one had anything to add, either.

"When I agreed to bring you out here, it's because I figured whatever heat you'd gotten into, you and the kid could wait it out here at the Vault. Best guess was that you got into owing some chemist more than you could pay. But it's not like that, is it?"

Cass shook her head slowly, but didn't offer any more. Didn't even take her eyes from his. He pushed.

"This... whatever it is. It's not gonna go away on its own. And they're not gonna stop looking for you. Ever. That about right?"

She nodded.

"So. Is there anywhere left in the world for you to go that they won't find you?"

For the first time, Cass let her eyes leave his, dropped them to the table. She felt her shoulders slump reflexively. Three had asked her the one question she'd been asking herself for however long it'd been since she started running.

"I don't know who they are, but *they* wouldn't come looking for anyone out this far, yeah?" Jackson asked. "I mean, why would they?"

"That's a fine question. Cass. Why would they?"

She didn't look up from the table. Didn't answer.

"It's my fault," Wren said, in his quiet voice.

"Wren."

"It's OK, Mama. I don't mind."

Wren looked at Three, then away, like he was ashamed.

"It's me. I did something bad."

Cass kissed the top of Wren's head, hugged him.

"No, baby, you didn't do anything wrong..."

Three remained motionless. Didn't even seem surprised. Cass took over the explanation.

"You know Wren is," she paused, searched for the word, "special. We were on a job. My crew, I mean. Kostya, Fedor, Dagon, we were all on it. And it was a tough one, tougher than most.

"Tough because we didn't have much time to get it done, and there was this guy, this... individual, who wouldn't cooperate.

He was the key to everything. And I tried to get him to help us, I really did. But he wouldn't listen. He kept saying we didn't know who he was, what he could do, kept telling us what he was going to do to us... so one of ours went to work on him. Hard."

She closed her eyes, hated dredging up the terrible past. Who she'd been. What she'd done. And what she'd made her child part of.

"Wren shouldn't have been there. I didn't want him to be there. But he was, and Asher..."

She caught herself, stopped. Glanced up at Three. She'd said more than she'd meant to.

"He was hurting him," Wren continued. "Real bad. I didn't mean to."

"I don't know what he did," said Cass, almost whispering. "None of us do. But Wren made Asher stop. *Stopped* him. Long enough for the target to ship. We couldn't finish the job. After that, Asher wouldn't leave Wren alone. He wanted to know what Wren had done, how he'd done it. And Wren, you know, he just doesn't know sometimes... but he just kept at him, and I couldn't protect him forever... so we left."

"I didn't mean to," Wren said. "It was an accident."

Cass hugged him again.

"I know about RushRuin," Three said. Cass silently cursed herself for slipping up, revealing Asher's name. If Three knew about RushRuin, he'd know what they were capable of. And there was no way he'd stick around to help them now. "And I know they're not in the business of running Sec/Nets."

"I never said they were."

"Said it or not, you let me believe it. Just as bad."

She didn't argue the point.

"Who's RushRuin?" Jackson asked. Cass had almost forgotten he was there.

"Brainhackers," Three answered, eyes still on Cass. "Some of the best."

"*The* best," Cass said. "I don't know another crew that does the kind of damage they do."

"And you're one of them?" Jackson said, obvious awe in his voice.

"*Was*. I don't do that anymore."

For a moment they all just sat in silence. Jackson stunned by the truth, Cass relieved to have admitted it, and Three trying to figure out what it all meant.

"Bottom line," Three said at last, "I shouldn't have brought you out here. Not without knowing the facts."

Cass felt stung, though not surprised.

"So you'd rather us be dead? My son and me?"

"I shouldn't have gotten involved, Cass," he said with a shrug. Never one for diplomacy. "But because I am, I'm telling you I shouldn't have brought you out here, to the Vault. If I had known what you were running from, there might have been better options."

"If you had known what we were running from, you wouldn't have helped us."

"I'm not gonna lie to you, girl. When you walked into that bar, you were just some skew with some kid you couldn't take care of. Same story, seen it a thousand times. And you're right, if I had known, no way I would've put my life on the line for you. But–"

If she hadn't been so tired, she would've stopped herself. At least that's what she let herself believe. As it was, Cass slapped Three across the face, hard. He took it, didn't even try to stop her. He worked his jaw, tested the inside of his mouth with his tongue.

"But," he continued, seemingly unfazed, "none of that makes any difference now. Right *now*, we're together, and we gotta figure out how to keep it that way."

Cass wasn't sure what he was saying. Or didn't want to let herself believe that maybe, hope against hope, he was saying he wasn't going to leave them, even now, even knowing what they were really up against.

"You really gotta stop hittin' me."

Cass chuckled in spite of herself. It all seemed suddenly ridiculous, that she should be sitting here, in this place, with these people. She was weary, weary beyond imagining, but she was with her son, and right now it was enough. She was instantly sorry she'd hit Three, but couldn't bring herself to say it.

"When you left, where'd you think you'd go?" Three asked.

For whatever reason, she didn't care anymore. If Three knew about RushRuin, he might as well know everything. She owed him that much.

"Morningside."

For a split-second, Cass almost thought she saw something like surprise on Three's face. Jackson was more obvious.

"Morningside?" he said, looking like he might fall backwards out of his chair. "That's on the other side of the Strand!"

"Yeah, I know where it is, Jackson."

"But... that's... there's no way you'd ever make it."

Cass glanced at Three, tried to gauge his reaction. As usual, nothing. He sat in stony silence, though his eyes were lively, active. Wheels turning.

"I mean... Fourover, Swingbridge, there's plenty of big towns to get lost in this side of the Strand. What's Morningside got worth the risk?"

She thought, weighed the options. She'd given up trying to guess Three's way of thinking, or motivation. No real reason to hold back.

"Wren's father."

And somehow, once again, Three had made a decision without ever having had a choice. He was kidding himself if he thought he could leave Cass and Wren behind to fend for themselves. It might've been a mistake to get himself involved, but that was one mistake he could live with. Leaving these two alone to face Dagon, and Fedor, and this Asher, whoever he was, wasn't a mistake he was willing to make.

It made some insane sort of sense. At least, tactically.

"Morningside, huh?"

Jackson chimed in.

"Why don't you just hide out here? There's plenty of everything you need. You try to cross the Strand, there's no way you'd make it."

"There's no way they'd expect us to try, either."

The more he thought about it, the more it seemed like the best way, the *only* way, to escape. He'd crossed the Strand before, once out, once back. He could do it again.

"There's a train, still runs out of Greenstone."

"Greenstone?" Jackson cried. "That's just as bad! Maybe you could do it, but no way you could take them. No way."

Jackson was growing agitated, Three noticed. He chalked it up to loneliness. The kid had been through a lot. They were probably the first people he'd seen since the Weir had come.

"Easy, kid," Three said, shooting Jackson a glance. He looked over at Wren, who was staring blankly at his shuttlecar. "Mister Wren, you alright?"

Wren looked up through glassy eyes, and nodded.

"You look like you could use some sleep."

"I'm OK," Wren said, immediately suppressing a yawn.

"Cass, how about you let your boy get some rest, while you and I work out details?"

He framed it as a question, though it wasn't a request. Cass picked up on the tone, seemed to understand. Nodded.

"I'm not sleepy, honest," Wren said.

"I know, sweetheart, but it'd be good if you could lie down for a bit. We'll have to leave soon, and I don't know how long it'll be before we'll have a real bed to sleep in again."

Cass kissed Wren on the top of the head.

"I don't wanna take a nap."

"Just rest then, OK? You won't miss anything, I promise."

Cass looked to Jackson, who was bouncing his legs up and down, anxious, restless. He looked like he wanted to be anywhere but here.

"Jackson, you think you could sit with him? So he's not alone?"

Jackson glanced around the room, sucked his top lip, nodded.

"Sure. Yeah, sure, no worries," he said, standing and offering a hand to Wren. "C'mon, little one. We'll let your mom sort it out, yeah?"

Wren nodded, slid out of Cass's lap, and took Jackson's hand. Cass squeezed Wren's shoulder as he moved away. The two walked to the nearest exit, brothers in exile. Just before they disappeared, Cass called after them.

"And Jackson?"

"Yes ma'am?"

"Thank you."

"Yes ma'am."

Three watched Cass as her son disappeared. Corners of her mouth taut in that mix of emotion mothers so often feel as they watch their children leave a room: pride, love, warmth, sadness.

"He'll be fine."

"I wish I could believe you."

Jackson sat in a low Temprafoam chair at the foot of the futon where Wren slept soundly. A small lamp shone golden-orange in the corner, casting the room in a dull tribute to sunset. Jackson looked at Wren curled there, oblivious to the world in the way only children can be. Kid hadn't gotten much sleep, he guessed, and he couldn't really blame the boy. So young, separated from his mama, trapped in a pitch-black urban cavern with a probable lunatic. Now that he thought about it, Jackson had to admire Wren for taking it all as well as he had.

*He shouldn't be here. He doesn't belong.*

The voice was in his head, but it wasn't his own. He wasn't sure whose it was, or what it was doing there. But it was angry. They'd been starting earlier lately. And there seemed to be more of them than there'd been when he first got back. Or did he just think that? Not like he'd been keeping notes, or counting names.

*Make them leave. They'll only make more trouble for us.*

Jackson tried to ignore it. Sometimes that worked. He watched Wren's easy breathing. The contented look on the boy's face. Tried to imagine what his life had been like up to now, figured he couldn't even guess. His mama was pretty beat up. And gorgeous.

*She could be ours. She* should *be ours. We saved her.*

And the man, Three. Gev's friend. He'd come and gone as he pleased, seemingly content to wander in the open without any apparent obligations.

*He doesn't deserve her!*

Jackson wasn't sure what had brought the three of these people together, or who this RushRuin was that was chasing them. It didn't really matter. If the boy were gone, and the man, who would she have to turn to?

*Us! She would stay with us!*

*No, she doesn't belong!*

*We could make her belong! She could be one of us!*

He straightened the blanket that covered Wren. The boy was blond and pale, vibrantly pale in a way that made him seem more alive, more healthy, than anyone had right to be in this world. Jackson would've said angelic, if he'd believed there could be any such thing. And he had a sudden urge to smash the boy's face.

"No!" Jackson said aloud, to himself. The voices shrunk back at the sound of his, but only for a moment. Wren shifted.

*The boy. The man. Gone. We could console her. She could stay with us.*

He wanted desperately for the voices to stop, for Cass to stay, to be his own again, to give the voices what they wanted. His eyes clenched with the strain. Tears streaked. Pain.

"All I have to do," he said to himself, "is nothing. Just. Do. Nothing."

Jackson balled his hands into tight fists, felt his nails bite into his palms, his knuckles burn with the tension. This wasn't the first time. But it hadn't been this bad before. There seemed to be more of them. Angry.

*You know how!*

*Yes, do it! Make her ours!*

*We deserve it!*

*It's easy! The boy is sleeping, he won't fight!*

Too much. Jackson stood. Crept to Wren. Leaned over him. The boy so peaceful. Beautiful. A stained-glass window of all that was right and missing in the world. Unfair.

Jackson's hands moved of their own accord.


They'd made as much of a plan as they could. They'd leave at first light, and make for Greenstone. How they'd manage to get on the train, if it was even possible, they'd figure out once they got there. One thing at a time.

Without thinking, Three reached out, ran his thumb along Cass's cheekbone, gently. Felt her tense under his touch. But not flinch. He knew he should pull his hand back. Didn't. Her eyes flicked to his, searching.

"We gotta get you some rest, girl."

"If that's all you've got, save it," she said.

She swatted his arm with a backhand as he withdrew. Three found himself half-smiling without knowing why.

She blinked, slowly. Shook her head. She'd lied about her burn rate, he knew. She was holding it together well, all things considered, but he could see it. The paleness of her lips, the dancing pupils, the tremble of her hands that she tried to conceal. They'd have to find her quint again, no doubt. Shouldn't be a problem in Greenstone, if they made it that far. But it'd be nice to know just how long they had before she needed her next hit.

"Anything else you wanna tell me?"

Her eyes dropped, brow furrowed. She placed both hands on the table, palms down. Drew a breath.

"They want my son…" she started. No surprise there. Cass paused, lingered. Traced a small circle on the table between them. Three waited. Willed her to own up.

Come on girl, let's have it all. How long till your next dose?

The circles on the table got smaller, slower. Then, without looking up, she told him the rest of the story.

"They want my son," she repeated. "And I'm dying."

Somewhere, far below, an inhuman cry echoed.

# FIFTEEN

Cass bounded down the hall ahead of him, faster than he remembered ever seeing her move; she'd reacted nearly instantly to the scream. No, not scream. Screams. Two voices, one unholy shriek. It hadn't occurred to him before that he had no idea where Jackson might take Wren. Now he couldn't understand how he'd been so foolish.

The pair raced past the medical apartment and leapt down the stairs that led towards the primary living quarters. Cass hit the landing so hard she nearly fell, but managed to maintain her frantic momentum and streaked down the central corridor. Three skidded to a halt, dropped to a knee. Listened; strained.

A sound, at the edge of hearing. He whirled and headed down a side passage, hunched, trying to steady his breathing as he searched. There again. A faint sob. The corridor dark. Doors sealed. But the muffled cry growing more apparent with each step. Near the end, a dull orange glow seeped from underneath a door.

"Cass! Here!"

In three strides he was there, propelling his whole mass into the door, throwing it open so hard the doorframe separated from the wall. Then, froze. Scanned. Cass skidded into the room while Three tried to make sense of what he was seeing.

"Wren!" Cass shrieked.

She flew to her son, flinging herself around Three and onto the boy who lay crumpled on the floor, fetal, at the side of the bed. Hands over his ears. A bright, thin trail through his fingers: blood.

Three's eyes swept the rest of the room, saw the sole of one of Jackson's feet poking out from behind the bed. He prowled cautiously around the edge, one hand moving instinctively to the handle of his blade, though he doubted there'd be any need for it. Wren was the one softly sobbing. Jackson, so far, hadn't stirred.

"Baby, what happened? What happened?" Cass was pleading with Wren, cradling him to her, voice trembling with fear. "Are you hurt? Did he hurt you?"

Three rounded the bed. Jackson was there, lying in an awkward pose, one leg bent behind him with the other outstretched. Eyes open, but unseeing. Mouth slightly agape. Didn't seem to be breathing. Three relaxed, released his grip on his weapon. Shook his head. Wren was going to have to do the talking.

"Wren," Cass continued, "Wren, baby, please, talk to me."

Three moved to them, took a knee, looked into Wren's face. The boy's eyes were open, and they rose to meet Three's. He was scared, confused, but he didn't seem hurt. Cass was frantic. Three stretched out his hand and took her shoulder, firmly, to steady her.

"You OK, kid?"

Wren nodded, took his hands from his ears but didn't offer anything more. There was a wet smear along the side of his face where the cut on his hand had reopened, but from what Three could tell, he didn't seem to have any new injuries.

"Can you tell us what happened?"

Wren pulled away from Cass enough to sit upright, and wiped his eyes.

"Wren–" Cass said. Three caught her eye and shook his head. After a long moment Wren spoke quietly, like he was recounting a bad dream.

"I was sleeping. And I heard some people talking. But when I woke up, it was just him." He lowered his head. "I didn't mean to hurt him."

"Come on, let's get you out of here," Three said, standing and offering his hand. Wren stood on his own, Cass accepted the help. "Go on up to the Commons, maybe your mom could take a look at that hand. I'll be there in a few."

Wren nodded, trudged out of the room, careful to avoid looking in the direction of Jackson's body. As Cass moved by him, Three caught her arm, leaned in close.

"Can you check, make sure his signal didn't slip?"

She nodded and followed her son out. Once they were gone, Three returned to Jackson's side and crouched. Whatever the boy had done didn't seem to be external. There were no obvious bruises or even scratches. Jackson's leg position suggested he had been bedside and fallen slightly backwards, but mostly straight down. More than anything, it looked as though he had simply collapsed where he stood. Whatever Jackson had done had made Wren feel threatened, that much was certain. Beyond that, Three was at a loss. He looked into Jackson's staring eyes. Poor kid, to have survived the Weir only to be dropped by a harmless looking five year-old. He reached out and shut Jackson's eyes. At least he'd be at rest now. Finally.

Three ran his hand over his own head, over his stubbled face, pinched the bridge of his nose. One less person to worry about. But troubling questions to answer. Was it even safe to travel with the boy now? He exhaled loudly, stood to his feet. Dropped his neck to one side to crack it. Froze.

On the floor below him, Jackson's eyes had opened again.

Back in the Commons, Cass dabbed Wren's tiny hand with a medpatch, watched the foam seep into the wound, cleansing and sealing it. Wren winced at the sting, but held as still as he could. Neither had spoken since they'd left the room. They both stared intently at the hand until the tiny scouring bubbles had all but died away.

"There," Cass said. "OK now?"

Wren wiggled his fingers, closed his hand into a fist.

"It's cold. And tingly."

"That means it's working, sweetheart."

The questions were eating her up inside, but she didn't want to push him if he wasn't ready to talk. From what she could tell, Wren wasn't hurt at all. Scared maybe, but mostly, she could see now, frustrated. His mind was at work, replaying the events, trying to understand what exactly had happened and not being able to piece it together. He stared absently at his hand.

"How about something to drink?" she asked.

"I'm sorry, Mama."

"For what, baby?"

"I killed that man, didn't I? I killed Jackson?"

Cass put her hand along her son's cheek, felt it warm, soft.

"I think so."

"He was real nice to me."

She was dying to know what had happened, but just leaned forward, kissed his forehead, put her head to his.

"He was nice to all of us, sweetheart. But that doesn't mean he was good."

"He was good, Mama," Wren answered. "It was the other ones I didn't like."

Jackson's eyes swam, focused, shifted to Three. And in the next instant, Three was on him, blade in hand, opposite forearm across Jackson's collarbone, pinning him to the ground. Jackson squirmed weakly under Three's weight.

"Wait wait wait, it's OK, I'm alright!"

"Not necessarily."

"C'mon, you're chokin' me here!"

"What did you do?"

"*Me?* Ask the kid!"

Three shifted his forearm upwards, where Jackson's neck met his shoulder. Nerves pinched, blood-flow halted.

"Gah! Get… get off, I'll explain!"

Three raised up, grabbed a handful of Jackson's shirt, and hauled him up on to the bed. He didn't sheathe the blade.

Jackson sat for a moment, rubbing his neck, working his shoulder, swinging his leg. He glanced around like it was the first time he was seeing the room. Pupils dilated. Movement stopped.

"What're we doin' here?"

"You tell me."

"Why'd you bring me *here*?"

"I didn't. This is where we found you. This is where *you* brought Wren."

Jackson shook his head in disbelief. Then settled back, as if remembering.

"Not me. Whit."

Three had no idea who Whit was, but nothing about the way the kid said it suggested he was lying. He was telling the truth. Or at least what he *believed* was true.

"This is Whit's old room."

"He still around?"

Jackson chuckled humorlessly. "No. Not anymore."

There was more to the words than Three understood. He waited, knowing the silence was more likely to get answers than any questions he asked.

"That kid… Wren. What is he?"

"How do you mean?"

"I dunno," Jackson said with a shrug, shaking his head. "He… something he did. He fixed me."

"What 'others', sweetheart?"

"It wasn't just him. I mean Jackson was the only one, but there were others. Inside. I think they wanted to hurt us."

"And they tried? To hurt you?"

"He was right there, when I woke up. Standing there with a pillow. But he felt wrong, Mama. There was something wrong with him. I didn't want to hurt *him*. I just wanted the others to go away."

Wren was starting to get upset again, reliving whatever terror Jackson had put him through. Cass picked him up, pulled him into her lap, rested his head on her chest.

"It's not your fault, Wren. You didn't do anything wrong."

He sniffled. Crying, though she could tell he was fighting it. Trying to be brave.

"It's alright, baby. It's not your fault."

"Then why does it keep happening?"

"That's what I'm tellin' you," Jackson said. "They're gone. The kid did something to me, and they're all gone."

Three sheathed his blade, and dropped into the only chair in the room. As far as he could tell, Jackson was telling the truth. Whatever Wren had done had actually been a good thing, hard as it was to believe. Three looked at Jackson, still sitting awkwardly on the bed. Afraid to move too much for fear of what Three might do.

"Relax. I'm not gonna hurt you."

"So you believe me?" Jackson asked, shoulders visibly relaxing.

"Doesn't make sense. But nothing has, since I met those two."

Jackson scooted back up the bed, rested his back against the headboard, pulled his feet up under him cross-legged. He placed his hands in his lap, then picked them up again. Looked them over.

"I'm in bad shape, yeah?"

"You could use a bath, sure. We gonna be OK to stay here tonight?"

Down here, underground, with all the activity, Three realized he was losing sense of time. But he guessed there wouldn't be time enough to pack up and get to a wayhouse in the light they had left.

"Yeah, of course. You can stay as long as you like."

"Doubt that," Three said, getting to his feet. "I'm gonna go check on the girl and her kid. Why don't you take some time, get cleaned up. Gimme a chance to…"

He wasn't even sure what all he needed a chance to do. Think. Rest. Prepare. He had important work tonight.

"They thought I was dead, yeah?"

"Yeah. Better let me break the news. I think everybody's had enough shock for the day."

Jackson nodded, understood.

"I'll be up later."

Three nodded in response and then left Jackson to look after himself.

They were sitting together in an oversized Temprafoam chair, cuddling. Cass looked up with anxious eyes when Three entered. He grabbed a chair and dragged it up next to theirs. They'd both been crying.

"You alright?" he asked, though he himself wasn't even sure who he was talking to. Cass nodded, and he guessed that was good enough.

"So, Wren. Jackson's alright."

Mother and child both looked stunned, though Wren seemed more relieved, more hopeful than Cass did.

"You didn't hurt him. In fact, I think you helped him."

"He's… he's OK?" Wren pressed.

Three nodded.

"Better than OK, kid. Whatever was wrong with him before, you fixed."

Cass and Wren exchanged a look. Three waited expectantly. Finally Cass explained.

"Wren said there were 'others'. He thought maybe he'd made them go away."

"Sounds about right. Whatever happened, Jackson's up and about down there. Gettin' cleaned up. And we've got some work to do. You remember where the Treasure Room is?"

The last was addressed directly to Wren, who nodded his head emphatically.

"Then why don't you show me around."

Wren led the way down the twisting stairs, eager to get another glimpse of the so-called Treasure Room. Cass and Three trailed behind, and as the trio entered a corridor, Cass felt Three's hand close firmly around her forearm, drawing her close. He leaned in, eyes still on her son.

"We're not done talking yet," he said in a low voice.

"I know," Cass answered, nodding.

"How long till you need to dose again?"

"About negative eighteen hours."

He grunted a wordless curse. Wren padded ahead oblivious.

"Do you still have any more of your synth?" she asked, wishing she hadn't sounded so needy.

"Not enough. Your body's already figured out that ain't what it really needs. And at the rate you're burnin', same dose would be half as effective. Less."

He let go of her arm, pulled away. Shook his head. He was thinking it through, and it didn't seem as though he liked the conclusions. But he'd found ways before when there'd been no way. She hoped he could do it again. No. *Believed* it.

"Here it is," Wren said.

Three motioned Wren on in. "Lead the way, soldier. Let's see what we've got to work with."

Wren smiled, puffed up by Three's words. Cass didn't understand it, but she couldn't deny that Wren was reacting differently to Three, now. Normally her son would shrink from attention; with Three, he seemed to revel in it no matter how small.

She moved to follow Wren inside the Treasure Room, but Three stopped her with a hand light on her belly.

"No way we're gonna find quint between here and Greenstone. Any other chems buy you some time?"

"Duff would work, if it's just to maintain. I can't boost off it, though. And Trivex, if the dose is big enough."

"If we don't have any luck here, I'll have to raid medical."

Cass just nodded. She didn't have the heart to tell him she'd already done that. He stared for a too-long moment. Hand still on her stomach.

"We'll figure it out, girl." He sounded like he was trying to convince himself more than her. She nodded again.

"I know."

"Oh, cool," a voice called from inside. "Mama, look at this!"

Three held his hand out in an "after you" motion. Cass slipped in and found Wren standing at one of the many low tables, holding up a clear flexiglass ball, perfectly round, perfectly smooth.

"What is it?" Wren asked.

She'd never seen anything like it before.

"I have no idea, sweetheart."

"It's a strobe. Old miltech. Thing's probably older than your mom is."

"How does it work?"

Three walked over to Wren, dropped to a knee. It suddenly struck Cass how often Three did that, and how rarely other adults did. The man making himself the same height as her son. Almost equals. Three held his hand out, and Wren dropped the ball into it.

"You take it like this," Three said, wrapping one hand horizontally around the ball, as if it were a drink. "Then, you press the top and bottom, like this." He motioned with the thumb and middle finger of his other hand, pinching the air, but not actually activating the device. Then he handed it back.

"Like this," Three said. He helped form Wren's tiny hand around the strobe.

"How do you know what's the top and what's the bottom?"

"Doesn't matter," Three answered. "It knows how you're holding it. Then, pinch."

"Can I try it?"

"Sure, just close your eyes first. If it's still workin', it's bright as a star."

Wren closed his eyes, and Three guided the boy's other hand into position, shielding his own eyes with his shoulder.

"Might wanna look away, Mama," Three said.

Cass had just barely shut her eyes when her lids suddenly flared in white-blue, dazzlingly bright.

"It still works!" Wren shouted, as if trying to be heard over the brightness. The strobe pulsed, a stabbing flash followed by a momentary reprieve. Cass turned her back and was amazed to discover she could still see the flashing reflecting off the walls, even with her eyes closed.

"How do you turn it off?" she called over her shoulder.

There was no verbal response, but a moment later, the pulsing stopped. She turned back, after-images floating in her vision.

"Can I keep it?" Wren beamed.

"Ask your mother."

"I don't know, sweetheart. Jackson might want to hang on to it."

Wren looked disappointed. Three cocked his head slightly, dipped his eyebrows. Two against one.

"Alright. For now," she said, relenting. "But let's make sure Jackson doesn't mind."

"Mind what?" Jackson said quietly from the door. Instinctively, Cass stepped to shield Wren from him. She felt

Three move beside her, calm, as he stood and smoothly moved to the midpoint between Jackson and her. He faced them both, leaning back against one of those sturdy tables, like a careful negotiator refusing to take sides. Making himself the bridge, Cass thought. Or maybe setting himself in place to be the wall, if it came to that.

Cass could only see half of Jackson sticking into the Treasure Room. He hadn't committed fully to coming inside yet. From what she could see of him, though, it was clear he'd spent some time getting himself cleaned up. He'd bathed, put on fresh clothes that actually seemed to fit him, maybe even cut his hair. His fingernails were trimmed to a normal length, and for the first time he actually seemed to be standing still. She hadn't really noticed it earlier, but now that she saw him it occurred to her just how much he had fidgeted before. He lingered in the doorway, seemingly uncertain as to whether or not he was welcome.

"If there's something you want, you can take it. That's what it's here for."

"How you feelin'?" Three asked, though it sounded more like a statement.

"Good. Real good."

Cass felt Wren close behind her. He slid up next to her, pushed himself between her hip and arm, so that her hand naturally fell to his shoulder.

"Hey," Three said, "you have any old blankets?"

"Sure. Most of that type of stuff's in that back corner."

"Firebricks?"

That one threw Jackson for a second, and Cass too for that matter. Not a whole lot of use for open flames these days.

"Uh, maybe," Jackson answered. "If so, probably around the same place as the blankets."

"You can come in, you know," Three said. "Your place more than ours."

Jackson half-smiled at Cass, then looked to the floor as he came in and slowly circled around one of the many tables. He hadn't cut his hair after all, just pulled it back in a loose knot at the base of his skull. Cass noticed he was careful not to look at Wren.

"If you're headed to Greenstone, you should probably load up, yeah?" he said. "I don't think you'll find too many friendly shops down there."

"But... you're coming too, aren't you?" Wren asked, pulling away from Cass's side. Jackson glanced at Wren and smiled, though there was no cheer there.

"No, little one, I don't think so."

Cass looked to Three, wondering if he'd talked to Jackson about it before, but Three had already moved towards the back of the Treasure Room, and was scanning the various tables laid out there.

"It's... I mean, is it safe for you to stay?" she asked.

"Safe enough, I would guess. It's been OK so far."

Three began rummaging through the scraps on one table, but called back over his shoulder.

"Not sure it'll stay that way, kid. Might be safer if you move with us."

"I can't, Three. The Vault is home. Plus, you never know when some more travelers might come through, yeah? Be a shame if there wasn't anyone here to let 'em in."

"Did travelers come through before...?" Cass asked, but trailed off, not knowing how to finish the sentence without sounding callous.

"Before the attack? Yeah, every few weeks, here and there," Jackson answered. He picked up a biochem battery off one of the tables, rolled it over in his hand absentmindedly. "The Vault's out of the way and mostly out of view. It's always been an OK spot to make a trade, and a good spot to rest."

"To hide?"

He shrugged. "Nobody asked questions, too much, except Gev." He went quiet for a moment, and Cass didn't feel like she should respond. After a moment, Jackson set the battery down and continued. "Always had a good sense for people, you know? He kept this place pretty quiet and calm. Turned away the troublemakers, and kept an eye on the rest of us."

"Not all the troublemakers, the way he'd tell it," Three said from his corner. "Used to say you were a handful."

Jackson cracked a sad smile, remembering.

"More like two."

Three stopped his rummaging, turned to address Jackson.

"Hey."

Jackson looked over to him.

"He thought a lot of you, you know. Always called you a good kid." Jackson nodded, but dropped his gaze. Ashamed of something he'd done, maybe, or overwhelmed by Three's words; Cass couldn't tell. "And you said it yourself, Gev had a real good sense of people. You *are* a good kid, no matter what you may or may not have done."

"It's a nice thought, but you don't know what I've done."

Three returned to his rummaging, but wouldn't let Jackson have the last word.

"Doing and being are two different things, Jackson."

Jackson didn't respond, but Cass saw his shoulders sag, like long-borne tension had suddenly released. He was quiet for a long while.

Cass found Wren sitting cross-legged on the floor, right next to her feet, rolling his new strobe from hand to hand, staring at it as if there were some swirling color and light within it. To her eyes, it was simply a clear ball, but she knew that Wren's eyes often saw far more than hers.

"What are we looking for?" she finally called.

"Four days to Greenstone. Take what you need."

••••

They'd spent the better part of the afternoon scouring the Treasure Room for supplies for their trip, which Three organized now. Jackson had led them all to a long-unused apartment; sizeable, furnished with a large bed, a couple of chairs, and its own bathroom facilities, which pretty much made it the honeymoon suite of the Vault. Three'd laid all their supplies out across that bed. Warmer clothes, sturdier shoes, better backpacks, food that would travel well. And as requested, a few old blankets, and a pair of firebricks, though he wouldn't be packing those. They'd have to start at first light and travel hard to make it to the next wayhouse, and he didn't trust the others to pack their own bags.

He'd asked about ammunition, of course, but there'd been none he could use. Of course. A lot of inert shells, which he had plenty of already. A handful of small-time pocket protectors, 1-kJ jobs for back alleys and gamedives. Nothing for serious work. Jackson had offered an 18-kilojoule shell he'd been keeping with him in his "safe place", but it was too small to fit the chamber on Three's pistol and wasn't worth cracking open for parts.

It hadn't been all bad news, though. Jackson had managed to turn up a single jector of Trivex in an old trauma kit that had fallen down behind one of the tables nearest the wall. The jector's flexiglass casing was frosted with ages-old dust, and without doubt the chems were past peak potency, but the dose was almost enough to cover the trip to Greenstone. In a stroke of actual good luck, the same kit had contained three minijectors worth of the syntranq Somalin. Three'd run the numbers four separate times to be sure. Full jector of Trivex tonight, let Cass's system spin up on it while she slept. Mini of Somalin every 18 hours or so to slow the burn. If they kept up the pace, and didn't have any major shocks along the way, it just might be enough. It was almost enough to make Three think they were getting a little bias from the System. Almost.

Cass had gone with Jackson and Wren back to the Commons to scrounge up some "real" food while Three took care of organizing their packs. Running solo, organizing had never been much of an issue. Wits, water, and weapons. The Essential Three of the open, in proper order. Everything else was fluff. As the saying went, if you'd survived out in the open long enough to get *truly* hungry, you'd already outlived your life expectancy. But traveling with those two, well... they had a lot of fluff. He loaded as much as he could in his own harness, knowing every extra kilogram he could grit out was one less for the woman and boy to wrestle with. He'd tried to keep everything they might need close at hand, but he realized he had no way to know what they might *want* close at hand. This wasn't his way.

He shook his head. Kid's dad is in Morningside, and the girl's dying. Seemed like every answer he got just raised more questions. Who was Wren's father, and how long had it been since she'd seen him? Did he know he had a son? What did Wren know about his dad? And what did Wren know about Three? He'd said something about Three being "just pretend", which sounded too close to something Three didn't want them to know. And then there was Cass... dying how? How soon? Of what?

We're all dying, girl. All of us, all the time. What makes you special?

He heard the trio coming down the corridor, and busied himself with securing the packs and moving them to the floor. He rolled the blankets around the firebricks and placed those on top of his harness, out of the way.

"You can stay up here with us, you know," Cass said, as they entered the room. "We really don't mind."

Jackson shook his head. "I appreciate it, Cass, but I just... I think I'll sleep better down there."

Cass flopped Wren up on to the bed, helped him pull his shoes off.

"They're not trying to get in here anymore," Three added. "I watched them myself."

Wren scrambled up towards the top of the bed. Three noticed the boy still had the strobe in hand. Cass sat on the foot of the bed, mild observer to the conversation. She was exhausted, in pain, fading. And still her primary concern was her son. Something like admiration stirred in Three.

"Well, I dunno what it is. But I feel safe there, yeah? They didn't find me when they were... that night. No reason to risk it."

"Only thing different down there's the water, kid."

Jackson looked puzzled. So did Cass.

"The water's different?"

"Your 'safe place'. It's under the central water exchange for the Vault."

"Yeah...?"

Three shrugged. "Something about all the water, rushing through the pipes. Makes it hard for 'em to see. Impossible, sometimes."

Obviously news to Jackson. But Three saw the wheels turning in Cass's eyes. Thinking back to the storm water system, no doubt. If he wasn't careful, she was going to learn all his tricks.

"But if they're not coming in, they can't see you anyway," he continued. "So no need to sleep on a wet floor."

Jackson regarded Three for a moment, then glanced to Cass. Stared for a moment, as she was looking elsewhere. She caught his eye, raised an eyebrow. He looked back to Three too quickly. Eyes dilated. Slight flush in his cheeks.

Three smiled to himself. Looked like Cass had picked up another would-be suitor.

"Yeeeaaah... I just don't think I'm ready for that. Not yet."

"Suit yourself. But grab some blankets or something. Only thing's gonna change that room is you broadcasting out of it."

"Yeah… yeah, I guess that can't hurt."

He reached for the blankets on Three's pack.

"Not those."

"Oh. Oh, yeah, I'll just pull 'em from next door. You'll wake me before you go, yeah?"

"Course, kid. I've still got the morning to convince you you're coming with."

"Heh, right. Alright. Night, Wren," Jackson's eyes moved to Cass, held like they were taking a long last drink.

"Night, Jackson," Wren answered, voice already distant and thick with impending sleep. Cass waved limply from the foot of the bed.

"See ya, Three."

Three nodded. Watched as Jackson backed out, pulled the door to. Cass bent double and unbuckled her boots, slipped them off. Rolled her ankles, massaged her feet. Three watched her for a moment: small, tucked in on herself, with such fragile beauty his heart burned.

"Hey," he said.

She rolled her head his way, eyes bloodshot, lids heavy. Smiled so genuinely, with such unexpected warmth; dawn breaking through a hurricane night. Three found he'd stopped breathing.

"Hey back," she said, voice low. No more than a meter away. She locked eyes with him: deep brown, dancing, golden. Vulnerable. She leaned back, propped herself on outstretched arms, lithe, feline in her movement. Cocked her head. "You gonna fix me up or what?"

Three held. Evaluated. Wren's breathing was deep, steady. Cass just sat there, staring back at him with those dark, depthless eyes. He stepped to her, brushed the hair back from her face. Traced her jaw with the back of a finger.

"Lay back."

Cass lowered herself to the bed, slid her hands behind her head. Three planted a knee next to her, the inside of his leg firm against her ribs. Leaned over her. Wordlessly, he unfastened the first, then second clasp of her shirt. Lay back the left side. Her smile had melted into an amused smirk, but she never broke eye contact.

Three started at her collarbone. With his fingertips, he traced from the notch at the top of her breastbone, out to her left shoulder and back, stopping about three-quarters of the way to the slender curve of her neck. Her olive skin was warm, impossibly soft. Now he ran his fingertips downward, sliding along the inside of her breast. She watched from stillness.

He found a rib, placed a finger from his left hand there. Reached with his right into one of the many pockets of his pants.

"I hate to hurt you."

"I'm glad it's you."

She let her eyes fall closed. Drew a breath.

Three took the Trivex jector from his pocket, placed its pepperbox-tip just above his finger, in the soft notch between Cass's ribs. Aimed directly at her heart.

"Ready?"

Cass exhaled. Nodded. Inhaled. He fired. The jector hissed softly, punching its chems through the surface down deep into the center of her bloodstream. Cass's eyes clenched so tightly a tear streamed, but she made no sound. The jector fell quiet. Cass exhaled. Three instinctively placed his hand on her chest, just above the jector. She dropped a cool, damp hand atop his. Opened her eyes, fixed him with a steady gaze.

"Come on, cowboy. Just four more to go," she whispered. She patted his hand. He nodded, watched her close her eyes again. Didn't ask her this time, just fired again. When it was done, she barely paused.

"Again."

Three didn't want to jolt her again so soon, but he knew better than to ask. He fired the third dose. Three was no stranger to jectors, having had to dose himself during some of the more unpleasant times he'd endured. He'd also been stabbed, shot, jittered, slashed, and burned. Given the choice of the six, dosing from a jector ranked third.

"Go, do it."

Cass was trembling now under his hand, heart hammering against her ribcage. Sweat beaded on her exposed skin, as if a heavy dew had fallen across her. Three leaned closer, brushed her hair back from her damp forehead. Ran his hand over her scalp, soothing, and knowing the pain in her chest was overriding every other sense.

"Last one. You're doing good."

She nodded, but didn't speak.

"Need a break?"

She shook her head, furrowed her brow. She didn't want questions, she wanted to get it over with. He dosed her the fifth and final time. The jector hissed out the last of its chems; a single dose intended to shock a still heart to beating, to trigger adrenals to flood the bloodstream at full capacity. Three knew quint was the emperor of high-speed chems, but he'd also seen a man's heart explode from a double dose of Trivex. This little sister had strength beyond measure. He gently closed her shirt, refastened it.

"We're done, girl. Let's get you some rest."

"I don't..." she whispered, mouth parched. "I don't usually let people call me 'girl'."

Three smiled as he stood. He scooped Cass up off the bed, cradled her like an overgrown child. She didn't resist. He walked around the bed and laid her gently beside her sleeping son.

He hovered over the pair, thought back to that first day. The first time they walked into his guarded, disciplined, secure world. And he wondered at just how far out from that world they'd brought him.

Three switched off the light in the room, tugged off his shirt, and decided he was going to allow himself a long, cool shower.

Cass could tell from watching him that he'd assumed she and her son were sleeping. He'd already startled her once walking naked by the open bathroom door, and now Three seemed to be oblivious to any notion of being watched, which was surprisingly uncommon for the man. The Trivex was working its way throughout her body, juicing long-starved muscle fibers and nerve endings. She lay motionless not for fear of being discovered, but because every joint, muscle, and nerve stung with icy vengeance at the slightest provocation. But here, with Wren cuddled next to her, she was warm, and comfortable, and safe. For the first time in far too long. Her body was deathly tired, and she knew sleep would come soon. It just hadn't found its way to her yet. Outside, twilight was descending.

She watched Three in the dim orange light of the single bathroom bulb. Studied him, really. For all the miles they'd covered, and the trust she'd developed in him in spite of herself, she still knew so little of the man. He stood at the small basin in the bathroom, methodically shaving his head. His face. Careful, practiced strokes. Using a gleaming-edged knife not unlike the one Wren had cut his hand on. No, not methodical. *Ritualistic*. Preparation.

He wore no shirt, and from her vantage, Cass could see the rope-like muscles of his back, shoulders, arms. Not bulky, like those splicejob showboys. Just authentic, well-used, well-formed, like they'd been doing work for fifty years and would continue for twice that much more. "Go muscle", she'd heard Ran once call it, "not Show muscle". She'd seen more genetically perfect physiology before. But the history that Three wore upon him was more fascinating by far. His back and shoulders were a tapestry of crisscrossed scars punctuated by the occasional dark stain of ink where a masterful calligraphist had inscribed captivating ideograms upon his flesh, in lines vertical and horizontal, in circles, in spirals. She wondered at their meaning.

Three set his blade aside on the basin and splashed water over his face and head several times. After the final splash, he stepped back from the basin and knelt upon the floor, feet behind him, head slightly bowed. Cass watched as his breathing slowed to such a point that she began to wonder if he had ceased breathing at all. Several minutes passed, and his stillness amazed her. For a moment, she wondered if he had perhaps fallen asleep, and if he had indeed even intended to do so. She couldn't remember having seen him sleep at all since the beginning.

Three rose like a liquid shadow, grabbed his shirt and blade, and switched off the light. A very faint residual glow emanated from panels placed around the room, like the softest of moonlight, intended no doubt to create an atmosphere that encouraged sleep while staving off the fears that a pitch-black room made of concrete might otherwise inspire. In it, Cass could just make out Three's movements across the room to their loaded packs. The man was utterly silent, like a dark mist driven about by an unfelt breeze. It suddenly occurred to her that she might well just be dreaming the whole event.

He crouched, then rose soon after with a bundle in his arms. He moved to the door.

"Hey," Cass whispered.

Three halted. But didn't turn.

"Hey back," he answered finally, in a low voice. He waited. Waited for her to say anything more. That seemed to be his way.

"I know your secret."

He was silent for a time. Still. Cass felt sleep's heavy approach. She wondered briefly if she'd actually said anything at all.

"I doubt that, girl," he finally replied. "But we'll talk when I get back. Maybe we can start being honest with each other."

Three opened the door, and the dim light from the corridor framed him. Cass saw he had slipped on his vest, with his pistol and short curved sword in place. And she thought she could make out a bundle of what looked like blankets in his hands.

"Where are you going?"

Three inhaled, held his breath. She saw his shoulders go up, draw back. Frustration? No. Steeling himself.

He exhaled. Checked the blade at his back. Shifted.

"To see a friend."

And was gone.

# SIXTEEN

Three crouched atop the Vault as the final traces of day seeped from the heavens, unveiling the first stars. Clouds were rolling in, backlit by a half-moon on the wane, tinted red from the residual glow of the electric embers of the city beneath. The Weir cried to one another, some from a distance, others less so, the echoes reverberating through the steel and concrete sprawl. Three had learned to judge those calls, or rather not to misjudge them. Magnified by overpasses, twisted by alleys, muffled by high-rises. Misreading the sounds of the hunt could prove fatal. Or worse.

Jackson hadn't been eager to let Three back out of the Vault so close to twilight, but the kid knew better than to argue for long. And the fight had gone out of him anyway, once Three had explained. Now, out here on top of the Vault, the temperature was dropping steadily. A light wind swirled out of the surrounding alleys and moaned softly through the skeletal maglev structure, streaming like water over the top of Three's freshly shaved head. He thought briefly about grabbing one of the old blankets he'd brought with him, but decided against it. The chill kept him alert, and comfort was an enemy.

After an hour of waiting, Three allowed himself to sit rather than crouch. He massaged his calves, hoping to ease the burn. Sleep stalked.

Not now, he insisted. When it's done.

He had assured Jackson that the Weir had lost interest in breaching the Vault, and he'd been more right than he'd known. Though he could hear their sporadic croaking, he had yet to see even a hint of one below. Clouds masked the moon, making darker the night and heavier the looming silence of the cityscape. He could barely make out the outline of the old rusted, V-shaped piece of scrap metal he'd dragged near the front gate, with his two firebricks inside.

Three drew his pistol, flicked open its cylinder with practiced ease, considered the single shell within. Walking to Greenstone, of all places, with one shell in the pipe. As far as he was concerned, shooting was rarely a good answer to a problem. But when it was, it was usually the *only* answer. He shook his head with a smirk and flicked the cylinder shut, before sliding the weapon back into its well-worn holster. A few more slugs probably wouldn't be the difference between living and dying out here. Probably.

A shuffling noise from below caught Three's attention, and his senses snapped alert. He rose to a crouch and peered into the darkness beneath him. For a long moment, there was nothing more. No noise, no movement, no blue-glow aura that always emanated from approaching Weir. Three remembered just the night before, at how Dagon had appeared without warning. He slipped a hand to the grip of his blade. Instinct crackled. Something was there, in the darkness. Watching.

Three released the short sword, slowly took up his bundle, shifted away from the front of the Vault. Gradually he eased his way to the left side of the squat building, silently worked towards the edge. He carefully wrapped his bundle inside one of the blankets and then passed one end under an arm and the other over the opposite shoulder, tying the makeshift satchel securely upon his back. Then, there at the edge, he waited. There again, the shuffling sound. Footsteps. Definitely approaching. They sounded heavy for a Weir, shuffling rather than pattering as he was accustomed to.

Three lowered himself over the edge, spidered his way down the wall. Slowly. Silently. When he reached the bottom, the shuffling had stopped again. He dropped to a low crouch, forced himself to move with painstaking care, towards the front of the Vault. An inch at a time. His held his mouth slightly open to ensure even his breathing made no sound.

The shuffling began again, and Three could tell now it was just around the corner. Just at the front of the Vault. But moving away. Then a pause. Then shuffling again, towards the Vault. Then a pause. Three came up out of his crouch and slid around the corner. There, in front of the Vault, a hulking Weir stood with its blue-glow eyes fixed on the gate.

"Gev," Three said aloud.

The Weir's head snapped in his direction, its eyes rapidly scanning for him, sliding over him without seeing. Three stood his ground, studied the thing before him. This thing that had once been his friend. Three didn't know how many weeks had passed since Gev had been taken, but apart from the electric blue light flooding out of its eye sockets, the Gev-Weir looked virtually unchanged.

It flexed its hands, squawked a burst of organic-digital noise. Its eyes still roving.

"It's me."

The Gev-Weir hunched down, as if to pounce. But Three knew he was safe from its searching gaze. He eased a hand back and slipped his blade from its sheath. Somewhere deep in his heart, a hope that he hadn't even realized he'd carried died. A hope for recognition. But there was none, and Three knew his friend was gone.

"I'm here, old friend," he said quietly.

As he spoke, he threw his arms out wide. The Weir reacted to the sudden, sharp movement, and launched itself toward him in a frenzy. But Three's calmness remained. And just before the Gev-Weir was upon him, he whirled to one side and whipped the tip of his blade expertly through the back of its neck, just at the base of the skull, severing the spinal column in a single, swift stroke, without beheading it. The blue-glow eyes doused instantly. The Gev-Weir collapsed headlong in a weighty heap and was still.

Three flicked the acrid fluid from his blade, and returned it to its sheath. Then he untied the blanket from his shoulder, and unrolled it on the ground. With great effort and care, he lifted Gev's body and laid it upon the blanket, and then knelt alongside.

Three arranged Gev's heavy hands over his heart, and then placed his own on top of them. They were cool to the touch, the flesh rough but not yet the rubber-like texture that death so often brought. If Three hadn't just slain his friend, he could've convinced himself that Gev was merely asleep. Three covered Gev's face, and then wrapped the blanket tightly around the body. He did the same with the remaining blankets, and then heaved Gev's massive frame up over his shoulders.

He strained to carry the body over to the scrap metal pyre he'd hastily formed, but once there, he laid his friend as carefully as he was able into the V-shape, atop the firebricks. Three stood and regarded the tightly-bound form of his longtime friend. He felt that he should say something meaningful, but discovered he had no words to speak. There seemed to be none worthy of so final a moment. So in silence, Three ignited the firebricks. In seconds, they grew white-hot and soon flames of many colors engulfed Gev's remains, spreading golden-orange sparks heavenward.

And with the task at hand completed, Three lay down on the cold concrete beside his friend and wept.

••••

A light knock on the door roused Cass from a depthless sleep. She remained still, drew a long breath, waited for her mind and body to synch. Wren was curled next to her, his breathing even. Undisturbed. The knock came again. She checked her internal clock. Twenty-two minutes to sunrise. No sign of Three.

"Mama, Jackson's knocking," Wren whispered. Awake after all.

"Alright, sweetheart."

Cass sat up and swung her legs over the side of the bed. Tested them, glad to discover she could move without pain. It'd been a long while since she could say that. She padded over to the door barefoot and cracked it open.

"Sorry to wake you, Miss Cass. But, Three's about ready to get moving."

"He's upstairs already?"

"Yeah," he answered, then paused. "Sorta."

"Sort of?"

"I haven't seen him yet. He just asked me to make sure you guys were up and ready to go around now."

"OK, we'll be up in a few."

Jackson nodded, but lingered at the door. He tugged at an earlobe, unconsciously from the looks of it. He was nervous about something.

"Need any help?" he finally asked. "I can carry your gear up, if you like."

"No, that's alright. Just need to get dressed."

"I don't mind waiting."

Cass sighed to herself. She guessed he was lonely, that he was having mixed emotions about their leaving. Might as well give the kid something, however small.

"OK, give us a minute."

"'K."

Cass closed the door and switched on the light. Wren was already sitting up, legs dangling off the side of the bed, blond hair sticking up like a halo. His sea-green eyes shone wet as he squinted against the light.

"How'd you sleep, baby?"

"Good," he answered. He rubbed his eye with the heel of his hand. "This bed is nice. I wish it fit in my backpack."

"Me too. But when we get to Morningside, we'll each have our own bed. Own rooms, even."

She smiled as her son slid to the floor, wishing she believed that they'd make it to Morningside, that there would be an end to their flight, to the pursuit. Wren sidled next to her, wrapped his arms around her leg. He seemed taller than he'd been last night. She dropped a hand on his back, squeezed him against her leg in a one-handed hug.

"Come on, we should get moving."

Cass helped Wren pull a heavier overshirt on over the top of his thinner long-sleeved shirt. As his head popped through the top, she found him staring her in the eye with a look of serious concern.

"What's wrong?"

"Do we have to have different rooms?"

Cass felt her heart turn in her chest.

"No, baby," she said, kneeling to his height and drawing him close. "No, we can stay together. We can always stay together."

Her eyes welled. She squeezed tight, continued to hold him as he stood with his arms at his sides, empty sleeves limp and dangling. For a long moment, he just let her hug him.

"Mama?"

"Yeah, baby?"

"You're squishing me."

She smiled at that. Wiped her eyes quickly before letting go.

"Sorry."

"That's OK."

Cass helped her son pull his arms into the sleeves of his overshirt. He lost a sleeve in the process and the two worked together to fish it out, and to pull the inner sleeve back down his arm.

"Go ahead and get your coat on, then hop up on the bed," she said. "I'll help you with your boots."

As Wren wrangled himself into his new coat, Cass changed out of the shirt she'd slept in and into clean clothes that almost felt new. Slipping into the less-worn garments energized her, as if she were putting on armor for the journey ahead. She slid her feet into thick socks made for hiking, and then sank them into her boots, and buckled them up. She stood and felt strong.

Wren was already up on the bed again and Cass helped him put on his new boots. Boots without holes. Boots that fit. He dropped off the edge of the bed to his feet, and they stood together, ready to travel. Scavengers though they were, Cass couldn't help feeling rich. She couldn't remember the last time they'd had everything they'd needed, and some to spare. Looking at the packs by the door, the ones Three had so painstakingly gathered and organized, she realized that for the first time since she'd left RushRuin, she actually felt *prepared*.

Cass took Wren's hand, and moved to the door. She swung it open and jumped a little when she saw Jackson standing there. She'd completely forgotten he was waiting.

"All set?" he asked.

"Yep."

"Let me just get your gear."

Jackson pushed in and wrestled all three packs onto his shoulders, refusing any of Cass's attempts to help. He didn't seem to have much trouble with Wren's pack, or her own, but it took him nearly a full minute to pull Three's pack off the ground, and position it securely on his back. It was only as the three made their way up the twisting staircase that she realized this was a show of strength on his part. She didn't understand it, but she said nothing.

They moved up past the Commons, all the way to the flat, concrete entrance where the Gate stood. Still, there was no sign of Three. Jackson trudged to the gate and, red-faced and sweating, slung the packs to the ground just in front of the looming steel plate.

"Is Three meeting us here?" asked Cass.

"I'd guess so. He didn't really say."

Jackson moved over to the hand-crank, and paused to check the time.

"Should be good," he said to no one in particular. And then he began to crank. The early purple light of dawn spilled in beneath the gate, splashing across the floor and sweeping over their feet, carrying with it a rolling wave of morning air, sharp with the scent of cold frost. In its midst, a shadow stretched.

And as the Gate rose to height, Cass recognized the figure standing beyond: Three.

"Ready to move?" he asked, with typical grim nonchalance.

"Did you spend the night out there?" Cass asked, in disbelief, knowing full well the answer to her own question. Which was good, because he ignored it anyway.

"We're going to have to keep a pretty good pace. Sooner we get started, the better we'll do."

"Then let's go."

Cass swung her pack up onto her back, and clipped the harness around her waist. It fit her well, and though she was surprised at the weight, once it was in place, it was so well-balanced she hardly noticed it. Wren's was much lighter. She didn't even try to lift Three's.

Three strode in, and hoisted his pack without any apparent strain. As he buckled in, he spoke to Jackson, though he didn't look at him.

"I'd feel better if you came with us, kid. Hate to leave you behind."

Jackson shuffled towards the three, but lingered several feet away.

"I'd probably just slow you down," he replied. "Besides, I gotta be here to work the gate for anyone else who might show up, yeah?"

He smiled unconvincingly. If he didn't believe it himself, Cass couldn't understand why he wouldn't just come along.

"Please, Jackson?" Wren said. "Please come with us."

"We'd be happy to have you," Cass added. "Really."

Jackson blushed at that. Dropped his gaze to Wren, and ruffled his hair. Shook his head. He shifted on his feet. Still nervous.

"I can't. But come back any time."

He glanced up at Cass as he said the last bit, then quickly away. Sheepish. It clicked for Cass.

Oh, she thought. A crush.

"Go on," Three said to Jackson. "Say something, kid. I doubt you'll get another chance, and I don't want you chasing after us once we leave."

Cass glanced over at Three. He was straight-faced except for the slight downward turn of one corner of his mouth; a tiny expression Cass had learned to read as something of a suppressed smile. She guessed he'd figured it out a while ago.

Jackson just looked up at her again, and smiled awkwardly. He shrugged, uncertain of what to say, looked away, out through the gate into the city beyond. Cass walked over to him, took his jaw in her hand, and swiveled his face towards hers.

"Thanks, Jackson. For everything. You're a true hero."

Before he could respond, she kissed him quickly but firmly on the mouth. He stared at her, stunned, when she backed off. She could still feel his gaze as she joined Three and Wren. Something like amusement washed over Three's face.

Cass took Wren's hand in hers and waited.

"Say bye, baby."

Wren waved.

"Bye, Jackson."

"Goodbye, little one."

"We gotta move. Last chance, kid."

Cass glanced behind her, saw Jackson shake his head. He was beaming.

"Alright then. Stay safe."

"You too, Three. See you around, yeah?"

"Never can tell."

Three turned and held out his hand, letting Cass and Wren lead the way out. They headed out into the open, and Cass felt a hitch in her chest. Some mix of exhilaration and fear. Not quite equal parts, but she couldn't tell which she felt more strongly.

"Hey, pim me when you get to Morningside, yeah?" Jackson called from behind. "Let me know you made it."

"Sure," Three answered back over his shoulder. "I'll have Cass do it."

Cass didn't turn around then. She just shook her head. When they had walked maybe a hundred feet, Three slid in next to her, leaned close. Spoke in low tones.

"Doubt you'll ever see him again. But that kiss is gonna last him a looong time."

He nudged her with an elbow, and then moved away a pace or two.

"Is he going to be alright?"

"Hope so."

Cass noticed something behind those few words Three was willing to say on the matter. His usual stony gaze was shadowed by a slightly furrowed brow.

"You think it was a mistake to leave him behind?"

"Yeah."

He let it hang in the air, as if that was all he was going to say. But just before she pressed him further, he added, "Might've been a bigger one to force him along, though."

"He seems pretty sharp. If he survived that long with all the…" she trailed off, unsure of the diplomatic way to say it, "*trouble*… he was having, I'm sure he'll be fine. I don't think we need to worry about him."

"I'm not."

"Look, if you don't want to talk about it, just say so."

Three clenched his jaw, grimaced slightly. Frustrated with her, or himself, she couldn't tell.

"Biggest footprints a man leaves behind are the people whose lives he crosses, intentional or not. And there's no way to cover those tracks… I just hope he keeps his head down, at least for a while."

With that said, Three lengthened his stride and was soon several paces ahead of Cass and her son. End of conversation. Cass shoved the implications of his words to the back of her mind and focused on keeping pace, the thought of pursuit too heavy to pick up so soon.

Before long, they'd fallen into Three's natural broken rhythm, and begun their twisting but steady journey towards Greenstone under his ever-watchful eye. It was late afternoon on the third day of the journey when trouble came.

# SEVENTEEN

The sprawling city shell changed in small but perceptible ways as they followed their wandering south-easterly path. Fuzzy as she was from the Somalin doses Three insisted she take, Cass nevertheless felt that her awareness of her surroundings was growing sharper from the time she'd spent with Three. Wherever they went, he seemed utterly in the Now; never reflecting on what came before, or thinking of what might be ahead. Just fiercely, aggressively, rooted in the instant.

Cass worked to cultivate a similar mindset, to push the inconsequential past from her thoughts, to chase the imaginary, unknowable future from her daydreams. And over the course of the past few days, she'd noticed details in the world around her that had escaped her before. Some were of little value, such as the subtle changes in architecture, or shifts in the concentration of the residual signals that still haunted the abandoned buildings. Others were more important, like the widening of streets that offered less concealment, or the decrease in functioning tech that signaled the likely presence of scavengers, whether past or present. Even as the winds and temperature blurred the lines between late autumn and early winter, Cass felt more alive, more in tune, than she had at any time before.

And so it was, though Three had said nothing, that Cass knew from the shift in his demeanor that danger was near.

They'd been making good time up to that point, but he'd slowed the pace, taken to narrower alleyways. They were moving forward, but in lines far less straight.

"What's going on?"

Three waved vaguely towards an alley as his eyes roved the wide road ahead. Cass caught the barest glimpse of three figures moving along parallel to them.

"Bad guys?"

"They were headed the opposite way when we passed 'em the first time."

Cass hadn't even seen them before, but the fact that Three had, came as less of a surprise than it once would have.

"And there were four of 'em."

She felt the icy pinprick of fear stab at her heart. She couldn't boost off Trivex, and worse, Three had dosed her with Somalin, a tranquilizer, to slow her burn rate. She felt like she was moving at half speed: a poor quality if it came to a fight.

"What do we do?"

"Keep your eyes open. And keep moving."

He led them out of one alley, then down a corridor formed by one sagging high-rise leaning into another. Pace slow, but deliberate, like an icebreaker through a frozen sea. He seemed to be looking everywhere and nowhere all at once, eyes taking in everything without focusing on any one thing in particular. Cass pulled Wren close to her side, kept a hand on his shoulder. He'd gone quiet, sensing the danger even before she'd spoken to Three.

Ahead, Three halted, held out a hand behind him to stop them as well. His head swept slowly back and forth. Cass strained to hear any warning sound, but there was nothing, save for the soft sighing of the late-autumn breeze through the twisted steel branches bending above them.

Cass felt Wren pull away from her, and looked down to see her son creeping carefully to Three. He placed a hand on Three's elbow, and Three bent down so the boy could whisper in his ear. Three glanced up to windows on their right as he nodded, then pushed Wren gently but firmly back towards his mother. Wren clung close to Cass then, his head pressed against her hip, making himself as small as possible. Cass cursed herself silently for her helplessness. Worse, for the danger her helplessness presented for Three. She longed for quint, not because her body craved it, but because she wanted desperately to stand at his shoulder, strong and capable, not behind him, like some creature to be protected, or pitied.

"You might as well come on down from there, brother," Three called suddenly, in a booming voice that echoed within their confines. "We're not here to hurt anyone."

After a few seconds, something shifted in one of the windows, and Cass realized it was a man standing up out of the shadows.

"You can call your friends, too."

The man disappeared from view. In front of her, Three slipped his pack off and set it on the ground, then stepped a few paces away from it. Cass felt the air go electric. The familiar feeling she'd learned to trust as a sign of imminent danger. The sign she'd used as the signal to boost.

"Three..." she said, without knowing why. Ahead of her, he seemed simultaneously relaxed and coiled as a steel spring. Stance wider, one foot slightly ahead of the other.

The man from the window emerged from the building, and as he did so, the other three swung into view from the end of the alley behind them. From the looks of it, the man from the window was the pack leader. He was round but solidly built, greasy hair in a ring around his head where he wasn't balding. A coil of leather hung at his waist, some kind of whip, she guessed. He smiled as he approached, but not in friendliness. It was the smile of a predator who'd cornered its prey. A gap showed where one of his front teeth should've been.

"Out for a bit of walks, are we? On our way to a visit?"

Three moved closer to Cass and Wren, blocking them from the leader's view.

"Just passing through."

The other three men continued to close in, casual.

"Ones don't 'pass through' without paying the toll."

"Didn't realize there was one, or I would have. I've got some food. Couple of batteries. What's the price?"

"Treats."

The three men were close now, and Three pushed Cass and Wren around to his side, shielding them as much as possible from the group. Cass noticed the leader lick his lips, his eyes roving around her waist, searching her out hungrily, burning with naked lust. Her stomach turned in revulsion. If she'd been able to boost, she would've forked the eyeballs out of his skull.

"Not for sale. And it's probably best if you all just move on, and let us do the same."

The other three men flanked their leader, formed a semi-circle with Three at its center.

"Not for sale, because we ain't payin'," said one of the pack, a gangly redhead with a patchy beard. "That one's ours now. You can move on, or you can die."

"Gonna have us a good time either way," added another, this one with a strip of stained cloth tied around his face as a mask. "Before *and* after."

"That's not gonna work," Three answered. Steady, controlled. But Cass could hear the fire. Four of them. Three was good, but no way he'd handle them. She unclipped her backpack.

"Hey, come on fellas," she said. "I'm sure we can work something out here."

The pack looked to her as if her words were an unwelcome intrusion on some black business deal. The leader seemed almost amused. He opened his mouth to say something, but instead of words, a strange crackling hiss spilled out from the leader's throat. Blood burbled at the corners of his lips. Three was in motion.

As the leader staggered backwards, clutching his throat, Three was already upon the redhead. The redhead was doubled over, his head caught in Three's vice-grip hands, being used as a human shield to prevent the other two from closing the distance. Three jerked the redhead in one direction, then violently back the other, twisting as he did. There was a sickening snap, and the redhead ragdolled into the gurgling leader. Three didn't seem to be in any hurry, and his expression had not changed.

The masked man was next in line, and Three met him halfway, stomping the man's shin just above the ankle. It rolled and snapped, as Three twisted and connected with a perfectly placed hammer-fist just at the hinge of the masked man's jaw. Cass saw his eyes rolling back before he'd finished falling.

The fourth and final man seemed frozen in place, his hand drawn back with some sort of jagged club, and his eyes wide with fear. Three took one long stride and then buried his boot sole-first into the man's hip socket, folding him like a jackknife. The man fell backwards but still Three closed, grabbing the man's head at the top of his skull between his hands. Three drove downward with all his weight as the man impacted the ground, and Cass heard the cascade of pops as some unknown number of the man's vertebrae shattered. The man slumped awkwardly forward, his jaw slack.

The pack leader had just gained a knee by the time Three turned back to him. He stretched out a hand in a silent plea for mercy, but Three had none to give. Three drew up to his full height and then plummeted his fist and all the power of his body into the leader's temple, his knuckle so expertly placed that Cass knew the man would never again wake. The leader's skull bounced dully off the concrete, and all was still.

It was over in six, maybe seven seconds. Cass was no stranger to violence, but the scene she had just witnessed was like nothing she'd seen before. The warmth drained from her body, and suddenly, the safety she'd felt with Three melted away. She had killed before, out of necessity, but she was no killer. But he had just violently disassembled four men with his bare hands. Just as casual as he was now, lifting his pack and rebuckling his harness. Same practiced fluidity, same apparent ease. Same load on his conscience. Zero.

"Come on," he said, lightly grabbing Cass under an elbow. "We gotta move."

His touch repulsed her, and she reflexively pulled away. He blinked at her, not understanding.

"You hurt?"

"You killed them… all…" Her voice sounded far away. He quickly scanned the four bodies.

"Maybe, maybe not. I don't have much patience for their kind."

She couldn't process it. Whatever these unfortunate men had been looking for, surely it hadn't been worth their lives.

"No patience for beggars? For scavengers?"

Three's eyes narrowed, and Cass wondered what she'd missed.

"Slavers, girl. And they weren't interested in you. Or me."

Cass flashed back to the minute before, replayed the scene in her mind. The pack leader staring at her. No, not at her. At Wren, clinging to her. She glanced to the leader's crumpled heap, at the coil of leather at his waist. Not a whip, she saw now. A leash.

Her eyes suddenly burned, and a sickness crept into her gut. A despair she couldn't name settled over her. What hope would there be for her son, when she was gone?

"Cass," Three said. "We need to go."

He didn't reach out to her then. Just turned and started on his way without even a glance back. After Three had gone a few paces, Cass felt Wren's grip around her leg slacken, and he pulled away.

"Mama?"

Cass wondered if there was really even hope for them now, if Morningside was anything more than a desperate dream. Wren stood, staring up at her with his storm-green eyes. She nodded. Drew a deep breath. Focused on the Now. It was all she could handle. And together, she and Wren fell back into Three's shadow, trailing long behind him in the low afternoon sun.

"But you were so… fast," Wren said in a hushed voice. In awe. In fear. Cass sat on the small bed, back to the wall, watching in silence as Three taught her son.

"Not fast," Three answered. "Quick. You learn to see a man's intent, you'll be the quickest."

The two of them were in the central room of the wayhouse. Three was on a knee, arms resting across his leg, face to face with Wren. Cass had resisted the idea at first, but after the event that afternoon and Three's description of Greenstone, she'd given in. So she just watched, as Wren got his first lesson in self-defense.

"A man's eyes will tell you everything he wants to do," Three continued. He shot Cass a quick look. "A woman's, too."

Wren was intense, focused, soaking it all in.

"And his hands will be the ones doing it. So, eyes, and hands. Hands and eyes. Learn to watch those, you're already ahead of ninety-nine percent of folks out there."

Wren nodded slowly. Three reached out, and took Wren's hand in his, positioned the tiny fingers, adjusted the grip. The dose of Somalin clouded everything, made Cass feel like she was dreaming.

"OK," Three said. "Show me. Real slow."

For a few moments, the two just stared at each other. Then, Three moved at half-speed, reached out slowly, grabbed Wren by the shoulders. Just as his hands made contact, Wren's right hand came up clutching the unsharpened knife Three had fashioned for him. He jabbed slowly, once, down towards Three's arm.

"That's good. But you can do better. Don't wait. And don't stop with one. Move as soon as you see trouble, and keep poking holes until you can't find any more places to poke. Got it?"

Wren nodded again. Cass wondered numbly what kind of mother she'd become. But the reality that she wouldn't be able to protect him forever was weighing heavily. Maybe this was the best way. If not the best, maybe the only.

"One more time. Just relax, you're doing good."

Three slapped Wren on the shoulders a couple of times. Smiled. Wren smiled in spite of himself. Three reset. Again, the man and her son stared at each other. Then, quicker this time, Three moved to grab Wren. And to Cass's amazement, Wren moved almost simultaneously, bringing his little blade up and darting it onto Three's biceps, forearm, then shoulder, neck.

"See, look at that. You're a natural, kiddo. A real warrior."

Three tousled Wren's hair, and Wren smiled again, stared at his feet. Cass saw her son's smile slip away. Three noticed it too. More than noticed it. Interpreted it.

"Not fun though, huh?"

Wren shook his head.

"Doesn't feel very good?"

Wren shook his head again. Spoke quietly.

"I don't like it when people get hurt."

Three dropped a hand on Wren's shoulder. Squeezed it.

"Hey. Hey, look at me."

Wren looked up.

"That's good. That's *really. Good.* OK?"

Wren nodded. "OK."

"OK. Ready for a break?"

Wren nodded again. He looked to Cass. "Can I play, Mama?"

"Sure, sweetheart," Cass said.

As Three stood, Wren held out the little knife to him, but he waved it off.

"That's for you. You hang on to it."

"Would you mind keeping it for me? Just... for now?"

Three paused for a moment, but then smiled, and nodded.

"Sure, kiddo."

Wren gave Three the knife, and then clambered over to a small table nearby. Three walked the few paces to Cass, as she watched her son pull the strobe out of his pocket and place it on the table. He laid his head down on one arm, and stared at the clear ball as he rolled it gently back and forth. She wondered what invisible thing he saw in it.

Three sat down next to Cass, and leaned against the wall with her.

"I know you don't like it," he said. "I hope you understand it."

"I wish I didn't," she answered. "But I do."

For a long while, they just sat together, watching Wren at the table. Cass wondered what Three was thinking, what he might say. Though as long as they'd been together, she couldn't remember a time when he'd really started a conversation.

"I had a kid sister once," he said abruptly.

Something stirred in Cass's heart, some mix of surprise, confusion, and sudden compassion. She didn't know how to respond, so she didn't. After a while, Three added.

"So... I don't have much patience for their kind."

Cass watched him, noticed he was carefully intent on Wren.

"I'm sorry."

His head dipped forward, a hint of a nod. Another long silence followed, Three lost somewhere deep inside himself. Grim. And Cass wondered just how much loss Three had suffered in his lifetime. He resurfaced after a while, back to business. The brief window of emotion once again sealed off.

"We'll hit Greenstone tomorrow," he said as he stood. "You should both get some rest."

He was sliding into his harness again.

"What about you?"

"Gonna take a quick look around. Back in a few."

He moved to the door, activated the hatch above. Waited as the skeletal ladder extended itself to the floor. But before he left, Three looked back over his shoulder and caught Cass's eye. Winked. And even after the hatch had sealed behind him, her heart remained warm.

It'd been three days since Cass had left with her son, and with the man Three. And though he hadn't thought it possible, Jackson was starting to feel like the Vault had grown too big, too empty. Maybe he should've gone along with them after all. He trudged up the stairs, anxious. Today, he'd decided to walk the perimeter, for no reason other than to get out.

As he climbed, he noticed the air growing colder, a draft flowing in from the upper floors. When he reached the top, Jackson was aghast to find the gate already raised, the cold gray morning light spilling across the smooth concrete floor. And there, in the middle of the room, a man sat cross-legged.

He was short but stout with muscle, head shaved bald. His almond-shaped eyes were closed in quiet meditation, and he remained so still that had Jackson not known any better, he might've believed the man had always been there.

Jackson froze. He couldn't see them, but he knew in his gut there were others. Travelers weren't all that unusual. But they didn't usually let themselves in.

"Jackson, isn't it?"

The voice came from his left, and Jackson jumped at its sound, at how close it was. Jackson looked, saw him standing there, leaning against the wall. Jackson figured they were about the same age, though this guy was definitely the better dresser.

He was tall, draped in a long black coat of some expensive fabric. Smiling. Seemed friendly enough.

"That's a way to make friends, yeah?" Jackson said. "Might've tried knocking, yeah?"

"Sorry, we weren't sure if anyone was still here to answer."

"We met?"

"No, but we have some mutual friends."

Two others appeared at the entrance. One a tall, pale man. The other the most impossibly beautiful woman Jackson had ever seen. The man sitting on the floor still hadn't moved. Jackson's chest went tight. Bad things were at play.

"I'm sorry to have to tell you, but there's no one left here but me. Been a few weeks since…"

"Oh, our friends weren't residents. They were just passing through. Past couple of days."

Jackson tried his best to look thoughtful, then shook his head.

"That may be, but I don't think I can be much help. I've been locked up in here the past week or so."

The young man straightened up off the wall, smoothed the wrinkles out of his coat.

"You don't think you can be much help?"

"I doubt it. Ever since the Vault got wrecked I haven't been much for going out, yeah? But if you got questions, I'll try to answer 'em. Ask away."

The young man smiled. "That won't be necessary."

And with that, Jackson suddenly felt as though a great black cloud descended upon him, forced its way through his skull, enveloped his brain. A sudden stab of electric fire raced through his nerves, seared his mind, blinded his eyes. Someone screamed. Pain surged, as if all the blood in his veins had been displaced by boiling water. And as Jackson felt his mind ripping from its anchors, he realized the scream was his own.

# EIGHTEEN

Wren pulled the hood of his coat down more snugly over his head, hiding his face in the shadow it cast. Not against the cold. He was plenty warm even in the winds that swirled from seemingly every direction here among the tall buildings. But with his hood up, he felt stronger, ready for whatever came next. Mama was walking a few steps behind him. She said she was fine, but Wren knew she wasn't. She wasn't sick, exactly, but he knew she wasn't well. She needed her medicine, and soon. And until he could find it for her, it was up to him and Three to keep her safe.

Ahead, Three's face was hidden in the depths of the hood of his coat, but Wren could picture his expression; the same one he'd seen for the past three days. Focused, eyes slightly squinting as they actively searched out the paths ahead. Wren furrowed his brow, imitated Three's hard stare. After a minute or two, it kind of gave him a headache. He crammed his hands deeper into his pockets. In his right pocket, his fingers dabbled between the strobe and the practice blade Three had made for him. The cord-wrapped grip of the knife was rough against his skin. He wrapped his hand around the cool, seamless sphere of the strobe light. Pictured the swirl of tiny galaxies he imagined it could contain. Like having a star in a cage.

They walked on in silence for some time, but it wasn't long before Wren noticed a pressure, steadily growing, in the air, in his chest. And it just kept growing. The crush and churn of crowds. The silent hum, the motionless vibration of hundreds, if not thousands, of others, moving, thinking, *being*; broadcast across the invisible spectrum of signal that Wren felt without understanding. He squeezed the strobe. Dropped back, slipped his free hand into his mother's.

"We're close now, Mama."

And as though by speaking he had summoned it forth, there in front of them the first towers of Greenstone loomed. Hidden briefly when Three weaved through an angled side alley, they reappeared in full view at the end of the narrow corridor, and Wren gasped involuntarily. At the end of the alley where the three travelers stood together, the asphalt and concrete fell away in a gentle slope down into a wide basin where Greenstone stood, strong as an island mountain. Its high walls were mounted by small guard towers at regular intervals, punctuated every so often by massive watchtowers bristling with powerful lights and mounted weapons. Wren could see movement along the top of the wall: men on patrol.

"It's like a castle," Wren said.

"Or a prison," his mother answered.

"Started as one, became the other," said Three. "Still not sure which it is now." Three turned and dropped to one knee, placed his heavy hand on Wren's shoulder. "When we get in there, most important thing is to act like we know where we're going. You start looking around like you've never seen the place before, people are gonna start asking questions, and they might not be asking us. We don't want to stir up any traffic out of here."

"What's the plan?"

"First thing is to find a place to stay out of sight."

He turned his back to them, surveyed the fortress below.

"Walk like you own it," he said.

As he strode down the hill, Wren wondered who exactly Three had been talking to.

He hated to admit it, even to himself, but as Three led Cass and Wren towards the gate, a knot of fear grew in the pit of his stomach. Greenstone had proven to be a useful waypoint on many of his previous jobs, but for as many times as he'd visited, he still never felt he had control inside those walls. Too many variables, too many unknowns. The greenmen did an impressive job of maintaining security and some semblance of order, but it was understood that certain criminal elements were given run of their respective territories, as long as they kept their business relatively quiet. In reality, the bad guys outnumbered the good. It was just that the good guys were what kept Greenstone running. Not an uneasy peace. More like surface tension. Step too hard or too quickly, and you were gone.

Navigating that environment was tricky enough on his own. But with Cass around, and a kid in tow... Three shook his head, wondering if he was taking them all to their deaths. Or worse. Still, there wasn't much to be had in the world that couldn't be found somewhere in Greenstone, especially if you were paying Hard for it. At least they wouldn't have to worry about locating quint for Cass for much longer. Here, even the premium chems were about as hard to find as a vein on a juicer.

Thirty yards from the gate, he was still considering options, few as they were. They were running on a knife's edge of risk. This wasn't his way. He was used to working the numbers, knowing the angles, controlling the game. Risking everything, but leaving nothing to chance. But since he'd picked these two up, it was all fast and loose. It was bound to catch up with them at some point. And there wasn't much better a place for it than Greenstone.

Walk like you own it, he told himself. Nobody's gonna stop you as long as you look like you know what you're doing.

As they approached the main gate, a pair of greenmen stepped out from a small shelter. The big one held out a hand, motioned for them to stop.

"Afternoon," Three said.

"Sir," the big one replied. Professional, not friendly. "Where you comin' in from?"

"Here and there."

The second greenman stepped around to one side, his hand resting on some gunmetal chunk of tech on his belt. Three couldn't identify the weapon exactly, but he got the gist. Something mean. The big greenman looked the three travelers over, face neutral.

"You gonna make trouble for me?"

"No, sir."

"How long you plannin' to stay?"

"Three days, maybe."

"You bringin' any contraband with ya?"

"No, sir."

"Weapons?"

"No, sir."

The greenman gave a fleeting smile at that.

"Yeah," he said. The two greenmen exchanged a glance. Three reached deep, forced stillness. Greenmen were hard men: hard to read, hard to anticipate, hard to kill. Three realized the anxiety he felt over Cass and Wren was clouding his judgment of the situation. What was the glance? Was it "Get ready" or "What do you think"? The other greenman shifted on his feet, adjusted the Whatever It Was on his belt. Was he getting ready to draw? Did he even have to draw it to use it?

The muscle in the big one's jaw was working. His eyes were level, probing. Taking too long. Something was up. Could Dagon have beat them here? Three slowly flexed his left hand

and rotated his wrist, releasing the small blade from its secret housing, its grip sliding silently into his hand. The greenman's high collar had steel fixtures; might deflect the blade. Have to go for the eye. Shield, draw, fire. One shot, make it count.

Then the big one nodded.

"Alright. You folks have a real nice stay."

Three blinked, exhaled. Hoped no one noticed.

"Will do."

He pulled Cass and Wren ahead of him, nudged them along. As they passed the guards, Three quickly produced a pair of nanocarbon chips from his vest, and discreetly tipped the greenman a generous hundred Hard. Not required, but always appreciated.

"Cute kid," the second greenman said, as the two guards headed back to their post. "Keep him close."

Once they were inside, Cass dropped back a pace, and leaned in close.

"What was that?"

"Don't talk. Just stay with me. Stay *right with me*."

Three reached down and took Wren's hand in his, drew the boy close to him, right up against his leg. Cass fell in a pace behind, but tight. And Three locked his gaze forward, powered his way towards his destination, doing his best to look like he was on his way to kill the man responsible for leaving this woman and child alone in the world. And trying to forget just how close he'd come to killing two of the good guys.

Cass followed as closely as she dared without stepping on Three's heels. Fought to keep her eyes focused forward, her face grim, as if she'd been through these streets a hundred times before. For the first time, she had seen Three rattled, and that terrified her. Was it this place? Or had something happened with the guards that she'd missed? There was an electric edge, a lightning crackle around the fringes of each breath, that told her danger was on their heels here. Maybe all around.

She realized her fists were balled tight. Forced them to relax. She risked a glance around. It was different here. The buildings, the layout, the people. Greenstone was uniquely itself in the midst of a sea of sameness outside its walls. At its base, it was purely institutional: a cold gray concrete uniformity. Built for function. For control. Regular angles. Squares. Boxes. Bunkers.

And yet, life here had sprung up wild; lavish decorations covered every front, every window. Lights, paint, scrap welded into art. Some garish, some elegant, some shocking, some breathtaking. As if the populace, forced into a sterilized conformity, had rebelled in explosive individual expression. Celebrated it, even.

The people themselves, far from the rough-hewn and downtrodden survivors she'd expected, sported outfits of bizarre experiments in fashion. Tech as clothing. Faces tattooed into digital oblivion. A woman covered from head to toe in a color-swirling translucent plastifabric garment stood in apparent conversation with a small Asian man, naked from the waist up, who had circuitry embedded just beneath the surface of his skin in patterns like veins and arteries, giving the impression that if cut, he might bleed light.

Three strode purposely through the crowds, which were much denser than Cass had anticipated. It took nearly ten minutes to reach their destination. And to Cass's eyes, the destination didn't seem to be worth the walk. It was a narrow building that looked like it'd been wedged between the two on either side well after the other two had been built. The door was blacked out, and only about three-quarters the width of a normal door, and the front of the building was painted in a Japanese cartoon-styled motif, with a wild-looking samurai; shirtless, a piece of straw dangling from his lip, sword held high above his head, and a bottle of a well-known brand of

Irish whisky dangling from his belt. A hand-written sign lay propped against the wall, apparently having fallen off the door and never repaired. Scrawled in red paint both in neo-kanji and common English, it read "Samurai McGann". A dull, pulsing beat sounded from within.

Three paused, turned, and gently pushed Wren into her care.

"Keep to yourself in here. Clientele's a mixed bag."

"There isn't a better place we can go?"

"Lotta connections run through here," he answered, shaking his head. Then, after a moment, added, "And I need a drink."

He pushed open the door, and the droning sound grew louder. Cass realized it was some fusion-style of music. And she wasn't sure she liked it. She picked Wren up, and followed Three inside.

If Three had been worried about Cass getting them noticed, the fear seemed unfounded. As far as she could tell, no one in the place had even looked their way when they came in. The Samurai McGann was pretty clearly a bar of some kind, but beyond that it was tough to judge what exactly its business amounted to. There were tables, mostly occupied though not full, as well as hard-wire jacks and terminals for various transactions of questionable nature. Three found a booth off to one side of the place, and directed Cass and Wren in that direction. As she removed her pack and Wren's and stashed them in a pile, Cass kept an eye on Three. He approached the bartender, had a brief conversation, and then came over and joined them. He slung his heavy pack onto the bench and dropped into the seat across from Cass.

"Where's your drink?" she asked.

"Later. Gonna try to take care of some business first."

Cass cradled Wren in her lap. His eyes were wide, drinking in the fresh assault on his senses, but he seemed to be in good spirits.

"Got any food here?"

"Yeah, but I don't know you want it. Let's see how things shake out first."

Three was just turning to look back over his shoulder when there was a flash of motion. Three's head went down, the muzzle of a jittergun pressed hard into the side of his face. He went still, and Cass's heart stopped cold in her chest. It'd happened so fast.

Then, there was laughing. And the man with the gun was sitting at the table, grinning like a skull, and Three was half-smiling, shaking his head.

"Gettin' slow in your advanced age there, Numbers," the man said, apparently amused. "You get my letter?"

"No, Twitch. Still hasn't come yet."

An old, running joke apparently.

"Family man now?"

"Cass, her son Wren," he said, motioning to each in turn. "Friends of mine."

The man extended his hand, the stubby jittergun now safely in a holster he wore high on his belly, right next to its twin.

"jCharles," he said. He was tall, thin, with sharp features. Quick movements, but precise, like he could start and stop at the exact point he wanted to, but move at top speed in between. Almost mechanical. Cass couldn't help but wonder just how fast he could draw those jitters.

Cass shook his hand, as did Wren when it was offered.

"How long you in for?" jCharles asked, apparently to Three, though he was still looking at Cass.

"No longer than we have to be. We need some things."

jCharles nodded, checked over his shoulder to the bar, and made some vague motions. The bartender nodded. jCharles turned back to Cass, smiled.

"My place. If I'd known you were coming, I would've cleaned up a bit."

"What's the word on q-dose?" Three asked.

Straight to business.

"Tabs or jector?"

Three looked to Cass, prompted her.

"Tabs."

"No worries. Couple hours maybe."

"And how about these?"

Three placed a closed fist on the table, opened it slowly. jCharles swept whatever it was into his hand, swift as a magician. He smiled and winked at Cass again.

"*Spatz*, brother. Thirties?" he said. Then grimaced, glanced at Wren, then back at Cass. "Sorry, I have a filthy mouth."

Then to Three, slipping the item back to him. Cass figured it was an empty shell from Three's pistol.

"I don't think I can help you there. Eighteens I can do pretty easy. Maybe a couple twenty-fours at best."

Three nodded, seemed to be expecting that. Cass suddenly felt a pang of guilt over her reckless firing outside the Vault, and wondered just how precious a resource she'd wasted. Far more than she'd realized, that much was certain.

The bartender swung by and dropped off four beverages. Three small mugs of a golden-brown viscous liquid for the adults, and something aqua and fizzy for Wren. It smelled vaguely fruity.

"Can I try it?" he whispered.

"Sure, baby."

Wren leaned forward, and sipped out of the straw. His eyes lit up almost immediately.

"Good, huh?" jCharles said. "Made that one up myself."

Wren nodded, and then sat back against Cass. Shyness setting in. Probably exhausted.

"And the big favor," Three said.

"Yeah?"

"We need on the train."

jCharles actually looked stunned by that. He let out a low whistle. "That's quite a shopping list, brother." He shook his head. "I can try to arrange a meeting, but that's about the best I can do. Afraid you're gonna have to talk to Bonefolder yourself for that one."

"You can arrange it?"

"I said I can *try* to arrange it. No promises."

"Try hard. It's important."

"Yeah, I'd guess so," jCharles glanced at Cass and Wren again. A different look in his eye now. "Where you stayin'?"

"Nowhere yet," Three answered. "Just rolled in."

"Alright, I'll set you up," said jCharles. He swept up his mug, downed the contents, and then slammed it on the table as he stood. He moved like an animation skipping frames. "Drop upstairs if you want, Mol's in. I got some business to attend to this afternoon."

Three nodded, waved slightly, and jCharles was gone. Cass waited for Three to elaborate, but of course he didn't. Finally, she prompted him.

"So… Bonefolder? That doesn't sound like something we want to do."

Three just nodded. Took a sip of his drink, grimaced, shook his head.

"Sit tight for a sec. I'm gonna go see Mol, let her know we're here." He stood, scanned the bar. Then added, "And do *not* chug that."

Cass and Wren sat silently, Wren occasionally leaning forward to sip his drink. The Samurai McGann was a busy place, people coming and going, but mostly minding their own business. So it was strange when Cass saw the man by the door, staring at them. She didn't recognize him, and he looked away quickly. Though there was something vaguely familiar about his eyes. As he walked out, she noticed he walked with a limp, but thought nothing more of it. It wouldn't be until much later that she would place him.

# NINETEEN

Three climbed the back staircase with heavy steps. Weary. Far more so than he felt he should've been. He was used to being the one on the hunt, not the other way around. It was a slow burn, never being able to rest, never feeling safe; it was beginning to take its toll. He couldn't remember the last time he'd felt this fatigued. The guards at the gate… he shook his head. Losing his edge, when he needed it most. And he wasn't sure when he'd get it back.

He hoped he'd get it back.

The stairwell was poorly lit, and its corridor was so narrow Three had to twist his torso to keep his shoulders from rubbing the walls on either side. An iron door stood guard at the top, painted over with some kind of pale green rubberized coating. There was no landing. The stairs just dead-ended at the base of the door. Three stood on the last step, gathered himself. Mol was in there. Always tough to see her.

Before he had a chance to buzz in, heavy mechanisms slid and *chunked* inside the door, and it swung away from him, and light flooded into the corridor, and she was there. She gave a little yelp, and in an instant her arms were around his neck.

"What are you doing here? Did you just get in? Does Twitch know you're here?" Her perfume hit him: gentle, faint, but like a sledgehammer of memory. Like rain and moonlight on the ocean. And he was suddenly conscious of all the sweat and grime thick on his skin.

"Heya, Miss Mol."

He dropped his hand on the middle of her back, gave her half a squeeze. Careful to avoid the jack and steel housing at the base of her spine. She pulled back, beaming.

"Don't you 'Miss Mol' me! What are you *doing* here?"

"Passing through." He tried to smile. It came out broken.

"Well, get in here. You bring anything with you?"

"Yeah, more than usual. Couple of guests this time."

"Oh," she said, obviously surprised. "OK. Well bring 'em on up. You need help with your gear?"

"No, I got it. You sure it's alright?"

Her expression went flat, like he'd insulted her. She swatted his shoulder.

"Go get your gear and your friends. You see Twitch yet? I think he was heading out…"

"Yeah, on the way in."

"Good. That means he won't be gone all day. You sure I can't help you with anything?"

"You're helping me now," he said, and winked at her involuntarily. "Be right back."

She nodded and as he turned and headed back down the stairs, he could feel her watching him. When he was about halfway to the bottom, he heard the little whirs and clicks of her walking back into the upstairs apartment. The sound of the servos and micro-hydraulics that made her lifeless legs useful. The sound that broke his heart, every time.

He found Cass and Wren where he'd left them. Cass hadn't touched her drink. Wren's was empty.

"Hey," Cass said when she saw him. Her expression shifted. "You OK?"

He nodded. "Mol's waiting upstairs."

"Mol is...?"

"A sweetheart. jCharles's wife."

He grabbed his pack, swung it up on a shoulder. Reached down and took Cass's in a hand. Paused. Nodded towards Wren. "He ever seen a nerve-rig before?"

Cass thought, shook her head. "Not that I know of."

"It gonna be a problem?"

"Full rig?"

"Half. Just the lower."

Cass nodded, understanding. Something in her eyes said more than Three wanted them to. He had the disquieting sense that she was starting to get a read on him. She looked down at Wren, still sitting in her lap. Spoke quietly.

"Wren, the person we're going to see upstairs has a special machine. To help her walk. It might look a little strange, but we don't want to make her feel uncomfortable, OK? So we're not going to stare at her, or ask her about it, OK?"

"Is she sick?"

Cass looked up to Three. He shook his head.

"No. She got hurt. A long time ago."

A long time ago. As clear as yesterday.

"OK."

Three hoisted their packs, shook Cass off when she tried to help.

"This way."

He led them back up the stairs, letting the burden of all the gear focus his mind on something other than Mol. The first few minutes were always the hardest.

She'd left the door cracked open, so Three nudged it with the top of his head and leaned in.

"We're back."

He heard her moving around in the back room.

"Just throw your stuff anywhere," she called. "I'll be there in a sec."

Three pushed in, slung the packs in an out-of-the-way corner by the door. Glanced around the apartment. Pretty much the same. The door opened right into the main room; a large, comfortable space that somehow seemed wider inside than the building had looked on the outside. It was warmly decorated, with oversized furniture. Old, dark woods. A kitchen was off to one side, and the other side led to the back room where Mol was now, which Three knew had a storage area in addition to jCharles and Mol's bedroom.

"What are those?" Wren asked, looking at the one oddity in the apartment, across the room. jCharles's life's work, obsession, and personal treasure all in one, stacked on shelves that ran nearly the entire height and length of one wall.

"Books."

Collected, scavenged, rescued, and restored. Ancient works, last known copies in existence. Masterpieces standing alongside some of the worst specimens of the written word ever penned by man. All worth saving, as far as jCharles was concerned.

"What do they do?"

"They're full of words, baby," Cass answered. "Stories and things. From a long time ago."

He moved closer, touched the spine of a cracked leather-bound volume.

"Let's not touch them, sweetheart," Cass said.

"Oh, it's alright," Mol answered, coming in from the back. "They're meant to be touched."

She walked over to Cass with her hand extended. "I'm Mol."

"Cass. This is my son, Wren."

Wren turned away from the books, moved closer to his mother.

"Hi, Cass. Hello, Wren." She knelt with some difficulty down to Wren's level. "My goodness if you aren't the most beautiful thing I've ever seen. Any chance you're an angel?"

"No, ma'am," he said quietly.

"Ma'am? Now I'm *sure* you're an angel. Your mama must be quite a woman to be raising an angel. That is no easy task." She glanced up at Cass. "You might want to keep him away from that one, though." She nodded at Three, with a smile. "No telling what he'll teach him when you're not looking."

"I don't like what he's been teaching him when I *am* looking," Cass replied with a shrug, smiling back. "But he's been taking care of us so far."

"Yeah, he'll do that too."

Both women were looking at him now, and Three was suddenly uncomfortable. It was strange seeing them there, in the same place, right next to each other. Three's carefully separated worlds colliding. He glanced away, surveying the apartment again for no real reason. Changed the subject.

"Twitch stayin' out of trouble?"

"Have you met him?" Mol answered, lightly sarcastic. She struggled back up to her feet, and Three reflexively reached out to take her hand. She accepted the help, her hand warm and strong in his. Her blue eyes sparkled up at him. Even at her full height, she was nearly a foot shorter. Her voice dropped, tone warm and reassuring. "He's fine, Three. We're fine."

Mol's eyes held his steady gaze for a moment. Strong. But concerned. She looked away, to Cass and Wren.

"You make yourselves right at home. Bedroom and bathroom are back there. If you want to take a shower or anything, you let me know. Sleep, whatever you want. I'm sure you're exhausted."

Three realized he was still holding her hand. He let go, busied himself taking off his coat and harness.

"Thank you," Cass said. "This is really kind of you."

"Selfish, really. Place like Greenstone, we don't get a lot of chances to host company. Have to milk it when we can."

Three noticed Cass was standing with the fingertips of one hand pressed in on the arm of a chair. Subtly keeping her balance.

"It's alright if you wanna lie down, Cass," he said. "Been hard goin'."

Her eyes flicked to his. He knew she'd never admit it, but she needed it. He nodded.

"Go lie down," he said, firmly. No longer an option.

"Isn't there something I can do? I feel bad just coming in and taking over…"

"Sweetheart, go on back there and rest up," Mol said. "Bed's all ready. If you've been keeping up with this brute all day, I'm surprised you can even stand. Not to mention your little one."

"Yeah, it's been a long road," Cass replied. "We came all the way from the Vault."

Three winced, at least internally. He'd meant to tell Cass not to mention it. Forgotten. His expression must've caught her attention, because she looked over at him, and her face changed suddenly.

"The Vault?" Mol turned and looked back at Three, excited. "How's Gev? Big goon hasn't pimmed in like a month."

Three stilled himself. Kept his eyes on Cass. She understood now. Pressed her lips tightly together, in a silent apology.

"Wren, baby, why don't you come lie down with me for a little while?"

"I'm not sleepy, Mama."

"Wren."

The boy didn't know what was going on, but he understood his mama wasn't requesting. He slipped his hand into hers and let her lead him back towards the bedroom. Mol's gaze hopped from Three to Cass, and back again. Excitement beginning to drain.

"Three. Did you see Gev?"

In the back, Cass quietly closed the door. Mol didn't turn, just looked intently at Three. Her eyes different now. Wider, unsteady. Searching his.

He could feel himself telling her before he even opened his mouth. Tears had already started to well in her deep blue eyes.

"Three…"

"He's gone, Mol."

He heard the servos whine and click, and reached out to grab her elbows, supporting her before she sank to the floor. Pulled her close. She buried her face in his chest, clung to him fiercely. After a moment, shock gave way and her body began to shake with quiet sobs, her tears soaking his shirt. He held her for a long while, silently sharing the grief, tormented by her closeness.

Night had fallen, and outside the high and guarded walls of Greenstone the unearthly cries of the Weir echoed amongst the urban labyrinth, answers to their own calls. Together, jCharles and Three stood atop the roof of the Samurai McGann, looking down on the throngs flowing in the street below, snaking through each other like streams intertwined. The women and the boy had remained in the apartment beneath, leaving the men undisturbed to attend to their business.

"I don't know how many times I tried to talk him into coming here," jCharles said, more to himself than to Three. He took a pull on his stimstick, held it. He'd handled the news better than Mol, but Three knew it'd take him longer to actually come to terms with Gev's death. jCharles exhaled with the sudden puff of a humorless laugh. "Said he couldn't handle all the noise."

Mol would grieve hard and fast. Twitch, well… he had a history of holding on to things.

"Sure, much better to live playing doorman to a bunch of trash-hunters," he continued, "and *die* as one."

Three just stood silently, letting the distractions below draw his attention. Twitch wasn't talking to him so much as he was thinking aloud. Processing. No need to interrupt.

"The *noise*." jCharles took another drag on the stimstick, held it, let out a breath like an extended sigh. Flipped some internal switch, packaged up whatever he was feeling about Gev. He'd deal with it later. "So you settling down, or what?"

"What."

"Wouldn't blame you if you were. Cass… she's sharp. And a real looker, you know." Three shrugged. jCharles smiled. "Yeah, you know. Kid's cute, too. You don't watch it, Mol might squirrel him away somewhere, keep him for herself."

jCharles hadn't meant it that way, but Three felt the cut anyway. Mol had wanted her own for as long as he could remember. And she'd *had* one, for the briefest, cruelest time.

jCharles turned to face him, serious.

"What're you doing, man?"

"Standin' here listenin' to you, Twitch."

"I mean it, Three. This isn't like you. Traveling heavy. People in tow. I know it's not for the money, 'cause you'd never take a job like this. And you look tired, brother. *Real* tired. So what're you doing?"

It was the question Three still couldn't answer. Or maybe wouldn't. A woman in a yellow coat floated through the crowd below, with the flow but not of it. A bright leaf atop the current.

"The right thing, I hope," he said. "We'll see."

"Is it the good guys or bad guys chasing them?"

"Bad ones."

"You sure?"

"I'm sure."

jCharles leaned over the edge of the roof and spat, watched as it tumbled towards the street below. Another pull on the stimstick.

"Listen, man. You wanna do you the penance thing, that's your gig. But Mol and me, we never put that on you. You know that. We *never* put that on you. Don't pick it up on our account."

"It's not like that," Three answered, hoping it was true.

"I hope not. 'Cause no matter how it ends, Jakey's not coming back."

They stood in silence for a time, and Three wondered what outcome he was hoping for out of all this. He'd been too busy fighting for that next minute to stop and think what it'd be like when it was all over. Cass and Wren would be with Wren's father, whoever he was. At some point, Cass would die. And what? He would go back to living the life he'd led before they stumbled into it? No matter what else happened from here, he already knew that was impossible.

"Well, here's the deal," jCharles said. "Bonefolder's people are going to meet us tomorrow."

"Meet *me* tomorrow."

"Us. Tomorrow afternoon. You convince them you can make it worth their while, they'll kick it up the chain, and with some luck you'll be on your way out."

"I appreciate the introduction, Twitch. But stay out of the way."

"They won't talk to you without me," he replied, stern. "And if it goes bad, you're gonna need the help."

"That's why I don't want you anywhere nearby. It goes bad, I disappear, easy. They know where you live."

"Then don't let it go bad."

Three knew he couldn't argue it. It was Twitch's turf, he'd go where he wanted. "Fine. And the quint?"

"Stack I got her today was a street job. Bigger quantities, I'll have to go Downtown."

"We're going to need more than the stack."

jCharles eyed him. "What's she burning?"

"Told me fifty a day." jCharles let out a low whistle in surprise. Three hadn't even hit him with the real numbers yet. "But she was lying. Hard to tell, since I don't know when she boosts. I'm guessing one-fifty, maybe as much as two hundred."

"No. No way," Twitch shook his head. His tone was patient but dismissive, as if Three, not well-versed in the world of chems, couldn't be expected to know just how far off his estimate had to be. "Girl that size, that much would wreck her."

"Already has. But I dosed her with Trivex myself before we got here."

"Trivex is different–"

"A full jector, five doses. At once."

jCharles stopped arguing. "Guess we're going Downtown, then."

"Busy day."

"Yeah. It'll be interesting," said Twitch, deactivating the stimstick and sliding it into a thin pocket on the sleeve of his coat. "Like old times."

"Hope not."

jCharles chuckled and turned towards the hatch leading back down to the apartment. He called back as he walked away. "Get some sleep, brother. World'll look lighter and brighter tomorrow."

Three held his ground. "You sure you can't find us another place to crash? Doesn't have to be fancy. Cellhouse would be fine."

jCharles stopped, threw a look over his shoulder. "Don't do that. It's insulting." Three felt the admonishment, the hard tone. A tense moment lingered, jCharles letting Three know he was serious. Then, he opened the hatch and headed back inside, softening the blow as he went. "Besides, Mol would kill me."

Three knew it wasn't fair, coming into their lives and at the same time, trying to maintain distance. But the trouble on his trail now was like none he'd known before. And he'd sworn he wouldn't bring that to their doorstep. Not again. Never again.

He stayed on the roof late into the night, not wanting to face Mol again. Not wanting Wren to see him. Not wanting Cass to look in his eyes again. His mask was cracking, he knew. And he couldn't afford for any of them to see that for the first time in long years, Three was standing on the edge of tomorrow, and was desperately afraid.

# TWENTY

Sunlight streamed in through a crack in the shade, a pure white sliver that fell warm across Cass's cheek. Her eyelids fluttered, drew open heavily. She felt herself waking, slowly, awareness leaking in like warm water pooling in from under a door. And as she woke, she was loath to move. The bed was more comfortable than any she could remember ever having slept in before, the sheets and blankets a secure cocoon of warmth and comfort that seemed to have been arranged and fitted to her exact frame. Wren was gone, but Cass felt so perfectly at peace that her usual desperate need to know where he was at all times failed to kick in. In the other room, no doubt. Safe. She could hear the low tones of Three's voice through the door, a quiet rumble like distant thunder.

She rolled to her side and arched, stretching, scissoring her legs to different corners of the foot of the bed, feeling the sheets run smooth and cool across the bare skin of her legs. jCharles had given her a stack of quint the evening before, which her bloodstream had greedily accepted. Cass relaxed her stretch, accessed GST. It was nearly noon. She'd slept for fourteen hours.

She sat up, swung her legs over the side of the bed. Took a deep breath. A smile crept to her lips. She felt good. Better than good. She felt *well*. She slid out of bed, dressed, and padded barefoot into the adjoining room.

"Mama!"

The conversation stopped when Wren called to her. He hopped off the couch and ran over. She stooped to intercept him, and swung him up to hug him tightly. jCharles was sitting in one of the plush chairs. Three, as usual, was standing. Mol was seated on the couch, next to the spot where Wren had been moments before. She had a book open on her lap. Apparently she'd been reading to him.

"Sorry to interrupt," Cass said.

"Hope we didn't wake you," Mol answered. "I was trying to keep them quiet, but you know how boys are when you get 'em together."

"Thanks, Miss Mol, but I probably should've been up about six hours ago."

Mol shot Three a flat look. "Now you've got her doing it." Her eyes were red, slightly puffy. Cass guessed she'd been crying recently. "At this rate, you'll have Twitch calling me 'Miss' before you go."

Three was unmoved, his stone mask intact. He looked Cass in the eye without expression. Grim. Cass couldn't help but wonder what had transpired while she slept.

"So what's the plan?"

Three's look lingered for an uncomfortably long moment. Almost angry.

"Tryin' to work that out now, actually," jCharles answered. "We seem to have a timing issue."

Cass moved on into the room, letting Wren slide down to his feet as she did so. To her surprise, he went right back to the couch and plopped down next to Mol, close. Right up next to her. She dropped an arm around him casual, like family. Cass, aware of the tension in the room but unable to identify the reason, situated herself on the arm of the couch, neither sitting nor standing.

"Anything I can help with?"

"No," Three answered in his direct way. A look passed between him and jCharles. She recognized the look, the one that Three used to indicate there would be no further discussion on the matter. jCharles either didn't read it the same way, or didn't care.

"Actually–"

"I said no, Twitch."

"Options and time, man. We're short on both. Don't say no to me again unless you've got a solution."

"I'll go," Mol offered.

"Absolutely not," Three said without looking at her. jCharles glanced over, warm, but shook his head.

"I'm not a cripple. I can still handle myself."

Cass got the sense everyone was talking around her, and she didn't like it.

"I know, Mol, but I didn't come here to bring you into this–"

"If you're in it, *we're* in it," jCharles said, cutting Three off. He leaned forward on the edge of his chair, voice intense. "That's how it works. *Spatz* Three, do you have any idea how tired it gets, you playing this solo warrior gig all the time?"

"jCharles," Cass injected. "What's the problem?"

Three looked her way, but jCharles ignored him.

"Schedule. We've got to be in two places at once. And neither of them are pleasant."

"And I can't go to one?"

jCharles looked back to Three, eyebrows raised. Cass saw the muscle of Three's jaw working. Finally, he turned to her.

"I've gotta go see the Bonefolder's people. They won't talk to me without Twitch there. But he's got a chem drop lined up Downtown."

"Caught a lucky break on the timing," jCharles added, "but with the quantity they're moving, they won't wait around. And it might be a week before I can get a handle on that much again."

Cass understood now. And it offended her that Three wouldn't consider letting her take care of the drop. She stood up.

"Then of course I'm going," she said. "It's for me, it's my thing. I'll handle it."

"Too dangerous, Cass," Three answered. "Greenmen don't patrol down there. You don't know your way around. You're a wo–"

He stopped himself, but not soon enough.

"What, a woman? Who do you think I am, Three? I'm not some useless skew, you know. You think a crew like RushRuin picked me up because they felt sorry for me?"

If she hadn't been so worked up, she would've noticed the sudden look of surprise and concern that passed between jCharles and Mol.

"jCharles, just tell me where I need to be and when. I can handle it." jCharles looked back at Three, but Cass wasn't having it. "Don't look at him, he doesn't have a say."

Three smoldered but didn't reply. Cass took small satisfaction in knowing he didn't really have any other choice.

"One sec, lemme sig you the spot."

He bursted the location to her. She pulled up a satellite overlay, gipsed the path, scouted the area via the image projected directly on her corneas.

"That's what we call 'Downtown'."

Rows of concrete blocks were arrayed around a large central structure that looked like an old aircraft hangar. None of the wild color that painted the rest of the city was apparent Downtown. Everything was still cast in its original concrete gray. Cass realized the blocks were isolation units, individual prisons for what once must've been Greenstone's most violent and deadly citizens. From the looks of it, the neighborhood hadn't changed much. More garbage, maybe.

"How much product are we talking?"

"Forty-five hundred in tabs."

Cass couldn't help but jolt at the number. Even the labs she'd frequented back in Fourover never dealt in more than a thousand when it came to quint. Too potent. Too much risk to have all in one place. She was almost afraid to ask, but knew she had to. "For how much?"

"Three thousand Hard. But the first half's been paid." Cass glanced to Three, but he'd turned away from her now. He was busying himself with his pack and harness. No doubt he'd paid for the chems. Probably enough to last him a year the way he traveled. She felt suddenly wrong for what she'd said to him. And how she'd said it.

"The people to meet check out fine," said jCharles. "Not direct connections of mine, but they come with the right credits. It's just, you know, walking in with that much cold and back out with that much q-dose."

"I understand. What time?"

"An hour."

"It gonna be a problem if it's me and not you?"

"Nah, I'll send word. Even Downtown they respect Bonefolder's time. You show up with the money, they'll do the deal. It's these guys." He transmitted two pictures, which she flashed up. They were practically kids. Gangly, bookish types. "The long-hair's Tyke. His friend is Jantz. They'll have security. Tyke's the talker. Jantz is the nervous one."

"Anything else I need to know?"

"Yeah, open that shirt up a bit, you might get a discount."

"Twitch!" Mol snapped, and Cass jumped, having forgotten she was in the room.

jCharles shrugged with a sheepish smile.

"I'm just saying. They're chemists, Mol."

"Mol," Cass said, a potential hitch having just occurred to her. "Do you think Wren could stay here? While I'm away?"

"Of course, Cass. Absolutely. If it's OK with Wren here, I mean." She squeezed him once, smiled down at him.

Wren looked uncertain.

"Will you be OK without me?" he asked. His sincerity brought unexpected tears to Cass's eyes. Her baby. Her would-be protector.

"Yes, baby, I'll be fine. You stay here with Miss Mol."

"OK," he answered. "If you're sure."

"I'm sure."

"OK."

She walked over and kissed him on the head, then turned back to jCharles.

"Gimme just a minute, then I'll head on. I'd like to have some time to scout it out before I go in."

"Probably a good plan."

She glanced to Three who was still carefully ignoring the whole exchange. She couldn't see his face, but she could picture it. Cass returned to the back room and made the bed. She didn't know why, exactly. It just felt wrong to leave it a mess.

Afterwards, she went into the bathroom, ran cool water in the small basin, and washed her face. She pulled her hair back tight into a short ponytail. Looked at herself in the mirror. Her color was better. Her eyes steady.

"It's just a buy," she said to her reflection.

"It is and it isn't," said Three from the doorway. Cass jumped. Of course she hadn't heard him come in.

"Don't try to talk me out of it, Three."

He shook his head, looked over the freshly-made bed.

"No, I–" he started, then stopped. Eyes narrowed. Gathered himself. "Look, I didn't mean..." he trailed off. Made eye contact. Cass was surprised to find something behind his usually-unreadable dark eyes. Genuine concern. "You watch yourself. And if you see anything you don't like, you walk away. We'll figure something else out. You just walk away."

She nodded, moved again by his suddenly obvious concern for her.

"We'll be back before sundown," he said.

"Alright."

He nodded and withdrew. When Cass returned to the main room, he was nowhere to be found. Mol was reading to Wren again, and he sat enthralled. jCharles approached and put himself between Cass and the others.

"You shouldn't need this," he said in low tones, "but I'd feel better if you had it." He slipped her one of his stubby jitterguns. "You know how to use it?"

Cass gripped the chunky weapon, tested its weight. It wasn't as viscerally terrifying as Three's pistol, but its design was still a clear indication of vicious intent. Its some two-dozen slender barrels were tightly stacked in a squared-off housing. A classic close-range weapon for personal protection. Cass nodded and tucked it into her coat pocket.

"Just a precaution," he said. "More for me than you."

"Thanks, jCharles." She leaned around jCharles. "I'll be back soon, sweetheart."

Wren looked up, and quickly hopped down. Her wrapped his arms around her waist, buried his head in her hip. "Be safe, Mama."

"I will, baby. Take care of Miss Mol while I'm gone."

"I will." He slipped back away from her, and returned to his place on the couch. Snuggled into Mol. Cass couldn't remember him ever having taken to someone so quickly before. Mol smiled and nodded, and without another word Cass left the safety of the Samurai McGann and plunged into the stream of humanity that seemed to flow in every direction except for the one she wanted to go: towards the darkest corner of Greenstone.

Three stared up at the building that seemed to loom over them despite being only three stories tall. jCharles had gone in first to make sure everything got off on the right foot. As important as this meeting was, Three found it tough to focus on the task at hand. He wondered how Cass was handling the trek. Tried to convince himself she'd be fine. She was right, after all. She'd run with RushRuin. There was no doubt she could handle herself. She'd already proven how tough she was, fighting for her life and covering twenty or more miles a day without complaint. And she was back up and running on quint, which meant... well, it likely meant that even Three had no idea what she was capable of now. He was probably in more danger than she was, anyway.

Three surveyed the street and surrounding buildings for the fifth time since Twitch had gone in. This section of Greenstone was surprisingly quiet. Almost vacant. There were a few stragglers here and there, but they seemed out of place. No, actually, they seemed too *in* place. Too evenly spaced, too strategically positioned. Three watched a man in a long, rumpled coat pass by on the opposite side of the street, noted how careful the man was not to look Three's way, how careful to keep the coat closed. Perimeter security. Three wondered how much hardware the guy was packing inside the coat. Long gun seemed unnecessary for a two-man meeting. Then again, in Greenstone it never hurt to be over-prepared. Three reached inside his coat and checked his pistol, gave a slight tug to loosen it in its holster. Just in case.

What was taking Twitch so long?

The nearer Cass drew toward the Downtown district, the thinner the crowds got. Knots of people walked together here and there, others clustered together in doorways, on steps. Some glanced at her as she followed the internal beacon that guided her towards her destination, but most ignored her presence completely. She kept her head up, her stride confident, shoulders back. Anyone who looked her way found her looking right back. Experience had taught her that the projection of strength was more important than actual possession of it. Still, it helped her confidence knowing at least she could boost again if she needed it.

Though the walls and alleys still bore the occasional spray of vivid symbols marking territory, the color had otherwise begun to drain from the surroundings. And with the loss of that wild façade, Greenstone was looking less and less like a vibrant city and taking on more and more of its original personality. The street hadn't changed width, but the walls felt closer, taller, more dominating.

Further ahead, Cass could see the rounded dome of the hangar peeking above the concrete-gray horizon. She put her head down and focused on reaching her goal. Get in, do the deal, get out. She realized she was gripping the jittergun in a tight fist.

*Breathe*, she told herself.

"Problem." jCharles was back, looking grim. He moved close to Three, lowered his voice. Eyes roving the surroundings. "There are way more people inside than there should be," he said. "The fact they let me come back out makes me think they've got 'em posted out here, too."

"Yeah. I count six ground level, two up high. Probably one across the street, second floor window, overlooking the intersection."

jCharles flicked his eyes that way.

"Shutters are all pulled up there."

"Perfect vantage to the front and side entrances. They *should* have someone there."

"So what do you wanna do?"

As far as Three was concerned, nothing had changed. Not really. Dealing with the Bonefolder was always a trap, in one way or another.

"You walk. I'll go in."

"It's like this, Three. Bonefolder's in there. Looking for you. So either we're both going in, or we're both shooting out."

"Well. Then I guess we're goin' in."

jCharles stepped back and nodded, glancing up and down the street.

"Bartender's faster than he looks. The big guy is the last one to worry about. If it goes bad, start right, I'll take left. Meet you in the middle."

Three nodded, unfastened his coat, and forced himself to relax.

The closer she got to the hangar, the more apparent it became as to why that was the meeting point of choice. Cass had walked the perimeter twice, and noticed only two doors, each on opposite sides of the structure. The main gates had been pulled to and welded shut long ago, and there were no windows to be seen. It'd be awfully hard to surprise anybody on the inside and still be able to get away without being tracked by someone on the outside. The place was almost tailor-made for deals between untrustworthy business partners.

Cass checked the time. 13:27 GST. Soon. But enough time for one more lap. She'd run her first two perimeter checks clockwise, and started that way again, but something pricked in her gut and caused her to turn back. As she did so, she noticed a man in a grubby brown coat limping her way. When she turned, he hitched his step. The briefest eye contact. A hesitation. Slight, but as if she had startled him, despite being separated by more than thirty feet. He continued on his shuffling way, turned a corner and disappeared down a row of iso-units. By the time she'd reached the line of units he'd taken, he was nowhere in sight.

Paranoia, maybe. But something about the man stuck with her that she didn't like. Some unplaced familiarity. Or maybe he was just the kind of person she'd expect to find lurking Downtown. Three's words flashed back to her.

*You see anything you don't like, you walk away.*

It'd seemed like good advice at the time, but now it sounded so vague as to be useless. There was a lot down here she didn't particularly care for. And the deal. The deal was big enough for her to get well, be well, and stay well for good long while. No way was she going to walk away from that chance. She shoved the man out of her mind and finished her final walk around the perimeter.

"Either of you gentlemen carrying any weapons?" the neckless bodyguard asked.

"No," Three answered, despite the fact that his coat was open and his vicious pistol was widely on display.

The bodyguard smiled, a gleaming white split amidst the pale pink flesh of his face and head. Three hoped this was the "big one" Twitch had mentioned. The Big One looked like a mountain of flesh, poured in a pile and shaped into some vaguely human form by someone whose only experience with anatomy had been muscular. He was dressed in a three-piece suit that looked like it was ready to tear apart if he so much as turned his head. Though it was cleverly tailored and woven, Three could tell from the sheen of the fabric that it was fibrasteel, likely impervious to any stabbing or slashing that might occur.

"And that piece is, I suppose, decorative only?"

"Keeps the kids away is all."

"The Bonefolder understands the nature of the world in which we live, friend. We do not wish to deprive you of your protection. We mean only to inventory. I would, however, advise you to keep your hands away from your... *ornament*. This way, please."

The Big One led them both from the entryway into a large open room, set with a number of tables. There was a bar off to the left, where a man stood wiping down a counter with a rag. The bartender looked to be in his early 60s, and he tipped his head in greeting. Even across the room, the bartender vibrated with menace. An open staircase in the back led up to a second floor, where an open balcony surrounded and overlooked the first floor. Evenly spaced doors off the balcony hinted at some kind of upstairs living quarters.

A knot of men sat or stood around small tables in the center of the room. And there at the large central table, all alone, sat the Bonefolder.

"Gentlemen," said the Big One. "Be seated."

Three and jCharles sat themselves across the table from Bonefolder.

"May I have a beverage prepared for you?"

"Bittertonic might be nice," jCharles answered. "How about you Numbers, something to take the edge off? Good chance to taste something from the top of the shelf."

Three shook his head, kept his eyes on Bonefolder. He could tell from Twitch's eager casualness that he was wound tight. Quick count put them down four to one, not counting the Bonefolder. Not good odds even against poorly-trained gun hands.

"Very well," said the Big One. He motioned to the bartender, who began preparing a drink for jCharles.

Three took in as much about the Bonefolder as he could. High cheekbones, light brown hair that flowed in a steep cascade to just below her shoulders. Pouty lips drawn down permanently at the corners of her mouth. Gave her a look of constant, polite disdain. As he regarded her, she smiled, drawing her lips back fiercely in an almost upside down kind of way, that, rather than a frown, managed to be something of a smile while still communicating a sort of strained patience. She'd been a looker once. Maybe still was, to some of particular tastes. She seemed severe in every way.

The fact that a woman had grown into such a commanding presence here in Greenstone told him all he needed to know about her will. And the deference the men around her showed her hinted at how she exerted that will. Her men exhibited the kind of fear and respect one might expect to see shown to a queen. Or an unforgiving goddess.

"This is the one they call 'Three'?" she said, with mild disdain, looking towards the Big One and waving her hand at Three dismissively.

"I am," Three answered for himself. The Bonefolder looked to him with mild disappointment.

"We see. Not much of a proper name, is it? It sounds simply ridiculous to us, to go about having others refer to you by number rather than name."

If she had intended to garner a response, she would be disappointed. Three sat without reply. The Big One left the table. The corners of the Bonefolder's mouth pulled downward.

"Well, we won't abide referring to you in such a manner, so here you will be identified as Mr Walker. Such seems suitable, from what we know of you."

"You can call me whatever you like, ma'am."

"How unexpected. It has manners." The Bonefolder paused long enough to sip from her beverage, a steaming, brownish liquid Three couldn't identify.

"Mr Walker, we understand you wish to make use of our train."

"Yes, ma'am."

The Big One returned and placed a bittertonic in front of jCharles, and then moved around to stand behind Bonefolder. jCharles didn't touch the drink.

"We had high hopes that we could reach some sort of an agreement on the matter. But it has been brought to our attention that an obstacle may have arisen between us already."

••••

There was no further sign of the limping man and as far as Cass could tell the area around the hangar was clear. Or at least, clear enough. jCharles hadn't told her which entrance to use, so she picked the westernmost. The door was steel, with thick white paint flaking off in strips. It didn't seem like the kind of place where you'd be expected to knock. Cass raised the bar that served to hold the door closed, and nudged the door open. Inside, the hangar was a dusty orange twilight of artificial light. Smooth concrete floor. A stale odor of mildew and something like kerosene. Same feel as the lab back at the enclave, where Fedor had nearly caught them.

She pushed the door open wider, and slid inside, careful to check both sides as she entered. Clear. From the inside, the hangar seemed impossibly large. The light didn't stretch high enough to reveal the roof, so looking upward into that looming blackness gave a sense of endlessness that made her dizzy. A small group of people stood in a cluster right in the middle of the hangar, soaked in a bright yellow-white light from the four vertical tubelights that formed a rectangle around them. The lights were a bit of a surprise, given the relative darkness that surrounded them. It seemed like inside that box of light, it would be nearly impossible to keep a clear view of what may be going on beyond its borders. She had to wonder just how experienced these guys were.

From this distance the tallest of the figures gathered in the center was no larger than her thumb. She knew that the eastern entrance was roughly the same span again from the center, which gave the hangar mind-boggling proportions. And she couldn't help but wonder what had ever been housed here.

Cass drew a breath, steadied herself, then started the long walk, her footfalls echoing mercilessly in the metallic cavern. Floorbox electric lights ran in a haphazard path the full length of the hangar, bathing the floor in dull pools of hot-orange between pockets of dusky hues. The cluster of people broke up slightly as she approached, two of the larger coming forward while the others remained behind. Separated as they were, she got a solid headcount. Six, altogether. Tyke, Jantz, and security. Seemed about right. Not great numbers for her, though, if it went bad.

When she was about twenty yards away, one of the bigger men raised his hand, indicating she should stop. It was tough to see him well, backlit as he was by the tubelights, but she could see enough of his silhouette to get the gist. She held her place.

"Can I help you, miss?"

Cass suddenly wished she'd asked jCharles for a little more info. Every chem scene had its own nuances, its own etiquette. Common greetings, sometimes elaborate introductions, even unspoken rules about distances to be maintained at all times. Play it wrong, and the other guys would know right off the bat you were an out-of-towner. That might just cost you an extra thirty or fifty percent. Worst case would cost you a whole lot more. On a whim, Cass reached up and nonchalantly unfastened her shirt a little lower.

"You boys keep it hot in here, don't you?"

"Are you looking for someone in particular?"

Dangerous question. In some circles, if you didn't have the right name, the deal would be off. In other circles, mentioning names was a quick way to get dusted off. She played cool.

"My boy from uptown sent me out for business, said he'd sent word."

"Why didn't 'your boy' come himself?"

"On account of his unexpected delay with the Bonefolder."

The mood suddenly shifted.

"Oh, you're McGann's little sister? Why didn't you say that, come on over here!"

Cass just smiled and walked to the group. As she approached, the light shifted enough that she could see the man who'd been talking to her. He was sporting the uniform of a Greenman, but it was ill-fitting. She saw him checking it out, and chuckled.

"Helps with the walk in," he said with a shrug.

"Long as you don't meet any greenmen, I guess."

He nodded, and led her to the others, who largely stood gawking. There was a small collapsible table set up in the middle of the lights. A case sat on the table. Behind it stood two young men she recognized from jCharles' pictures. Quick scan of the three other guards. One in red, one in black, one wearing a white coat with a backpack.

"This here's Tyke," said the guard, pointing to a tall and thin youth with long hair and a hawk-beak of a nose. "And that's his buddy Jantz." Jantz was shorter, but just as rail thin, with a shock of orange hair highlighted silver. Neither made eye contact. Both were staring at her chest.

"Boys!" the guard snapped, drawing Tyke's attention. He glanced up, wild-eyed, looking back and forth between the guard and Cass several times. Jantz lingered.

"Hi, yeah, sorry, sorry, little jumpy out here with all this material out here, you know, out here. We're big fans of your brother, Mr McGann I mean, big fans, I read all his stuff. Me and Jantz both do, all his stuff. Maybe, you know, maybe if we're all happy with this arrangement, you know, after we, you know, handle what we have to handle here, maybe sometime down the road we could actually meet him. If you're cool with that, I mean."

"I'm sure that'd be great, Tyke," she cooed, putting on the womanly charm. A little bit of skin seemed to have them all distracted. The sultry voice would probably have them completely mesmerized. Completely off guard. "He had nice things to say about you already."

Tyke let out something halfway between a giggle and a snort. A thin thread of phlegm flipped itself over his bottom lip and dangled there a moment before he wiped it away. Jantz lowered his head and stared at the table. Then slowly slid his eyes back up to Cass's cleavage.

"My understanding is that you've received the half up front?"

"That's right, and you can check the case if you want," he said, as he swiped a fingertip across a chrome strip. A mechanism hissed and the case unsealed itself. "It's all there, forty-five hundred, cut in stacks. We went ahead and cut 'em in stacks for you so, you know, so when you, you know, when you sell 'em off or whatever, they're easier for you to move, for when you sell 'em. That's a little extra service we wanted to provide to you on account of Mr McGann. For when you sell 'em."

"Well, I appreciate that Tyke. I'm sure Mr McGann will too."

"And you've got the money, right? In Hard?"

"Of course." She slung the pack onto the table. "Case is mine to take?"

"Sure, that's fine. Sorry to make you lug it all the way down here, that much Hard. But you know, this was kind of a hurry up kind of thing, and we don't usually work in this kind of, you know, arrangement, and so we're sorry, we would've rather done it some other way that was better for your brother, you know and you, but this was all we could work out to handle, you know, on such short notice, with that much, you know, that much q."

"It's really not a problem, Tyke. I know it's a lot of pressure on you guys."

A momentary cube of light flashed at the eastern entrance of hangar, someone entering quickly. Once the door clanged shut again, it was impossible to see who it was approaching, with the light from the tubelighting in her face.

"Don't worry that's just our moneyman. Like an accountant, you know, just to make sure we're all on the square and everything. He's with us, don't worry, he's one of ours. He's our moneyman."

A prickle of electricity raced along Cass's spine. That made seven. No matter how well things were going, seven to one was bad odds.

"I'm not sure what kind of trouble I could've caused you, ma'am," Three answered. "Just rolled into town yesterday, and haven't done anything untoward to anyone since I got here."

The Bonefolder sipped her beverage again, a dainty procedure borne of long years of practice and some kind of homage to traditions long dead. She replaced her cup on the table, adjusted it slightly so the handle was pointing exactly ninety-degrees to her right.

"This may be true. But we fear the offense came before you 'rolled into town', as you so *eloquently* put it."

Three could feel the tension pouring off jCharles. Without a doubt, he was already running through the scenarios of who to drop first when it all went down.

"Ma'am, I hope you'll forgive me, but I've had a long few weeks. If I've done you some wrong, you're gonna have to come right out and tell me."

She looked at him with disappointment, clearly affronted by his crass disregard for her preferred manner of speech. The Bonefolder took another sip of her beverage. Three already recognized the routine. Same quantity in every sip. Raise the cup. Sip. Pause. A long blink. Lower the cup. Adjust. Handle ninety-degrees to the right.

"A few days ago, Mr Walker, several of our business associates went looking to procure certain commodities that are at times in demand here within Greenstone. Four associates departed. Only one of those associates returned, Mr Walker, and he was notably less well than he had been when he first departed. His ankle snapped cleanly in two. Jaw dislocated. Only partial memories of the events which led to the unfortunate state in which we found him."

The image flashed through Three's mind immediately. The slavers. He'd told Cass he might not have killed all of them. Apparently he was right. Small comfort.

"It seems he spent the night in a culvert, wedged inside a drain pipe, Mr Walker, after having crawled there on his elbows, he says. Apparently, he had the less than desirable experience of observing the Weir as they savaged the corpses of his companions and then dragged them away. We fear he has been somewhat changed."

"Ma'am, I'm sorry for your loss, but I gave those men the only thing I had to offer 'em. I didn't know they were yours."

"Would it have mattered if you had, Mr Walker?"

"No ma'am, I reckon not."

"As we suspected," she replied. She pressed her lips together so that they disappeared into a perfectly flat, horizontal line. Cup up. Sip. Pause. Blink. Cup down. Adjust. "Under normal circumstances, we fear we would have no choice but to make an example of you. Greenstone is a challenging place for a woman of any standing, let alone for one of our particular age, you see."

Close to go time. Three casually surveyed the bartender. He was cleaning a glass, but watching intently. The Big One stood statue-still behind Bonefolder, hands behind his back. The rest arrayed in a half-circle that nearly enclosed Three and jCharles. Four to one. And the Bonefolder. Three didn't know how she'd earned that name, and he didn't want to find out.

"So what's the procedure here? I assume you want some kind of restitution, else I'd be swinging from a post already."

"Oh, isn't it a sharp one?" she said. "We understand you desire use of our train that you may travel to Morningside. Is this accurate?"

"It is."

"It is to your great fortune, then, that we have need of a courier for just that very destination. A messenger."

"So I hop on your train, deliver your message, and we're square?"

"We require a message be delivered to the governor of that province. A man by name of Underdown."

Under the table, jCharles spread his fingers wide, stretching them, then relaxed them into his lap. He bowed his head slightly, let his eyelids droop. Ready. On Three's move, Twitch would unleash.

"And the message?"

"The message is his death. After we receive confirmation, we will allow your woman and child to join you."

An icy shock went through Three, and he saw jCharles' eyelids flutter. How did she know about Cass and Wren?

Three forced himself still. Calm. Cool. Controlled.

"Ma'am, I'm afraid that doesn't work."

"Mr Walker, by now we have your woman and child in our custody. Your decisions are reduced only to this: deliver our message to Governor Underdown of Morningside, or die. We do not care, but recompense must be made. Your death plus the woman and the boy are calculated a fair exchange. The sum is equal to the cost of the zeroing of Underdown. This is business. What is your decision?"

The electric feeling didn't subside as the man approached from the hazy darkness. There was a shift in the crowd, as well. Cass felt the ring tighten ever so subtly.

"Our moneyman," Tyke continued. "Just taking care of the money, and we should all be on our way, just like that. I hope you'll tell your brother what good business partners we are, how well we held up our deal, and how eager we are to serve. We're fans of his, we read all his stuff, me and Jantz."

The man finally reached the perimeter of the lights, and Cass recognized him instantly. The limping man from before. But more than that, she saw it now, all of it. The man she'd seen in the Samurai McGann. The one with the familiar eyes. She'd seen him even before that, out in the open. He'd been wearing a mask over his mouth then, when Three had broken his leg and knocked him to the ground like a dead man. Not dead after all.

Cass stepped back involuntarily, and felt the fake greenman close behind her. Seven to one. Very bad odds.

Tyke changed his tone immediately, apologetic now.

"We didn't have nothing to do with it, I swear. You tell Mr McGann we didn't have nothing to do with it, we wanted the deal just like we said, just like we said, and we didn't want to have nothing to do with the Bonefolder!"

Hands gripped her upper arms tightly, surprising in their strength. The pressure applying so smoothly, so steadily. The uniform wasn't the only thing fake about the greenman. Servorganical arms, at least. They gripped with steel certainty.

The Limper approached, got right in her face with a damaged smile, and without a word he slapped her, hard. When she looked back, he spit on her mouth.

"Easy", the fake greenman said. "Bonefolder doesn't want her damaged."

"She said alive. Didn't say nothin' about damaged."

The Limper grabbed her shirt at the top and ripped it wide open. Seven to one was bad odds.

"There is no decision," Three said, quick to grab Twitch's arm under the table. "The woman and boy are yours if you want 'em. But I'm not going to handle Underdown. Killing a governor's not my idea of repayment. So look, you take the woman, you take the boy, what's that leave between us? A few thousand?"

The Bonefolder hitched, the slightest hint that something had taken her by surprise.

"These terms are unacceptable."

Three knew jCharles was straining with all he had not to open up on the crowd and see how far he could get before they cut him down. If they were going after Wren, that meant they were going after Mol. And the thought of that seared Three to the core. He could only imagine what Twitch was feeling.

"Then forget it. Keep the woman and the boy, and we don't bother with the train. We'll call it even." Three stood just quickly enough to make everyone flinch. He snatched jCharles' bittertonic and downed it.

Four to one, plus the Bonefolder. Ranges were all wrong. One shot for the bartender to open, and after that, it was all close work. Had to assume everyone was packing hate of one form or another. Even at his most desperate, Three had never tried something so obviously guaranteed to end with his death. Why had Twitch come? Even if they managed to clean house, there was no way they'd make it out of the building alive. And then what would happen to Mol? And to Wren? Where was Cass? What were they doing to her?

"Come on, Twitch, we're done talkin'."

jCharles stood, slowly, smoothly, all eyes on him. And then, Three did the most dangerous thing he could possibly think of.

He turned his back and walked out the front door.

It was obvious to Cass what was going down. The Bonefolder had arranged for them to be separated. For whatever reason, the Limper was here to handle Cass. She could only assume that meant Three and jCharles were in the heat. And the thought flashed: what if they'd sent someone for Wren? The fake greenman's fingers were beginning to dig into her flesh. The Limper obviously had plans for her body. She made plans of her own.

"Wait, stop, listen," she said, suddenly frightened, shrinking back into her captor. "Take the quint, take the money, I don't care, take it all."

"Too late for that, missy," said the Limper. "Bonefolder says I gets to have you, so that makes you mine."

"You can have me," Cass answered. She pulled her shirt fully open, letting it fall down her shoulders, her thin compression top the last line of defense. "Take me, take me, just leave my son alone."

She stepped toward the Limper, felt the greenman's grip loosen as she went docile. Cass reached up and slid her garment down, baring her breasts.

"It's OK, take me," she whispered. The Limper stepped forward, mouth hanging open, hand raised.

She boosted.

They made it out of the building, and picked up the pace to cross the street, both walking as if slightly drunk, hoping any first shots would miss. Across the street, alley twist, another alley twist, and they broke into a full run.

"What was that?!" jCharles shouted.

"We gotta get back to Mol first! Back to Mol and take it from there!"

As they punished the pavement with heavy footfalls, fast as they could deliver them, they crashed through the increasing crowds, knocking people aside and to the ground. Three's heart pounded with icy fire at the thought of Mol confronted by Bonefolder's thugs. She would never back down to them. She would do anything to stop them from taking Wren, and that thought, that knowledge, terrified Three.

They'd get to Mol first, find Wren. They were priority. After that, they'd find Cass. If she was alive.

She waited in stillness, as his hand approached. Fingers flexed, shaking in anticipation. The final half-inch. So close she could feel the heat off his palm.

He never touched her.

Cass flashed with her palm, drove it upwards into the Limper's nose, felt the bone shatter and the cartilage slide back and in. The Limper choked and burbled a blood-filled cry as he stumbled back, lost his footing, and went crashing into the table. She covered herself, and surveyed the scene. With the quint racing in her bloodstream, everything seemed to be taking twice as long to fall. Cass felt faster than ever. The Limper's head was just above the table, his neck hard against its edge. Cass stomped forward, snapping his neck in an instant, and then reversed the kick and folded the knee of the fake greenman behind her. She spun as he fell, saw his head at her waist level, and struck down on the side of his face with her open palm, ensuring his impact with the planet would finish the job.

As she pulled the jittergun from her coat, she saw with crystal clarity the guard in red drawing a black device from his belt. Two gleaming points shone from the tip, and she recognized it instantly as a stunner. She brought the jittergun to bear on the security man in black across the table. Just as the red guard fired, Cass squeezed the trigger on the jitter, felt it hum in her hand, saw the guard in black's chest explode in red puffs from the impact of dozens of micro flechettes. In the same instant, she twisted, snatched the stunner's dart-like probes between two fingers. Whipped them back at the red guard. Tips buried in his neck, the live current of his own weapon knocked him writhing to the floor.

Cass leapt to the table, and off again, plunging from eight feet in the air down onto the last guard, who seemed frozen in fear. Her impact dropped him to the concrete, crushing the air from his lungs and knocking him out cold. Without losing momentum, she rolled to her back and let loose with the jitter, shredding Jantz's left calf. Before he'd finished collapsing, Cass was up and had Tyke's head on the table, with the jittergun tight against his temple.

He was crying.

"Bonefolder! The Bonefolder, we didn't want none of this, you take it you take it I'm sorry, we love your brother, man we love him!"

Jantz was screaming on the floor like a hysterical woman. Cass had to take a second, let the bloodlust lose its edge. She shouldn't have done that to Jantz. It was payback for staring at her, she knew, and she knew it was wrong. Tyke was quivering under her grasp.

"Take all of it, keep the money, we don't want it. Please, just take it and go!"

"Maybe you find yourself a new line of work, alright, Tyke?"

"Yeah, alright, definitely, yeah."

Cass left the pistol pressed against his temple while she resealed the case. She threw the money pack back over her shoulder, and picked up the quint. She nudged the shrieking Jantz with her foot.

"Hey, Jantz. I'm sorry, kid. Wrap it up tight, you'll be OK." She tapped Tyke on the head with the jittergun, and then slid it into her pocket. "You stay clear of the Bonefolder."

Cass walked to the eastern entrance, and didn't look back. Once she'd crossed through the outer edge of Downtown, she turned down a narrow alley, dropped to a knee, and vomited.

Three had led for most of the way back, but Twitch had covered the last hundred meters faster than Three had ever seen anyone move. He crashed through the front door of the Samurai McGann, and Three was only a few steps behind.

"Mol!" he shouted, "Where's Mol!"

The bartender leapt over the bar and intercepted him before he could get too far, grabbed him by the shoulders, held him fast.

"Twitch!" the bartender tried to get his attention. "Twitch!"

"Mol! Mol, baby, where are you?"

"Twitch, hold on now, hold on!" said the bartender, but jCharles wasn't having any of it. He lifted the man bodily and threw him into the bar, and raced towards the stairs.

Three followed closely behind, certain his heart had stopped in his chest. Halfway up the stairs the door swung open, and Mol stood there looking terrified. jCharles swept her up in his arms so violently, they both nearly toppled into the room.

"Twitch?! Twitch, what happened, are you alright?"

"Mol, baby, are you OK? Where's the kid?"

She was pale with fright, confused.

"Wren? Wren's right here. Wren, come here, sweetheart."

Wren poked his head out from the back room, wild-eyed and clearly confused.

"Twitch, calm down, what is going on?"

Three stood at the door, scanning the apartment. No signs of a struggle. Everything seemed as they'd left it.

A commotion sounded on the stairwell, and without hesitation, Three drew and was on target in less than a blink. The poor bartender nearly fell back down the stairs.

"Nimble! What's going on!?" jCharles yelled from the top of the stairs.

Nimble, the bartender, crept up the stairs almost apologetically. "That's what I try'a tell ya, Twitch. Got some down here for you see."

Three reholstered, straightened up. jCharles went back and hugged Mol.

"You sure you're OK, baby?"

"We're fine. We're completely fine. What happened, Twitch?"

He kissed her hard on the mouth, then on the forehead, then left her in the room. Nimble led them back downstairs, down the length of the bar, and around the corner to a large end booth. Two rough-looking gentlemen sat shoulder-to-shoulder next to each other, surrounded by seven much rougher-looking gentlemen. Three recognized the seven as regulars.

"These ones here," said Nimble, wagging a finger at the two men pressed in the middle of the booth. "Come run in ask about Miss Mol, say the Bonefolder needs talk to her. I tell 'em get faffed."

"Faff off, ye!" one of the regulars shouted, for no apparent reason.

"And 'ems start get rowdy. Actin' for show, y'know. And ol' Nimble say nay go round here, no sir." He looked at the two men for emphasis. "NAY. GO. ROUND HERE."

Twitch let out a laugh then, a genuine laugh of relief and joy. He slapped Nimble hard on the back, leaned his forehead into his bartender's in some version of a hug. Started handing out backpats to the regular seven.

"Well thank you, Nimble. This is why I let you run the place. You take better care of it than I do. Open the bar up for everybody."

"And about 'em?"

Twitch thought about it for about two seconds.

"Strip 'em. Tie their arms around each other. Let 'em walk back to Bonefolder."

"Aright then."

"Make sure they're facing each other. And tie 'em tight."

"A course, sir."

Twitch led Three back to the main room, where the bar seemed to be carrying on as usual.

"Good people, Twitch."

"You gotta have a few, Three. What now?"

"I gotta go find my girl."

"Let me tell Mol–"

"No, you stay."

"We're not doing this again, Three."

"Good reason this time. They might try again, I'd feel better if you stayed. I'll move faster without you."

"Alright, I'll buy that this time. But if they've got her, don't you go in there on your own. You come right back here, and we'll get my boys up a right proper army, you understand?"

"Fine. I'm gone."

"Godspeed, brother."

Three turned and strode to the door, half a catastrophe averted, the other half unknown. He reached for the door, and it flew open, catching him in the chin and forehead. He saw stars.

And then, he saw her.

Cass. Alive and well. Carrying a case and a backpack.

He grabbed her and pulled her in, holding her as tight as he could, wishing he could bring her even closer.

"Three?"

He pulled away, looked her over. "Are you alright, Cass? Did you have any trouble?"

She looked thoughtful for a moment, shook her head.

"No. No trouble. You?"

"Maybe."

"Is Wren OK?"

"Yeah, he's upstairs. You get everything you need?"

"Yeah, we're good."

"Good. Cause we're gonna have to move again. Now."

"Like, right now?"

Three nodded. Brain already racing to do the calculations. They were going to have to disappear, fast. Train was out, no doubt about that. Only a few hours of daylight left. Not enough to go far. But there was no way they could stay in Greenstone now.

And what about Mol and Twitch?

"Come on," Three said. "Let's get upstairs. We gotta get this sorted out."

He slipped his hand along the small of Cass's back, and steered her through the bar, up the stairs, into the apartment. And as he watched Cass drop to a knee and Wren run into her arms, Three knew, and let himself know, that he loved them both in a way he'd never thought possible.

# TWENTY-ONE

The apartment was a whirlwind; explanations colliding with improvised plans and haphazard packing. Mol was busy in the kitchen, preparing some fragrant dish that Cass thought couldn't possibly be finished before they had to leave.

"You just left? They just let you walk right out the front door?" Cass demanded.

jCharles threw a bundle of chemlights across the room to Three, and chuckled. "Shoulda seen the look on that old crow's face when you turned around. I think she got stuck trying to calculate the odds of you actually doing what you were doing."

"Any more time we spent in there was time we weren't usin' to get to you. The drop? They let you keep the money for charity?"

"It was recommended I take both."

"Recommended? You still got any of that goo?" Three asked Twitch, mid-sentence, then switched back. "This is serious Cass, how many were there, how many did you leave, and in what state?"

She flipped through the high-def images in her mind, like a reel of still frames, perfectly preserved. Even the pattern the blood-spit spray made out of the Limper's mouth when his head hit the table.

"Seven total. Two dead, one stunned, two unconscious, one crying, one screaming."

jCharles shot her a concerned look.

"Tyke crying, Jantz the screamer. I took a little meat out of his leg, but he'll be fine. They're both alright. Big fans of yours, too, by the way."

He nodded, but didn't smile. "I'd heard. Here," he threw three packets from the storage room over to Three. "Probably tastes terrible by now, but it should still get you there. Four ounces, three times a day." Then back to Cass. "They set you up?"

Cass shook her head. "I think the Bonefolder got to them after you'd made the deal. Saw an opportunity."

"Opportunity's her game."

"The ones you left unconscious?" said Three.

"One was Tyke's friend, I'd guess. About the same age, had a backpack. When it all went down, he just stood there with his mouth hanging open. The other, not sure. Servorganic arms at least. Not sure if he was Tyke's hired man, or Bonefolder's."

"Big guy? Fake greenman outfit?" jCharles asked.

"That's the one."

"Unconscious, or dead?"

"Not sure, but I'd have to guess unconscious. I dropped him pretty hard, but I didn't stop to check."

jCharles flicked a look to Three.

"Problem?" Three said.

"Bonefolder's nephew. She lets him handle the easy jobs. Might've been kinder to put him down."

"Mama?"

The quiet voice captured the chaos, stole the energy from the room.

"Yeah, sweetheart?" Wren stood next to the couch, looking tiny, lost. Verge of tears.

"I don't think I can leave again."

Cass crossed to him, sat on the couch, pulled him close.

"Baby, what's the matter?"

The others held still, just observed, afraid to disturb the delicate balance of the moment. Wren just shook his head.

"Are you tired?"

"No," he answered, quietly.

"Did you take a nap while I was gone?"

"No."

"Maybe you should lie down for a–"

"No!" he barked, with the sharpest tone Cass had ever heard from him. She slid back involuntarily. "I don't wanna lie down, I don't wanna a nap! I wanna stay here! I don't want to leave!"

And then he broke into sobs, deep, soul-shaking sobs, and Cass wrapped her arms around him, and he stood there with his arms at his sides, just weeping. Cass saw Mol, realized she'd come from the kitchen, hovering. Wanting to help, not wanting to interfere. Cass caught her eye and motioned to the back room, and Mol nodded.

Cass gently lifted Wren up, and laid his head on her shoulder as he let it all out, weeks of terror and confusion and exhaustion. She took him to the back room and as she was closing the door, she saw Mol there, watching them the whole way, a sad look in her eye. Compassion. Longing. Cass motioned to her, for her to join them. At first, Mol refused, but jCharles nudged her, and she finally relented; joined the mother and child in the room. They sat on the bed together, Cass on one side, Mol on the other, with Wren tucked between. And they let him cry and cry, and would let him continue until he had no more tears to give.

The kid had stopped squalling almost an hour ago, and Three was anxious to get moving. They were losing daylight by the minute, and he feared that once the Bonefolder got word she had neither the woman nor the child, a plan B was bound to come knocking.

"Hey." jCharles was sitting in his oversized chair drinking a cold beverage of questionably high chemical properties.

"Yeah?"

"We got you all loaded up?"

"Yeah."

jCharles took a pull, let it settle in his mouth. He swallowed, and then exhaled, mouth open, a vaporous sigh.

"So. Where do we go?"

"You know."

jCharles shook his head. "There's got to be something else. Something we've missed."

"*Wanting* to have missed something doesn't mean you have. Bad options aren't so 'bad', when they're 'only'."

"I'll go with you to the steam tunnels..." said jCharles, trailing off.

"You've done too much already, Twitch. The Bonefolder's gonna come looking for you, and you can't say I'm not to blame for this one."

jCharles made a dismissive noise and waved his hand. "Bonefolder's got her friends and turf, but there's a reason she doesn't do business downstairs. You don't worry about ol' jCharles."

"She won't come after you for this?"

"She might have some power. But me? Me, I have *influence*."

"This is serious, Twitch, I need to know."

jCharles sat forward, suddenly serious. "She moves on me, the networks she uses to run all her gigs suddenly disappear. In fact, just planning a move on me would guarantee I know about it ahead of time. So, no. No, she'll sit over in her little palace sipping her little drink, and she'll go looking for some other way to keep those books balanced.

"But don't you let her people catch you in town. She snags you and whisks you off, no way I'll be able to track you down before she's done with her work."

"Well, I appreciate it, Twitch. You're a good man. And a better friend."

"Don't make it a goodbye."

"'Fraid it's gotta be."

jCharles stood, and the men embraced awkwardly, but sincerely.

"I can come as far as the steam tunnels. Maybe even a little further out."

jCharles was grim, but there was a paleness at the corners of his lips, extra clicks in his words that signaled a dry mouth. Even the bravest men feel fear.

"No, Twitch. Stay here, with Mol. Stay here, and you love her with all you got."

jCharles nodded. And then, there seemed to be no more words. Three gave a little nod. Turned to his loaded pack. Checked his harness, his pistol, his blade. Everything was ready to go. Whenever it was time.

"Mol's gonna want you to get one last good meal in, you know."

"I know."

"Hurt her feelings if you don't let her."

"I know."

Three glanced out through the window, but couldn't get a good gauge on the sun, because of the random buildings stacked in the way.

"Hey, what time you got?"

jCharles accessed the global. "14:31 GST."

"Sundown?"

"18:02."

About that time, the door to the back room open, and Wren stepped out, with Mol close behind, her delicate hands on his shoulders. He looked a little embarrassed, as children often do after a good cry. Mol nudged him forward.

"Twitch, Wren had something he'd like to ask you."

Wren took a timid step forward, and Three saw now he had a book in his hand. The one Mol had been reading to him earlier.

"Mr jCharles, sir. Would you be interested in trading this book, for this?" He stretched out his other hand. Three recognized the sphere that filled that tiny palm. The mil-spec strobe he'd picked up back at the Vault.

jCharles bent over, and made a good show of examining both pieces, as if comparing quality. He stood, and thought. Took a swig on his beverage. Cass came out of the back room as the appraisal continued. Then at last, he bent low again.

"I'm sorry, young master Wren. Can't do it."

Wren was obviously disappointed, but he took it like a professional. "OK, thank you for considering it."

Wren moved to put the book back on the shelf, even in the right location, but jCharles interrupted him.

"I said I wasn't interested in trading, young sir. You can't trade for a gift."

Wren turned back, obviously hopeful, but not quite understanding.

"You go ahead and take it, sweetheart," Mol said. "It's yours. We want you to have it."

"Really?"

"Really."

Without reservation, Wren wrapped himself around Mol's waist, nerve-rig and all, and squeezed, and smiled. "Oh, thank you so much."

And to everyone's great surprise, he rushed right over to jCharles and hugged his leg just as ferociously. "Thank you so much, Mr jCharles."

"Easy kid, you break my leg off, I might just take it back."

Mol kissed Wren on the head as she passed him, and made her way to the kitchen. Whatever it was she'd prepared smelled delicious, and was apparently moments away from completion.

"You guys can stay for another twenty minutes, right? If you eat fast?"

Three surveyed the scene. Wren, so hopeful, Cass trying to look ambivalent, but clearly hoping for a good last meal. jCharles with his head inclined that one way he did it to let you know you weren't really being given a choice.

"Yeah, alright. But let's be quick about it."

They all bustled together then, setting the food out, finding enough chairs to fit around the tiny table. And once everything was set, Mol stood at the head of the table, and encouraged everyone to hold hands. The only one comfortable with the idea besides Mol was jCharles, but they figured it out.

Mol bowed her head and said, "Sweet Lord, we thank you for all your many goodnesses to us, and we're mindful of all the blessing you've bestowed upon us with these friends, old and new, and we ask your hand be upon them as they go out, and we ask you bring 'em right back to us again. Amen."

Then she set to serving up something from a large pot that was reddish-brown, and thick, and almost smelled like it had real onions in it. Real, out-of-the-ground onions, not the vat-grown ones that tasted like some chemical engineer's idea of how an onion *should* taste.

"It's not much, I know, but Twitch found an old onion bulb long ago, and believe it or not, he managed to nurse that thing back to health enough to pop us out an onion every now and again. I thought this was a special enough occasion to break out the good stuff."

"You ever had a real onion before, Wren?" jCharles asked.

"No, sir. I didn't know they grew…" he trailed off, suddenly distracted.

"Well, you are in for a real treat, then, buddy."

Wren didn't respond. He was staring at the wall, at the window, at nothing.

"Wren," Cass said, but she already knew. His eyes went wide.

"Leave, we have to leave!" He was up out of his chair, backing towards the wall.

Three reacted instantly, pouncing to his gear, swinging on the harness, the pistol, the blade, the coat, the pack, like a whirlwind. He was fastening his coat while Cass was still moving to grab her pack.

"What's going on?" Mol asked, up, half-crouched out of her chair.

"Something bad," Three answered. "We gotta go, Mol. Thanks, as always, for everything."

He didn't approach her, so she came to him, and wrapped her arms around him. Tight.

"You be careful out there. And you come back," she said. Then lowered her voice. "You come back to me, Three. I mean it." And kissed his ear as she drew away.

"Wren, come on baby," Cass called to him, and he skittered to her, accepted his coat and pack. Eyes searching, wired.

"Twitch," Three said.

"Yeah."

Cass and Mol embraced, warmly, like sisters at parting.

"I left something for you in the storage room. It's nothing really, just a little thanks. We can't ever repay you."

"Mama."

"OK. Yeah, we're going."

"You sure you know the way?" jCharles asked.

"Yeah got it."

"Travel safe. Stop by on your way back through, let us know you got it sorted."

Three made eye contact with jCharles, and in their own way, they said their goodbyes. And with that, Three, Cass, and Wren, were once more on their way.

With the afternoon sun draining from yellow to golden, the trio set a quick pace, and stayed huddled together.

"Stay tight to me, keep your eyes open. They might make another try at us."

"What about the greenmen?"

"Can't trust 'em now, either."

They pushed hard, walking as fast as they could without running, less concerned about attracting attention than they were about getting out. Their path led them in the direction of Downtown, but veered off at an angle that eventually led them to some sort of outdated, non-functional industrial sector that seemed to be nothing but pipes for the sake of pipes. The place was completely deserted, and smelled strongly of human waste.

"Steam tunnels," Three said, as if that explained it.

"What are they for?" Wren asked.

"Some busted geothermal system. Right now, they're for getting out."

Three scoured various endcaps, and found one about the size of an adult at full crouch.

"Let me know if you see anyone around."

While the others kept watch, he twirled the caps in three specific areas, and then stepped back. There was a click, and a whine, and the endcap slowly swung to a side. Before it was even fully open, Three shoved his pack in first.

"We're going in there?"

"All the way," Three answered, as he pushed his way in. Beyond the pool of light that fell within the first six inches of the pipe, it was like looking into a starless outer space. A depthless dark, so complete its end could be an inch from your face, or a thousand miles distant.

"Come on, we don't want anyone seeing us headed in here."

Cass helped Wren up, noticed his frantic eyes. Remembered the last time he'd crawled in a dark tunnel and ended up separated from his mother and held captive.

"It's alright, baby, we're with you the whole time. Three in front, me in back. We'll make sure you're fine."

Wren didn't respond, but he climbed in as well, pushing his pack ahead of him as Three had done. Cass was the last one in. The pipe wasn't quite high enough for her to move on all fours properly. After the first few meters, she discovered if she lay on top of her pack, she could pull both the bag and herself along at the same time, instead of in two stages.

Thankfully, after a few minutes in the impossible dark, a yellow-green light flared. Three lit a chemlight and tied it to the back of his coat. As they crawled for what seemed like hours, it never occurred to Cass that the chemlight didn't shine forward, but backwards. It was for their benefit only.

They continued in silence of voice, escorted by the eerie echoes of their scraping progress down the "tunnel". The air was coolly damp, reminiscent of the storm drain tunnels that Three had first led them to. Cass hoped Wren wasn't too cold, but dared not ask for fear of the cacophony it would create.

Then, suddenly, out of nowhere, Three spoke.

"This is it."

There were movements, and grindings, and a muffled curse, and then a thin ring of light, which grew, and grew into a tiny sun all of its own. And as Cass's eyes adjusted, she saw the exit. Three pushed out first, then turned and pulled Wren out with him, and set him by his side. He pulled Cass's pack out, and then held out his hand and steadied her as she slipped out of the pipe.

Then the three stood together on a little shelf of soft gray dust, and the weight of the history of a world gone wrong settled on them with all the gravity and terrible awe of a cataclysm. There, before them, lay the Strand.

Another meeting had been hastily arranged, shortly after the disappearance of the man some called Three, but that the Bonefolder insisted upon referring to as "Mr Walker". No sign of the woman or child he had been travelling with either. It was in fact, a work of chance that this meeting had come together at all, that the man standing in front of the Bonefolder at this very moment had just happened to overhear a tale that led him to this place. A tale of a particular chemdrop gone awry. A tale of a woman, and perhaps a child. And it was in this meeting that this gentleman fully intended to have his way.

The Bonefolder sat in her usual place, with her usual steaming cup of brown fluid. The bartender leaned against his bar nearby, carefully intent. Poised for action, it seemed. The big bodyguard behind the Bonefolder stood as one might expect a butler to do so. However, this particular big bodyguard had all the classic signs of a juicer, and it would be foolish to assume the vast graft-musculature on his frame was purely for show. Two lazy gun hands flanked the Bonefolder, trying to look important, but mostly revealing themselves to be poor maintainers of their weaponry and thus, likely, undisciplined in the practice of their craft.

The final gun hand, however, strutted about as though he was the spokesman for the group, broadcasting his opinions on how business should be undertaken, particularly on account of what had befallen several of his associates in a previous matter.

"Sent 'em tied up NAKED. My pardon, ma'am, but it's true, that's what they did, and it's not right. It's not right to shame good men for trying to uphold some sense of honor and justice in this world.

"And then this fella here. Walking in like he's some kind of prince with all his finery, and his entourage, thinking he's going to presume upon our charity to see him through to his destination. Well it just makes me mad, ma'am, to see disrespectful youth speak to you in that manner."

The Bonefolder sipped her tea, as per usual. Up. Sip. Blink. Hold. Down. Adjust.

"I'm sayin' we're done with these types. This isn't a shuttle service we're runnin' here, this is a privately-owned transit system now, no matter what the old laws say. The Bonefolder saw to it that the line got back to running, and it's hers to do with as she sees fit. And coming in here with that attitude and that smile, like you're going to charm something from us? From *her*? Son, I tell you what I know, if you don't start showing some respect in here, I'll take you out in the street myself and let your friends learn a real good lesson in manners at your expense."

"Thank you, Domino, we do appreciate your passion and concern, if not your manner of speech."

"Yes, ma'am. I just don't like 'em, ma'am."

"Yes, thank you, child Domino," she said with a gentleness that felt somehow firm as a slap. She adjusted herself upon her chair, and addressed the visitor. "We're afraid this Mr Walker has caused some consternation amongst some of our associates. We cannot guarantee that Mr Walker and his friends will in fact go to Morningside. As long as you understand that our agreement is based solely upon transportation to the destination, with no guarantee whatsoever that Mr Walker will be found there, we believe we can afford you and your colleagues passage by way of our train. Under certain, highly profitable business arrangements."

"Certainly, of course," Asher said, leaning forward to rest his hands on the back of the chair he'd been offered. He let his eyes casually sweep the upstairs balconies. No surprises there. Good. Had to be sure, since he was the only one they'd let inside. "I understand that you'd like to maximize your potential upside with this arrangement. I'm just not certain that the quoted price is optimal."

The loudmouth started up again. "Whatever price that gets you on *our* train is optimal, partner. Every time she goes out, that's a risk on us. And I haven't heard nothin' yet out of your mouth that says what you can do for us."

Asher scanned the room with his easy smile. "You know, you're right, sir. I'm sorry, I have been rude. My apologies." He bowed just the right amount to seem gracious, and not at all condescending. "Please allow me to elaborate on exactly what is that I can do for you."

Asher smiled warmly. Waited. The Bonefolder smiled slightly. He watched her intently. Smile. Wait. She raised her tea cup. Took a sip. Her eyes closed.

And Asher revealed himself, awesome and terrible. The bartender was first, as Asher stretched out across the electromagnetic mist and seized him through the cortex, driving a single command through his nervous system like an iron spike.

*Cease*.

Like a river suddenly dammed, the bartender's brain simply stopped responding and left him a body with no mind.

The Big One was the easiest. Asher hacked his adrenals, and dumped them all at once while activating the man's chem stores. There was a dull thump inside the Big One as his heart exploded.

The two gunmen at the table got a generic treatment, deserved for their laziness. Asher pierced their minds and locked their muscles into one-hundred percent contraction, simultaneously cutting off their breathing, their heartbeats, and any chance either of them had to scream.

And finally, the mouthy gun hand. Asher penetrated the man's mind and crackled its own signals across it, throwing the gun hand into a very specific seizure: one which would guarantee he would choke to death on his own tongue.

The Bonefolder opened her eyes from her long blink. Set the cup on the table. Adjusted the handle. Oblivious that the men who were only now beginning to fall around her were already dead.

# TWENTY-TWO

The Strand.

Of course Cass had heard of it, seen scans of it, even projected to it once. But there at its very edge, confronted by the sheer, inexorable scale of it all... she found herself sitting without being able to recall ever having sat. She didn't know how it had come to be known as the Strand, who had first named it so, but seeing it now in person made it seem there was no other name it could be called. It was as if some great ocean of destruction had rolled its unyielding tide through the city and then, upon its terrible recession, left behind only a shoreline of concrete sand and crushed humanity.

Even Three stood silent, despite the urgent pace he'd set before. He stared out over the vast, broken plain with tears in his eyes. Wren moved to Three's side, and the man placed a hand on the boy's shoulder.

Cass scanned the horizon, its gray, fractured features rounded by wind and rain and time. It seemed endless. And impossible to cross. She understood now why Three had taken the risk of Greenstone and the Bonefolder. Without the train, the chances of making it to Morningside seemed farther away than ever before.

"We'll never make it," she heard herself say.

"It's not impossible," Three answered. "Difficult, but not impossible. I've done it before."

285

She glanced up at him. He was still surveying the terrain, but his eyes were clear now. Purposeful. Already he was looking for solutions. And, she hoped, finding them.

"Forty miles across, if you keep straight. Miss your mark, it can get a whole lot farther. I've heard of Runners who've made it through in under five hours. But I've heard of a lot more who don't make it through at all.

"Out there, there are no wayhouses. No maglevs. No functioning water systems. The Weir own the Strand, and there's no place to hide."

"Which part of that was supposed to be the good news?"

"Just want you to understand what we're about to do. If there's any good news, it's that the Weir don't much expect to find people in their stomping grounds. If we move quickly, keep quiet, and get lucky, we'll make it."

"I've never known you to trust much to luck," Cass said.

He turned and went down on a knee, facing them both. "They track you by your signal. That's what they see. In a way, it's what they smell. Everywhere you go, you leave a trail they can follow. And *will* follow."

Looking at Three there, kneeling by the edge of the Strand, it suddenly clicked for Cass. She'd come to suspect it based on fragments she'd picked up: Wren's comments about not being able to feel Three, about him not being real, the strange markings and scars on his back, the ease with which he seemed to be able to take life. Now she understood how he could walk the open, day or night.

"But they can't track you," she said. "Because you're disconnected."

It was punishment of the cruelest sort, usually reserved for repeat offenders or, as in Dagon's case, those deemed too dangerous to remain part of society. They called it *sanitizing*. Though, these days, the State wasn't necessarily the only one with the power to unplug someone. Not that there was much of a State left.

His eyes met hers; held steadily. He didn't seem surprised at all that she knew, or had figured it out. And she could see she was right. He shook his head slightly, but as was his way, he didn't elaborate. "We're losing daylight. We're gonna push for an hour. Then we're gonna find a place to hide."

She wondered again just how deep and dark this man's past really was. And she couldn't help but wonder now if all he'd done for them had really been for himself. Some kind of atonement for deeds he'd never mention, and she'd never imagine.

"Running low profile, like you are, is gonna help us. But one active pulse, they'll be on us. And we'll never shake 'em. So both of you lock it down from here on out. Don't try to gips a path, don't pim anyone, don't even check the time. We clear?"

Wren nodded. Cass stood, and gathered herself.

"We're clear."

Three gained his feet and looked at her for a long moment in a way that made her suddenly self-conscious. He placed a hand on the top of Wren's head, drew a deep breath and exhaled slowly. Then turned and faced the Strand.

"Stay close, stay quiet. And just maybe we'll slip through."

The bottom of the sun was just hovering above the horizon when Three found a place for them to stop. It couldn't have been more than an hour, but Cass was already exhausted. The dust of the Strand was like soft gray sand; fine, and shifting under foot. She couldn't face the idea of another thirty-something miles of that kind of travel. Wren was riding on Three's back, having been unable to keep the pace that Three demanded. But now Three let Wren slide down off his back, and waited for Cass to catch up the few steps.

When she approached, he leaned close, spoke in low tones.

"We'll stop here for the night."

There were a few burned out and collapsed structures, none more than nine feet tall. One in particular, though, actually had two walls standing and a third fallen over the top that almost made something like a shelter.

"You don't want to push on a little further?" she asked. "See if there's something a little more..." She trailed off, not being able to find the word.

Three shook his head.

"Better to dig in here. There *may* be something sturdier another mile in, but it won't do us any good if we're staring at it when they come."

Wordlessly, he went to work, and they spent the next twenty minutes tunneling a small nest for themselves back in the darkest corner of the shelter, and filling in holes where they could with debris. Cass suspected hiding would do little good out here. She eventually realized Three was going to so much trouble in an effort to give them an impression of safety, even if there was none to be had. By the time they'd finished working, they had a fully enclosed space with a narrow entrance. It would be a tight fit.

Three threw their packs down first, and then had Wren climb into the urban nest on top of them. Once Wren was inside, Three crouched at the entrance and reached inside, rustling Wren's hair.

"You get some sleep, Mister Wren. We've got a long walk ahead of us tomorrow, OK?"

"OK," Wren said. He nestled down as best he could atop the packs and lay on his side; curled, still, eyes open.

"Hey," Three said. Wren looked at him, moving only his eyes. "You got your knife in there?"

Wren didn't nod or take his eyes off Three. He gently rocked back just enough to show his tiny fist beneath his body, already clutching the grip of the blade Three had made for him. Three nodded, and Wren rolled back into his previous position, and stared at the wall.

"I'm gonna talk to your mama for a minute, alright?"

Wren just nodded. He blinked once, long and slow. Three stood and tugged Cass away from the entrance.

"How're you doing?" he asked.

Cass shrugged. "Tired. But I'm fine."

"You good to boost if you have to?"

She nodded. "I'm still running the first stack jCharles gave me. Still got a couple of shots left in it if I need them."

"You won't need 'em," he said, too quickly. "Just wanted to be sure you were set." He looked at her for a long moment, as if he had more to say. But then, he just added, "Alright. Let's get you in there."

He turned back towards the little shelter, but Cass stopped him with a question.

"Three, what'd you do?" she asked. He stopped. Just stood there for a moment. Still, the way only he could be, like he'd just turned to stone. Or had always been. "To get disconnected, I mean."

He turned slowly, with a grim look. Wrestled. With the confession, she assumed.

"Whatever it was, I can handle it. You can tell me."

"I know," he said. He stared at the ground for a long breath, then inhaled sharply through his nose. Held. Then looked up, and answered.

"To be *dis*connected, you gotta be *connected* in the first place." That took Cass by surprise. There was no way Three was old enough to have been born before they'd gone genetic, before connection had become inherited, like brown eyes, or high cheekbones.

"I... don't understand."

"You're not supposed to, Cass. No one's supposed to."

"What, both your parents were sanitized or something?"

"I don't know," he answered, stepping closer. "I don't know who my parents were." He looked to the ground, then away to the horizon. Another step closer. "But I'm not what you think."

"Then tell me what you are, Three. Tell me *who* you are."

He turned his shoulder to her then, leaned against the broken wall, slid down it until he was seated. And suddenly he looked desperately weary. After long moments of silence, Cass sat down next to him.

"Back… before," he started. Then, he raised a hand and swept it over the Strand. "*Before*. I was born into a very particular family. Raised for a very particular reason."

She sat in silence, sensing that Three was fighting himself. Wanting to tell a story, *his* story, one that he'd kept secret for perhaps as long as he'd been alive.

"I lied before," he said. "When I told you I had a sister. There was a girl, but she wasn't my sister. I loved her like one. At least, I loved her the way I'd guess you might love a sister. We grew up together, in the same House anyway."

He put a curious emphasis on the way he said *house*, as if it meant more than the building in which he'd grown up.

"We grew up together. We were the same. And they taught us, they trained us, to do certain things, to be certain things. When everyone in the world is connected… well, I guess there were uses for people like me. But then the world changed, Cass. And my House fell. And all those things we'd been trained to do didn't matter anymore. Not in the same way. And they didn't help me protect her. Not when I needed to most."

He went quiet after that, and still, and the sun continued to slip below the horizon. After a while, he broke the silence.

"How long do you have?"

Cass understood the question, wondered how long he'd been wanting to ask it.

"A few months, I'd guess. Give or take."

"Nothing to do?"

She shook her head. "It's the quint. A body can only run so hot for so long."

"Not even genework? Nerve replacement?"

"No. Believe me, I've looked. But no. When I went chemic, I knew what I was in for. But when you're fifteen, living to thirty seems like forever."

"That how you got hooked up with RushRuin? Pulling speedruns and security?"

Her turn now. It was only fair. She took a breath, and started in.

"It wasn't RushRuin when I got started. There was a man, and I was young and scared. He wasn't nice, but he was strong. And he liked me, so I let him."

She hadn't thought back to those early days in a long time. It seemed like someone else's life.

"Called himself Zenith," she said, with a scoff. All these years, it still sounded ridiculous. "Thought he was the 'true peak of man'. He put a crew together, and let me tag along as his showpiece, used me when it suited him. Wasn't too happy when I turned up pregnant."

"And this is the guy you're taking Wren to?" He sounded skeptical. Maybe a hint of shock, or anger.

"No, he wasn't Wren's father," she replied. Hesitated. But they were being honest now, and it somehow felt right to tell the whole story. "He was Asher's."

Three didn't respond, not verbally, but she could feel the realization sweep over him.

"Asher's your son," Three said. His tone even, controlled.

"Wren's brother," she added. "Well... half-brother."

He made no further comment, and Cass suddenly felt compelled to fill in the blanks. "Zenith's crew was pretty good in the small-time, back when we were running standard jobs. Sec/Net stuff mostly, identity spoofing sometimes. That's when I started dosing. Making myself useful, you know."

She didn't say it, but she couldn't forget the terrifying nights she'd withstood from Zenith, just to keep Asher safe.

"Eventually, we started getting attention from some big players, and Zenith brought in people like Jez, and Fedor and Kostya. They were fresh on the scene then, but they'd already dusted off some important people."

"And that's when you started the brain gigs?"

Cass shook her head. "Not until Wren's father showed up. He was light years ahead of everyone else. Not just in our crew, everyone. The whole scene. As far as he was concerned, Sec/Net was doing things the hard way. He'd figured out how to go straight to the source. Right into someone's head, find what you need, get back out.

"He was elegant, though. His way was to do the job so no one even knew he'd been there. Zenith hated him from day one, but he knew a moneymaker when he saw one." Cass paused. She hadn't really thought back to those times, not in a long while. Back to when she was young, and he swept in and changed her life. Old feelings stirred like autumn leaves rolling. "He was good. And he was a good man. That's when we went big time. RushRuin. After a couple of runs, Ran and Dagon came on board. The Mountain and the Grave. They were at the top of the game back then. Freelancers. Everybody wanted them, and they came to us."

"One big happy family."

"Until Wren."

"Not Zenith's. And he knew."

"Everybody did. Except the father."

"He left you there? With Zenith?"

"There was a… disagreement. He couldn't stay. I couldn't leave."

"So your new man walked. And Zenith did what?"

"Got what was coming. Finally got too rough with me one night. Dagon was there."

She grimaced at the image. The pain. The flood of relief. And regret. Three hadn't looked at her since she'd started the tale. He was busy studying the horizon. Only the top quarter of the sun remained. She could see behind his eyes though, that he was busy putting the pieces together, processing.

"And Asher runs the show now," he said. "It didn't bother him that Dagon killed his father?"

"He was running jobs by the time he was ten. At first, because Zenith made him. But after I had Wren, he... changed. Started asking, begging to run jobs. Even ones Zenith wouldn't take. Sometimes, Asher would do them anyway. After Dagon... after Zenith was gone, he just sort of took over. Didn't miss a beat. Like he'd been groomed for it. And everyone seemed OK with it."

"Except you."

"I was never OK with any of it."

Three nodded.

"He's after Wren," he said. "Because Wren is... Wren is something else entirely."

"Wren shut him down, Three. Locked him out. At age five. No one else has ever been able to do that. And Asher can't live without knowing how Wren did it, and Wren..." Tears started coming now, thinking about her boy, lying in a hole in the middle of the Strand. All because he didn't want to see someone hurt. "That's my baby he's after. My baby. He doesn't know how he did it, he can't tell Asher what he wants to know. And Asher won't stop... it's an obsession. A disease. He wants to take my boy apart."

"They're both your boys."

It stung to hear him say that, but he didn't seem to have intended it to be anything more than a factual statement. Or maybe he was, for the first time, processing out loud. He looked to her, as if he suddenly realized how that had sounded. Placed a gentle hand on her forearm. She wondered that such rough hands could touch that gently.

"Hey, I'm sorry. I didn't–"

"No, it's OK," Cass said, wiping the tears off her face. "It's true. Technically. But Asher ceased to be my son years ago. He's more like his father now. And he wants everything his father had." She dipped her head, looked straight into his eyes. "*Everything*."

Three seemed to understand. But nothing seemed to shock him. She guessed he'd seen too much of the world to be surprised by any depths of depravity anymore.

"So we get to Morningside, and you find Wren's father, and then?"

Cass was surprised to feel her heart drop under the weight of the question. Up until a few weeks ago, she'd been unable to imagine any other person in the world she could trust Wren to, once she was gone.

"I guess we hope he's still as good a man as he once was."

Three just nodded again. The sun's final orange rays were tinting red now.

"Alright, girl," he said. Her heart stirred when he called her that. "Let's get you some rest, and we'll see about getting you to your man."

He stood, and lent her his hand, helping her to her feet. They stood close for a moment. He looked down deep in her eyes; she felt he was searching for something, and found herself wishing she knew what it was. Right now, she felt like she would tell him anything. Then he stepped back, moving out of her path to the shelter.

"It might get a little noisy tonight. But don't worry. I'll be watching over you."

Cass only nodded in response, but somehow hearing those words, in that voice, with that certainty, gave her hope, comfort. She moved to the shelter, and worked her way in through the narrow opening. Wren was already fast asleep. As she settled herself in beside him, she heard Three moving near the entrance, and then it was suddenly dark.

"Three?" she called in a forced whisper. Orange light reappeared, and he looked in through the opening.

"Yeah?"

"Are you coming in?"

He shook his head. "I'm going to seal you in. Cover you up completely, just to be safe. I need to be able to see what's going on."

"Will you sleep?"

He smiled. "Later." He started to cover over the entrance again, and then paused. "Hey, Cass. Wren's dad. What's his name?"

It struck her as an odd time for the question. Especially since he hadn't seemed interested before.

"Underdown," she answered. His expression wavered momentarily in some passing cloud of emotion. Then he smiled again, and nodded, and covered the entrance, and all was dark.

# TWENTY-THREE

After the first hour of the distant, circuit-laced wails, the exhaustion finally won out, and Cass dozed off. But just minutes after she'd fallen asleep, she was startled awake by a scrabbling noise just outside the shelter. Heart pounding, she fought to control her breathing, to shield Wren, and most importantly to be *still*. Something was right outside, right next to the wall, picking along it, picking *at* it. Dust crumbled onto her cheek.

*Still*, she thought. *Be still*.

There was a noise of something shifting away, and a flow of cold air rolled over her. It was dismantling their shelter.

"Cass," Three whispered. "We're gonna need to get movin' in a few."

Her mind rejected the concept immediately. Moving through the Strand at night was guaranteed to get them all killed. What time was it anyway? She went to check the time…

"Cass!" Three whispered more urgently. "You awake?"

His second call was enough, and snapped her to full awareness. She wouldn't mention just how close she'd come to giving them all away.

"I'm awake," she answered in a whisper, fearing the Weir were near. "What's wrong, did they find us?"

She rolled over, and found Three peeking in through their narrow entrance, face backlit by a dull gray light.

"No, it's almost daybreak. If we're gonna make it out of here today, I want to get a jump on it. Just over ten hours of daylight."

"It's morning already?"

"Yeah, close enough. You sleep?"

"Apparently."

"Well, take a minute to get sorted out, and then we need to move, OK?"

"OK." He looked tired. And sweaty. There were flecks of something dark spattered under his chin. "Are you alright?"

"Sure, fine. Just be ready to move."

Cass pointed at his chin. Three touched it with his fingertips, and drew them back. Scanned them.

"Yeah…" he said. "Busy night." He flashed a weak smile that seemed filled with an endless fatigue. "Let me know when you're ready. Sooner is better." And then he withdrew.

Cass sat up as best she could inside their hiding place, rolled her neck and shoulders. Frustrated that she'd slept for hours and felt it had been no more than a few minutes. She hoped Wren had slept better. She looked at him there, curled tight in a ball, a long coat draped over him like a blanket. She blinked at the coat. Mind still groggy, but processing. She didn't remember the coat from before. Three's. He must've checked on them in the night.

Cass reached over and ran her fingers through Wren's golden-white hair gently, and cooed his name the way only mothers can.

"Wren."

He stirred.

"Wren, baby, it's time."

Her boy fidgeted under her touch, and then his green eyes appeared beneath slowly receding eyelids. Gradually focused. He lay still.

"Wren, sweetheart, we need to get going, OK?"

Wren inhaled deeply, his mouth inverted. A quick ex-halation, another deep inhalation; corners of his mouth quivering. She realized he was trying not to cry.

"It's alright baby, we're alright."

She leaned over onto him then, wrapped her arms around him and hugged him tightly. But he squirmed away. Cass sat back up, and Wren sat up with her.

"OK, Mom."

The 'Mom' hit her like a mild slap. It sounded too old to be coming out of Wren's mouth. He was already up and tucking his little blade back inside his belt, hidden by his coat, suddenly looking very much like a man in miniature.

"OK, baby," she said. And then she too was up on knees, checking gear and refastening her boots. Three reappeared and started tearing down a section of their hide to open up the entrance. An electric howl sounded from far too close for Cass's comfort, but Three ignored it.

"Farther than it sounds," he said, apparently seeing her concern. "Sound carries in strange ways out here."

He helped her out of the shelter, and then Wren, and then reached in and pulled the packs out.

"It's early yet. There may still be a couple of 'em out and about, so stay sharp. But if we don't get started now, I'm afraid we'll run out of time on the other end. And that wouldn't go well for us."

Cass nodded, as did Wren.

"It's going to be a hard push today, alright? Set your minds to it. It's going to be hard. But once we're on the other side, there's gonna be a place to rest. We can rest for a couple of days. Fed, warm, safe. So you push with everything you've got today, and we'll make up for it after, alright?"

"Alright."

"OK. Here," he said, handing them each a silver-foil package. Cass took hers, and couldn't help but notice how it seemed to ooze in the middle. Three ripped the top corner of his and squeezed some kind of congealed substance out of it into his mouth. It looked like a mix of coagulated grease and wet sand. He grimaced as it went in, and swallowed hard. Seeing her look, he explained. "Supposed to be the perfect chemical balance of proteins and carbohydrates to keep you running all day. If you can keep it down."

She nodded, and squeezed a portion of her packet into her mouth. The taste wasn't quite foul, but if not for Three's explanation, it never would have occurred to her that this substance was intended to be consumed by humans. Machines, maybe.

Wren gagged on his, and coughed it back out. It fell in a wet pasty lump into the cold, gray ash-sand of the Strand. Three knelt next to Wren, and they both stared at it.

"Tell you what," Three said after a moment. "You get half of one of these down, and I'll carry you when you get tired."

"I don't think I can…" Wren said.

But Three coaxed him with a hand on his back. "You can do it. It's not food, it's fuel. It's power. Just get it in there and swallow as soon as it hits your tongue. Don't even have to chew it."

Wren nodded, and gingerly squeezed another half serving out. It dangled for a moment above his open mouth, then plopped suddenly full force onto his waiting tongue. He swallowed in an instant, and dry heaved, but nothing came out. Nothing but a few tears of disgust.

Three stood, and patted him heartily on the shoulder, rustled his hair.

"There you go, buddy. Just like a soldier."

Wren looked up and gave a strained smile, no doubt still dealing with the semi-acrid aftertaste of whatever it was that was sliding down into his belly.

It came so fast, Cass barely had time to scream.

"Three!"

A streak of gray-blue leapt, and Three knocked Wren clear the instant before impact. Wren fell hard, and rolled up shrieking at the writhing mass that fought and strove just inches from him. Cass reacted, reached down, snatched him by handfuls of his coat. Jerked him away with such force she lost her balance. They tumbled together, backwards to the ground. Helpless spectators.

It was so fast, so savage, Cass couldn't make sense of what was happening until she saw the Weir's clawed hand flash up bloody, and down again. Three whipped back and forth on the ground like he was lying on hot coals, his arms folded up like a mantis. The Weir flailing as if caught in a web. Terror gripped Cass's throat, her spine, paralyzed her, even as Wren was screaming, screaming, like a child in the throes of a nightmare, screaming for her to help.

There was a sudden snap. And then, somehow, it all stopped. And all was still. And all was quiet, save for the sobbing child. Her child. What had happened? Where had it come from?

Then, movement. The Weir. Rising up. Rolling over. Flopping onto its back. Three lay still. Breathing. Heavy, labored, but breathing.

Wren was the first to his side. Three held up a hand. Bloody, impossible to tell if it was his or the Weir's.

"Bad start," he said through gritted teeth. "Bad start."

He rolled up to an elbow, awkwardly pushed himself to sitting. Cass got to her feet, edged her way to him. Realized she was trembling. From somewhere out on the Strand, a cry pierced the pre-dawn gray and was answered in kind.

"So much for keepin' quiet."

Three forced himself to his feet, shouldered his pack. There was blood on his lips.

"You sure you're alright to go?" Cass asked.

"Doesn't much matter. Let's move."

He turned and started the march with long strides. Forced, determined steps. Not the smooth glide she was accustomed to seeing. He was hurt, and she had no idea how badly. Cass took Wren's hand and together they followed as quickly and quietly as they were able.

The sky above was growing lighter by the minute, but Cass couldn't escape the grasping fear of the shadows on their heels. The suddenness of the attack on Three had her shaken. It'd come without warning. Taken Three by surprise. And if Three could be taken by surprise... she didn't want to think what that might mean for them out here. She replayed it in her mind, realized she couldn't find the starting point, couldn't picture where the Weir had been when it leapt. Only that it had leapt. Three knocking Wren to the ground.

Not to the ground. Out of the way. The Weir hadn't been after Three. It had been after Wren. And Three had saved him. Saved *them*. Again. She wondered at what cost. But the man that forged ahead of them made no signs of slowing, no hint of injury, or fear. Cass set her mind to keeping pace. And she swore that no matter what may come, she would never again let surprise render her helpless. Next time she would stand at his shoulder. Next time, they would fight together.

Three had told them it would be a hard push, and he kept his promise. For the first four hours, he refused to let them stop for more than three or four minutes at a time. There was a dull ache deep in his side from the impact with the Weir, and the pain got sharp if he inhaled too quickly, or too much. But he fought back, forcing his mind back to the now, to that moment, that footfall. And he fought to keep his bearing, knowing the human tendency to circle obliviously. They'd survived one night in the Strand, but not by accident. They wouldn't survive a second.

At times, he'd switched packs with Cass so he could carry Wren. Another promise he'd made. How many had he made to them now? How many kept? How many more could he keep?

The wind had picked up that day, gusts swirling gritty dust into their eyes and mouths. They passed most of the journey in silence, each focused on the peculiarly personal misery the Strand seemed to impose upon anyone who crossed it. There was a presence in the place, an ominous weight that bore down on the spirit, and made footsteps heavy. At one point, Three realized Wren was quietly weeping. No one asked why.

By noon, Three reckoned they'd traveled maybe eighteen miles, which was good, but not great. If they kept pace, they'd clear the Strand in time. But keeping pace was a hard task, harder than the one they'd accomplished that morning. They stopped then, and took another round of the goo that jCharles had provided. It wasn't the physical fatigue that concerned Three the most, however. It was the draining of the soul, the sapping of the will that he feared. The early morning attack had rattled Cass. She kept Wren close while they rested, but her eyes were vacant, staring. Hunted. He'd seen that look before, back when he'd first met the two.

"Hey," he said. "We'll make it…"

He cut himself off before he finished, and realized he'd been about to make it a promise. Cass smiled emptily and nodded. Three didn't know which worried him more. Her look, or the fact that he couldn't make the promise.

They got on the move again after that, but within the first hour he knew they were in trouble. The pace was slacking, and no matter what he tried, he couldn't pick it up. It was as if some cruel headwind had set itself against them, as if the Strand itself had bent its will to preventing their escape. By mid-afternoon, he'd discarded Wren's pack, and soon after he offloaded most of Cass's and his own as well. He carried Wren on his back the rest of the way, fighting hard to ignore how the boy's knee drove into his side and sent waves of electric fire radiating through his chest.

Three strove onwards, willing himself, willing Cass and her son, willing them to race the slowly gathering dusk. But with less than an hour of daylight left, he estimated they still had another five miles to the fringe. It didn't matter. There were no other options.

He looked back at Cass, hunched over, forward, leaning into the journey as if she really were facing a physical wall of wind.

"Almost there, girl," he lied. "Just a little further."

Cass didn't reply, and as he turned back and resumed his plodding steps, he wondered whether she hadn't heard him, or hadn't believed him. She was no fool, and the sun was impossible to miss. It was already sinking into the horizon. He thought briefly about telling Cass to run for it. To boost, and to take Wren and just run, run as fast and as far as she could. But he knew it was a fool's wish. She wouldn't know the way. All the speed in the world wouldn't save them if she ran back to the heart of the Strand.

As the sky faded purple and the first stars began to appear, he began preparing. The adrenaline kicked in then, for both of them, and they covered those last couple of miles at a better pace than they started the day with. But it wouldn't be enough. The first calls were already sounding in the night.

"Three," Cass said, and he heard it in her voice. She knew what was coming. And to his surprise, she sounded strong.

"We're in some trouble, Cass."

"I know."

He set Wren down. Cass slid next to them, picked Wren up, hugged him close. He was strangely calm.

"Are we going to die now, mama?" he asked sleepily. Three didn't wait for Cass to answer.

"No, Wren. Now we're going to fight."

Heart full of fire, Three scanned their surroundings. There wasn't much to choose from, but as the cries of the Weir grew louder, he spotted one structure that might actually give them the slightest chance. It had been taller before, perhaps much taller. Now it was little more than two stories. And the top story was mostly exposed, its walls largely crumbled away. There was a corner of protection, and it afforded them height. Maybe it'd be enough.

"This way," he said. Grabbing Cass by the arm, he pulled her along and together they raced across the broken terrain, fear and adrenaline granting them new speed. They reached the skeletal building, and Three wasted no time. He grabbed Wren away from Cass, and then leaned into one of the crumbling walls.

"Climb," he said, as he laced his fingers together at his waist. She understood immediately, and stepped into his hands. Three boosted her and she used his shoulders as another foothold. He felt her press down, and then spring off him. Quickly after, she called down.

"Wren!"

Three grabbed the boy around the waist and lifted him until Wren was on his shoulders. He stepped close to the wall, held steady while Cass got a hold on him.

"Help me, Wren, come on. Climb up!"

"I'm trying!"

The calls weren't just getting closer now. They were growing in number.

"Go, Wren, go!" Three called, and as if his word alone was enough, Wren's feet lifted off his shoulders and were scrabbling up the side of the wall as Cass pulled from above.

As soon as Wren was clear, Three moved back about six feet, and then dashed towards the wall. He leapt and planted a foot in the middle of the wall and then pushed off and stretched upward, catching the lip of the upper story by just the fingertips. Stifled a grunt of pain as something cracked in his side. He strained upwards, and as he pulled himself high enough to get an elbow atop the wall, four hands grabbed him and hauled him further along. He scrambled onto the top level with the others.

"Back," he said, "back to that corner, small and tight as you can."

There was a gaping hole in the floor, but it was to the opposite side of the remaining walls. Wren slid into the corner first, hunched into a little ball, knife in a downward grip and at the ready, just as Three had taught him. Cass curled herself around Wren, shielding him completely from view. Three put his back hard against them both, blade unsheathed.

They were all panting.

"Still now. Still as you can."

He fought his own heartbeat, his lungs, the molten pain searing his ribs on one side. Deeply bruised or maybe cracked, if not broken. He raised his arm and slapped the injury. It made him suck in his breath, but he didn't convulse or scream. Not broken then.

In the distance a dark shape moved across the rolling destruction of the Strand. The first Weir of what would be many, he knew. But it was headed away. He hoped that would be the case for them all.

The first two hours were filled with the silent tension of a black storm cloud. And then, just as the moon was coming high, it broke.

Three saw it first, noted how it crouched below the structure and scanned it, as if assessing it. The moon was light enough for him to see it clearly, and he noticed immediately how different it was from the Weir he'd encountered on the other side of the Strand. This one was almost indistinguishable from a human, except for its blue-glow electric eyes humming in the darkness. It was fully clothed, fully featured. Not the gaunt corpse-like creatures from before. But no less deadly, he guessed. Perhaps moreso.

It didn't make any noise. No static-burst squawk. It just crouched there, in the darkness, watching. Soon enough, Three understood. A second Weir appeared, off the opposite corner, slipping silently like a shadow across the ground. Then another scuttled to join the second. The realization spread like a slow dawn, and Three was amazed. And terrified.

They were coordinating.

In the next moment, two Weir sprang over the edges of walls simultaneously, and Three reacted. The first one's head was already falling down to the ground below as the second turned to face its companion. As Three plunged his blade through its chest, he thought he saw something that almost resembled surprise. The Weir burbled as Three withdrew his blade, and then he struck again, sending the creature toppling through the hole in the floor.

Three heard a clattering sound, and as he turned he saw Cass flash from the corner to intercept the third Weir. She shot out a stomping kick that connected at the Weir's hip, crushing the socket, and folding the Weir towards her. As it fell, Cass caught its head between her hands, dropped to a knee and twisted. The Weir's neck snapped as its body cartwheeled off the second floor and landed with a meaty thud in the dust below.

"Just the beginning," Three said.

"I know," she answered.

He handed her a long knife from his boot. "You still got that jitter?"

Cass nodded.

"Don't be afraid to use it. Hate to die with ammo left."

"You think about that yourself," she said, pointing to his pistol. Wren stayed crouched in his corner, knife at the ready, shivering with fear. His eyes were wide.

"They're coming."

A second wave came almost immediately after. Four this time. And as if to confirm Three's worst suspicions, these four fought together. Not as four wild animals, striving to be the first to the kill, but as four limbs of a single mind. One would feint, and the other would follow through, and in the first exchange Three felt the sting as claws rent the flesh of his shoulder. But Cass was there suddenly, suddenly everywhere it seemed, and as she forced them back, Three seized each opportunity to strike, and soon the four lay motionless.

Three checked the wound along his shoulder where the blood ran freely, and knew it wouldn't be the last of the night. He looked to Cass, radiant and fierce in the moonlight, glistening under a thin sheen of sweat and speckled dark from the war at hand. Her once fragile beauty replaced by strength, and raw will, and a dark-eyed gaze full of unquenchable fire. And for the first time, he knew they were going to make it.

The next group attacked about three minutes later. The night became a blur for Three then, a smear of gray and blade, the cries of Weir mixed with Cass calling out, his own voice sounding distant. They fought like demons atop a mountain, like lions among wolves. With loud cries and savage strikes, they threw back their enemy. The attacks came in a broken rhythm, sometimes one right after another, sometimes as much as a half hour apart. Each clash brought a new rush of adrenaline, a clarity of focus that seemed impossible to maintain. And after each battle, the fatigue came crushing down, an iron fog that promised the next fight would be the last. They were wounded, slashed, clawed, even bitten. But somehow, some way, Three and Cass fought back to back, shoulder to shoulder, and still they fought, and still they fought.

As the bodies of the Weir fell and piled around them Three got sudden flashes, almost still images of his blade slashing through a Weir, or Cass's knee crushing into the skull of another. Even little Wren stabbing, fighting like a cornered wolf cub, teeth bared and tears streaming. The sky almost seemed lighter.

But then another wave crashed, and there were too many. Too many. Three fought and slashed and felt more than one impact that he knew meant he'd been punctured, if only the adrenaline had let him feel the pain. He killed the two closest Weir. Moved to a third, stepped into its attack and severed its arm at the shoulder. Threw his body into it, flinging it out into the air and crashing to the ground below. And then Three spun, instinct firing a warning and reflexes answering, and he saw it, coming up through the hole in the floor, leaping up from below. Cass facing the other way. Three screamed her name, but heard nothing. A roar of blood in his ears. She reacted, turned, twisted to dodge the strike but too late. Three saw the claw enter her side, and tear out through her abdomen in a spray.

Wren saw it too.

"MAMAAAAAAAAAAAAAAAAAAA!"

The scream tore through the melee and Three felt something pass through him like a shockwave, and suddenly all the remaining Weir spasmed in near unison and collapsed like they'd just been switched off. Wren just stood there, near the corner, eyes wide, face pale. Staring. Panting. And all else was still.

How Three got from where he was to Cass, he didn't recall. The next thing he knew, he was dragging her into the corner, slipping in the trail she was leaving behind. His heart cold with fear, with a fear so familiar, so cruel; a fear he'd sworn he would never feel again.

He pulled her into the wall, propped her up. Wren moved in close.

"Mama?"

"It's alright, baby. They got me a little, but it's alright. Go over there and keep watch for us, OK? Let us know as soon as trouble comes."

He nodded, tears in his eyes, but didn't move.

"Wren, sweetheart. It's important. We need you to keep watch, OK?"

"Go on, son," Three said. And at that, Wren nodded again and moved away, crouching low near the edge and peering into the waning night.

Three reached down to examine the wound then, tried to move her hands away. Cass resisted.

"Three," she said calmly. Much too calmly. He wouldn't look at her.

"Move your hands, let me see it."

"Three," she said again. And the fear rose, and the strength left.

"Move your hands, Cass! Move them!"

"Three, it's OK."

And then she lifted her soaked hands and took his. He felt the hot gush, and she squeezed his hands with such strength, with such warmth, and his heart shattered in his chest.

"Cass, don't. Come on, girl, come on, we're gonna get out of here. We're all going to get out of here."

She smiled, and shook her head.

"Not all. Take Wren, Three. Take Wren and go. Right now."

"No, Cass. I'm not going to leave you here."

"More will come, Three. More will come, and we'll all die. But not if you take my son and go."

He ripped his hands away from her then, and pulled her shirt up, expecting to staunch the wound. And stopped cold. He understood now. The gashes were severe; deep, and black with blood, which meant her liver was torn. But worse, her receptor was destroyed. Only a few fragments and thin cables remained, the rest lay scattered across the floor. Her supply of quint was gone, permanently. And there was no telling how much she'd just burned through in the fight.

"Just take him and go. Tell him I'm right behind you."

"No, Cass. I'm gonna save your life."

"Wren *is* my life, Three."

Three looked at her hard then. So much to say. So much he should've said before now. Her golden-brown eyes already fading. And he realized, looking into those eyes, how badly he'd wanted to let himself love her. And how much he loved her now. Now, at the end. He grit his teeth then, turned his heart to stone. It was dead now anyway. But there was one more thing to be done.

"Wren, come here."

Her eyes went wide.

"Three, no, don't…"

"You let him say his goodbyes. Only chance he's gonna get."

Wren crept to his side, laid his hand on Cass's hands. A cry sounded from not far enough away. They were coming.

"Wren, we have to go, and your mama's not coming with us. So you go on and say goodbye."

Cass couldn't hold it together then, and the tears sprang forth.

"Mama?"

"We don't have much time, Wren," Three said firmly. Lock the feelings away. Lock them away, deal with them when it's safe. "Kiss your mama goodbye, we've got to go."

"Mama?" Wren exploded in a sob now, and wrapped his arms tight around her neck. "Mama!"

Another cry answered the first. They were circling. But holding back. Waiting for reinforcements, maybe. Three still didn't know what had happened to the last few. He couldn't count on it happening again.

Cass and Wren sobbed and held each other, Cass stroking his hair, kissing his face and ear where she could reach him. Then soothing him.

"Wren, it's OK. It's OK, baby. Go with Three, sweetheart, he's going to take care of you. It's going to be OK."

The Weir called out again, closer now. Closing in. They were out of time. Three grabbed Wren around the torso and pulled him away. Wren screamed and writhed, inconsolable wails of his heart crying out for his mama, but Three pulled him in close, held him tight. As he stood, he exchanged a look with Cass that said nothing he wanted it to. She reached behind her and produced the jittergun. Her face hardened in raw determination.

"Go."

And Three went.

He turned and didn't look back then, clutching Wren to him. Together they dropped through the hole in the floor, and then Three ran. The last vestiges of adrenaline fired up as the sounds of the Weir closing in magnified, and were soon joined by the buzz of the jittergun firing off bursts.

But as he ran, Three knew something was wrong. His legs were heavy, and he was going cold. Too cold for it to just be the pre-dawn air. The sky was getting lighter, there was no doubt. But he couldn't outrun the Weir. His breathing was labored now, every inhale sizzling pain through his side, every exhale ragged. He willed himself on, and found even that was not enough. He stumbled once, then again. The third time, he couldn't catch his balance, and went down hard on his knees.

Behind him, there were no more sounds of the jittergun. Which meant pursuit was not far behind. Three laid Wren down on the ground in front of him, and the boy laid still, shock having silenced him for the moment. And sure enough, behind them now, Three could just begin to make out the first footfalls of the approaching Weir.

He drew his pistol then, checked the cylinder. One shot. Three's head swam, and he was suddenly lying on the ground, next to Wren. So cold. Three lifted the pistol, slid its heavy barrel along the ground. Lined it up with Wren's golden hair.

The Weir were closer now. Less than a minute, they'd be upon them. Three placed his finger on the trigger.

"Three?"

"Yeah, Wren?"

"Are angels real?"

"I dunno. I hope so."

Wren sat up on his elbow. Three struggled to adjust his aim. Thirty seconds.

"I think they're real."

"That's good, Wren. Maybe we'll see some."

"I see them now."

Three didn't see any angels. But now he heard something strange. A single note sung out, high and clear. And beautiful. A simple melody floated on the wind, and it stirred his heart. Maybe there were angels after all.

He shifted his gaze in the direction of the sound, and saw shapes in the distance. Three of them, approaching steadily. Gliding, it seemed.

"They're beautiful," Wren said in awe. In reverence.

And then all was dark.

# TWENTY-FOUR

She was there. Before anything else came back to him, Cass was there, looking down at him. Watching over him... No. Cass was gone now. She was gone. He had left her.

Something moved in the darkness. A presence. Watching. Waiting. Evaluating. Lie still. A steady patter, just at the edge of hearing. Boiling water? Sharper. Rain upon a roof. Inside, then. The presence shifted, slipped away. Low voices in the distance.

Three felt his eyes open thickly, felt them strain to focus in the gloom. An orange-hued darkness; dusky, warm. The walls seemed too tall, the ceiling too far away. He turned his head, or rather let it roll to one side under its own weight. Across the room, a small canister sat on the floor radiating a dull orange light. Soothing, but unsteady. Fire in a bottle. Three's clouded mind struggled to identify the device, nagged him for his inability to find its name.

A shadow moved across the room. Feet gliding into view, backlit by the light. The presence. A person. A woman. She knelt down, but only in silhouette. Three realized he was lying on the floor. No, not the floor. On some sort of mat on the floor. The woman pressed a hand to his forehead, her skin smooth and cool.

"Cass?" he heard a voice whisper. A voice like his, but weak, ragged. His tongue felt too large for his mouth.

She made no reply. Not Cass. Cass was gone. She moved her hands, and he felt them on his shoulder, on his chest, then a stab of white pain slashed his vision. He wanted to cry out, but there was no air in his lungs. The woman stood quickly and disappeared again, as spots floated in Three's already blurry vision.

Wren. Where was Wren?

Footsteps outside. Louder, but somehow more distant. Darkness closed in.

A lantern. It's called a lantern.

In his dream, and he knew it was a dream because he was with Cass, they were back in the agent's office, back where Three had killed Kostya thinking he was Fedor. Except Kostya wasn't there now, and the agent was away. Cass sat on the agent's desk, and Wren stood by her, driving his shuttle car amidst the clutter. And she watched her son, smiled at him, smiled with her sudden warmth like the sun breaking through a storm cloud. Three wanted to reach out to her and found he couldn't move. Wanted to call her name, but found he couldn't speak. She noticed him anyway, she looked to him, surprised, startled. But then her eyes danced with some secret delight, and her lips moved with a subtle curl at the edges. A whisper. She spoke, but Three couldn't hear her.

She slid off the agent's desk, landed lightly on her feet. Glided to him, so close he could feel the warmth of her, so close but never touching, and she passed by and slipped through the door and walked down the long marble hall, impossibly long, without looking back. Three strained to call out, fought to chase after her, to catch her one last time before she disappeared, but it was no use. The office grew steadily warmer, steadily darker, and as Three tried to draw a breath, it was like sucking air through a heavy blanket.

A dream. Only a dream. And some part of Three's mind,

the part that knew he was dreaming, knew just as well that something was terribly wrong.

There was commotion, and a fiery brand of raw pain shot from between Three's ribs into his chest cavity, forking like a bolt of lightning, shocking him awake. He struggled to escape, to twist away from the hurt, but they were holding him, they were holding him down, and there were too many to escape, and he was too weak to break free. The Weir. It had all been a dream, and he was only now waking to find the Weir were upon him.

No, there were hurried words. Three's mind fought the confusion, the disoriented thoughts scattered by fatigue and trauma and pain and loss. Cass was gone. He had left her.

A face loomed into view, serious, concerned, but human. Fully human. A man. Old, early sixties, Asian. Bright eyes peered into his, as a voice floated into his consciousness.

"...relieve the pressure there..."

There was still pain, but Three found breathing easier. The man nodded, withdrew. Three's vision swam, his limbs went suddenly warm and tingly. He fought it, but knew he was going under again. The man reappeared, calm, soothing.

"Rest. You are safe here. Your son is here, safe." Three felt a pressure on his shoulder. A comforting hand. "Rest now. Rest."

Three felt a question forming in his mind, but couldn't grasp it before the darkness came, and he knew no more.

Oddly, it was hunger that brought him around. A dull but deep ache in the pit of his stomach dragged him from whatever bottomless sleep he had fallen into. And in that in-between space between sleep and wakefulness, a sound entered his consciousness. Soft, subdued, but clear, haunting as it was hopeful. Singing. A woman's voice, like a winter's wind in high places, or the sharp brilliance of the night sky. He'd heard it before. There, at the end.

Three let his eyes open. He was still on the same mat, staring at the same ceiling. The searing pain from... before, however long ago it had been, was gone now, replaced instead by an low-intensity but widespread ache, as if every muscle in his body had been bruised or strained in some way. He shifted and felt his elbow bump something that sent a jolt of pain through his ribcage on the left side, forcing a reflexive inhale. Glancing down, he noticed a clear tube inserted between his ribs. A long hose, snaking away. Before he could follow it, he realized the singing had stopped.

His eyes instinctively flicked to the corner of the room, and he saw her there. For a moment, she was Cass. But then, no, taller, lighter hair, fairer skin. Blue-eyed, blue as a glacier. She didn't approach.

"I'm sorry, did I wake you?"

Three swallowed, and realized his mouth was painfully dry. He settled for shaking his head.

"Do you think you could take some water?"

He nodded. The woman dipped her head slightly and disappeared. A few moments later she returned holding a small blue bowl. She set it on the floor beside Three, and knelt. He curled himself up, clenching his jaw against the onslaught of his senses, forced himself through the discomfort and disorientation. The woman seemed surprised, and as he raised himself to a sort of hunched sitting position, he realized she'd intended to lift his head to help him drink. After a moment, she just handed him the bowl.

"Thank you," he choked out, surprised by the hollow sound of his voice, like the wind through rusting beams. He raised the bowl to his lips and sipped tentatively. The water was cool with hints of mint and citrus, and though his body screamed for him to drain it all in one breath, he forced himself to take it slow. Testing. A little bit at a time. The woman watched intently, hesitant. Or expectant. Maybe she was waiting to see if he'd collapse backwards. He wouldn't.

As he sipped the water, he traced the tube from his side, followed it to where it punched through some rubbery membrane down into a jar half-filled with water. The end of the tube was submerged. He watched as the hint of a bubble bulged, released, and floated to the surface. The woman followed his gaze, anticipated the question.

"Your lungs collapsed," she said. "But they seem to be stabilizing. Chapel thinks we should be able to pull the tube out tomorrow, maybe."

Three meant to respond, but only an exhale escaped, and even that seemed to take more effort than he'd expected. He closed his eyes and took another sip of water.

"Shall I bring your son?"

It took a moment to process. Wren, of course. Three didn't have the energy to explain. He nodded. At least, he felt like he did. There was no telling how perceptible the movement had actually been. He heard her rustle, and knew she was standing. Three opened his eyes in time to see her slipping out. Almost floating. She had an easy grace in her movement that made him think of silk and falling snow.

Gravity seemed to have tripled since Three last noticed it. His body started to sink slowly back to the floor, but he refused its motion. Instead, he turned, slowly, painfully, until his back was against the wall, and crossed his leaden legs. It wasn't even slightly comfortable. He sipped the water again, longer this time. Two, three swallows. The room was smaller than it had first seemed. Long enough for him to lie down, but not much longer. And not as wide. Wooden walls, wooden floor. Simple, but well-fashioned, and well-maintained. A craftsman's work. He noticed as well the door was on a track, with neatly-hidden rollers that kept it nearly flush to the wall when opened. Clean, efficient, space-saving.

Three's gradual evaluation was interrupted by Wren's sudden appearance. The boy slipped in quietly and stayed close to the door, in the corner. Like a child expecting punishment. Or at a funeral. His eyes were wide, expectant. Hopeful. But far too heavy for a boy his age. The woman did not return with him.

The two waited in brief silence, neither knowing what to say, or if anything should even be said at all. Finally, Three motioned with his head to the space next to him on the mat. Wren slipped over and sat down with him, and for a time they just sat together in the dusky gloom. Three offered his bowl of water to Wren, but Wren shook his head. Three nodded, and sipped again, and struggled to find the words. But it was the boy who broke the silence.

"They thought you were dead," he said. "At first, I mean."

Three grunted. "Not too far wrong, I'd guess."

Wren looked down at his hands, tugged on the fingertips of one with the other.

"How long has it been?"

"Five days, I think."

"And they've been taking care of us?"

Wren nodded, and looked up at Three with unexpectedly bright eyes. "They have tomatoes."

An odd detail, and a surprising one. "Real ones?"

Wren nodded again. "And some green things too, but they don't taste very good."

An underground farm, perhaps. Could explain the small room, the use of the lantern. But no, they'd need UV lights. That would mean generators, electric light. Three took another swallow of water. Still about half the bowl left.

"What happened?" Three asked. "When they came? The last I remembered, the Weir were…"

He trailed off, unsure of Wren's state, suddenly concerned of waking memories that might have been best unmentioned. But while Wren dropped his gaze back to his own hands, he answered readily.

"The Weir ran away."

"What do you mean, 'ran away'? They didn't follow us?"

"Oh, no they found us, but they ran away."

"Was there a fight?"

"No," Wren shrugged, but answered matter-of-factly, as if it was no big deal. "I think the angels scared them."

"Who are the angels, Wren?"

"Lil. And Mister Carter. And Mister Chapel, I guess. They're not really angels, I don't think. But they can look like them. When they want to."

Three's mind swirled, still off-balance from the damage he'd suffered, the time he'd been under. He drank more deeply. Steadied himself. Ravenously hungry, but daunted by the idea of trying to stand. Real tomatoes. That would be something.

Angels. Something else entirely.

# TWENTY-FIVE

Three jerked awake, not realizing he'd nodded off. The bowl sat in his lap, empty now of its water. Wren hadn't moved, just sat motionless, hugging his knees and staring at the wall, sea-green eyes dull and unfocused, somewhere far away. Three stretched his legs out in front of him. The motion drew Wren's attention back to reality.

"Think I dozed off," Three said. Wren nodded. "You hungry?"

Wren nodded again. Three looked again at the tube inserted in his chest, and wondered what would happen if he stood. He'd never had a collapsed lung before, let alone two. His list of injury firsts was growing ever shorter. "Well. Why don't we see what we can find, huh?"

Three reached out tentatively and took hold of the jar of water that held the other end of his chest-tube, moved it gingerly as if just touching it might somehow reignite the pain. He lifted it and brought it closer. Another bubble had just begun to form. Like a bead of glass. It made sense. Pressure from his chest cavity forced air through the tube, relieving the strain on his lungs and enabling them to re-inflate. The water jar acted as a cheap one-way valve, letting pressure out, but not allowing any back in. Clever. Three couldn't help but wonder if he ever would've thought of that on his own.

The jar was interesting, but it was mostly an excuse to avoid the hard work of standing. Three thought about calling for the woman again, or sending Wren to fetch someone, but quickly dismissed it. As long as he was still conscious, he would ignore the creeping fear of vulnerability. Fake it. People can't tell the difference anyway.

"Right," he said aloud, and stirred forward, tucking his legs beneath him. Wren clambered to his feet and stood by as Three began the process of working his way up. It was nearly a full minute before he could be considered standing, and even then he had to lean against the wall to steady himself. He couldn't remember a time when he had been this weak.

"Are you OK?" Wren asked quietly. He formed it as a question, but the tone made it a statement: *you're not OK*.

"Sure, kiddo. Just a little woozy." Fake it. Whether proving it to the boy or to himself, Three forced himself off the wall then, and refused to let his body collapse. It was more of a fight than he would admit. One step. Then another. Hold. Focus. Don't dare fall. More like walking a tightrope than it had any right to be. Three was so focused on getting one foot in front of the other, he didn't see it coming through the door.

Something hard jabbed into his elbow, the impact just enough to force his arm into the tube leading into his chest. There was a lightning stab of pain between his ribs, and a sudden roll of fire down the front of his leg. Something shattered in the distance, though Three knew not as distant as it sounded. It went dark, and he inhaled sharply, reflexively, caught the doorjamb to keep from collapsing. It was several moments before he realized his eyes were squeezed shut. He slid them open slowly, scanned for the source of this new pain.

The woman. The woman was back, holding a small tray, with a bowl partially filled with some sort of thin broth. It was steaming. Three guessed the bowl had been much fuller moments before. That would explain the burning leg. The woman stood in the hall, eyes wide, mouth open, trapped somewhere between stunned and mortified.

"You're back," he said, because it was the first thing that came to mind.

"What're you doing?" she asked almost breathlessly.

"Hurtin'."

"I mean, you shouldn't be up… you shouldn't be *able* to be up."

For some reason, watching the dawning of thoughts and emotions play across the woman's face struck Three as amusing. He felt his mouth curling in a subdued smile. She was only just now realizing what had happened. And suddenly she was a flurry of activity, but obviously uncertain of what needed to be done.

"I'm sorry. I'm so sorry!"

"It's alright, ma'am," he answered. It was too warm. "Not much for soup anyway." Getting warmer.

"Oh no…"

Three followed her gaze, scanned the floor. The end of his chest-tube lay in a puddle amongst shards of glass. At some point, his jar of water had slipped from his hand. The shattering noise. Why was it so hot?

The woman no longer had the tray, she was standing, hands up towards him. Her mouth was open, moving. Probably saying something. Three felt his lips forming a curse as he realized all the work of standing and walking to the door was about to be for nothing.

When he woke the next time, there was a man sitting on the floor near the lantern, across the small room. Vaguely familiar. From before. He'd been the first to tell Three that Wren was safe. He didn't seem to notice that Three was awake, so Three remained still. Let his eyes rove, pick up the details. His focus was sharper now. Same room. They hadn't moved him. At least, not far. And the tube was gone from his chest, replaced now by some gauzy bandaging with a faint pink spot in the center. Something about the way it wound around him spoke of something else familiar; clean, efficient. A craftsman's work. The same hands that had constructed this room.

Three's eyes went back to the man in the middle of the room. He had something laid across his lap and was intently working on it, though the backlighting made it impossible to see what he was doing. His movements were small, exact. An etcher's hand. Or a surgeon's.

"You a doctor or a carpenter?"

The man didn't stir, but smiled slightly, as if he'd been expecting Three's comment. "A little of both, I suppose." He looked up at Three then. "But not as much of either as I'd wish." Bright-eyed, kind. Deeply intelligent. There was a weight to the man's stillness, like a great stone in a deep pool. "I am called Chapel."

His voice wasn't particularly deep, but it had warm, rounded edges that reassured, like a grandfather's.

"That your name, or just what you're called?"

Chapel's smile widened. "Do you only ask questions, or do you answer them as well?"

"What do you think?"

"I think you're recovering. How's your breathing?"

Three tested it, drew a long, slow inhale. There was internal pressure, an automatic hesitance to deep breathing, but the only pain he felt was in the stretching of the flesh where his tube had been. "Fair. Your work?"

Chapel nodded and then shrugged. "Not all of course. You've required many caretakers since you arrived. But the blame for the hole in your chest is mine alone."

"I appreciate it."

Chapel inclined his head in a slight bow, a precise movement that graciously acknowledged Three's gratitude without accepting any credit. Three hadn't even begun to process how much he owed these people, this man in particular, but somehow in that one moment, it was as if all expectation of repayment dissolved.

"I imagine you're quite hungry. Shall we find you a proper meal? Something other than soup?"

Three nodded, and steeled himself for another attempt at moving. As he rolled up to his elbow, Chapel rose to his feet with surprising ease and fluidity, almost as if falling in reverse, though completely controlled. The next moment he was at Three's side, offering a hand. Not as a nurse to an invalid; as a man to his friend. Three took it and, after a brief struggle, was standing.

"You lost quite a bit of blood," Chapel said. "I expect you'll find yourself unusually weary for the next few days." He extended his hand, holding out the object that he'd been working on, offering it to Three. "This may help, until you've gotten your balance back."

Three accepted it with curiosity, and realized it was a walking stick, carved of a smooth, stout wood. Three, maybe three and a half feet in length, it was well-balanced, with a subtle but elegant arch. Delicate markings near the end seemed to be an incomplete etching at first, but when he rotated it in the meager light, they revealed themselves to be an understated image reminiscent of bamboo. Minimalist detail that captured the essence perfectly. Whole lot of effort for a stick. Chapel seemed to anticipate Three's thoughts.

"A foolish habit of mine," he offered. "But the rude etching shouldn't interfere with its effectiveness as a stick, at any rate."

Three gripped it, tested his weight against it. For a walking stick, it felt good in his hand. Solid. Natural.

"It's good. Thank you."

"This way."

Chapel led Three out into a narrow corridor, slowly but firmly, setting a casual pace, Three's every other step sounding

with the dull *thunk* of his walking stick on the floor. The corridor
wasn't wide enough for them to walk side-by-side, so Chapel
kept a pace ahead. As they walked, Three noticed other sliding
doors on his left. Most pulled closed. Other rooms, like his, he
guessed. There were no doors on the right. Just the occasional
orange-glow lantern mounted on the wall. Mindlessly, Three
ran his free hand along the wall, noticed it was warm to the
touch. Some kind of geothermal heating system, he guessed.
More sophisticated than he'd first thought.

After about twenty feet, the corridor took a sharp right,
and continued on. Further down on the right however, was
a large double-door. When they reached it, Chapel slid one
door partially open, just wide enough to pass through. Three
followed, surprised to find the air suddenly cold and crisp,
and more surprised to discover it was the middle of the night.
Chapel closed the doors behind them, and started out across a
small courtyard.

"Where's Wren?"

"Sleeping, I imagine," Chapel answered. "He's been staying
with Lil and some of the other children in one of the shared
rooms."

"How many children do you have here?"

"Twenty-two, including your son."

Three marveled at that, wondering just how big a place it
was. He couldn't remember a time he'd seen that many kids all
in the same place. "He's not my son, you know."

"Oh?"

"I'm taking him to his father, in Morningside," Three said.
"We were traveling with his mother."

He covered the sudden tightening in his throat with a forced
cough.

"I see," Chapel answered, with such weight that Three felt
he really did see, that he'd absorbed the entire message, both
said and unsaid. They walked in silence a few moments, as if

Chapel sensed Three's need for the chance to compose himself. And then, the moment before it would become awkward, he spoke up again. "You are of course welcome to stay as long as you need. Though as you regain your strength, we may ask you to assist with some small tasks here and there. We're a small community, each with responsibilities."

"Sure. Of course."

Three scanned the surroundings, surveyed the compound, though somehow compound seemed to be the wrong word for it. It felt too open. There were a number of structures of varying sizes, each lit with lanterns of various sizes, spaced at differing intervals. As they walked, Three realized there were others moving in the darkness, near what he guessed to be the outer perimeter. And as they turned and made their way towards a rectangle-shaped, low-roofed building, he noticed at last the wall that surrounded the area. It was barely three feet tall, with gentle, drooping curves. More for aesthetics than protection.

"How close are we to the Strand?" Three asked.

"Quite close. We are on its border, by most accounts."

A figure approached from the darkness.

"No secure structures, no walls. How do you live out here, exposed like this?"

The figure, a man draped in a heavy cloak of some kind, passed quietly, exchanging a brief nod. As he moved by, Three noticed the hilt of a blade under the man's cloak.

"Vigilance and discipline are our walls," Chapel answered. "We are not animals that we should live in a pen."

"Sounds nice. You tell that to the Weir?"

They reached the rectangle building, and climbed the few steps to its porch. Chapel paused outside.

"They do come, from time to time. So far, they are disappointed."

Chapel's lips moved in the subtlest hint of a smile, and then he slid open the door to the building. Inside there was a large, open central room, with a number of long tables with benches, as well as a few smaller tables with chairs.

"Take a seat. I'll see what food we have on hand."

Three eased into a chair at one of the smaller tables. When he sat, he rested his forearm on the table, felt it shift slightly. A sudden flood of memory caught him by surprise. The bar. The shifting table. The first time he saw Cass. He closed his eyes against the images. Would she be alive now, if he hadn't gotten involved? Would it even have mattered? Either way, she would've been gone. But now she was his burden to bear, terrible and beautiful.

Approaching footsteps forced him back to the moment, and he opened his eyes with relief, with regret. The memory of Cass seared and soothed, brought a comfortable pain that Three found himself reluctant to let go. Chapel slid a spoon and a bowl of thick brown stew in front of Three, and sat in a chair opposite.

"I hope you'll find it suitable. It was the first thing I came across that didn't require significant preparation."

"I'm sure it'll be great, thank you," Three said. He picked up the spoon, found it strangely unsteady in his hand. Trembling. He took a bite. Utterly amazing. Best he could tell, there were potatoes and green beans in there, among other things. *Real* potatoes, not the synthetic mass-produced starch compound that people sometimes likened to potatoes. Not a mass of goopy proteins and gelatin carbohydrates whose flavors were customizable by the 99.9% of the world with the hardware to dial it in, that may as well have been ashes to Three. It was likely the first meal that he had ever truly tasted.

Three's belly strained well before the stew was gone, having gone days without solid food, but he force-fed himself anyway. When he finished, he looked up to find Chapel watching him with a hint of amusement.

"Would you care for more?"

"I would," Three said, "but I think my gut would split."

Chapel smiled. "It'll take a day or two for your body to remember food, but we have plenty for you. We should be certain to focus on iron-rich meals; spinach, lentils, beans, that sort of thing. It will accelerate your recovery from the blood loss."

Three nodded. "You have all that here?"

"We grow quite a bit. Perhaps tomorrow I can give you a proper tour. If you feel up to it."

"That'd be great."

Chapel nodded with his subtle smile, but then his mood suddenly darkened, brow furrowed. Deliberating. The first time he seemed uncertain. After a moment, he drew a breath.

"I should tell you," he said. "After we found you with the boy, we tried to recover her. The boy's mother." Chapel paused for a moment, seemed unsure of his words. "Mr Carter went to find her. He found many slain Weir. I'm afraid he was unable to locate the woman."

He was, in his own way, sharing hard news in a soft manner. Three had of course already known, but hearing it confirmed still had impact. The Weir had taken her. Had taken Cass. He had left her. He clenched his jaw against the raw emotion. Stilled himself.

"Her name is Cass. Was. I appreciate you looking."

Chapel nodded. Gaze dropped to the bowl. Again, giving Three space.

"How did you find us, anyway?" Three asked.

Chapel looked up, eyebrows raised, momentarily surprised. Three wondered what new information he had just given away.

"You called us."

Three's turn for confusion. He definitely didn't remember crying out for help at any point. "Not sure I follow, considering we didn't know you were out here."

"Perhaps 'called' isn't it exactly, though I'm not sure how else to describe it." He thought for a moment, then shook his head with a slight shrug. "For me, it was like the passing of a wave. For Lil, a cold wind. There are no windows in her room. Mr Carter described it as an urgent pressure in his chest. Somehow we knew you were out there. And we knew we needed to come look for you. Though we didn't know what we would find."

"Wren," Three answered. It must've been Wren. "The boy's something special, Chapel. Not sure anyone knows just how special. Including him."

"I suspect he's not the only special one."

Three ignored the prompt. Kept the conversation focused on Wren. "Just before I blacked out. Before you came, I guess. He said he saw angels. Said you, and Mr Carter, and Lil were angels. When you wanted to be."

Chapel's brow furrowed again, puzzled.

"When we go out into the Strand, when we must face the Weir or expect to, we broadcast. A technique I learned long ago. It changes the way the Weir perceive us. Frightens them, in a way. I have taught the others here, but it's nothing you can *see*…"

He trailed off as a thought occurred, eyes widening slightly, the first hint of a breaking dawn.

"Told you he was special."

"I suppose he is."

Three hated to admit it, but he already felt wiped out. All those days unconscious, and the only thing he wanted to do right then was sleep. Chapel seemed lost in thought. Three interrupted.

"I hate to seem lazy, but I think I'm gonna need to lie down for a bit."

Chapel snapped back to reality, returning to the role of gracious host. "Yes, yes, of course. More than anything, you need rest."

Chapel escorted Three back to his room in the large L-shaped building, and promised to bring Wren to visit sometime mid-morning. Back on the mat, Three extinguished the lantern, and as he slipped into darkness, his last thoughts took him to Cass, pale, beautiful, broken. Gone.

The train-line didn't actually go all the way to Morningside, ending instead about a half-hour's walk away. As far as the guards at the gate were concerned, there was no reason to refuse entrance to the well-dressed and amiable people that showed up one late afternoon, hoping to stay a few days in the legendary city. And there were always rooms available to respectable-looking folks with well-funded and verified pointcards on hand. The four men and their woman-friend had found a nice second-story, three-bedroom apartment above an upscale clothier, not far from the Governor's compound. No one had seen much of them since their arrival.

"They should've been here by now," Dagon said. He stood at the window, looking out into the brightly-lit city under the deep night sky. It'd been three days since they'd arrived.

"Maybe, maybe not," Asher answered. He was sprawled casually on a short couch, his feet resting on the arm. "It's a long walk. No telling how many more secret hiding places the man knows."

"Why don't we see Underdown?" Fedor asked. "Or send word that we are here?"

"Not yet," Asher said. "I don't want him to know we're around. Not until I know what he's up to."

"He's running a city, Ash," Jez said from the adjoining bedroom. "What more do you need to know?"

"They're coming," Ran said. He was sitting on the floor, legs folded in some sort of meditative position.

"Finally." Asher sat up, swinging his legs off the couch and moving smoothly to standing in a single fluid motion. He grabbed his coat and threw it on as he moved to the door.

"No, not her. The Weir."

Asher stopped for a moment.

"Here?"

Ran nodded. Asher finished pushing his arms into his coat sleeves.

"Well. This should be interesting. Where are they coming from?"

"The east."

Asher moved to the door.

"Come on. Let's go see what happens."

The five remaining members of RúshRuin left the apartment and moved out into the street below. As usual, Asher took the lead at an aggressive pace, with Fedor at his elbow and Jez close behind. Dagon and Ran shadowed the others from a space removed on opposite sides of the thoroughfare. The calls of the Weir were dulled by the great wall of Morningside, but the sound was unmistakable. A force was gathering out there, and the screams of those outside the wall grew in intensity.

Asher led them towards the easternmost gate at a determined pace. A crowd had already formed by the time they arrived, tense little clusters of Morningside's citizenry waiting in strained silence for someone to rescue them.

They didn't have to wait long. Dagon spotted him first, moving along the top of the wall.

"There he is," Dagon said with a quick nod. Moments later a cheer went up from the crowd as Underdown strode the length of the wall. Beyond it, the surge of static voices grew.

"How many?"

"About thirty," Ran said. Asher raised his eyebrows appreciatively, nodded slightly. Atop the wall, Underdown strode with purpose, flanked by six of his black-clad personal guard. Asher pushed his way through the crowd towards a set of stairs along the wall, followed closely by the rest of his crew.

He took the steps two at a time, racing to get a view of the event before it resolved.

By the time Asher reached the top of the wall, Underdown had stopped above the gate and was now facing outwards, arms stretched out to either side. His eyes were closed, his brow furrowed in painful concentration. Down below a crush of outcasts pressed against the gate and wall, clinging to one another in fear as the electric horde descended upon them.

"That's going to get messy," Jez said.

But just before the savage wave crashed upon the helpless, Underdown cried out in a loud voice. In that instant, the Weir halted their advance, as if repelled by some unseen wall. Underdown trembled with the effort, straining like a man lifting a great weight. But as he did so, a remarkable thing happened. The Weir began to fall back. Slowly at first. And then in numbers, they turned and fled back into the night. And at their retreat, a great cry went up from outside the wall, from the outcasts who had moments before been facing certain death, now rescued.

Underdown lowered his arms and stumbled backwards. Two of his guardsmen caught him immediately and steadied him. As they escorted him back towards his compound, the Governor waved weakly at the crowds below on both sides of the wall who were now chanting his name. Extolling him. *Worshiping* him.

"They should've been here by now," Dagon said.

"Then go look for them," Asher replied, a sinister smile spreading slowly across his face. "I have business with Underdown."

Over the following two weeks, Three's strength slowly began to return, and he and Wren found themselves steadily becoming more a part of this frontier community. True to his word, Chapel showed Three the extent of the grounds, including the fields hewn from concrete where crops were now grown. He also returned all of Three's gear, his harness, pistol, and blade, explaining how he'd kept it safely locked up until he was certain of Three's intentions. Three met Mr Carter, a man of few words who seemed to carry the weight of the world and who possessed the strength to do so. And Three became better acquainted with Lil, the woman who had cared for him, and scalded him with hot broth.

After a time, Three was able to assist with a number of the daily tasks that kept the group thriving in the midst of the once-urban wasteland, though they would not let him keep watch despite his willingness to do so. Cass's death continued to weigh heavily, but the sting of her loss gradually lessened, and Three found himself occasionally able to think of her without being crushed by sorrow and guilt.

Wren's spirits lifted as well, as he was at last able to live in safety, to play with other children, to have something like a childhood again. He was plagued by sudden waves of grief and longing for his mother, but he nevertheless improved as the days wore on. Lil especially seemed to have formed a special bond with him, and the two were regularly together throughout the day. Most nights, Wren would sleep on a mat next to Three, in their small but adequate room. But occasionally Wren would ask for permission to stay with Lil, and Three never refused.

By the start of the third week, Three felt nearly himself again. And one night, after a hard day's work and an evening of hearty food and good company, he found himself lying on his mat with Wren by his side, beginning to wonder if maybe, just maybe, there was a life for them here. Here, in this unimaginable community, this boldly defiant explosion of life and freedom on the edge of the Strand.

It was just as he drifted off into the space between wakefulness and sleep that the attack came.

# TWENTY-SIX

He felt it first, more than heard it. A sort of creeping, electric dread that caused his heart to pound, a sudden heightening of his senses that told him adrenaline was pouring into his system, readying him to fight, or to flee. It had been Wren, of course. The boy had suddenly tensed beside him; a reaction Three had quickly learned to interpret as a dire warning. Wren fumbled for Three's hand. Found it, squeezed. Three knew well by now that Wren would say nothing, would make no sound. And he knew far too well that the boy was terrified. Something was out there, ominous, brooding, like a black thundercloud waiting to burst.

A sliver of light seeped in from lanterns in the hall that had been turned low, dull like the final heat of a dying ember, perceptible only because Three's eyes had adjusted to the otherwise complete blackness. He stretched out his hand in the darkness, gently felt for the boy's face, his cheek newly wet with tears.

"Wren," Three said, parting his lips just enough for the breath to escape in a whisper. "Is it Asher?"

He felt Wren shake his head.

"Weir?"

A nod. Three expected to feel some sort of relief, but instead felt only a sickening knot tighten in his gut. His last encounter with the Weir had left him more shaken than he cared to admit, and not only because of Cass's death. These Weir from the Strand, their coordinated movement and attacks, were entirely new to him, something he didn't understand. Without understanding, there was no way to prepare, and in his usual way of life, being unprepared was essentially the same as being dead. Then again, nothing about his way of life had been usual of late.

"We need to get out," Three said. "Don't want to get caught where we can't move."

Three rolled to his feet, and had to pause momentarily to pull his hand free from Wren's. He patted the boy's arm firmly, then crossed to the corner where he kept his harness and weapons, trying to ignore the stiffness in his shoulders, the dullness he felt around the edges of his perception. Sliding into his harness, there was a tremble in his chest, reminding him of his injury, of his too-recent weakness. He'd slipped in his time here, allowed softness to creep in. Soon enough he'd learn when he'd have to pay for it.

Three crept back to Wren, found him lying in the same position, still as death. He lay a hand on the boy's arm, and squeezed it.

"Come on, kiddo," he whispered.

Wren answered only by picking himself up off the mat and grabbing hold of Three's arm. Three stayed on one knee, cupped Wren's head in one hand, drew him close so that their noses nearly touched.

"Stay close," he said. "Like always."

He felt Wren nod. "Like always."

Three swiveled into a crouch and slowly drew open the door, thankful for the workmanship that kept the movement silent. The hall was empty, quiet, dark save for the dots of dim red light from the lanterns. He moved out into the corridor, probing with all his senses, with Wren pressed hard against him. There was no sound of trouble, no smell of blood or fire, nothing to see but stillness and the trick of darkness on the eyes. But there was tension in the air, a tangible, crackling pressure like a bone flexed to the point of breaking.

The two continued cautiously down the hallway, around the corner, to the set of double doors that led outside. Three slid them open carefully, felt the crisp air splash across his face. The courtyard was bathed in the pale blue-gray of the half-moonlight, spotted by pools of dim orange where lanterns hung. In the middle of the courtyard, Three could see the inkblot shape of a lone figure, standing upright, facing away.

Tall, stretched thin, utterly still yet somehow fluid, like he could melt into shadow at any second. Even from this distance, without seeing the man's face, Three knew him.

Dagon, the man they'd called The Grave. It wasn't hard to imagine why; Three pictured Dagon emerging from some dark pool of shadow and dragging his victims back down with him, for the earth to swallow. A dead man, doing death's work.

There was no other choice. Three stepped out into the courtyard, with Wren clinging to the back of his shirt, practically tripping to keep close. Dagon turned at their approach, but in the instant of his movement, Three could tell something had changed. There was an edge in Dagon's motion where none had been before. And when their eyes met, Three recognized well the look of the hunted.

They stood maybe twenty feet apart. Three rested his hand on his pistol, hoped his draw hadn't suffered too much over the past few weeks. One chance before Dagon could close the distance. One shell left in the cylinder. One shot to kill or be killed.

"Took too long," Dagon said in a rasping voice. He was rattled, almost out of breath. Not nearly the casual killer he'd seemed before. His eyes were hollow, like he hadn't slept in days. He laughed sadly.

"Where's Haven?" Dagon asked.

Three didn't answer. Just held steady. Not even wanting to blink.

"Spinner. Where's your mom, kid?"

Three felt Wren tighten around his leg, tried to ignore it. Focus. Wait for the moment.

"I can't get you out of this one anyway. Not now. I just wanted to see her."

"You'll see her soon enough," Three answered.

There was a cry in the distance, a man's voice shouting an alarm. Dagon flicked a glance in the direction of the warning reflexively. Three anticipated, drew, squeezed the trigger–

And stopped the instant before the hammer fell. Dagon had reacted to his sudden motion, twisted, rolled, just enough for Three to doubt himself, to hesitate. And the chance was gone. Dagon melted from the ground to his feet, suddenly fluid shadow again, putting a lantern between himself and Three. In the next instant, he evaporated into the darkness that had deepened suddenly, from the lantern light shining in Three's eyes.

Three cursed himself for faltering, but didn't have time to linger. Dagon was gone, and chaos took his place. A chorus of electric screams split the night air, and Three found himself running with Wren in his arms, towards the centermost building in the compound.

As he ran, other men from the compound emerged from their quarters, rushing headlong towards the growing sounds of battle. When they reached the building, Lil was already outside. Three practically tossed Wren to her.

"Keep him safe!" he yelled, and before she could respond, he whirled back and joined the flow of men rushing to the eastern side of the compound. He was vaguely aware of the fading sound of Wren screaming his name as he ran. He secured his pistol back in its holster, and slid his blade from its sheath.

But whatever Three had done to ready himself, nothing had prepared him for what he now saw.

They were coming over the wall in a cascade, like a surging tide overrunning its bounds. The greatest number of Weir he had ever seen at one time. Maybe more than he'd seen his whole life. In a flash his mind counted hundreds, though he told himself it was fear that made the multitude. And then the wave swept into him, and past him, and he screamed in rage and with his blade he made himself known among them.

The first he simply grabbed by the face as it ran by, slamming it backwards headfirst to the ground, crushing its skull with its own weight and momentum. He buried his blade to the hilt through the creature's midsection before whirling and lopping off the legs of another just below the knees. A few of the Weir faltered, surprised by this sudden motion that materialized and slew their fellows, but they quickly recovered and moved to attack him. He met them with fists, knees, and elbows, and his short sword ran slick. Three let loose the raw fury of his pain, invited the anger and pure emotion he so often held in check. Awakened wrath and ruin poured out rage on the inhuman throng that had stolen Cass from him.

How long he fought and how many he killed, he didn't know. But at some point in the frenzy, he found himself nearly shoulder to shoulder with Mr Carter, who was armed with a sword in one hand and a long hammer in the other. The two weapons were in constant motion, never interfering with the other's arc, never failing to find a target to devastating effect. Mr Carter's shirt was torn and splayed open, showing at least one jagged gash across his midsection. There was too much blood and other dark fluids splashed across him to know how severe or numerous his injuries actually were, and he fought with such intensity that Three was sure Mr Carter didn't know he'd been wounded at all.

Though they never directly acknowledged the other's presence, the two fell into a coordinated rhythm and together they cut a wide swath through the surge. Soon they were joined by a third man, and then a fourth, and gradually a small knot of warriors formed in the midst of the battle, briefly staunching the flow of Weir. Even so, Three began to feel the tide turning against them. In the span of a few minutes, they were giving ground again, despite the hard posture they fought to maintain.

The man immediately to his left dropped to a knee with a cry and before Three could react, one of the Weir tore the man's jugular. Three slashed the Weir, but he knew the man was beyond saving. Their eyes met for the briefest moment, and Three expected to see fear and desperation. Instead, there was only grim determination, as the man surged upward one final time, and impaled a Weir before collapsing together with it and becoming still.

In that instant, Three became suddenly aware of a voice, cutting clear and high above the combat. A woman singing. Her words were lost in the chaos, but the melody carried unmistakably on the air, and ignited his heart with strange passion. The same voice he'd heard the night they'd saved him. Lil's voice.

He risked a glance over his shoulder, and was startled by how close they were to the central building. She was there, standing at the top of its steps. And he saw then enough to know there was battle raging across the courtyard as well. A coordinated attack. The brunt had come from the eastern wall, but another contingent had joined from another direction. The Weir were pushing towards that building. Towards the building with Lil. And Wren.

Without thinking, Three leapt forward into the Weir, drove them back with sheer will and fury unleashed. A hoarse cry sounded behind him, and suddenly Mr Carter was by his side. They fought together again then, each renewed by the other's strength. Those men that had fallen back surged forward yet again, and though they suffered many wounds, they once again rejoined Mr Carter and Three.

And suddenly, something within the Weir broke. There was no fear, no panic, no obvious signal of retreat or defeat. The attack simply dissolved and fell away. The Weir nearest Three backed away, and then turned and fled back over the eastern wall and into the night. As they went, Three realized there were far fewer of them remaining than he'd thought only moments before.

He and Mr Carter and the few men with them stood in stunned silence before they came to their senses and realized that others were still fighting near the western side of the central building. Three led the way, and they raced to lend aid. But by the time they reached it, there was only a handful of Weir left. They stood in a semi-circle, facing a single figure, around whom many slain were arrayed.

Chapel. He held a long-bladed sword with both hands, but its tip drifted off so far to one side it was nearly behind him, and hovered just above the ground. Clearly exhausted from the battle, Chapel waited in utter stillness, as if already resigned to his fate. Three stepped forward to help him, but felt Mr Carter's heavy hand on his shoulder. Three stopped. Watched.

Four Weir remained, though Three knew from painful experience that they could essentially act as one. They hesitated, however, and he wondered if it was due to Chapel's broadcasting, wondered how they saw him now. Whether the face of a great avenging angel, or perhaps some ravaging demon.

It came in an instant, the swift collapse of the four Weir upon Chapel, and Three knew it was over. The Weir were just too fast, striking from too many angles. But in the span of two forward steps and a half-turn, only Chapel remained standing, watching as the Weir fell to the ground. The whole scene had unfolded like a choreographed dance, the way Chapel escaped the crowd with unhurried strokes of his blade sweeping up, out, and down again. It was several seconds before Three realized Mr Carter was no longer restraining him.

Three and the others moved forward to regroup with Chapel. As they approached, Chapel whipped his blade quickly to one side to clear the ichor, and then smoothly sheathed the sword. Lil had stopped singing, though Three couldn't remember when. He saw now that most, if not all, of the citizens of the compound were huddled in that centermost building. Or rather the women, children, and elderly. He couldn't help but wonder how many men they'd lost that night.

Wren came charging down the stairs, and Three didn't hesitate to pick the boy up. For a long while, no one spoke. There were just no words. And for a long while, Three just shut his eyes and held tightly to Wren, unsure whether he was offering comfort or receiving it.

When morning came, the damage was somewhat less severe than had been feared. Three learned there had in fact been three attacks: two simultaneously from the north and the east, and a third coming from the southwest after most of the men had already engaged. Chapel alone had defended the central building from that attack, though he was quick to downplay the numbers that he had faced and to give credit to the valor of the other men.

All told, they counted over sixty dead Weir, though Three knew the number slain could easily have been more than twice that. The Weir rarely left their dead behind, though no one knew why. Most stories suggested they ate their own. Three had never met anyone who had any evidence for that explanation. For their part, the compound had seven dead, and twelve wounded.

Had it been a legend, the story would have read as a heroic victory, for so few to stand against so many. In reality, it was a heavy blow for such a small community to bear. Seven husbands, seven fathers, seven guardians, all lowered into the ground. Even Three had shed tears during the simple ceremony they'd held. He himself had dug the grave for the man who had fallen by his side just hours before. Kirin had been his name, though Three hadn't learned it until he'd heard the man's wife crying out.

And all the while, while he'd carried the wounded, and dug the grave, and done what he could to help, Three couldn't shake the feeling that somehow it had all been his fault.

"Strange that they would choose now," Chapel said, late that afternoon, as they ate together. "We've been attacked before, of course, but never by so many. Never like this."

Three hadn't told anyone of Dagon's appearance, wasn't sure if there was a reason to do so. There couldn't be any connection between Dagon and the Weir, of course, but there was no doubt that whatever had happened, they couldn't stay. He and Wren had to leave.

"Chapel, I don't really know how to say this," he started.

"You're leaving."

Three nodded.

"I understand," Chapel said.

"No. You don't," Three answered. He stared down at the food in front of him, knowing he needed the nourishment, but having no appetite for it. "But I made a promise. And I've brought far too much trouble on you here."

"Nonsense. You've been a great help to us."

"It was selfish to stay. You and your people paid for it."

"By all accounts, we would've paid much more without you. Everyone agrees it was your actions that prevented complete tragedy. Even Mr Carter."

Three shook his head, but couldn't bring himself to elaborate. He wanted to believe the Weir would've attacked whether he'd been here or not, but his gut told him otherwise.

And Dagon. Would he bring Asher here, to these people? The only hope Three had now was to get Wren to his father in Morningside, the hope that this man Underdown would have the will and the means to protect his own son. And then... well, Three didn't know what then, except that he'd be back in control of his own life, and maybe then he'd be able to figure out how to become the man he'd once been, able to forget all the calamity he'd endured and created because of one simple decision to help a woman and a boy in distress.

"How soon will you go?" Chapel asked.

"First light. How far to Morningside from here?"

"Twenty-five miles or so, if you know the way."

"And if you don't?"

"We'll make sure you do."

They ate in silence for a time, and then Chapel excused himself to attend to the wounded. Three finished his meal alone, dreading having to break the news to Wren. He spent an hour or so preparing his gear for the journey, though it didn't really take more than fifteen minutes to do so. As evening was coming on, he trekked over to the central building, where he knew Wren was keeping close to Lil.

Sure enough, he found them together, sitting on the floor, playing a game of some kind. Three watched them from the door for a moment, watched their easy interaction, the obvious comfort they provided one another. He'd wondered before, but now he was certain that she'd lost a child of her own. She'd been a mother once, to some fortunate son or daughter. Maybe to many children. Three couldn't help but feel that he'd missed an opportunity with Lil, if nothing more than to get to know her. But the wounds Cass had left him with were too fresh, and Lil stirred the memories too strongly. He'd encouraged Wren to spend time with her, while he'd kept his own distance. Now he wondered if that'd been a mistake.

He entered, and knelt down beside the two.

"Hey, kiddo. Ma'am."

"Hi, Three."

"You really shouldn't still be calling me ma'am," Lil said, her eyes wrinkled at the corners with a hint of a smile. She looked exhausted, but genuinely glad to see him.

"Hey, Lil," Three answered. "Can I interrupt for minute? I need to talk to Wren."

"Sure, of course," Lil said. She started to get up, but Wren stopped her.

"Can you stay?" he asked quietly. "Please?"

Lil hovered between staying and leaving, looked to Three for a cue. He shrugged and nodded. He'd have to tell her at some point anyway. Might as well get it over with. Lil sank back to the floor. Three drew a breath to explain, but it was Wren who broke the news.

"We're going away, Lil."

Her brow furrowed in confusion, and she looked to Three for confirmation. He nodded again.

"But... what? Why?" The tears were already welling in her pale blue eyes.

"It's not safe," Wren said.

"I know last night was scary, but there's no reason to think it's going to happen again–"

"It's not safe for you." Hearing the words come from Wren's mouth, in his tiny voice, made them sound all the more terrible. Three had expected Wren to scream and cry and fight. Watching the boy now, calmly delivering the message himself, Three wasn't sure if he should feel proud or frightened.

"I don't understand," said Lil.

"And we can't explain," Three answered. "Just know that we'd stay if we could."

Lil blinked back at him, searching for words she wouldn't find. A tear dropped and splashed on her cheek.

"Is it OK if I stay with Lil tonight?" Wren asked.

"Sure, kiddo. If it's OK with her."

Lil wiped the tears from her eyes, and nodded. "Of course. Of course it's OK. I'd like that."

"Can Three come too?"

Her eyes flicked to his then, and he saw the flash of unspoken hope, the slight reddening of her cheeks. Then she looked quickly at the floor, afraid she'd given herself away.

"That'd be nice," Three said. "But I've got a lot to do to prep for tomorrow. And you need a good night's sleep."

"OK."

Lil nodded and smiled at him, but he could see the lines of disappointment, despite her efforts to conceal them. She was a good woman. Maybe a great one. But not for him.

Three tousled Wren's hair and stood up.

"Early morning tomorrow. Don't stay up late."

"OK."

"Night, kiddo."

"Good night."

"Good night, Three," Lil said, looking up at him from the floor. She had a sad smile on her face.

"Ma'am."

Three was up before the first hint of daybreak, and he spent the final hour of darkness sitting on the steps of the central building. He found himself shivering in the cold, sharp air. He was filled with a nervous energy that nagged at his mind. Three needed focus now, needed clarity. He needed to move.

As the sky was brightening to pale purple, Lil appeared with Wren in tow, flanked by Chapel. A small but sincere send-off. Wren slid in next to Three, stoic but not quite awake.

Three extended his hand.

"Chapel."

"Three," he said, taking Three's hand in a firm, warm handshake. "You're a good man. We hate to lose you."

"Wish I could do more to thank you."

"Come back some time. That will be enough."

Three nodded, and turned his attention to Lil. "Lil. Take care of yourself."

She smiled weakly and nodded. Wren took his cue and approached her. She knelt to his level, and he wrapped his arms around her tightly, then kissed her on the cheek.

"You always kiss the lady goodbye," he said. "So she remembers you."

"I could never forget you, Wren," she replied, with a broad genuine smile. "Not even if I tried."

She kissed the top of his head, and sent him back to Three. As the two turned to go, though, Three saw a third person crossing the courtyard.

"Mr Carter," Chapel said, "has insisted on taking you to Morningside."

Sure enough, as Mr Carter drew closer Three could see he was outfitted to travel, despite the fact that he was heavily bandaged.

"That's not necessary," Three said.

"He insists. You can try to refuse him if you like, but he'll follow you anyway."

There was a brief exchange between the men, but in the end Three relented, and as the first rays of sunlight began to crest the horizon, Three and Wren set out once more, each knowing full well that danger lay about them on all sides.

# TWENTY-SEVEN

For the first hour, they walked mostly in silence, and Three was uncomfortably aware of an ethereal dullness that seemed to surround and follow him like a personal fog. Whether he hadn't fully recovered from his wounds or instead had lived in comfort for too long, he wasn't sure. But out here in the open, he knew in his gut that he'd lost his razor-edge. He hoped it'd come back quickly.

Mr Carter led them east and south, through squat ruins and gutted shells of structures that may once have been homes, or schools, or shops. If the Strand were the unbroken sand after a recent surge, these were the remnant sandcastles along the fringe, rounded and bowed by the tide, but not completely destroyed. Though Three had passed through the Strand before, he had forgotten how similar the landscape was on either side. It was perhaps a redder brown here in the east, as opposed to the more dominant, cooler blue-grays of the west; some of the faded fonts and markings were rounder. But by and large, taking it all in at once left one with more or less the same impression. Urban. Decayed. The corpse of a once-unbroken cityscape.

As they walked, shadows receded, the air lost its bite, and the landscape gradually grew around them. Buildings stood taller, scattered bits of tech remained intact, signs of other travelers began to reveal themselves. By midday, they were well clear of the borders of the Strand, and on into what would relatively be called civilization proper. They stopped to rest, taking shelter from the sun in a rusted-out kiosk that may once have sold the day's latest technical fashion, and now stood gaping and gutted. At least there was no broken glass on the floor. They ate from their rations, but before Wren was halfway finished, he began nodding off.

"How much farther to Morningside?" Three asked.

"Three, maybe four hours," Mr Carter answered. "The child has time to sleep."

Three nodded and Wren needed little encouragement to curl up with his head on his pack. In short time, the boy's breathing was deep and regular with heavy sleep.

"You've been before?" Mr Carter asked.

"To Morningside? No," Three said, shaking his head. "Heard the stories, of course, but never had much need."

Mr Carter nodded.

"Are they true?" Three asked.

Mr Carter stroked his beard along his jawline with the back of his hand, tilted his head slightly from side to side, weighing his response. "Some yes, many no. It is a place of great wonder. And mischief."

"Have you been often?"

"I lived there for many years. Before I met Chapel. I have not gone back."

"Too much mischief?"

"It is a safe place, of a sort. But it is also difficult to live life on one's own terms there. A certain exchange of freedom for security, which I could not continue to pay."

Three nodded and sipped water. He let his eyes rove the surroundings, scanning for whatever might catch his attention. The fog was still there, but he felt it thinning. His senses were sharpening, focus returning. Being on the move stirred their awakening.

"How will you find the boy's father?" Mr Carter asked.

"Shouldn't be too hard. Name's Underdown." Mr Carter's eyes widened slightly at the mention of the name. "You know him?"

"If you mean the Governor Underdown, yes, of course."

"What do you know of him?"

Mr Carter glanced off at his surroundings, took a long pull of water. Shook his head. "A hard man to know."

He trailed off, as if that were all he had to say, but Three saw the man's eyes flicking back and forth over the landscape as he again drank from his canister of water. Three waited.

"Things changed when he arrived. Better, in many ways. Order. Safety. He is the reason the city flourishes. Its savior. But in some ways, its captor as well."

"Savior's a pretty strong word."

Mr Carter looked back to Three then.

"The Weir..." he paused, searching for the word, *"fear* him. If they can feel fear. Before he came, Morningside survived because of its size, like Fourover. But now... it's like a strong light turning back the darkness. Night still comes, but the light keeps it from the city." He shook his head again. "I'm sorry, I'm not making any sense. I don't really know how to explain it."

Three glanced at Wren, sleeping peacefully nearby. Memories flashed: how Wren sensed when the Weir were close, how he knew that Three wasn't wired, or the night Cass fell, when the boy's cry for his mother seemed to steal the very life from her attackers.

"I know what you mean," said Three. And for the first time, Three felt a certainty that this was all going to be alright. A man like that, a man like Wren, but who understood and could control his gift... well, surely such a man was better equipped and able to raise and protect this boy than Three would ever be. He felt a pang then, at the thought of leaving Wren. In spite of himself, he'd grown fond of the little guy. But knowing he was safe, with his own real father, that would be enough. Time would heal the rest.

"We'll move on in an hour," Mr Carter said, interrupting Three's thoughts. "Give the child time to rest."

Three nodded, took another long drink of water. Another hour, and they'd be on the move again. And by tomorrow, he just might have his life back.

The sun had just begun to blur the border between late afternoon and early evening by the time the trio reached the outskirts of Morningside. Here, the urban landscape took on a striking contrast to the surrounding sprawl. Order, it seemed, extended even beyond the walls of Morningside. Clearly great pains had been taken to clean, repair, and in some cases even reclaim the remnant city that surrounded the thriving township.

"We're very close now," Mr Carter said. "We'll start seeing people soon. Don't be alarmed."

Three just nodded. He felt Wren move closer beside him, and felt the boy's tiny hand slip into his. Within ten minutes, it was just as Mr Carter had said. Here and there were signs of people living out here, beyond the wall. Soon enough, they saw the people themselves. Those they encountered responded in their own way; some with flat stares, some with a nod of greeting, others with indifference. But none seemed hostile, or even surprised.

"Squatters," Mr Carter explained. "Most of them have been expelled. Underdown allows them to stay, under his protection."

"Expelled?"

"As I said. Within Morningside, it can be difficult to live life on one's own terms. During the day, the gates remain open, these here are free to do trade. But come evening, they return."

"And if they don't?"

"Punishment."

They continued on in silence for another fifteen minutes, until there before them loomed the wall of Morningside. Standing there under its lengthening shadow, even Three couldn't help but feel the awe the place inspired. He'd been to the largest of towns west of the Strand: Fourover, Swingbridge, Greenstone. Now, even Greenstone's fortress-like design seemed childish by comparison.

The wall itself ran nearly thirty-feet high, but unlike Greenstone's prison-inspired structure, Morningside's wall had been built with an eye for aesthetics. There were no watchtowers, no mounted weapons. At least none that could be seen. Instead, fiberlights ran throughout, enmeshed with the steel fabric of the wall, so that the entire barrier seemed to glow with an internal, vibrant green-blue that shifted like the sea. Like Greenstone, Three could see people moving along the tops of the wall, but they were no guards. He realized they were citizens, walking along as one might expect in a park.

Beside him, Wren stood with his mouth slightly open, eyes wide and drinking in the astonishing display before them. From somewhere atop the wall, there was music, tumbling down with the faint but unmistakable raw emotion of live players, supported by a crowd singing along, nearly in time and almost on key. A large gate stood open, tended by a trio of guardsmen, and a handful of people trickled in or, if they were among the unfortunate, out.

"I trust you can find your way from here," Mr Carter said abruptly.

"You won't come in?"

Mr Carter shook his head, but offered no explanation. His eyes were on the wall, but unfocused. Thinking of something beyond, or within. Three noticed a thin, dark shimmer along the front of Mr Carter's shirt, guessed his bandage had bled through.

"Why don't we camp together tonight, then? We'll see you on your way in the morning."

Mr Carter smiled and turned to face Three and Wren. "A kind thought, but one I must refuse. Talk to the guards at the gate. They should be able to help you." He knelt and placed a hand on Wren's shoulder. "Wren, you are fine boy, and you will be a great man. Maybe one day you could come visit us again."

Wren nodded and surprised Mr Carter by wrapping his arms around the man's neck. "Thanks, Mr Carter. I'd like that."

Mr Carter patted Wren firmly on the back, and then stood, and shook hands with Three. "The same stands for you as well, Three. The village is as much a home to you as you choose to make it."

"I appreciate that, Mr Carter. Just may take you up on it some time."

"Please do."

Three looked down at Wren and gently slapped him on the shoulder with the back of his hand.

"Come on, kiddo. Let's go see if any of these stories about Morningside are true, huh?"

"OK."

Three looked back up and exchanged final nods with Mr Carter, and the three parted ways.

After they'd walked about halfway to the gate, Wren spoke in his quiet voice. "Why won't he stay?"

Three glanced back over his shoulder, saw Mr Carter's silhouette in the fading light, shook his head. "I don't know, Wren. Every man's got a story. I'm sure he has his."

Wren didn't respond. Just slid his hand into Three's again. Three tried not to think about how natural it had become, holding that tiny hand in his own. Tried not to think about what it might be like to let go of that hand a final time. Deal with it later. When it's done. They walked those final steps towards Morningside, together, in silence.

As they drew closer, the sounds of the town grew louder, more distinct. The music became more apparent, bits of conversations became discernible: vendors making last minute deals, friends calling to one another. The atmosphere was pleasant, inviting, and Three wondered if they'd arrived on the night of some festival, or if this was just a typical evening in Morningside.

The guards at the gate stirred as they drew near, and one guard, shorter than the others, casually motioned for Three to stop just outside. The short guard approached with an easy smile. None of the guards looked as grim or hardened as the greenmen of Greenstone, but they all held themselves with the bearing of men of authority.

"Evening," the guard said.

"Evening," Three answered. He felt Wren step closer, the boy's shoulder lightly pressed against his leg.

"Been to Morningside before?"

"No, sir. First time."

"Where you comin' in from?"

Three felt a twinge in his chest. The slightest knot of pressure, born of frustration, the first hint that here, even now mere inches from his goal, there was a dangerous game to be played, a chance for misstep. He dare not lie, but how much of the truth was necessary?

"A long way off, sir."

"I don't doubt it," the guard said with an understanding nod. "You gents look like you've had a bit of a rough go."

One of the other guards sidled up, an older man, hands behind his back. Curious, but not enough to get involved. He stood back a couple of paces, greeted Three with a dip of the head.

"What brings you out our way?" the short guard asked.

"The boy. We need to see the Governor."

The guard's eyebrows raised slightly at that, his expression one of... what? Surprise? Something prickled in Three's instincts, but it was too vague, to fleeting to identify.

"And why's that, if you don't mind my asking?"

"Beg your pardon, sir, but I don't think I can explain. It's a private matter."

The guard nodded thoughtfully, his lips pressed together and jutting slightly, as if weighing his options. There was something. Something Three should've noticed. Or was there? There was too much noise, too many things going on. His focus was dull.

"I see," the guard said. "Well, I'm not one to pry. How long you expecting to be in Morningside?"

"Shouldn't be long. Just have some business with the Governor, then I'll be gone."

Wren pressed further into Three then, hard. Tense. The thought of being left alone in this strange city with a man he'd never met must've been sinking in. Three wished he'd chosen his words a little more carefully.

The short guard took a knee in front of Wren, leaned forward slightly with a lowered head. Gentle. Disarming.

"And how about you, little one? Will you be staying with us?"

Wren made no answer. Three glanced back at the older guard, still standing there. Watching without emotion.

"Here, boy, lemme take a look at you," the short guard said, reaching out with two fingers extended to raise the boy's chin. "How old are you now? Five?"

"Six," Wren answered. "And three-quarters."

A ripple of thought ran through Three's mind… he'd never thought to ask Wren's age. Just assumed his initial guess had been correct. Almost seven, still looked five. Small for his age.

"Six and three-quarters. Practically a grown man."

Everything about the situation seemed fine, and Three could find no reason for his unease. But he was nevertheless uneasy.

"And that's a fine coat," the guard said, rubbing the lapel of Wren's coat between two fingers.

Three thought back, replayed the moment he'd said he needed to see the Governor. The guard's expression… eyebrows up, pupils constricting, twitch at the corner of his mouth, at his temples. Not surprise.

Recognition.

Where was the third guard?

The realization struck in the same instant that the guards moved. The short guard snatched Wren by the front of his coat, jerking the boy away, tearing him free of Three's leg. As he did so, the older guard brought his hands up, pointing some kind of dull metallic box at Three. He heard Wren cry his name, shrill, terrified, followed by a muffled thump.

Three twisted, reaching into his coat to draw his pistol, but something dull punched into his upper chest, sent him sprawling. He absorbed the fall as best he could, rolled to his feet. The older guard was still standing with his arms outstretched, a look of shock on his face. Three went for his pistol, but before he could get it free of his holster, massive arms wrapped around him from behind, pinning his own to his sides. Three instinctively whipped his head backwards, felt the impact, the crunch of cartilage that told him he'd just broken someone's nose. But still the arms squeezed. He snapped back again with his head, and then again. The arms released for half an instant.

But before he could exploit the moment, he felt the vice-grip clamp around his neck, cutting off the blood flow to his brain. He had seconds before he'd pass out. Time slowed.

The older guard was running at him now. The shorter guard fought to control a squirming Wren. Blood rushed in Three's ears. Cass flashed in his eyes. She'd trusted him with her boy. With her life. He'd come so close. Too close.

A deep redness started closing in from the edge of his vision. He fumbled, felt his fingertips brush the grip of his pistol. The red became blackness. Sound suddenly snapped to an unearthly sharpness. Wren crying out. The shouts of the guards.

There. The pistol hard in his hand. He drew it, felt it slide with intolerable slowness. Darkness nearly complete. Numbness. Was he still holding the gun? The old guard was two steps away.

A low *whoosh… whoosh… whoosh*. Louder each time. The last strangled rush in his blood-starved brain. Something cracked wetly. The grip around his neck fell away. Hard impact on his knees, his pistol clattered away. And as his vision returned, there were the feet of the older guard floating up off the ground, backwards, up and away from Three. And in the next instant, time returned to its proper flow, and Three saw the old guard slamming backwards to the ground, and Mr Carter there.

As the old guard impacted, Mr Carter followed him to the ground, dropping his knee into the man's chest. Mr Carter spun, swept something up from the ground behind Three, where the third guard lay bleeding from his face and side of the head. His hammer. He must've thrown it.

Three's fogged mind fought to catch up as the events unfolded before him at lightning speed. The short guard cried out in pain, and dropped Wren. As Three gained his feet, he saw the man clutching his arm, with crimson spots welling up in three separate locations. Wren crouched back, his tiny blade gripped tightly, gleaming wet in the fading light. Tears streaming down his face.

Three covered the distance to the guard in three steps and buried the sole of his boot in the man's solar plexus. The guard buckled to the hard ground, and Three was on him the next moment, delivering a devastating fist crushing down into the man's jaw. Three saw the guard's eyes go blank under the impact, out cold.

Wren's sobs suddenly caught Three's hearing, and he turned to see the boy standing there, knife in hand, arms dangling at his sides, wailing in terror, and confusion, and who knew what other raw emotion. But there was a commotion near the gate, and Three knew that more guards were surely on their way.

"Run! This way!" Mr Carter yelled, and in the next instant, Three had Wren in his arms, and they were running, running again, away from Morningside, back into the open, back once more into the gathering night.

# TWENTY-EIGHT

Following Mr Carter's lead, Three raced back through the outskirts cradling Wren tightly to his chest. Three was still lightheaded from the attack, and his lungs strained for air as they threaded their way through the eerily sterile urban remains. Through the alleys and side streets, they fled like thieves, like men with hounds at their heels. The night fell down around them, a heavy shroud upon weary shoulders. They ran long past the squatters, out through the crisp borders of Morningside's reach, into the fuzzy border between the open and the looming township.

At last, Mr Carter slowed his pace, and then soon after ducked into a brick shell of a building. Mr Carter moved through the first room quickly, scanning the surroundings. Towards the back, a darkened corridor ran to a second, windowless room. Mr Carter stopped at the entrance of the corridor, and waved Three and Wren on through. Three pushed his way into the dusky room, immediately reminded of his small room back at the village. He set Wren on his feet, and dropped to a knee, sucking air into his burning lungs. His hands were clammy with sweat, shaking. Behind him, Mr Carter leaned against the doorframe, doubled over, hands on knees, panting as well. Wren stood as stone, staring blankly, his hair matted to his head by Three's sweat. It was minutes before anyone spoke.

When Three had recovered enough to know he wouldn't pass out, he took Wren's face in his hand, and sought out the boy's eyes in the darkness.

"Are you hurt, boy?"

Wren made no sound, but Three felt the boy's head shake slightly from side to side. Three dropped his hand onto Wren's shoulder, squeezed it.

"What happened?" Mr Carter asked from the corridor.

"They tried to take Wren," Three said. After a moment, he added, "and I almost let 'em. I let 'em get the jump on me. If you hadn't come back…"

Three trailed off, suddenly reliving those near-final moments. Trapped. Blacking out. Wren struggling in the guard's grasp. Three, powerless to prevent it.

"The child," Mr Carter said. He paused, searching for words. "He… *called*."

"Are they dead?"

"I don't think so. The one that had you, the big one… maybe. It was not my intent…"

"My fault. Should've been more careful." Three shook his head, then snorted a humorless chuckle. "Been on a bad run with guard-types lately." He thought back to the attack, but much of it was a jumble in his head. Too many things happening at once. One guard grabbing Wren, the other hitting him with… what? "One of them shot something at me. Knocked me down. But not much more. Any idea what that was?"

Mr Carter thought for a moment, and shook his head slightly. "Many of them carry dislocators. But a shot from one of those would've done more than just knock you down."

Dislocator. Made sense. Intended as a non-lethal weapon, a dislocator fired a semi-rigid projectile that caused massive overload of one's datastream on impact, incapacitating the target without causing any significant physical trauma. But

Three wasn't wired. That would explain the surprised look on the guard's face.

"Maybe it was a dud," Three offered. He didn't know if Mr Carter was aware of his disconnected status.

"Could be. Fortunate, if so."

Three got to his feet and moved his hand from Wren's shoulder to the top of the boy's head, where he gently tousled Wren's blond hair. Behind him, he heard Mr Carter stir, and moments later the soft glow of a chemlight spilled through the room. Mr Carter entered carrying his light held out slightly before him. He moved gingerly into the corner where he let his pack slide to the floor and then sat more heavily than Three expected. Weary. Wounded. Three wondered just how much pain the man was silently bearing.

"We gonna be safe here?" Three asked.

Mr Carter closed his eyes, and leaned back against the wall. After a moment, he nodded, drew a deep but strained breath. "Far enough out, the guards won't come searching. Not tonight, anyway."

"And the Weir?"

Mr Carter shrugged weakly. "Close enough to Morningside. We hope."

He was still and quiet just long enough for Three to think that was all he had to say, but he eventually stirred and added, "I'll stand watch. I just need a few minutes' rest."

Three gently turned Wren and walked him over towards Mr Carter. It was only then that Three at last realized the lightness of his own harness. His hand shot reflexively to his holster, even as his mind made the connection.

His pistol. Gone.

He remembered now. The grip around his neck releasing; the impact of falling to his knees. The pistol skittering across the concrete. And Wren in trouble. He'd grabbed the boy, and left the weapon behind. A sort of quiet despair sank into

Three's heart then, like the death of a long-time friend, or loss of a beloved pet, or both. Its heft had been a comfort. And it had saved his life more than once. He cursed aloud, startling both Wren and Mr Carter.

"What's wrong?" Mr Carter asked.

"My pistol. It's gone."

"The guards?"

Three nodded.

"I'm sorry. It was a rare and fine weapon."

"Still is. Just someone else's now."

"Hard earned."

"Not hard enough."

Three smoldered at the thought of one of Morningside's guards sporting his pistol, ignorant of its legacy and worse, its power. It was all too easy to imagine one of them squeezing off a round and blowing a hole through some unfortunate citizen's home. He was roused by Wren's quiet crying.

"It's alright, kiddo," he said, thinking the boy was blaming himself. "It wasn't your fault." But Wren just stood there, facing the wall, sobbing.

"Hey. Wren." Three turned Wren around to face him, and took a knee, looking into the boy's eyes. "Wren, what is it? What's wrong?"

Wren didn't speak, just wept. But he held his hand out for Three to see. It was dark and sticky with blood. Three took the hand and searched it for injury, until it clicked, and he then understood. Not Wren's blood. The guard's.

"Oh, Wren," he said, and instinctively he pulled Wren close to him, and held the boy tight to his chest. "It's alright. It's OK, Wren. You did the right thing."

For a time, he just held Wren, and Wren stood there crying, letting himself be held. Eventually Wren's crying ebbed into a quiet sniffling. Three let go, eased back to look at him again.

"Here, come over here."

Three led Wren to across the room to another corner, and got out his canister of water. He took Wren's hand, splashed water over it, scrubbed it with his own. Wordlessly, Three repeated the process, carefully washing Wren's hand until there were no traces of blood remaining. Then he took both of Wren's hands in his, dried them on his own shirt, and rubbed them vigorously to warm the tiny, chilled fingers in the cold night air.

"Better?"

Wren nodded.

"You OK now?"

Wren shook his head.

"Are you hurt somewhere?"

Wren shook his head again. "I'm sorry I hurt that man."

"He was going to take you away, Wren. He would've taken you if you hadn't hurt him."

"I'm still sorry."

"OK, buddy. It's OK to be sorry. It was a bad situation. For everybody." Wren nodded at that, and Three picked him up. "Tough day. Let's get you something to eat, and then get some rest, alright?"

Three led him back to Mr Carter's corner. Mr Carter had dozed off, and Three didn't disturb him. He dug through his pack and pulled out some of the food Chapel had provided for them. They ate, though neither seemed to have much appetite. After they'd finished, Three pulled blankets from their packs and made a pallet for Wren to lie down on.

Rolled in one of the blankets, Three discovered a device; brushed steel, rectangle-shaped with rounded edges. It took him a moment to realize it was an old military heatcoil. When activated, it radiated a gentle warmth similar to natural body heat. Whether Chapel had slipped it in the packs, or Lil, it was truly a gift out here in the open. Three activated the heatcoil, and tucked it in with Wren. He laid his coat over the boy, and rested his hand on Wren's head.

"Try to get some sleep, alright?"

Wren nodded and closed his eyes. Three sat with him for a while, rubbing his back because he didn't know what else to do. After a time, Wren's breathing was deep and even, and Three quietly got to his feet and walked to the door. He stopped at the entry, and stared down the corridor, into the darkness, wondering what the night might bring.

He heard shuffling from within the room, and soon Mr Carter appeared.

"I don't understand it," Mr Carter said, voice lowered. "What reason would they have to seize the child?"

Three shook his head. "I told them we needed to see the Governor. The guard reacted."

"As if they had been expecting you?"

Three remembered the guard's expression. Reflexive, but controlled. "Like they'd been warned."

"By whom?"

"Asher," Wren said quietly, apparently not asleep after all. He had said it so flatly, with such lack of emotion, that Three thought he'd misheard.

"What?"

Wren didn't stir, didn't open his eyes. "Asher's there. In Morningside."

"What makes you think that?"

"I know."

Three wanted to argue, to tell Wren he was dreaming it, or imagining it, or just scared, but he knew better. If Wren *knew* it, then it was true. Asher was in Morningside, waiting for them.

"Who's Asher?" Mr Carter asked.

"The kid's brother," Three answered. "The one we've been trying to escape."

It didn't seem possible, but at the same time, it made too much sense to be wrong. Pieces started falling together. Dagon showing up at Chapel's commune. They could've tracked Cass and Wren to Greenstone. Probably convinced Bonefolder to let them on the train. Rode into Morningside, and just waited for their quarry to show up. But after Three's delay, maybe they got nervous, and sent Dagon out into the Strand after them. And in the meantime did what? Tell Underdown Three was on his way?

Bonefolder had offered him a contract on Underdown's life, after all. Sure. Man shows up with a kid, says he's got private business with the Governor. Not likely to be a lot of people rolling into town with that story. And what story had Asher told? That Three was a kidnapper? A slaver? An assassin, using a child as cover?

*Kill the man, rescue the boy? My baby brother?*

Three laughed then, in spite of himself; a sad chuckle at first that started as a rumble in his chest, and grew slowly into a full throated laugh devoid of humor, and hope. "All of this," he said. "All of it, and we're right back where we started." He squeezed his eyes shut, pinched the bridge of his nose, tried to keep the weight of inevitability from crushing down. Cass flashed before his eyes, weak, pale, life flowing from her. Not much different than when he'd first laid eyes on her, and her son, harried, frightened, desperate for help. "Except somewhere along the way, I lost something I never even wanted in the first place."

Cass. She'd given her life to get her son to Underdown. What would she have done now?

"This man Asher," Mr Carter said. "He is dangerous?"

"Worse. Deadly."

"Then you should return with me. We will hide you."

Three shook his head. "They already know about you. One of his men showed up night before last."

"Then we will protect you."

"They'd kill every man, woman, and child in your village, Mr Carter. I was afraid they might do it anyway, but once they hear what happened to the guards, they'll know we're nearby."

Three's mind ran through the scenarios. Dagon had tracked them down outside the wayhouse, to the Vault, and somehow through the Strand to Chapel's village. How long would it be before he found them hiding here? Would he come alone this time? A sudden thought struck Three then, and he cursed himself for not thinking of it sooner. He'd assumed that after their last meeting, Dagon had rushed back to report their location to Asher. But what if he had merely trailed them from the village? The hair stood up on the back of Three's neck, and a rage kindled in his heart.

This wasn't his way. It hadn't been from the start. Everything he'd been trained for, all the years he'd spent honing his senses, every scar he bore, it was all building him to be the predator, never the prey. And now, here, at the end, he found himself in little more than an urban cave, cornered.

He'd sensed it, back on that afternoon when she'd walked out of the bar, and he'd followed; he knew deep down that somehow this was the decision that was going to get him killed. And now he knew why. Because everything he'd done to this point had gone against his carefully cultivated discipline. His code. His *way*.

No more. If death was coming, Three was wise enough to know he was no match for that ageless enemy. But he was done sitting around, waiting for it to show up. It was his turn to stalk.

"Enough," Three said. "Enough of this."

"What will we do now?"

"Now?" Three answered. "Now, I'm going to do what I was made for."

# TWENTY-NINE

The night air was cold, cutting and clear, like a knife's edge bitten by frost. A half-moon hung high in the sky, bathing the ruins on the outskirts of Morningside in a soft white-blue light. For a time, Three just crouched atop the roof of an abandoned and gutted building, staring at Morningside and its wall. Getting a feel for the flow of its people, the unique rhythm of the life inside. He let his eyes float unfocused, drinking in the cityscape without fixing on any one detail. From here, with the slope of the terrain and his elevated vantage, he could see glimpses over the wall, though he was too far away to make out specifics. Still, it was the big picture he was after, the subtle signals his subconscious would record and later recall unbidden, when the time was right.

The city was lively, the citizens inside oblivious to the dangers that plagued the rest of the world. Distant troubles, far removed. Even the outcasts and exiles that lived outside near the wall seemed unconcerned by thoughts of the Weir, or slavers, or any of the thousand other deadly things that lurked in the night. Three couldn't help but wonder at this man Underdown, whose leadership and power extended so far beyond physical boundaries. Would such a man be approachable? Even if Asher had reached him first, would he have entertained discussion, or might he have cast Asher out with all the others that now huddled against the cold?

There was only one way to be certain. Three would go see for himself. He stood slowly, careful to make no sound; let the blood pump again after his hour or two of stillness.

Wren had been asleep when he'd left, and he had decided not to wake the boy. Three'd left Mr Carter watching over him, with clear and specific instructions. He'd said he'd be back before dawn broke. But if he didn't show, Mr Carter had agreed to take Wren with him back to the village as soon as the sun was up. Three knew that if something happened to him, there was no better place for Wren to be than under Chapel's watchful eye. And the thought lingered that even if *nothing* happened to him, Chapel's home might still be the better place.

Now, perched on the roof's edge, Three wasn't sure whether he believed he'd be able to return or not. At the time he'd made the deal, he'd certainly intended to. But out here, looking at the city, a sense had begun to settle on him that it had been foolish to expect it. Morningside loomed luminescent, and he felt as if he were staring at a vast ocean, preparing to walk into its depthless waves.

Admittedly, he wasn't even sure what he intended to do exactly. Find Asher, certainly. And most likely kill him. But he didn't know where to begin. After the fight with the guards at the gate, surely news would spread. Asher would know they were near. And then what? Send Dagon after them? That was most likely, assuming Dagon had returned from the village. Asher himself wouldn't be out doing the grunt work. He had people for that. Three would have to go to him.

Jez, and Ran: Three didn't know enough about them to make a guess. They seemed to stay near Asher for the most part, so maybe they weren't worth worrying about yet. Though if he spotted them, they'd be worth following. Jez he remembered well, with her ice-blonde hair and precise movements. More of a stalker than a tracker. And her beauty probably afforded RushRuin a level of charm it otherwise lacked without Cass around; all manner of authority could be circumvented with the right wink and smile. Ran he wasn't sure he'd recognize just from Cass's description. They'd called him the Mountain: a man as dispassionate and immovable as a wall of stone. There was danger there, an unknown variable.

And then there was Fedor. Fedor he knew plenty well. A hound. Not a tracker of Dagon's caliber, Fedor was probably the one Asher sent out when the prey was near. An attack dog. And they still had unfinished business.

Fedor, then. Dagon was best avoided anyway, if possible. Three would start with the genie, and work his way back from there. Track down Fedor, see what doors opened up afterwards. It wasn't much of a plan, but it was a start.

He checked the blade at his back, and moved his hand to his holster out of habit, before catching himself. There was little hope of recovering his pistol, but it was one hope he allowed himself to indulge. Maybe, before this was all over, he'd get a chance to use that last shell.

Three inhaled deeply, and slowly released a long, controlled settling exhalation. It was time. He climbed down from his makeshift watchtower and followed the narrowest alleys towards Morningside. He had little concern of being stopped or engaged by any of the people outside the wall, but Three saw no need to draw attention to himself if it could be helped. He kept to the shadows and the dark places as he approached the city.

Getting into Morningside was actually easier than he'd anticipated. Though the wall looked smooth from a distance, it was in fact pieced together from all manner of steel plating, and presented plenty of sturdy hand- and footholds for a climber as skilled as Three. His biggest risk had been his own silhouette as he picked his way up the softly radiant wall. Few people would be interested in what was above them, however, and he'd chosen to climb a seam where two sections of the wall met, giving himself the best chance of escaping discovery.

The section of wall he'd selected afforded another advantage as well. Along the top, a garden of sorts had been planted; delicate-limbed trees and carefully arranged shrubs, lit softly for nighttime strolls. As he crested the wall, he realized now that the plants were all of course artificial, but the effect was not wholly lost. And most importantly, he was able to slip into them without notice.

There was a distinct pathway through the atrium, and a few citizens strode along it leisurely, some in pairs, some alone, some in small knots of hushed conversation. Three crouched in the shadows, waiting for the right moment. After a minute or two of observing, he simply slipped out onto the path and joined the flow, walking as a man deep in thought amongst the gentle beauty of the replicated garden.

Undoubtedly, the wall was lined with sensors that would've screamed at the intrusion had Three been connected. As it was, he was inside and unnoticed. It was up to him to keep it that way. He knew he'd have to err on the side of caution, not knowing how far or wide a description of him may have spread. But it was to his advantage that he had been seen fleeing back out into the open. Certainly the guards posted at the gates would be on the lookout, but no one had reason to search for him within the city wall. At least, not yet.

Three set an easy pace for himself as he moved along the top of the wall, hands clasped behind his back, head up and soaking in the surroundings. The wall itself was perhaps twenty feet wide, leaving plenty of room for the path and its garden-like surroundings without feeling crowded. And at this height, he had a good view of the town sprawled below. It was well-lit, and people moved freely throughout the streets, though his eye was quick to note the presence of pairs of guardsmen patrolling through the crowds, casual in pace but ever alert.

As he walked, Three absorbed the layout as best as he could, forming a rough mental map. He followed the wall in a slow, steady gait, soaking in the environment, letting his mind work out the plan of action. After a time he came to a gently winding set of stairs that doubled back on themselves, and he took them down to ground-level, where he blended in amongst the people. Here, moving with and through the citizens of Morningside, Three was struck by how clean, and healthy, and happy they were. Certainly there were those among them who had come from the open, but many were seemingly untouched by the hard living beyond the wall. They seemed so *soft*; a people from a different world. It both amazed and sickened him.

For an hour or so, Three moved through the streets with casual confidence, stilling himself whenever he passed a patrol. His attire and rough look drew a few glances, but he was not so strange as to draw attention. And as long as he seemed to know where he was going, no one else seemed to pay him much mind. He wandered towards the center of the city, correctly guessing that the Governor's dwelling would be located there. When he arrived, he couldn't help but be impressed. It wasn't just a compound as he'd expected; it was more like a miniature city of its own.

Guards patrolled an octagonal outer wall, which had main gates facing northwest and northeast, and a third narrow gate on the southern side. Towers loomed at each of the corners of the wall, though it was difficult to tell whether there were men in each. Three made a single lap, taking in what he could without appearing like he was casing the place, and then circled back towards the section of Morningside he'd already walked.

It was impossible for Three to gather all the information he'd need in the few hours before daybreak. But he turned his focus towards finding the most likely scenario of what he was up against. Wren had said with certainty that Asher was here. Once Asher had discovered Morningside was their destination, he would've had to have known that Cass had meant to take Wren to Underdown. Whether he'd made contact with the Governor or not, then, it was a safe bet that he was nearby.

Dagon had found them just the night before, and had likely backtracked from Morningside into the Strand. There was no telling how long it had taken Dagon to track them, but from the look of it, he'd been out for days at least. It was possible that Dagon had returned the previous night, and that RushRuin had traveled out towards Chapel's village that morning, whether in part or in whole. But it seemed unlikely that Asher would spread his crew too thin. And if, as Wren said, Asher was here, it would make sense to expect that the others were here as well.

If Jez and Ran were still with him, what would Fedor be doing then? Three thought back to the first time he saw Fedor; the intensity of his pursuit, the aggression in his every move. Fedor would be straining the leash, anxious to bring the quarry in, and perhaps even more so to pay Three back for his injury. Without the threat of the Weir, would he be out beyond the wall, searching?

No. It was unlikely that the guards would open the gates after dark without good reason, and it most likely would be unwise for Asher to draw too much attention from the people of Morningside. And they had tracked Wren this far. If anything, Asher was probably savoring the night, fully expecting to have his brother back under his control by tomorrow. And Cass. Three couldn't help but wonder if Asher had sensed Cass's death, or if he was still expecting to find her, too. Dagon had asked to see her just last night, after all.

Dagon. Dagon was still unknown. Unpredictable. He could be anywhere. And this was the hardest part. Embracing the unknowable. Accepting it. Acting in spite of what might be.

Three had gathered all the information he needed for now. It was time to let instinct drive.

No matter how much his training had drilled it into him, nor how many times he had seen it work, it was still challenging every time he needed to let go, to trust. But the subconscious had a way of noticing details that shouldn't matter and making sense of them anyway. Of completing pictures even before the mind's eye could see.

He had once survived a surprise attack from a then-trusted colleague because of it. At the time, it had only been a sudden dread that warned him. A feeling of danger. And while his mind tried to explain the fear away, his friend had turned with blade in hand. It wasn't until much later that Three recalled the detail his subconscious had noted and processed in a flash: the closing of a window. There'd been no need for it, except to prevent the noise of his death from spilling out into the street below.

It was to this inner mind that he now turned, allowing his gut to set his course. The night was growing late, and the temperature fell so low that he could see his breath. For a moment, he thought of Wren, and Mr Carter, and hoped they were warm, and safe. And then pushed them from his mind.

The crowds had thinned, and trickled from the streets into pubs and tea-houses along the main walkways. But though there were fewer people out, Morningside kept its lively thrum, as music and laughter seeped from nearby establishments. Three chose one at random, or at least could find no logical reason for his choice; a tea-house called the Green.

It was not far from the Governor's compound, but the separation was noticeable, as if the aura of law and order emanating from the city's seat of power faded out, and this was its edge. Patrons talked loudly and loosely, and none paid him much attention when he entered. He chose a high table just off-center in the room, neither too near the back, nor too close to the entrance. A harried attendant stopped barely long enough to take his order, and only hesitated a moment when he offered Hard for payment. Unusual here, but not unheard of. Just another recent addition to the citizenry. The woman left him with a small cup and a pot of the house special; some combination of green tea and rice wine. Or synthetic approximations of those age-old delights.

Three poured himself a cup and downed it quickly, enjoying the rush of heat down his throat, to his belly, radiating outwards to his wind-chilled arms and legs. He poured another. This, he left on the table before him, watching the steam curl and rise, cultivating the image of a weary traveler lost in his thoughts. He *was* weary. And a traveler. But his senses remained sharp, and alert. He sipped from his cup, eyes low, and stretched out with his hearing, taking in scraps of information without judging or analyzing.

How long he sat, he didn't know. Between the alcohol and the warm buzz of a dozen conversations, Three felt almost adrift. But he kept finding himself focusing on a group of men two tables away, just over his left shoulder. Old-timers, the same here as anywhere, exchanging news of the day, swapping familiar stories, arguing about trivial details, and griping about newcomers. Through them, Three learned of the most recent Weir attack, some two weeks before.

According to the tale, the wave had broken and turned back when Governor Underdown appeared on the wall. There was much speculation about the power he seemed to wield against them. Some argued it was the memory of battles Underdown had fought long ago that caused the Weir to flee. Others said it was the efficiency of his command. And one suggested there were darker things at work, though he was quickly booed to silence. It all had the feel of a common refrain, as though the men had rehearsed it a thousand times before. Whatever the truth, Three made a mental note. He'd seen Wren do things he couldn't explain; perhaps Underdown could explain them.

It was another hour before Three heard what he'd come for, and it was from that group of men that it came. A snippet of conversation floated to him.

"…big fella, with an arm all broke…"

He missed the next part because his attendant returned and loudly asked if he'd wanted anything else. It took a long moment to send her away, but once she was gone, he focused in.

"…well, it just ain't right. Him hanging around, leering at folk like they don't belong," one of the men was saying. There was a pause, and then Three heard the emphatic bang of a bottle set too heavily on a table. "*He* don't belong."

"Maybe *you* don't belong, Vel."

"Ah, shut yer face, Arlen. You know what I mean."

There was some good natured ribbing from the crew, and over the course of a few minutes, Three had what he needed. He poured himself a last cup of the mixed brew. It was barely warmer than room temperature now and had started to turn bitter, but it wasn't important. It was the finality of that last drink he wanted. Three drained the cup, placed it firmly on the table, and made his way to the door.

Fedor paced the narrow side street that ran along the three-story building Asher'd put him in. An apartment, on the top floor, all to himself. It was nice to have his own space for a change; nicer still that the accommodations had been well-furnished by the Governor's own staff. But they'd been in Morningside too long, sitting idle. Asher assured them all that they'd be back to business soon, that Haven and her pup would be back under control, or dead, matters resolved either way. But even after the man had shown up at the gate and escaped into the night, Asher remained with the Governor inside the compound instead of finishing the pursuit. Fedor's apartment had become a prison.

He seethed, anxious to be done with this waste of time and energy. Haven was an asset to be sure; one of the best. But she was a chemic, and nearly burned at that. She could be replaced. Would *have* to be replaced, eventually. And the boy. Just a boy. Though, Asher's half-brother. Fedor understood something about brothers.

It was vengeance that stirred him so. Asher's dalliance annoyed him. But here, now, the man that had killed Kostya, his dear brother, was almost within reach, and yet Asher refused to let him finish the job. That was infuriating.

A sudden noise caught Fedor's attention, the crunch of glass underfoot, somewhere in the dark behind him. He turned and scanned the street, irritated at the interruption. But there was nothing. One of the useless locals, most likely.

Fedor squeezed his dead arm with his left hand. The man. The man had taken his arm when they'd fought. But when Kostya was killed, that man had taken Fedor's heart. His baby brother, by three minutes. Scores would be settled. Fedor would rip the man's own heart from his chest, and eat it still beating before his dying eyes.

Images of vicious and glorious revenge were why Fedor was out on the street at this hour. He had worked himself up enough to contemplate disobeying Asher, and hunting them down on his own. But not yet enough to abandon his post. They would come on their own, Asher said. But why wait? They had waited long enough. Chased long enough.

The wind washed over the buildings on either side of him, making a hollow sort of sound in the narrow alley, like shadows scraping across the rooftops. And Fedor suddenly felt that he was being watched.

He quickly checked up and down the alleyway, straining his eyes in the heavy shadows. A single light glowed around the front of the buildings, spilling softly into the mouth of the side street, but creating strange pools of darkness along the sides. Fedor listened for any hint of sound, but detected none.

Until the whisper.

It was barely more than a rasping wind through the alley, but there was no mistaking what it said.

"I *am* sorry about your brother."

Fedor ran protocols, just as Asher had taught him, casting a wide net into the datastream that would tell him if not who was there, at least where they were. In an instant, the results came back. Empty.

"I thought he was you," the whisper said, this time from the opposite side of the alley. Closer.

Fedor searched frantically. It was the man, undoubtedly, but *where*? He reached inside his coat and drew out a wicked whipcoil baton, with a vicious pyramid-tip designed to puncture flesh and strip bone. It didn't matter. Anger surged, adrenaline flowed. Vengeance was at hand. The man would appear, and then Fedor would rip him in pieces.

"Come, little dog."

"I'm here."

The whisper came from behind, so close Fedor could feel the breath. But even as he spun, he felt the blade bite just above the elbow of his good arm, felt the explosion of pain, the severing of bone, tendon, artery. Something metallic clattered away against the wall of the building, and something thumped wetly nearby. The arm. The other arm. Gone. Fedor stood face to face with the man, and the pain could not diminish the rage kindled.

With a roar, Fedor lunged with a lightning head-butt, but the man melted backwards, downwards, and Fedor felt a hard impact on his throat and in the same instant on the back of his neck. A wave of warmth rolled down his back. His breath came out in a whistle. And looking down, Fedor saw the hilt of the man's blade just below his chin. Fedor tried to speak, but something hot and metallic bubbled out of his mouth instead. The man stared back at him passively. Quietly. Peacefully.

Fedor hated him.

••••

Getting back out of the city had proven even easier than getting in had been, and Three made his way nimbly back through the outskirts. There were no others out now, no one watching the roads at this time of night. By his guess, he still had four, maybe five hours until the sun came up, bringing with it whatever storm he had called upon himself. Killing Fedor had brought him no joy, nor relief, but it was finished. It was done. The message had been sent.

There was still no clear plan in his mind, but he knew the next step: get back to Wren. He'd figure it out from there. At the very least, he had shifted the game. Made himself known as dangerous prey. Unpredictable. Maybe it would buy them some time.

Three slowed his pace as he approached the tumbledown building that Mr Carter had chosen for their hideout, and made a wide, careful arc, looking for any sign of trouble. Though he couldn't imagine anyone would have followed him, he doubled back just to be sure before making his way inside. As he crept through the front of the building towards the corridor, he hunched down, making himself small in the near-absolute darkness.

About halfway down the hallway, he stumbled over something heavy that hadn't been there before. Three managed to catch himself without too much noise, but even as he recovered, he knew there was trouble. The floor was gummy, and the thing he'd tripped over was warm, though not as warm as it should've been.

Mr Carter. Dead.

Three whipped down the hall, knowing what had happened, knowing that the room he was about to walk into would be empty, that Wren would be gone. But he couldn't stop himself. He burst through the doorframe and stopped short.

The chemlight glowed warmly at the head of Wren's pallet. Wren was there. Sleeping. Three blinked, mind trying to process, fighting to understand. If he hadn't been so frantic, he might've heard it coming.

An iron vice-grip seized him, pinned his arm behind him with searing agony, and twisted and jerked his head around to the absolute farthest point just before his neck broke. There was a grim whisper, hot in his ear.

"Easy, brother. Let's not wake the boy."

# THIRTY

The air outside seemed colder now than it'd been only moments before. Dagon had released Three and let him walk out on his own, but he'd hovered the whole way, tense, ready to pounce if necessary. Three knew better than to try anything in that narrow hallway with Dagon so close behind. During that short walk, his mind had jumped into hyperdrive, flying through options, knowing they all led to the same outcome. Though if Dagon had wanted to kill him, he'd be dead. He might be dead in the next moment, or the next, but for *this* moment, stepping out into the night again, he was still alive. Still a chance, however slight.

Dagon had the initiative, but Three wasn't going to cede control. As soon as they crossed the threshold, he stung Dagon the only way he knew how.

"Cass is dead, Dagon."

He heard Dagon stop behind him, and Three kept walking, gaining critical distance.

"That's far enough."

Three stopped and turned slowly back to face Dagon, taking an extra half-step back.

"Haven isn't dead," Dagon said, matter-of-fact, hollow.

"I couldn't save her and the boy. I tried but…" Three trailed off, shook his head. Measured the distance.

••••

Dagon shook his head slowly, his eyes unfocused for a moment. Imagining. Or remembering. In that instant, Three swept across the gap and drove his fist through Dagon's jaw.

A lesser man would've blacked out on his feet, gone straight to ground. Instead, Dagon staggered with the impact, but managed to twist, catching himself with his left hand on the ground and whipping his right around in an arc. The stance was nearly impossible, contorted, like Dagon's back had broken and his shoulder dislocated. Yet as Three deflected the blow with his shoulder and forearm, he was surprised at its power. Dagon rebounded, switched direction off the impact and struck twice, once at Three's knee and the other stinging the front of his thigh.

It was a small thing, but significant. Three knew from the angle of Dagon's attack that he'd been aiming for the saphenous nerve along the inside of his leg, a strike that would've crippled him. But he'd missed. Even as Three was bringing his elbow down, he wondered if Dagon had ever missed before.

Dagon, still crouched, managed to partially intercept the strike with the flat of his hand, taking the blow in the upper shoulder instead of the back of the neck. He surged upwards, a brute force tackle that lifted Three off the ground. But the two were tangled, and Three reflexively brought his knee hard into Dagon's solar plexus, felt a dull crack. Dagon's breath exploded out in a wheeze. As the two crashed backwards, Three twisted at the last moment, dumping Dagon face first onto the concrete.

The impact broke them apart, and Three scrambled up to a knee. Somehow, Dagon was already up, blood in his mouth, hands outstretched. But Three's body was in motion. The sword was out, speeding to target. Dagon's hands clapped together on either side of the blade, catching it mid-thrust. Try as he might, Three couldn't budge his sword any direction. Dagon's grip held it locked: a human vice.

And for a moment, the two stood frozen, locked together, brothers in blood. Then, Three felt his blade release, and Dagon spread his hands.

"Got me."

Three saw now. Dagon had stopped his sword, but not soon enough. The first quarter of his blade had found its mark. Judging from the angle and the depth, just under the ribs, Dagon likely had a punctured lung and a gashed right ventricle. He was already dead. He just hadn't admitted it yet.

Dagon stepped back, sliding himself free of the blade with a spurt before he pressed his palm over the wound. Three watched, waited for some sudden movement, but Dagon just stumbled backwards, propped his back against the nearest wall, and slid to sit on the ground. Weary. Broken. Three's blade may have finished the work, but something else had delivered the crushing blow before they'd fought.

In the soft moonlight, Dagon stared at Three with the hint of a smile curling his cracked lips.

"I'm glad it was you," he said at last. Three stood from his crouch at last, relaxing. But didn't approach.

"Feels honorable, somehow. This way."

Three just held still. It wasn't that unusual. Dying men often felt the need to say something there, at the end. But he'd seen Dagon move too fast to trust him even now.

"We're brothers in a way, you know. More ways than you'd guess."

At that, Dagon reached up with his other hand and pulled the neck of his shirt down low, exposing the pale flesh of his upper chest in the moonlight. Three couldn't make out what it was he was supposed to be looking at from that distance. Dagon waited. Three took a few cautious steps forward. It was recognition that stopped him again.

Markings swirled across Dagon's flesh, intricate tattooing of ideograms in lines and patterns not altogether similar but far too familiar for Three's liking. Dagon saw Three's reaction and was satisfied, released the cloth and let his hand fall to his lap. Still he smiled.

"What clan?" Three asked, at last.

"The Empty Frost," Dagon answered, with a wet cough. There was a rattle in his chest. Fluid building. "You?"

"House Eight."

Dagon grunted, a sort of impressed chuckle, mixed with pain. His gaze floated off down the street. "The Old Ones. That explains a lot."

"Frost was a good house." Three meant it. The Empty Frost clan had never been an influential one, but before the Falling, it had been known as a house of integrity and honor.

"Was."

Three stepped closer and took a knee. "How'd you end up with RushRuin?"

"Lack of conviction," Dagon said. A half-joke. "Tried for a while, you know. But…" He trailed off, either lost in thought or momentarily overwhelmed by pain. After a moment, he shivered, or shook himself. "Just easier." He blinked heavily, changed the subject suddenly. "…I wasn't going to kill, you know."

Three flashed back to the moment he was drawing his blade. Dagon standing with his hands outstretched. Not preparing to strike. Motioning to stop.

"You killed my friend."

"He didn't give me a choice."

"And what *were* you going to do?"

"I don't know," Dagon looked back to Three then, into his eyes. "You're a better man than me, Three. Doing what I could've done. Should've done. A long time ago."

"You loved her."

"I *wanted* her. If I'd loved her, I would've protected her." Dagon's gaze dropped back to the ground. Three didn't respond. They sat in silence for a long moment, Three listening as Dagon's breathing shallowed and became forced.

"How you doin', Dagon?"

"Can't feel my legs, Three."

Three slid around and sat down beside Dagon, back to the wall. It all seemed so foolish now. So wasteful. So few things to have changed for the two of them to have been friends instead of enemies.

"Strange pair, aren't we?" Dagon said, his voice thin. "The elite of the damned."

Three nodded.

"I guess this is the part where other people would ship," Dagon said. Nearly a whisper.

"Yeah."

"Will you sit with me? Until after?"

"Yeah."

After a moment, Three added, "I'll do more. I'll remember you, Dagon, of the Empty Frost Clan." It wasn't a platitude. It was an oath, and a blessing. A pledge between brothers. And a comfort from a fear Three knew in a vague way, a fear he knew Dagon was feeling the full force of now. Something they'd each learned from their own houses, long ago.

They weren't wired. There was no digital afterlife for them. But as long as a brother remained, they would be remembered.

Dagon smiled faintly. His breathing slowed. And quietly, Dagon, the Grave, died.

After a time, Three rose and went into the back room of the small building where they'd been hiding, and roused Wren. The chemlight still glowed softly. He was surprised to see how soundly the boy had slept that night, when so much danger had been so near. Even now Wren moved sluggishly, hair matted to the side of his head with sweat, looking as if he could sleep through the day. It was several moments before he noticed.

"Where's Mr Carter?" he asked suddenly. There was no way to soften the blow, so Three didn't.

"He's dead, Wren. Dagon killed him last night."

"Where's Dagon?"

"Dead too."

"You?"

Three nodded. Wren hid his hands in his face, but not before Three had seen the glimmer of tears welling. The boy cried silently, and Three let him for a time. But there was work to do.

"Come on. I need your help."

In those bitterly cold hours before dawn, with Wren at his side, Three worked to scavenge and build a makeshift metal basin. Together, they prepared and wrapped the bodies of Mr Carter and Dagon. Three lay the bodies side by side in the basin, then stood back, with Wren close by.

"Want to say anything?"

Wren was quiet and still. But just before Three stepped forward again, the boy spoke.

"Mr Carter was a great man. He was kind, and strong, and he always made me feel safe." He paused. And to Three's surprise, he added, "Dagon was a good friend. He did some bad things, but I don't think he really meant them. He was a good friend." He looked up, eyes and cheeks shining in the weak light. "Do you want to say anything, Three?"

"I think you covered it, kid."

Wren nodded, and as the sun was just beginning to redden the sky, Three stepped forward and set the bodies alight. They stood in silence as the flames took the remains. Wren watched deep into the fire.

"We're going to fight today, aren't we?" the boy asked.

"Yeah."

Wren thought for a moment. Wiped his cheeks, his eyes. Nodded.

"OK."

••••

It was still early morning when they set out, headed back towards Morningside. Three couldn't help but wonder how long it would take Asher to find Fedor, and to react. And what that reaction would be. Today would decide everything. Three had accepted that. Embraced it. It was the end, however it turned out.

"What do you think, Wren? Ran or Jez?" Three glanced over his shoulder at the boy following a step behind. His eyes were downcast, but he seemed to be standing taller than Three remembered.

"Jez," Wren said after a moment's hesitation. "But you'll have to be careful. She's got… magic. Or something."

"What kind?"

The boy shrugged. "She talks to people. They do stuff."

"Why not Ran?"

Wren didn't answer.

"Is he stronger?"

"He's nicer."

Three wanted to press the issue, but decided it didn't really matter. He'd have to deal with them all at some point anyway. The order didn't seem to make much difference. Except Asher. He'd be last.

"I think maybe – maybe we won't have to fight Ran," Wren added. "At the end."

"Are they together now?"

"No."

It was a new approach. At first, Three didn't think it'd be possible. Then, when he'd realized Wren's gift, he hadn't wanted to risk it because he'd feared it would give them away. But now the risk… well, this close to the end it didn't seem to matter one way or the other. Whatever came, he would deal with it.

It had taken some convincing. At first, Wren was afraid to try, was afraid he couldn't do it, but Three had coaxed him into it. Sure enough, he *could* do it. *Was* doing it. For the first time since this had all begun, Wren was tracking *them*. Masking his own signal, tracerunning theirs. Leading them to the very people that had been hounding them for so long.

Wren wouldn't go near Asher, not even across the digital, but the others he seemed more confident about. They were still in the city, but they weren't holed up in the Governor's compound. They were roaming the streets. Searching.

"Got your knife?" Three asked.

Wren nodded. "But I don't want to use it."

"You might have to."

Wren swallowed. "If I have to."

They pressed on towards Morningside as the outskirts of the city began stirring into life. Three scanned the surroundings, searching for signs of danger, soaking in the feel and flow of the people that were just beginning to appear. The outcasts, or those deemed not worthy to live within the walls. The closer he and Wren got to Morningside, the more active it became, as the men and women outside prepared for another day of bartering inside. Wren took quick steps to catch up and grabbed Three's hand with casual familiarity.

"What do they sell?" Wren asked suddenly.

It was a good question. There didn't seem to be much that the people outside of Morningside could provide to those inside. Hand-crafted trinkets, perhaps. Something just endearing enough to attract the charity of a wealthy city-dweller. But Three's quick eye saw little in the way of goods among those preparing to enter the city. It clicked for him, then. Most of the outcasts that made a living in Morningside probably did so by selling themselves, in one way or another. Indentured servitude. Freedom for security.

"Don't know, Wren. Maybe they're all musicians."

"That sounds fun," Wren said. Then with barely a pause added, "How do we get inside?"

"Quickly," Three answered. "And with big smiles."

Wren looked up, not understanding. Three just looked down and winked. Wren held his hand a little tighter.

Within a few more minutes, a gate was looming ahead of them. Not the same gate they'd entered before, though not far from it either. A steady trickle of people had already started making its way into the city.

"Hold on a sec," Three said, stopping. Wren turned to face Three, and in the next moment Three had him under the arms and was picking him up. Three lifted the boy up over his head and set him on his shoulders.

"Won't they be looking for us?"

"Yeah," Three said. "But we often see what we expect, and miss what we don't."

As they approached the gate, Three moved up alongside a woman who was carrying two large cases, one stacked atop the other. She was a few years older than he was, with wrinkles just starting at the corners of her eyes. Brown hair pulled back in a loose knot, with wisps floating on either side of her face. Not particularly attractive.

"Ma'am, we're headed the same direction," he said, smiling. "Can I carry those for you?"

The woman smiled faintly but shook her head. "Oh no, I can manage. I do it every day."

But Three was already taking the top case. The woman tried to protest, but she needed both hands to hold the other, so there wasn't much she could do. Three fell into step with her, close enough so their shoulders brushed as they walked, and just kept smiling.

"Whew, one of these is heavy enough," he said. "You must be the strongest woman in Morningside."

"It's really OK," she said, though already he could tell she didn't mean it. "I can manage."

"You already said that," Three said with a wink. "Day in, day out, you manage it. You deserve a break."

"Well, thank you."

"It's my sincere pleasure, ma'am."

They were maybe fifty feet from the gate. Three counted four guards. One more than the other gate had last evening. The guards were scanning the people as they passed, but so far they hadn't stopped anyone.

"I usually come in through the south side," Three said. "Do they always post four on this gate?"

"Just one most days, sometimes two," the woman said. "I don't see Jonas, though. He's always here."

"Day off maybe."

Thirty feet. Three slowed his pace just enough to let another pair of travelers catch up. The woman instinctively matched his stride without even seeming to notice.

"No, yesterday was his day off. Something must be going on inside."

"Parade for the Governor, I bet."

The woman snorted. "And me in my work clothes."

"You look lovely, ma'am. If you don't mind me saying so."

"I do mind, because it's not true," she said with a slight frown. But then a smirk appeared. "But keep talking anyway."

"If those are your work clothes, I'd hate to see you in your finery. I might be tempted to flirt."

"I don't remember what that's like."

"Neither do I, ma'am."

They shared a laugh then, though only the woman's was genuine. Fifteen feet. One guard was scanning the horizon in an unfocused way, two of the guards were looking at the pair of travelers that Three had let pass. But the other was staring right at him.

"How you doin' up there, buddy?" Three asked Wren.

"OK."

"You smilin'?"

Wren didn't answer, which meant the answer was no. Ten feet. The guard's eyes narrowed. His hand went down to his belt. So Three did the only thing he could.

He lurched forward suddenly, fumbled the case, and went sprawling on his hands and knees right at the guard's feet. The woman gasped, and Wren let out a little yelp. But somehow the boy managed to land on his feet just a step or two beyond the guard. Though a trained eye might've picked up on the way Three had kept Wren from falling, or how gently the case went to the ground without tipping over or spilling its contents, to the surrounding crowd it looked entirely as if he'd just tripped over his own feet.

Three burst into laughter then. A raucous, foolish guffaw that guaranteed all eyes were on him as he rocked back on his knees and hung his head in mock shame.

"Honey, are you alright?" the woman asked.

"Fine. I'm fine." Three looked up at the guard, locked eyes with him. Smiled. "Just an idiot."

The guard searched his face for a moment. Then quickly reached down and took his arm. Firm.

And helped him to his feet.

"Sure you're OK, sir?"

Three kept smiling, and clapped the guard on the shoulder. "Broke my pride, but I think that's it." He picked the case back up and dusted it off.

"Well, try to be more careful," the guard said. "Lucky your son's so quick on his feet."

"Yes, sir, I am. Lucky to have him. You have a great day," Three answered with a nod.

And with that, Three and Wren breezed inside the city. They walked with the woman to the tea-house where she worked, Three alternating between apologizing and flirting the whole way there. By the time they parted ways, she'd made not so subtle invitations for him to meet her at sundown, and suggested that some kind of repayment was in order for his kindness. Three assured her it was not, and made as clean a getaway as he could.

Once they were back out on the street, he took Wren by the hand.

"Sorry if I scared you," he said. "I wasn't gonna let you get hurt."

"I know," Wren said.

"You OK?"

Wren nodded.

"Ready?"

Wren nodded.

"Alright. Where is she now?"

"This way." Wren tugged Three's hand, and gently guided him through Morningside's elegant streets and walkways.

There was a heavy sleepiness to the city, as if the citizens were waiting for the outsiders to take care of the morning. The further they moved away from the gates, the fewer people they saw. Wren led Three through an unfamiliar quarter, heavily shadowed by the wall at sunrise. He stopped suddenly, and drew Three to one side, slipping into an alley between two darkly-windowed buildings.

"She's there," the boy said, pointing to a squat, one-story building further down the path. It was quiet here, almost untouched by the distant murmuring of the rest of the waking city.

"Is she alone?"

Wren shook his head. No point in going in, then. Three scanned the area. It was too open here. But further down the alley...

Three crouched down on a knee, and put his hands on Wren's shoulders.

"I need you to do something brave," he said.

Wren stared back with his deep sea-green eyes, intent but watery. Afraid, but trying desperately not to show it. The boy nodded.

"I need you to let her see you."

Wren stood utterly still. Eyes wide, jaw clenched. His breathing quickened.

"Stand here at the end of the alley. As soon as she sees you, just turn and walk down there." Three pointed back down the alley between the two buildings, to where they backed up against the city's great wall. "I'll be right there, waiting. I'm not gonna let her hurt you, OK? Don't run. Just walk. Even if she calls your name, don't run or turn around. Just keep walking. Think you can do that?"

A long pause. Then Wren shook his head slowly.

"I don't *think* I can," he said. "I *can*."

Three squeezed Wren's shoulders. Ruffled his hair. "I'll be right there."

Wren nodded. Three took to his feet and walked down the length of the alley. Forty feet, maybe. It opened into a small sort of courtyard between the buildings and the wall, though the space seemed mostly unused. Three was relieved to find there were no windows back here. He turned and looked back to Wren, who was watching him. Three nodded and gave the boy a thumbs-up. Wren waved and disappeared around the corner.

The next few minutes were the worst Three had suffered since the night he'd lost Cass. He hadn't meant for Wren to leave his sight, and he cursed himself for not telling the boy that explicitly. But there was nothing to be done about it now. He couldn't risk getting caught out in the open, not when Wren might turn the corner at any second with Jez close behind. The seconds crawled by, and Three fought to still himself, fought to silence the voices screaming in his head at how foolish a plan he'd made, how he'd endangered Wren, how Jez had probably already caught him. What was taking so long? Three slid low to the ground and risked a peek around the corner. Where was Wren? How much closer to the building had he gone? There was a distant sound, a high pitch, muffled. Was that Wren, calling out? Three stood back up. This wasn't going to work. Wasn't working. He cursed himself for not thinking it through, for putting Wren in harm's way. He had to get him back. Three was just stepping into the alley when Wren rounded the corner at the opposite end, walking carefully towards him.

The boy's face was bloodless, ghostly white, and even from this distance, Three could see he was shaking. But he held strong, kept his pace steady. Three motioned for him to keep coming, and then slipped back into the shadows of the courtyard.

He could hear the boy's shuffling footsteps echoing down the alleyway. Closer. Almost there. And then.

"Wren?" A woman's voice. Warm. Tender. Not at all what Three had expected. "Wren, sweetheart, is that you?"

But Wren did just what Three had told him. His pace didn't falter. A few seconds later he came into the courtyard and headed straight for Three. Three pressed a finger to his lips and waved Wren into the far corner, furthest from the entrance. Wren nodded and moved there quickly, curling himself into a tight ball, hands over his ears and terror in his eyes.

Three crept silently to the edge of the nearest building, moved into position, poised to strike. He could hear her approaching cautiously, footsteps falling fainter the nearer she got. Then, silence. Three strained to hear her.

"Wren?" she said again.

She had stopped about two-thirds of the way down the alley. But it was alright. Either she'd come all the way to investigate, or she'd wave it off and turn back the other way. If she didn't come to him, Three could cover the distance and take her down before she made it back to the street.

"Is there someone back there with you, sweetheart?" It shouldn't have mattered, but Three couldn't help but notice the perfect quality of Jez's voice. Rounded and full, pleasantly deep. Resonant. "Why don't you come out where I can see you?"

Without even realizing it, Three started edging towards the alley. He caught himself.

"It's alright," Jez said. "I want you to come out."

Her voice seemed to come straight from inside his own head, a honeyed droning that filled Three with a sense of complete calm. And he remembered how beautiful she was. Vividly he saw her in his mind, her perfect features, her perfect form accentuated by her fitted bodysuit. Three felt himself sliding dreamlike, even as one part of his mind raced to analyze what was happening. Some kind of vocal implants, most likely. Wren had warned him. But the most common ones worked through connection, like a virus for the mind. Three had never experienced anything like this before.

"Come out. I just want to see you."

He knew exactly what was happening. The frequency of her voice was being tuned to modulate the electrical impulses in his brain, inducing a dream-like state that left him dangerously open to suggestion. And even knowing this, he couldn't keep himself from stepping into the alley.

"There you are," Jez said with a suppressed smile. Seductive. "I'm *so* glad to see you."

She took a step closer. Three's arms hung limply at his sides, while the tiny part of his mind that was still his own screamed for him to act. He would have to destroy her... but not yet. He wanted to hear her, to see her, just a little longer. He felt so warm, so comfortable. She started walking toward him now. Not the stalking, bird-like movements he'd seen before. Fluid. Feline.

"I was hoping I could be the one to find you, you know," she said, her voice low. "I wanted to be the one."

Her smile. Her eyes. Everything about her said she loved him. *Desired* him. But Jez was going to kill him. He knew it. And he accepted it. It would be alright.

"Asher will *love* me for being the one."

Six feet away.

And suddenly an arctic light pierced the veil, a pulse of blinding white shocking him back to himself. He reflexively shielded his eyes. In the next instant he glanced back to Jez, who was momentarily stunned by the flash. Their eyes met for a split second, and as she opened her mouth to speak, Three closed the gap and lashed out, striking her across the throat with the web of his hand.

Jez reeled backwards choking, but as Three advanced she snapped her head around, whipping her long braids towards him. Not realizing the threat he tried to strike through the attack, but felt the sudden impact and sting across his face as the razortips woven in her hair bit deeply into the flesh of his cheek and neck and brow. The shock blurred his vision, and he missed his target.

Three followed with a forearm, but Jez slipped the blow and swiped upward with her palm, aiming for his eyes. Three threw his head back, narrowly dodging the attack. He snatched her wrist with one hand and wrenched her elbow with the other, using the leverage to slam her face-first into the alley wall. Before she could rebound, he drove his knee into her lower back. And as she arched backwards from the strike, he grabbed her head in a lock and twisted nearly to the point of breaking.

It hadn't been that long ago that he'd been in her position, a fraction of an inch and a few pounds of torque from dead. Jez started to go slack, and Three forced her down on to her knees, keeping a strong stance behind her. Another day, in that critical moment, he would've snapped her neck without hesitation. But the sudden realization that if not for Dagon's mercy he would be dead was enough to give him pause. Locked together as they were, his cheek pressed hard against the back of her head, Three could hear her choking breath as

Jez's throat continued to spasm from his blow. The whole left side of his face was wet and sticky with blood, one eye blinded with it.

"Please," Jez rasped, barely forcing the word out through his chokehold. The power of her voice was gone. So, it seemed, her will to fight. Jez wasn't like Fedor or Kostya. She wasn't a fighter. She was a manipulator, a seductress. And somehow, now, caught in his arms that were so much stronger, she seemed suddenly fragile. Not altogether unlike Cass.

At the far end of the alley, towards the city, the white light continued to pulse. Three recognized the source now. Wren's strobe from the Vault. He'd forgotten the boy even had it. Three glanced behind him with his good eye. Wren was there, standing in the courtyard. Watching. Three loosened his grip on Jez.

And suddenly–

"Asher, he's here!" she called out in her damaged voice.

Three strengthened his hold.

"Wren," he called. "Look away."

He left her body behind the building and together with Wren fled towards the center of the city. They were careful to dodge other citizens until Three could get the bleeding stopped and the blood washed off his face. Crouched behind a one-story clothing shop, he used a maintenance pump to splash ice cold water across his latest wounds, and scrubbed them clean as best he could.

The cuts sprayed across his face were thin but deep, the kind of precision pain only a razor can deliver. The one across his eyebrow was the worst. He was fortunate not to have lost the eye completely. Wren stood quietly by, pale with fear, brave in his silence.

Three wiped his face and shook his hands dry as well as he could, and caught Wren's eye. "You OK?"

Wren nodded slightly.

"Where's Ran now?"

Wren's eyes unfocused for a moment. "Heading back towards the middle of the city."

"Governor's compound?"

Wren shrugged. "I guess. Yes, that seems right."

Three wondered why. Why Asher wouldn't send Ran after them immediately. Frightened? He probably didn't know about Dagon yet, not for sure. But he'd lost Fedor and Jez within eight hours. Maybe in his panic, he was calling all security back home. But Three's hope of that was quickly lost. The next moment, all across the city, alarms began to blare.

Wren reflexively stepped into Three's body, buried his face against Three's neck. Three threw his arm around him protectively.

"They're coming!" Wren said in a terrified whisper. He gripped Three so tightly, it nearly choked him.

"I'm not gonna let 'em take you, Wren. Not now."

It was a promise. He said it, and he meant it, even though he had no idea how he was going to keep it. His brow still hadn't stopped bleeding yet, but if they were alerting the whole city there was no reason to worry about that now. And there was no way to figure out a plan, no time to strategize. Three didn't know how many guardsmen a city the size of Morningside had, but it was likely in the hundreds. They had to move.

"Come on, Wren," Three said, picking the boy up.

Morningside's security forces would most likely seal the gates, and work their way from outside in. That made the Governor's compound literally the last place they'd look. And maybe he'd get a shot at Asher before all was said and done.

They raced together through the streets as citizens began flooding out of their homes, and it didn't take long before Three realized something else was going on. Something terrible. The citizens of Morningside were in a panic, fleeing together in a mad rush, a churning human current that swept Three and

Wren along with it, all going in the same direction. Towards the Governor's compound. And then above the cries of panic, Three heard a shriek that pierced his heart.

The Weir were attacking.

# THIRTY-ONE

Three and Wren were among the first of the crowd to reach the Governor's compound, and as they approached, Three slowed his pace. Already a thin line of citizens was pressed against the gate, pleading with the guards on the other side to let them in. The guards stood dispassionately, clad in black, grim-faced and motionless. Their only job to protect the Governor, not his subjects.

"Governor Underdown! Governor, we need you!" came the cries. "Governor, please!"

From the clamor of the crowd, Three picked out news that the eastern gate was already overrun, that the guards had been cut down before they could seal it. The Weir were inside.

Three's mind reeled at the prospect. He had walked the open for decades and never once seen the Weir roaming in daylight. Images flashed from his walk through the streets the night before, images of the people he'd passed. So clean, so carefree. Soft. He could only imagine how quickly the Weir must be cutting through them now.

Wren was sobbing on his shoulder, sucking in choking breaths, gripping Three's coat in his trembling fists. "Asher. He'll know. He'll know I'm here!"

"I know, Wren," Three answered. "We're counting on it."

The crowd swelled as more citizens joined the ranks, crushing together around the compound, piling against the gates, clamoring for Underdown to appear. Their Governor. Their savior. Three kept clear of the crowd, held steady around the edges, alert for any sign of the Weir. Watching for Asher.

"Tell me if Ran shows up," Three said. Wren didn't respond, so Three dug the boy's face out of his shoulder and looked in his eyes. "I need you to do that for me, OK?"

Something shifted in Wren then. He caught his breath, wiped his eyes and nodded, and though he lay his head back on Three's shoulder, he didn't hold on so tightly.

Moments later, a cheer went up from the crowd. Both Three and Wren looked to the mob of people, then followed their collective gaze up to the wall. There, next to one of the towers to one side of the gate, he stood.

Underdown.

He was tall, nearly six and half feet by Three's guess, with pale blond hair and a powerful frame. Even from this distance, the resemblance was striking. If there'd been any lingering doubt about whether Cass had told the truth about who Wren's father was, it was dispelled. The Governor could have been Wren, thirty-five years older. Whatever catastrophe was about to befall Morningside, Governor Underdown had arrived to thwart it. Silence fell over the throng of citizens, though in the distance Three could hear the cries of the Weir approaching.

Three started to press his way into the crowd, a new idea forming. If he could just get close enough, maybe he'd be able to force a confrontation between Asher and Underdown. But as he neared the Governor, he stopped. The look on Underdown's face was not the cool confidence Three had expected. Nor the grim determination of a seasoned warrior before battle. The eyes too wide, the lips colorless. The look of a man caught in a lie. Powerless.

He opened his mouth to speak, and closed it again wordlessly. At a loss. Somewhere nearby a Weir shrieked its electric call. Three figured they had two minutes, maybe three.

"People of Morningside!"

Another voice now. Younger. Cocky.

Asher.

"People of Morningside, you have been deceived!"

He strolled along the wall, making his way towards the Governor casually, hands clasped behind his back. Three had never seen him before but he knew him instantly. Shaggy brown hair, sharply handsome, he had just enough of Cass in his cheekbones to make Three hate him. Seventeen, maybe eighteen years old, he walked like he owned the world. Now that Three saw him, he couldn't believe this was the little punk they'd been running from for so long.

"Your beloved Governor is a fraud," he said, with a smirk. Like it was some cruel joke he'd pulled. "Tell them, *Governor*. Tell them how you lied."

The silence of the crowd was intensified by the growing sounds of chaos gathering from the distance. The stream of citizens had ceased, which meant they'd either taken to hiding in their homes, or they'd been cut off by the advancing Weir. On top of the wall of the compound, Underdown remained speechless. Asher slid next to him.

"Tell them!" he barked, suddenly furious. Three saw it now. The trait which made Asher so frightening, though Three was not frightened by him. There was a strange mix at work; a malevolent childishness, like a spoiled prince with the power of life and death in his hands. No doubt he was powerful, to see how Underdown cowered before him, to know how men like Fedor, and Kostya, and Dagon had served his will. And in that moment, Three understood... Asher cared nothing for Cass, his mother, or for his baby half-brother, Wren. They had defied him, and for that alone he could neither forgive nor forget them.

Three's vague plan had been to let Asher sense Wren in the Governor's presence. He saw now his plan was falling apart spectacularly.

"He doesn't protect you from the Weir," Asher called. "He brings them upon you!"

Murmurs rose from the crowd even as the Weirs' crying grew nearer. The tension strained with panic just beneath the surface, but some mix of curiosity, and dread, and belief that Underdown would still save them seemed to hold the people at bay, even if against their will.

"He calls them forth, and sends them away again! Behold! Your *savior!*"

And with that, the first of the Weir appeared in the streets, coming from the east, loping towards them like wolves on the hunt. New screams rose within the crush of citizens, and they surged against the gates of the compound. Three started to force his way back out, clutching Wren close as he fought to push through, away from the people. He'd rather die fighting in the open than get trampled in a mindless panic. Apart from the crowd, they'd have room to run, or at least maneuver.

The sight of the Weir was terrifying to the people of Morningside, who'd likely never seen them at all, and certainly not without a wall separating them. But Three could tell something was off with the creatures. They moved more slowly, heads weaving back and forth, like men stumbling through a heavy fog. The sunlight, he guessed. Three was nearly out of the knot of people, threading his way to the edges where those near the back had given up hope of gaining entry to the compound and were so less pressed together.

"Save them, Governor! Save your people, as you have so many times before! Save them now, if you can!" Asher mocked him openly now, robbed Underdown of any last sense of dignity or power. "Why won't you save them, Governor?"

And then without warning, Asher put his foot on Underdown's back and shoved him from the wall. It was a fifteen foot drop onto concrete, and Asher's kick had sent Underdown sprawling. The Governor had no way to cushion his fall. With a sharp cry he impacted with bone-shattering force and lay still, mere feet from the throng of men and women who moments before had been his adorers.

A sickly sort of paralysis overcame the mob then. The shock of their beloved Underdown broken on the ground, the shambling horde that approached, this brash new man on the wall who had cast their Governor down... it was as if their collective mind had ceased to process or respond.

"Three..." Wren whispered.

"Now, citizens of Morningside, watch," Asher said, "and know true power!"

Asher leapt from the wall and landed just beyond Underdown's motionless form with a lightness that surprised Three. He strode towards the Weir, his long coat billowing behind him like some great cape, and then halted, awaiting their final approach. There were thirty or so by Three's quick count.

"Three," Wren whispered again, urgently. "Ran. Ran's coming."

Three nodded, and started backpedaling slowly. But his gaze was still drawn to Asher and the Weir. The Weir had seemed to fix on Asher alone then, and they gathered towards him. Twenty feet. Fifteen. Ten.

And then Asher raised his hand, palm out, and cried in a loud voice:

"FALL!"

And as if a towering wave had crashed over them, they did. The Weir were thrown back to the ground, where they lay dazed. Asher lowered his hand. Adjusted the sleeves of his coat. And as the first shouts of relief and amazement and joy from the crowd were just beginning, he turned and pointed directly at Three and Wren.

"Stop them."

Three turned to run, but it was no use. They hadn't cleared the mob yet, and those nearest pressed in. In the next instant the crowd swirled around them. Too many hands clutched and grasped at them for Three to get away. Wren fought to hold on. For a split second, Three considered trying for his blade, but didn't, fearing what would happen if he didn't hold Wren with both arms.

In the end, it didn't matter anyway. They were forced apart, and Three felt Wren sliding away from him.

"Wren!"

"Three," the boy shrieked, terrified.

"Wren! Fight, Wren! Fight!"

Three's rage surged, and he channeled his fury into those around him. Like a thunderstorm against a mountain range, he threw himself at those who in their ignorance had dared to lay hands upon him. For a moment, he was free and a small space opened in the crush, the bravery of the mob briefly broken. But as he reached to draw his blade the crowd parted and a short but grim man strode towards him as if he were wading through shallow water.

Ran.

The blade was halfway from its sheath when the blow landed, and Three knew no more.

After the crowd had pulled him away from Three, Wren hadn't fought. He hadn't done anything, except cry. There, at the end, when Three had needed him most, he had cried. And they had taken Three away, and with him they had taken everything. The journey into the Governor's compound was mostly a blur in Wren's mind, a tangle of rough hands and strong voices. He was ashamed.

It was quiet now, here, in this little room they'd locked him in. A strange room to be inside such a fancy building. It had a small bed, and a table with a chair, and a high window sealed over with colored glass that made Wren think of winter stars. A room that would've seemed more at home in Chapel's village than here in this big city.

He wasn't sure how long it'd been since they'd brought him. He felt he must've cried for a long time, and thought he may have fallen asleep at some point. Asher hadn't even spoken to him, just ordered that he be put away to be dealt with later. Wren shuddered. Asher was scary. You never knew what he might do, or how he might treat you from one minute to the next.

Wren remembered once, before he and Mama had left, how Asher had carried him on his shoulders, running around and laughing and tipping from side to side like they might fall over together any second. And afterwards, when they were both panting, Asher had set him down and stared at him with a smile.

"Oh Spinner," he'd said. "Oh, little, beautiful Spinner."

And then his smile had gone away, and he got The Look on his face, the one he had when you just didn't know what he was going to do and it could be anything or nothing at all. And then he'd said, "How I hate you, you stupid little boy."

That's how it was with Asher. And that's how it was going to be from now on. Wren couldn't help it then. He started crying again, crying for his dead mama, for Three. Even for Dagon. He had no one left.

The first sensation Three had was that of floating in a cold fluid; too thick to be water, too dark to be real. He pushed his way to the surface with heavy legs. Realized he was coming into consciousness. Harsh light. Brutal pounding in his skull.

He was seated. Arms bound behind his back. He was damp with sweat. Left eye crusted and sticky with oozing blood. Alive. He chuckled at that, out of disbelief. Out of a lack of other options. His head swam as he lifted it. Concussion, maybe. Coat, harness, gear, all gone of course. Still dressed, at least. That was something.

He was in a room lit with gray light that nevertheless seemed too bright. The room was large, much larger than seemed necessary. Smooth gray walls, a high ceiling, pillars. Sparsely furnished, it had only one other chair on a dais, about fifteen feet away. Almost a throne room. Too cold, though. Sterile. Three was vaguely aware of a deep, distant humming, like a vibration in the walls. But he couldn't tell if it was real or imagined.

Movement in his periphery.

"Oh good, he's awake," the voice rang in the room. Asher. He crossed the room with long strides and flung himself casually sideways into the chair on the dais, with a leg dangling over the arm. Six guardsmen accompanied him, dressed in sleek black outfits that bore the subtle silhouettes of embedded body armor. Two flanked him on either side of the "throne", two posted up by the entrance, and two took position on either side of Three. Ran flowed in after them like a heavy fog, silent but substantial. His silent grace made the others seem clumsy, his motionless strength made them seem childish.

Asher scratched his forehead absently and sniffed impatiently, as if Three's unconsciousness had kept him waiting unfairly.

"What's your name, exactly?" Asher asked. Three didn't feel like answering, so he didn't. After a moment, Asher cocked his head, as if Three were being unreasonable. "I don't get it, you know. Why someone like *you*," – the emphasis here was somewhere between condescending and dismissive – "would want to have anything to do with someone like *me*. Stupid? Sure. Obviously. But at first I thought 'He just doesn't know who I am'."

Slowly, Three worked his hands and arms, testing to see how he was tied, and with what. They'd bound him with some kind of synthetic cordage that cut into his wrists as he twisted them; he couldn't get a read on the knot they'd used. Heatwrapped, maybe. Melted instead of tied.

"Kostya, I get. Self-defense. But why did you get involved at all? Did you think you could save her? I don't understand why you would think there was anything worth saving." He spoke quickly, obviously not expecting any response to his questions. "Is that what it was? The woman? Haven?"

It was stupid, sure, to invite pain, but Three had to test.

"Her name is Cass."

For the first time, Asher looked at him. A smoldering stare. Three held the gaze, returned it without fear. There was little left that Asher could do to him now.

"Her name is Haven. Idiot."

The childishness of the insult, its ineffectiveness, caught Three's attention. Asher didn't just live among dangerous people, he was their captain. To hold sway over such individuals... Three wondered what danger lay in Asher's power, or skill, or cunning.

"And to run. To run for so long. After you killed Kostya, you had to know I wouldn't just let you get away. And now. Now look at where we are. Fedor. Jez. Poor Ran probably thought he was next on the list."

Three glanced at Ran, who stood motionless and emotionless to one side. Ran returned the look with a flat stare. Fearless. But something behind the eyes...

The guard standing to Asher's left, or rather what would've been Asher's left had he been sitting upright, shifted his stance, drawing Three's eye. And there Three saw it, hanging on his hip. His pistol. *Three's* pistol. He wasn't the one from the gate. Captain of the guard, then? Asher's trusted man. The captain followed Three's gaze, and laid his hand over the gun with a smirk. A "*this is mine now*" look.

We'll see, Three thought.

"And the boy," Asher continued. "Spinner?"

"Wren."

"Spinner!" The response was sharper this time. Agitated. "My kid brother. What claim do you have to him? None! He's *my* brother! He's nothing to you!"

Three's heart burned at that false accusation. Wren had been nothing to him at one point. Now, he was everything. Slowly, Three fought to turn his hands together behind his back so his palms were touching. He felt the binds bite his flesh. Hoped the bleeding wouldn't attract any attention.

"And Cass?" Three said. "Your own mother."

"She's whatever I want her to be. Whatever *I* decide." Asher sat up straight in his chair and leaned forward, resting his elbows on his knees. "You're *going* to understand that. If not now, very soon. *I* decide."

Asher flicked his finger, and the guard to Three's right struck Three across the belly with some sort of rod, knocking the wind from him. Blackness closed in from around the edges.

Wren lay on the bed, curled in a ball with his coat over him, trying to cry some more, but he just couldn't. Even reliving those last, terrible moments of being pulled away couldn't bring out any more tears. It was still so clear, so fresh in his head. Maybe even clearer now because he'd stopped crying. Three fighting in the crowd. Fighting on all sides. And Three's final words echoed in Wren's head.

*Fight, Wren! Fight!*

And here he was, lying down instead. Lying down. Wren felt suddenly guilty, and foolish. After all Three had done for him, all he'd taught him, and he was just lying here being sad. He sat up, swung his legs over the side of the bed, feet not quite reaching the ground. Felt inside his coat. Found his knife. No one had thought to search him for anything.

Wren held the knife, turned it over and over in his hands. He remembered when Three first gave it to him outside the Vault. The first time Three had needed his help. How Three had called him a soldier. A *soldier*. Soldiers didn't sit crying in their beds. Soldiers did whatever they had to do.

Three was in trouble. And Mama wasn't here. She wasn't going to come back and fix everything. It was up to him, now.

He slid off the bed, and put his coat on. Slipped the knife into his belt, where it wouldn't poke. Took a deep breath. And then stretched out beyond himself, from the place of his brain that did things he didn't understand, things he just did without knowing how. Someone was sitting in the hall outside his door. One of the guards that wore black. Wren could feel him. Could *see* him. And the door. The door was locked.

And then it wasn't.

Three's vision cleared again, and he made a mental note. Guard to the right had a weapon. Asher had leaned back into his chair again, was watching with some mix of amusement and judgment.

"It's a shame we got off to such a bad start," Asher said. "A man of your talents… I could've had use of you."

Three rolled his head to the side, popped his neck in the spot that always seemed to need it. Tried to relax his shoulders. The burn was intense, muscles screaming for relief from the way his arms had been contorted behind him. He'd managed to get his hands around so his palms were touching, which helped ease the pain and improve the blood flow. He could tell now that the binding was some kind of brittle synthetic. He rolled his hands into fists, knuckles together, increasing the tension on the bands around his wrists.

"Didn't expect you to try to cross the Strand. I'm amazed that any of you survived. I would've guessed you'd all end up like Haven."

So he did know. Asher seemed to read Three's thoughts.

"I didn't have the heart to tell Dagon. Figured he'd discover it on his own at some point. And until then, his obsession was useful. I was kind of hoping he'd blame *you* for it. I assume he's dead too?"

Three didn't answer, but flicked his eyes to Ran. Dagon's trusted friend. Ran made no hint of response.

"Just as well, I suppose," Asher said casually. "I think he might've gone mad if he'd known what happened to her." Asher ran a hand through his hair. "He was the one that reminded me of Underdown, you know. I'd almost forgotten him completely. He was only with us a few months. Didn't get on too well with my father."

Three felt the back of his chair with his thumbs, found a ridge where two joints met to connect the back to the seat. He positioned the cuffs over that raised point.

"If we'd known what kind of man he really was, I think we may have kept him around. Spinner's father, you know. Speaking of which. Ran."

For the first time Ran took his eyes off Three, and looked to Asher.

"Go get him," Asher said.

Ran stood motionless for a moment, staring back at Asher without any discernible emotion.

"Go on!" Asher said, louder. Ran dipped his head and turned to go. But as he did, his eyes slid across to Three, and the two exchanged the briefest of looks. Three had no way to interpret that look, didn't have the information to know what was going on, but he had the distinct impression that something significant had just happened. Some kind of momentary breakdown of Asher's hold over Ran, or the first signs of its erosion. Asher watched him as he exited, and then turned his attention back to Three, shaking his head slightly.

"Dagon was the one who guessed it, when I found out you were headed to Greenstone," he said. And then added with a wolfish grin, "Your friend at the Vault wasn't much for keeping secrets."

Three remembered Jackson, imagined what Asher must've done to him. Burned with anger.

"I suppose Haven thought Underdown might remember her?" He shook his head again. "Women and their fantasies. I can imagine it now, the way she must have. Underdown learning of his precious son, Spinner. Falling in love with her again. Bringing them both in as his own. And I wonder what she expected of you, then. Maybe the three of you, living here together under his *protection*. Ha!" He spat a laugh.

Three tightened his fists. Reminded himself.

*Guard on the right has a weapon.*

And with a sudden motion, he swung his arms behind him, away from the chair, and then slammed them forward again. Already flexed tight, the binding on his arm impacted the ridge of the chair and split. The captain of the guard's eyes were just going wide when Three crushed his fist into the groin of the guard on his right. The man reacted, and Three rocketed up, wrapping one arm around the man's head and snatching the weapon from him with the other hand. Three whipped down and whirled, snapping the guard's neck and dumping him to the floor as the others converged. Continuing the motion, he struck the closest guard across the temple with the rod. Two down, four to go. The captain of the guard leapt from the dais as the two guards from the door rushed towards Three. But the captain hesitated, as if he'd just remembered he had Three's gun. He fumbled to get it out of its holster. Three closed the gap before he could draw it.

Three snatched the man behind the neck, forcing the guard's head down into his shoulder, and whipped him around, putting the captain between Three and the other guards. With his free hand, Three trapped the pistol, and pressed its barrel against the captain's stomach. Lined it up, and squeezed the trigger. The shot thundered in the room, tore through the captain, and dropped one of the guards from the door. Three slung the captain's body to the floor and leapt at the next guard, intercepting the man's jaw with a flying knee. Three rode him to the ground. As they landed, Three bounced the man's skull off the floor, knocking him out cold.

Three whirled back to his feet, facing the throne with the rod in one hand and his pistol in the other. Its bulk was comforting. He'd missed it. Asher was sitting bolt upright in the chair, but his face was more one of disappointment than fear or surprise. The last guard stood trembling by Asher's side. Asher looked at him.

"Well. Go on," he said. The guard looked at Asher, and then at Three. And then back to Asher again. Asher sighed. "Useless." He looked hard at the man, and the guard suddenly cried out sharply and collapsed to the ground as if his muscles had simply switched off.

Asher stood then, casually, confidently. "I told you I could've used a man like you. Too bad, really."

"Bring Wren to me, and I might not kill you."

"Oh… no, I don't think I'll do that," Asher said. "The people of Morningside thought Underdown was something special, you know. Allow me to show you why."

The guard had been asleep when Wren had quietly opened the door. A lucky break. Wren didn't know what would've happened otherwise, and he hadn't wanted to kill the man, after all. He'd shut the door behind him quietly and locked it back. For at least ten minutes, Wren had wandered the halls, listening for people approaching, sometimes hiding. The place was vast, with confusing hallways and passages, and voices seemed to come from funny places.

There was no way for Wren to track Three, and he didn't dare risk trying to pinpoint Asher. So he did what Three had taught him to do.

*When in doubt, trust your gut.*

Wren followed a corridor down a long set of stairs, and kept descending, and descending. And the lower he got, the more terrible he felt. A growing, creeping fear crawled over him. He stopped several times on the steps, fighting the urge to turn around and at the same time trying to convince himself he was going the wrong way anyway. But each time, he knew in his heart that he had to go down those stairs. Three had once told him that it wasn't bravery if you weren't scared. So he gripped his knife in slippery palms and tried to ignore the trembling in his legs.

He passed a couple of landings as he went down, but no one seemed to be on the stairs. It didn't seem like anyone had used them in a long time. Wren forced himself to keep moving, told himself there was nothing really to be afraid of. And all the while the dread grew. A terrible, terrible feeling like sweating and being cold and wanting to throw up all at the same time. It was like something he'd felt before, but the feeling was one he couldn't quite place.

And suddenly, the stairs stopped. And there was a hallway. And at the end of the hallway, there was a door. Wren did not like that door.

There was a humming sound deep in the walls, a low drone that he noticed now seemed to vibrate in his chest. Wren sat down on the bottom step and hugged his knees. The door stood, staring back at him. Like so many doors Mama had gone through before. And nothing good had ever been behind them.

Wren cried a little then, silently, the tears rolling down his cheeks and dripping off his chin. He had to go through it. No matter what, he had to. He wished Three could be there with him. But he missed his mama most of all.

Finally he stood, and wiped his nose on his sleeve. And took a bunch of deep breaths. Then he started walking. It was the hardest few steps Wren had ever taken in his life.

The door was cool to the touch. Heavy, and a dull green, with big rivets around the edge. Locked. And then somehow it was open, and Wren knew he had opened it without really even meaning to. It was getting easier to do that. He pushed on the door, and it swung silently, smoothly inward. Inside there was only a dim reddish light, and it was hard for Wren to make out more than shadows and silhouettes within. He stepped inside, squinting. A wave of fear rolled over him, and he stood there shaking uncontrollably. In here, the hum was louder. No, not louder. Stronger. Or at least, he could feel it more. His eyes finally adjusted enough for him to make out what he was looking at.

There were boxes. Huge boxes, made of metal, with metal bars. As tall as Fedor. Rows and rows and rows. It made him think of the Vault, the first night he'd fallen inside.

And for all Wren's fear, curiosity finally built up enough for him to take a few more steps inside to get a better look at the boxes. Though, boxes didn't seem like quite the right word for them. And just as he approached the nearest one, his hand reaching out to touch it, he realized... not a box.

A *cage*.

From deep inside, near the back, two pale blue lights shone back at him. And just as a scream began rising in his throat, something clapped over his mouth and dragged him suddenly backwards.

In the wall behind the throne, a panel shifted quietly and slid to one side, revealing a dark passage behind. Though his mind couldn't comprehend, it didn't take but a moment for Three to recognize the aura emanating from it. The moonlight glow of a Weir's eyes, growing as it approached, ascending stairs from below. Asher stood to one side, watching impassively, with except perhaps a look of muted pleasure on his face.

"They thought he was some great warrior. Or wizard. Or both, I suppose. Feared by the creatures. But he was neither." He turned and looked at Three then. "He'd built a machine, you see."

The Weir's eyes became visible in the darkness, two soft stars in the gloom. The creature paused before entering the room, its other features hidden in the shadows.

"He hacked them. More or less. He could call them, he could drive them away. He even has a place to keep a few of them. But he never really understood them. He was about control, you see. Always *control*. Never got much beyond using them to secure a place of power for himself." Asher returned to his seat, relaxed into it. "And that is why I am sitting here, and he is not."

Three's vision swam, his balance shifted awkwardly, though whether it was from the shock of this news, or from the injuries he'd sustained, he couldn't tell.

"You look like you need to sit down." Asher smiled. "Underdown was an innovative man in some ways, but he wasn't terribly clever. Summoning the Weir and then driving them away again, for show. A one-trick pony. It took *me* to realize the full potential of his creation." He looked vaguely over his shoulder to the creature behind him. "You can come in, my dear."

The Weir stepped forward, something familiar in its movement. The creature snaked fluidly around the throne, and then poured itself seductively into Asher's lap. If not for the eyes, Three would've sworn the woman was human. Her flesh a healthy olive tone, her hair dark and untangled. Her features perfectly preserved. Just as he'd remembered her.

Cass.

Three felt his legs go out, and he fell backwards, collapsing heavily on the floor, his weapons clattering heedlessly next to him. It was her. Cass. A violent chill shook him, and he nearly vomited. It *was* her. And yet it wasn't. The she-thing looked back at him without recognition, without emotion. It wasn't Cass, not anymore. Just a slave, using Cass's body.

Asher ran his fingers through her hair.

"Beautiful, isn't she?" he said. "I've always thought so. And the Weir, the Weir are fascinating, you know. Not at all the wild animals you think they are. They found her. Repaired her for me. *Optimized* her. And when directed, they are capable of… things beyond your imagining. No mind of their own, of course. But with *my* mind…" he stopped and smiled. Robotically, the Weir-Cass turned its head and kissed Asher's head.

Three felt feverish, felt like he might lose consciousness at any moment. He fought to hold on. Seeing her again, seeing her like this, was more than his heart could bear.

*No, not her,* he told himself. *Cass is dead. That is a thing. An abomination.*

"So, I guess in way, it's all worked out just like she wanted," Asher continued, running his finger along her jaw. Along *its* jaw. "All back together again. And so what do we do about you, then?" He made a show of considering it. And then shrugged. "I suppose you get to die."

Cass stood then, and stalked towards him.

They stood in the passage outside the door, Wren shaking violently, Ran holding him in his arms.

"You shouldn't be here, little one," Ran said with gentle firmness. "This is a terrible place."

The door was closed now, but Wren couldn't stop trembling. He was freezing cold. Ran had managed to stifle his scream, and had quickly moved him back out into the passageway, Wren was sure that at any moment the door would open and *they* would flood out.

"Come, little one. I'll take you to him."

"Ran, please," Wren said, his voice breaking as he fought back the tears. "Please, I don't want to go back to Asher."

"I know," Ran said. "I will take you to the man. The one who brought you. And then we will see."

The fear, the shock, the relief, it was too much for Wren to absorb. He burst into tears and went limp, letting Ran bear him back up the stairs. Back to Three.

Three scrabbled backwards on his hands as Cass approached. Her hands had looked normal at first, but as she closed the distance, claws had extended from the tips of her fingers. Not true claws; some kind of blades embedded beneath the nails. Deadly, either way.

He was just gaining his feet when she moved to strike. And it was all he could to slap the attack away, to get himself clear. The assault came furiously, and no matter what he did to break contact, he couldn't keep distance. Three's mind flashed back to the last fight, the night she'd fallen, the way she'd fought when she was healthy, and juiced on her chems. It was like that now; raw fury and surprising power, like a lioness defending her cubs.

But no matter how much he fought to tell himself this creature was no longer Cass, that *she* was gone, Three could not bring himself to harm her. He struggled to defend himself from her relentless advance. But he couldn't bring her down.

"Asher!" a loud voice called. And in an instant, Cass stopped her attack. Ran stood at the door, Wren in his arms, and a look of horror on his face. "Asher! What have you done?"

Asher waved dismissively. "It's none of your concern, Ran. She's mine to do with as I please."

"You... you *did* this?"

"Are we having a problem, Ran?" Asher said, his tone rising.

"Mama?" came Wren's weak voice. Ran instantly covered the boy's eyes, pressed his head back down on his shoulder.

"Don't look, little one."

"Let him look," Asher said. "He'll be seeing a lot of her from now on."

"*Mama?*" Wren cried. "*Three?*"

"You demon!" Ran shouted. Asher rolled his eyes. In the passage behind him, a blue light grew. And more of Asher's Weir emerged. Six of them. Well-muscled. Deadly. They moved to either side of Asher, like wolves protecting their own.

Ran put Wren down, and slid the boy behind him.

"Three, what's going on? What's happening?" Wren called.

"Don't worry, Wren," Three said. "We're gonna work it out."

He started towards Wren and Ran, but in that instant Cass renewed her attack. Three managed to stop the first swipe, but the second caught his side, raking across his ribs. As he redirected her strikes, he caught a glimpse of her passionless face. Hollow. There was nothing of her in there.

She stopped again, but remained poised to strike.

"You're boring me," Asher said. "Are you just going to let her kill you?"

Three understood. Asher didn't care how the fight turned out. It was the sport he wanted, the sheer torment of watching Three fight this woman he'd come to care so deeply for, and the pleasure that Asher derived from it.

"You have no power over me, Asher," Three said, knowing it would enrage him. "I won't fight her."

"You *will*," Asher said. "Or the boy dies."

The six other Weir advanced, towards Wren. Three made a move to intercept them, but Cass was there, cutting him off, knocking him away, keeping him cornered.

"Your choice," Asher said.

The Weir collapsed as one, lunging for the boy.

But Ran was there. He flung Wren away, into the corner, and with all his fury unleashed his fury upon the six.

Wren tumbled to the ground, and scrambled over to the corner, where he balled himself against the wall. Hands over his ears, he screamed and screamed and screamed at the chaos around him. Ran fighting so many. He was bleeding so much. And

Three fighting Mama. But it wasn't Mama, not anymore. What had happened? What was happening?

Cass attacked and attacked, and Three had shifted gears. He struck her in the legs, in the arms, in the torso. Anything to slow her down without doing any real injury. But he was getting tired. His wrists were bleeding, his shoulders were still stiff, and his head was still pounding. Everything was taking its toll, and Cass started landing strike after strike. His pant leg was soaked with blood from numerous wounds, and he was starting to get lightheaded.

Across the room, Ran still fought, though two of the Weir were on the ground now. But every attempt Three made to help him was stifled by Cass.

Wren tried to shrink back further into the wall, to get away. To get away from all the screaming, and the sounds of fighting, and the utter chaos. All the blood. And Asher. Asher sitting on his tall chair, watching it all. Watching.

It was Asher. All of this was Asher's fault. And without Asher, maybe it would all stop. And that's all Wren wanted now. He just wanted it to stop. He wanted it all to stop.

"Stop," he heard himself say. "Stop!" He was standing now. Louder. "STOP!"

Three's legs were heavy. His steps were off, his kicks missing targets. And Cass was tireless. How fitting, he thought, that after all was said and done, she should be the one.

Amidst her attacks, Three was vaguely aware of Wren yelling something, and Asher got off his throne and strode across the room. But there was nothing Three could do to reach the boy. In between clashes with Cass, Three saw Asher backhand Wren across the face.

••••

"Shut up, Spinner!" Asher yelled.

"My name is Wren!" Wren shouted back.

Asher struck him again, harder this time. Wren tasted blood in his mouth. And then Asher's hand was around his throat. He had The Look on his face.

"Shut. Your. Mouth," Asher said, his face an inch from Wren's. Wren felt his feet go out from under him. Asher was picking him up. He couldn't breathe. His hands fumbled at his belt.

Wren found it, the grip cool against his palm. Just like Three'd taught him. Wren plunged his knife into Asher's forearm, and then into his upper arm, and then his shoulder, and then his neck. Asher dropped him, stumbled backwards in shock.

Behind him, four Weir stood over Ran, his body torn. Three, pale, cut, and bleeding, was losing ground. And Mama. Mama.

Asher gathered himself, a dark look on his face. "You stupid little boy." The four Weir turned and stalked towards Wren. And in his chest, a quiet fury sparked.

"Asher," Wren said, though he didn't know why. And then again. "Asher!" he called. The fury was swelling, and Wren felt like he might explode. The Weir were almost on him, and his anger was so great Wren could do nothing but scream.

"AAAASHEEEEEEERRRRRRR!"

And in that moment, something burst inside him. The four Weir collapsed instantly to the ground. Asher's hands flew up to his head, and Wren could see it now. Could see all of Asher, who he was and what he thought, and what he did, and what he would do. Asher looked up at him now, eyes wide in horror, in true, uncontrolled fear. And from a quiet place within the storm, Wren spoke a whisper.

"Be gone."

Asher screamed then, a shrill, otherworldly sound, and fell backwards, and was still.

Across the room, Three had fallen to his knees.

"Mama," Wren said, gently. The Weir that looked like Mama advanced towards Three.

"Mama, stop," Wren called again, just as gently. He walked towards her. She stopped the second time, turned to face him. He reached out, touched her. "Mama. Come back."

Three lay on the ground, bleeding from too many wounds to count. Too weak to even sit up. He couldn't tell if he was hallucinating or not, if what he was seeing was real. Wren stood by him, and the Weir that had been Cass was kneeling next to him. His vision was blurred, dark at the edges.

The Weir peered down at him with its blue-glow eyes. But different now. Clearer. Recognition.

"Three," she said. "I'm here."

There was too much to process, too much pain, no words even if he could have spoken.

"Mama, is he going to be OK?" Wren asked.

She looked to Wren. Concerned. Bit her lower lip, just slightly. She was back. Cass was truly back. Three's heart leapt within him.

"Not this time, buddy," Three managed. Wren dropped to his knees next to Three. Tears in his eyes. Cass reached down and lifted Three gently into her lap, cradled his head in her arms.

"Three?"

"Hey, girl."

Tears brimmed in her altered eyes, caught and swirled the light emanating from them, like moonlight on snow. Beautiful. Three's eyes flicked to Wren.

"You used your knife."

Wren nodded. "I had to."

Three managed a smile. "You did good. Real good."

"Three, I don't want you to go," Wren said. Three felt Cass's arms squeeze him tighter. He nodded, or at least tried, and felt like he did.

"Why didn't you fight?" Cass let the tears fall then, let herself cry. "I was in there, Three. I was in there, trapped. Watching. Why didn't you just kill me?"

"I promised to protect you," he said. She bent over him then, pressed her wet cheek to his forehead. Wren started crying, and tiny hands squeezed Three's. He let himself be held, savored the feel of her arms around him, the rhythm of her breathing, Wren's warm hands around his fingers. Cass was back. Back with Wren. And for Wren. They were going to be alright now. It was going to be alright. Three felt the life slipping out of him. It was time.

"I'm gonna have to go now," he said.

"Three," Wren said through his tears. "You gotta kiss the lady goodbye. So she remembers you."

Three smiled to hear his words returned to him. They were going to be alright. Cass bent further, brought her lips gently to his. Whispered to him.

"I will *always* remember you."

"Be good, girl."

Three squeezed Wren's hand. "Take care of your Mama."

Wren nodded.

And with that, Three closed his eyes, and did not open them again.

# EPILOGUE

They built a great pyre for him on the grounds of the Governor's compound. Wren remembered the rituals Three had taught him, and had prepared and wrapped Three's body just as he had been shown. They waited for dusk before he set the pyre ablaze, hoping it would be a fitting tribute to the man who had never feared the night. They sat together for long hours, Wren in Cass's lap, watching until the last embers died quietly in the night, having taken into the wind the final traces of the man they had both come to love.

It was some time before the people of Morningside understood what had happened within the Governor's compound. One of the guards inside had regained consciousness in time to witness the events, though few believed the story no matter how accurately retold. But of all the rumors and stories that swirled, one thing was universally agreed upon: Governor Underdown's son had come to take his place, and things were going to change for the better.

Ran died of his many wounds, and was buried in a cemetery reserved for those who had given their lives to protect the Governor. He was greatly honored by the citizens of Morningside in his death, for the sacrifice he had made to save Wren.

Of all the changes, Cass was the most difficult for the people of Morningside to accept. She rarely left Wren's side, serving as his counselor and his most trusted bodyguard. Many found her a terrifying reminder of the day that everything had changed. But she was the mother of Underdown's son, mother to the one who had set things right, and if the people did not love her, they eventually came to accept her. And, after a time, she became known as the First of the Awakened.

# ACKNOWLEDGMENTS

As anyone who has ever written, well, probably just about anything, will tell you, though writing is often a solitary adventure, it is never truly done alone. Many people have contributed to this work, but here's a short list of those to whom I owe the most. My most sincere and heartfelt thanks to:

... Jesus, for your calling, equipping, provision, and enduring faithfulness.

... my wife and children, for your constant love, encouragement, support, and for making my every single day a blessing.

... Jeff McGann, for your patience and for being Reader Number One. If not for you, I would never have finished this novel. I'm looking forward to seeing yours in print.

... David Mooring, for your advice and encouragement, and for being the brother I didn't have.

... Richard Dansky, for your long-suffering guidance and genuine friendship, and for giving me a place to practice and grow as a writer.

... Christopher Stout, for your patient instruction, the 80s montage-worthy training sequences, and the Gumby t-shirt.

... Ed and Cindy Bagwell, for your unfailing support and generosity, and for letting me remain part of the family even after I quit my lucrative programming job to become a writer.

… Mom and Dad, for your innumerable sacrifices and constant love.

… Marc Gascoigne, Lee Harris, Mike Underwood, Darren Turpin, and all the Robot Overlords for taking a chance on me and helping this work become more than just a really big text file on my laptop.

# ABOUT THE AUTHOR

Jay is a narrative designer, author, and screenwriter by trade. He started working in the video game industry in 1998, and has been writing professionally for over a decade. Currently employed as Senior Narrative Designer at Red Storm Entertainment, he's spent around eight years writing and designing for Tom Clancy's award-winning *Ghost Recon* and *Rainbow Six* franchises.

A contributing author to the book Professional Techniques for Video Game Writing, Jay has lectured at conferences, colleges, and universities, on topics ranging from basic creative writing skills to advanced material specific to the video game industry.

*Jayposey.com*
*twitter.com/HiJayPosey*

From *the author of* The Shining Girls

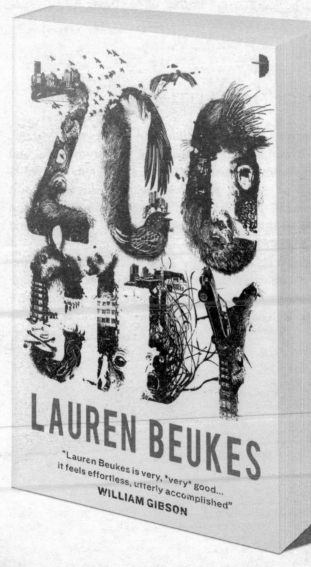

LAUREN BEUKES

"Lauren Beukes is very, *very* good...
it feels effortless, utterly accomplished"
**WILLIAM GIBSON**

"The only serious successor to Michael Crichton working in the future history genre today."
*Scott Harrison, author of* Archangel

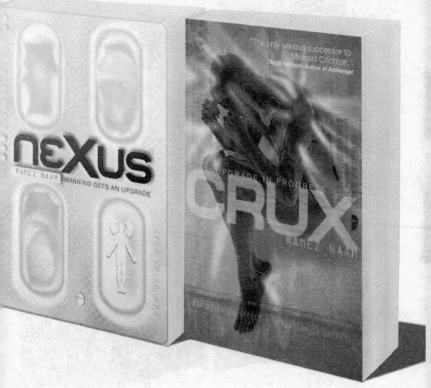

"Wesley Chu is my hero… he has to be the coolest science fiction writer in the world."
*Lavie Tidhar, World Fantasy Award winning author of* Osama

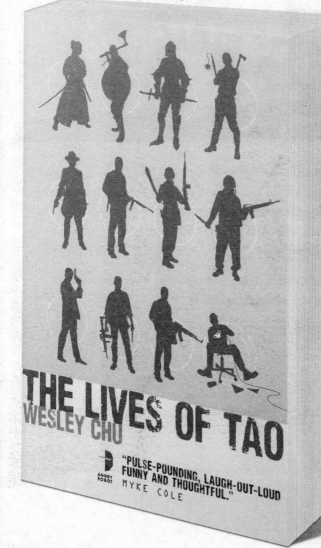

THE LIVES OF TAO

WESLEY CHU

ANGRY ROBOT

"PULSE-POUNDING, LAUGH-OUT-LOUD FUNNY AND THOUGHTFUL."
MYKE COLE